THE LEGMAN

Mike Kerr

CONTENTS

FOREWORD

This is a fiction work leveraging historical fact. Specific true events and real-life people are detailed in the Author's Note section at the end of the book. The plot is told in classic mystery/thriller style. The story is set in 1969, a tipping point for Chicago as it moves from its motto, The City That Works, to the murder capital of America.

Give me your tired, your poor, your huddled masses is the promise of a big city, not small town or rural America. The problem is someone is always already there and they don't want to move over or give anything up.

CHAPTER 1

June 1969

M ost know, the smart ones; the neighborhood is waiting to break, like a piñata, spilling its treasures to those with the quickest hands. Get yourself ready to grab or get out of the way are the only two moves to make. Her family did neither; that's why she was in a place she never should have been.

Today, the beginning of summer vacation for Effie Alexander before her sophomore year at Austin High School on Chicago's West Side, her appearance rivals Crazy Marie who endlessly parades the streets arguing out-loud with herself. Hair gathered high, away from her neck and makeup-less face, she is braless under a gray t-shirt and wearing two-year old pajama bottoms that she's long outgrown. Her sneakers are past redemption. That was the uniform needed to complete her assigned chores. Who's around, and what's left of the day, are the next order of business.

She slides off the round elastic tie that holds

her almost-black hair on top of her head, letting it fall to her shoulders. One victorious through-with-all-that shake and it's free. She scoots over to the living room window, careful not to be seen, looking as she does. In the corner near the wall, the curtain serves as a prudent shield. Her index finger bends a few inches of fabric at eye-level to allow a glimpse of Laramie Avenue in hopes of spotting a few friends. Instead, what she sees, shocks her.

There's no explanation for it!

She abandons her protected position for a better view. Placing her hands on the radiator in front of the window, she leans forward, left cheek pressed against the glass. It can't be, but it is. There are no colored people here, right here, none that live here and none, except for a well-known few, that even work here. Wherever colored people are and wherever they go, it's not here.

Dozens of blacks pointedly march down her street, 3-4 abreast, taking up the entire width of the sidewalk. Their length stretches over several houses. She's seen blacks marching on television, but they carried signs and chanted slogans. These marchers do neither. She's also seen the news film of the riots following last year's assassination of Martin Luther King, but this is not that either, although they are menacing to her.

The marchers turn their heads giving scornful looks to those neighbors who watch from their front lawns and porches. Part of what's threatening is that they don't rush. Rather, they pass slowly like a river flooding at night sending its black water over the banks to pour smoothly down streets, drowning anything in its path.

One marcher, older, catches her eye. He gazes differently, without emotion, cold but penetrating, like a Doberman. As he passes her, a marcher directly behind him trips, his foot stubbing on a section of the sidewalk slightly elevated by the force of a tree root. He steadies himself by grabbing the back of the shirt of the older marcher, exposing his lower neck. The older marcher quickly yanks it back into place and turns his head looking to see who noticed.

Effie saw something there, on his neck, a mark. She looks closer at his neck, now covered, trying to remember when she suddenly notices that the marcher's eyes are now on her. They glare in anger. The skin around his eyes has an aged mahogany color and starkly contrasts the rest of his face, which is the color of unbleached flour.

She sees his eyes move downward. In a frightening realization, she understands that he's examining her, taking in everything: the length and style of her hair, her features and — *Oh, God!* — what she's wearing! Her lungs constrict for a moment. She backs quickly away from the window. *What did he see?* She glances down at her breasts which move slightly under her t-shirt. Her nipples are more visible, extended by fear. Panic. *He saw more than a strange boy should? And he was a man! What if he chases me?*

Too afraid to look back, she races to her room, quickly finishes dressing and grabs a square paper-weight with sharp corners. She holds it ready, but wonders whether she could really fight him, with that black face and those odious eyes. And there was that mark. He was stamped with a triangle or arrowhead or something. The minutes pass. He doesn't come. She places the paperweight back, relaxing, but still unnerved.

◆ ◆ ◆

The ten o'clock news fills all tv stations ex-cept Channel 9, which is running a movie about World War II that is so boring. Her younger brother, Paul, covered by a blanket mom retrieved from the closet, sleeps on the couch. Mom, curled up in the sofa arm chair, does the same. The late evening tem-perature brings a chill to the air. Effie closes all the windows, gives in to her drowsiness and retires for the night. She's done her best to not even think of her moment with the marcher, let alone discuss it, but as the hours pass, the inevitable happens.

She dreams of the black man with the blank face and the light skin except by his wicked eyes. He's hiding on her front porch in the dark waiting until she falls asleep to enter. If she calls the police, he'll hide. Then he'll come back. Like the boy who cried wolf, the police won't come a second time, if she calls. Then he's outside her bathroom door while she takes a bath. If she moves, he'll hear the water and know where she is. If she doesn't and he guesses, she'll be caught, naked. Then she dreams that he's entering her room. He's come through the back, by the alley. Her room is very dark, out of reach of the Laramie streetlamps. He's inching toward her. She desperately wants to get up and run, but her legs just won't move. She can't scream. She pulls herself forward by grabbing the bedsheets with her hands. She stretches her arm toward the handle of her dresser drawer, but her body rises, floating in the air and pulling her back toward him. She knows that she's not getting away. *Where is mom? Why can't I yell?*

Then she feels it. A knife cuts deep into her back. She trembles feeling the warm blood seep over her. She can't breathe. Her lung is pierced. He is coming still closer. *What's he going to do? I am going to die.*

Effie awakens with a jolt. She rips back the covers and stands up, and away from everything, in the center of the room, her heart racing. If she looked, she is sure that she would see it pushing out, trying to escape by bursting through her skin. She looks for him. Her eyes can see just enough for her to imagine his shadowy silhouette in every corner, behind the dresser and at the foot of the bed. She wants to scream for her mother but restrains herself.

Whoosh! The sound fills the house, freezing her. It's the furnace. The fire has lit. Normally, it's a comfort; warmth soon is coming. Tonight, it's a husky laugh rising up from the basement, mocking her fear, and telling her that she is right to be afraid.

◆ ◆ ◆

In the early morning hours as Effie prepares herself for the day's work, she hears her mother, Electra, outside, talking to Mrs. O'Reilly, who lives next door. O'Reilly saw it all and gives her an earful on the march. "Intimidation, " Electra spits out with disgust for such behavior.

"Aye, and they know it works, but we have to stick together. If we don't leave, they have no place to move in, " adds O'Reilly. The two women lock eyes, reading each other, but don't speak.

It's a poker game. Fold, and you lose the hand for sure. Stay in, and it may cost you everything. To Effie, it means he's coming back. What she doesn't know, and couldn't have seen, is that yesterday, when she pulled away, his eyes moved to the center of her front door where, prominently displayed, is her address.

CHAPTER 2

T he phone rings at the tiny office and printing spaces of the Central Standard Times (CST), a low-circulation weekly that squeaks by selling ad space to local businesses. Micky Mulvihill, lead writer as well as publisher and owner, momentarily breaks his focus. He squints to inflect his hostility at the offending receiver, hoping to coerce it into submission.

Acknowledging its determination, he yells, "Kath, can you get that?" No response. He options to stretch out a few feet of slack in the black cord and stuff the phone into a desk drawer. The muffled ringing gives him a Cagney-like grapefruit-in-the-face exhilaration.

He returns to drafting a news article on the recent surrender of serial bomber, Frank Kulak, the 'Mad Bomber', as coined by the Chicago press. The Kulak story is hot news in the city. Before he surrendered, he killed two police officers and wounded six more in a deadly 6-hour shootout at his home where he kept an arsenal of weapons: military rifles, sidearms, grenades and homemade bombs. Ultimately, a hero cop put his life on the line, walked right up to the front door of his apartment and convinced him to give himself up.

The policeman's bravery has been the story, so far, by the big papers. That, and the confessions to the many other bombings. People want the grit. They're intrigued by the story of a Korean and World War II veteran, a weapons specialist, trained to destroy, whose bombings were anti-war messages. Mad. Lethal.

Micky understands the appeal, but it's covered. And he's looking ahead, to accountability. The Kulak defense, he estimates, will play on the crazed veteran angle. He thinks it'll work, that Kulak will likely be acquitted of criminal charges 'by reason of insanity'. His current lawyer, public defender, Gerald Getty, has already provided comment that a psychiatric evaluation is needed. The gist of Micky's draft is, 'Don't excuse him. He's a cold-blooded killer.'

Poor guy. War is hell, and now he needs to kill more people to help extoll that notion. Sure, we all understand. Kulak's off his rocker, way off. He can't even see his rocker from where he's at. And so, he should get 'treatment' at a hospital where he can be 'cured' instead of jail or execution. Not to me, he shouldn't.

Frank Kulak, willfully and with ruthless intention, made detailed plans to maim and kill. In particular, let me tell you about Frank Aldrich who had all 5 fingers one hand, 3 fingers on the other and half his face blown off in front of his wife and young son while looking to pick up a toy at Goldblatt's. Kulak set a "tip bomb" inside a paper bag. It triggers with motion, just to be sure, extra sure, he would hurt someone.

Aldrich, curious, looks inside the bag. Is there a toy in there? It's sitting on a shelf next to other toys, in the toy department. Boom! Maimed for the rest of his life. Think about trying to be a dad that your 6-year boy old can look up to when you have two fingers and half a face.

Revenge won't help Frank Aldrich, you say. It's not a matter of revenge. Enforcing the law is a deterrent. The next guy who wanders from his rocker may have the sobering thought that the consequence for his actions isn't group therapy to help him release his inner demons before everyone settles in for the evening movie and popcorn in the tv lounge. Rather, it's a jail cell, a dark and lonely place where you can play with your demons for as long as you like.

Not bad, he thinks. It gets to the point he wants to make; you don't do something so evil that you're not accountable. More later. Has to fit the space. Soon he'll need to head out to his other job, the one that pays the bills, legman for investigative reporter, Jim Diamond, who is somewhat of a legend in Chicago news circles. If you ask Micky, though, he'd say Diamond's just been around a long time.

The phone! A persistent pleading , like a victim begging to be released from the trunk. "Kath. Please." She comes rushing forward, opens the drawer and answers.

She listens, nods and gives a yes, her mouth slowly curving to a smile, almost a laugh. "For you, Mick. It's Electra Alexander. "

Kathleen Noonan is one of three highly-deserving and just as highly underpaid staff on CST. She's a Journalism student at Wright Junior College, Working for Mulvihill, who's a legman himself, she's, essentially, a wannabe to a wannabe. Micky thanks her, calling her, again, by her name. Her nickname, Forty-Eight, based on her height (4'8"), is too long to say except in third person references.

Electra, whom Micky has known a very long time, pleads with him to please come over and listen to her daughter, Effie. It will make her feel better. She tells him that a hundred blacks marched

11

right in front of her house, just to scare people. And they did. Effie is terrified that they're coming back. Micky wants to help.

He only has a little time before he must head out to recover, and handle, the incoming mail for Diamond, but the Alexander place is close, a short walk. He'll get back to the Kulak story late tonight or early tomorrow. "Yeah. Sure. I'll just walk right over now, if that's okay, Mrs. Alexander." Okay, and, it was clear to him, very much appreciated.

Micky checks for his keys and wallet, then stuffs a notebook and pencils into his backpack. He's lines up his next steps: talk to Effie, walk down to the train and head East to the Daily News building, get the mail, check messages, head back, eat and read/sort the mail. —March? *A hundred blacks? Down Laramie, just a block over from here? Well, in the next couple years, the majority of these homes will be sold, to blacks. Maybe someone is impatient?*

◆ ◆ ◆

The space Micky rents, on Leamington, for CST is in a large apartment building that extends 3 doors down, all the way to Chicago Avenue. The street-level is designed for businesses. The two upper floors are apartments. It's too far from the main drag to garner customers from foot or car traffic. His office has failed other businesses. The rent is, accordingly, low. His product doesn't rely on such window shoppers.

Laramie, the next street over, is a "busy street", as Micky has always heard parents say in warning their children to be careful of its traffic. They distinguished it as such because it has stoplights and city busses. There's very little in the way of businesses keeping it busy. None, in fact, on the block where Electra lives.

He always marvels at how each home differs from the one next to it in style and age. The Alexanders live in two-story red brick century-old Victorian built a good twenty years before Austin was annexed to the city. Just next door to their building is a brand-new single-story and centrally air-conditioned ranch home. On the other side there is a two-story asphalt-sided World War I era A-frame. The back yards are equally mixed with fences made of wood, thin wire and stainless steel. There's even a couple that use metal pipes held together with elbow joints.

In the back of the Alexander home, instead of a garage, is a two-story brick carriage house with a loft where once hay was kept for the horses. There are two large wooden doors that meet in the middle and swing outward to open into the alley. The garage for the ranch next door uses a folding aluminum door that is remote-controlled. Micky imagines the story that any one of these houses could tell of who was here, what they built and why it served their need, each in their own time. For a hundred years, Austin has had generations of families migrate in and contribute.

Electra anxiously greets Micky whom she believes will solve her problem. He's like a doctor making a house call come to help her little girl.

"Hi, Micky. Hi. Hi. Come in. Yes. Please. Thank you. She's inside."

The smell of the morning's doubtless hearty breakfast lingers, but the dishes and any other cleanup would be long gone if he walked back to the kitchen. Electra covers the necessary chores of the day the way a latex glove covers a surgeon's hand, very tightly and snapping into place.

She is sole support for herself and her two children. Mostly she works from home doing tailoring and alterations for two nearby dry cleaners, and in her own side business, Alexander Master Tailors. It's just her. A husband, whose story is a mystery to Micky, may have been in the business with her at one time. She's known Micky, 22, now a brawny 6'2" tow-headed blonde ex-Marine with skin color not much shy of Casper, since he was a skinny spot of white-yellow bristles for whom she hemmed Confirmation pants.

The Alexander apartment is on the first floor. The apartment above her is occupied by the owner, Ron Williams, a widower who prefers the second floor. He doesn't like the sound of people walking above him. Every Catholic Easter, he gives the Alexanders a cake in the shape of a lamb. They respond with a bowl of red-dyed hard-boiled eggs on Greek Easter.

"Hi, " says Micky, waving to Effie and Paul. Effie, hands clasped together on her lap, smiles nervously. Electra motions him to sit in an armchair adjacent to the couch where the kids sit. She stands, arms folded across her ribs, off to the side, slightly leaning against the wall.

"So, Paul, what're you, twenty now?"

"I'm eleven."

"Very close, not even a decade off." Paul smiles. It's a joke, but he also thinks it's cool that Micky said he was twenty.

"And I assume that you've just finished college?" he asks, looking at Effie.

"I'm fourteen. I'm a sophomore at Austin," Effie says, proudly, for being a sophomore.

She hates going to Austin and wishes she were back at Greek school, but that only goes until 8th grade. There's a trace of a smile. That's a start, Micky thinks.

"Paul," Electra interjects," why don't you go outside and play?" She wanted them to say hi to Micky. That's her etiquette. If you come over to her house, you see the kids. Then they can be released, like now. It should just be the three of them talking.

Paul is only too happy to take this suggestion. He fires off a goodbye, hardly looking and is nearly running by the time his hand pulls down on the doorknob.

"Okay. So, Effie," Micky begins, jumping right into it. "there was some kind of march that you saw? You want to tell me about it? What time of day? What exactly you saw? Just like that. Take your time."

Her mother glares. She's counting on her to be strong and grown up. She expects a lot of her children, always. Electra enjoys the envious position of having her children's love and respect, while still maintaining their fear. The combination gives her great leverage. Raising them alone is arduous, but she simply isn't going to let them fail.

Slowly, with her head down at first, Effie begins to recall the details. Afternoon, coloreds, silent, not like television marches. "They" frightened her. She is afraid to admit that her fear is really just from the one.

"Nothing distinctive then, to identify any of them, if the chance came," Micky asks? Effie shudders at the idea of such a chance. The thought of seeing that man again pales her complexion. Electra has her under the microscope. No movement or emotion escapes her notice.

"I mean, for ME to identify them, to find them," he clarifies, emphasizing himself.

Electra scoffs, raising both arms with her palms up, "How you describe a colored man, to tell him from another colored man? Is hard. I mean, they say—"

"I saw something, like a drawing, on one of them. Like a tattoo. It was on his neck. I think it was an arrowhead. It was shaped like a triangle." If she hadn't spoken right now, she might not ever have had the nerve. She shivers under the intense gaze of her mother.

Electra, who didn't know this detail, previously, streams out something excitedly to her in Greek. "Because you'd go crazy. I did see it. My eyes are very good," Effie answers with emphasis. Total silence follows. Electra, again in Greek, asks her if she was seen. Effie, not answering her question, turns to Micky.

"He...He fell. I mean, the one behind him fell, pulling his shirt. I saw it. His head turned. I saw his face. He had...on his chin..." She strokes her own chin with her fingers, fumbling for the word.

"A goatee?"

"Yes! A goatee, and mean eyes, evil eyes." She puts her head down, nearly cracking under the memory. Electra moves to sit near her side on the couch. She now knows this man did see Effie. That's why she's been so scared.

"Micky, " Electra begins, "They didn't do anything. I can't call a police. I call you. Everyone sees them. Who they are? What they want? Why they are doing this? Can you do something?"

"I'm going to try, Mrs. Alexander. I'll ask around to find out who knows what. Then, we'll see."

"He was a little older," Effie add, meekly.

"How old," Micky asks?

"I don't know. More than 21? Maybe 25 or more? I don't know." She asks as much as tells. He asks her about height, weight and clothing. He's tall, taller than Micky. His weight is average. His shirt was white with a mock-turtle neck.

"Anything else?" She shakes her head.

"Effie, he's gone. You'll never see him again." She looks at him. "I promise, and everything is all right. You're completely safe," he says. It helps a little. Electra is grateful for these assurances. "And it's good that you told me all this. "

Micky decides not to press further. It might be better to talk with Effie when her mother isn't around. He knows, too, that Mrs. Alexander's children don't do much that she doesn't know each, and every, single thing about, much less have an encounter with a black man who was angry and try-ing to intimidate. Effie was in for a serious grilling. Something more might come from that, too. Elec-tra would tell him.

Micky, saying goodbye, thanking them both, walks out. He dismisses the fear that Effie's feels. She's just a young girl who saw a scary looking guy. It's the march itself that has him concerned. There are a lot of young white guys that hang on street corners. There could be serious trouble if they run into a march, especially if they hear about one and prepare. And then, afterwards, the talk of any fight would only further spook a neighborhood that al-ready has one foot on the gas pedal. The march. He knows that it didn't just happen. It's a message.

The steps of the Alexander Victorian are wooden two by fours with an infinite number of grey layers of paint. He walks down them slowly. It feels like its slipping away. *How many feet have walked these stairs bringing home how many problems or how many joys? How much longer will he be able to walk these streets.* He decides to knock on a few other doors on Laramie and see what anybody else saw. First stop, at the next corner, is the 3-story, six-unit orange brick building that old man Hogan owns and lives in. He was a precinct captain years ago. Hogan knows the inside of everybody's house.

"I didn't see it myself, Mick, but people have stopped to tell me things, here at the house, up at the National, " he says referring to the grocery store," and just on the street."

"Was there a leader, Mr. Hogan? Did anyone say that?"

"No one saw it that way, Micky, no."

"Was anything said? Did they have any gang jackets or colors?

"Nothing like that, I'm afraid. It's a show of force, like marching the troops right through the middle of town so everyone knows you're there, and it's yours. " Hogan's reference is to his WWII experience.

"Right, like this neighborhood is ours now," Micky offers to show he understands. Hogan nods an agreement. He's not invited Micky in. They're standing, rather, at the front door. Apparently, he intends to hold the entire conversation here. Everything Micky can see, looking at Hogan and slightly past him into his apartment, is the same, right down to Hogan's suspenders, where he always pinned his political buttons.

"There's been other things, too."

"Other marches?"

"No, other trouble. The Italian fella, Citelli? He had his garage spray-painted, "Stones Run It." Can you imagine such a thing? Here's the kicker, it was painted on the inside, on the side facing the house, so he'd have to look at it. That's what they wanted. 'Read this, every day with your eggs and coffee.' They turned over a few garbage cans, too. Heard that one a couple of times now. And Sean Gibbons, you know him," he says getting a nod from Micky about the man who owned the building Micky grew up in. "His girls, they're both grown. Jean, who's married, is over. She walks to the store to get something for her mother. It's dark and here comes a Buick Riviera with a muffler the devil would have, yelling at her, scared her half way to glory-be."

"Did she get a plate?"

"No, she wasn't thinking about no plate, but if Sean sees that Riviera, those hooligans are gonna get a plate, in their head." Great, Micky thinks. That should start the fire sale. Although, if it were one of his sisters, he'd do that and more.

Micky doesn't mention the tattoo. It's what someone else knows, not what he tells them. He makes a note to talk to Citelli and Gibbons. It's the same story everywhere he stops. No descriptions. Just black. No one saw them North of Division. *How did they get here? How did they disappear?*

When he gets some more time, he'll talk to others who live south on Laramie. It would be easier for them to have disappeared down there by Lake Street where the elevated train, the "L", barrels through all day and night, limiting the types of businesses that can make it work . It's only the small manufacturing types where people are buried deep within their own world and who wouldn't notice the walkers, anyway, especially if they broke ranks to avoid being a spectacle.

He walks toward Lake to catch the train, thinking about who else he'll ask when he has the time. It's likely a dead-end, unless it happens again. *Which it will, something will. Who is doing this? Why?*

CHAPTER 3

"**G**entlemen, please rise for His Honor, the Mayor of Chicago, Richard J. Daley." Daley strides in briskly, making minimal eye contact. He's not wasting time with handshakes and hellos. A quick thank you to everyone for coming and he gets down to business. Reverend Charles Moore, senior minister at Chicago's Garfield Park Baptist Church, grants Daley one virtue; he works hard.

An invitation to this meeting was extended to Moore by the City of Chicago Office of the Mayor because he is known and trusted by the city's black gangs whose violence and criminal activities are epidemic. Daley has, in total, reached out to more than 30 public officials to plan and implement a solution.

Over the next two hours, the dialogue repeats from the previous meetings. The phrase 'gang structures' is used multiple times by the Mayor and by his State's Attorney, Edward Hanrahan. Charles' patience wanes. Nothing's new, or good enough. Nearing the end, Daley provides his two-minute summation, monotone and staccato as ever, that is, effectively, the entire meeting.

"I am calling for an all-out war against gang structures. The city has seen an upsurge in murders and other crimes committed by gangs near the schools and in the neighborhoods. We can't continue to have these senseless killings that we've seen in Chicago. We must stop the extortion of adults and school children and community leaders. All of society must rise up to these challenges. We owe it to the future generations to take a positive and firm stand. We are asking the public to cooperate with us in identifying the offenders. We will provide adequate protection to them with the constituted authorities."

He backs away from the escalating rhetoric for a brief, and to Charles, idiotic moment. "It is my hope that we can reason with some of these people and channel them into positive activities, like recreational activities." *Honestly! Does he really think that these young men will give up the opportunity for power and quick wealth to play basketball at the YMCA?*

Daley's next words show that he's ready to crush people if his appeasements don't work. "If we can't control and curb these gang structures, society will demand that we take the necessary actions. I hope it doesn't come to that. Today—" *I know your history, all the way back to the Hamburg Social and Athletic Club. Let's spell out it out for everyone.*

"Excuse me, your honor. What do you mean by the necessary actions, the ones that you hope it doesn't come to, Mr. Mayor, " asks Reverend Moore in a clear breech of protocol?

Daley glares sternly. He seethes. He recognizes Charles but continues, not responding directly. "All constituted authorities will use the means at their disposal to reason with and negotiate with the gangs. The hope is that this works."

"The city has had other gang structures, " interrupts Charles again, emphasizing the Mayor's words to effect sarcasm, "that extort and murder and have done so for longer than anyone can remember. These are white gang structures, organized crime, the Chicago Outfit. The black gang structures follow that model because the society you speak of hasn't left them much choice. It sounds like the city is prepared to flat-out kill these youths whereas the white gangs can just go about their business. How many Chicago business are being extorted by the Outfit?"

Several bodyguards and police move toward Reverend Moore sensing an oncoming rage that the press will eat up and make things worse. Seeing them, Reverend Moore asks, "Going to kick me out, with the constituted authorities? And the press here?"

Daley gives a slow blink that indicates an acceptance to letting Reverend Moore continue. "There has to be an alternative, for the young. Those who are in gangs now, are in them. Those coming up need to see a choice. They need an entire community. Integration has failed. We need a model that builds that community."

"Thank you, Dr. Moore, " begins Daley misidentifying his title, then disinviting him to continue. "The city looks forward to your ideas on how to do that. " Right, thinks Charles, about as much as they look forward to repeating the blizzard of '67.

◆ ◆ ◆

"He's equal parts ignorance, desperation and bigotry...a trinity of incompetence." Moore says of Mayor Daley, to his wife, Olivia, over breakfast, still frustrated with yesterday's meeting. He tugs loose a sadistic tie that he wears with his conservative black suit. He walks to the closet to retrieve his jacket. Not ready to don it yet, he hangs it on the back of a kitchen chair, leans against the counter and folds his arms across his chest. Unmistakable. He wants to vent.

"Charles, this is the third of Daley's meetings that you've attended. You hate them. Why don't you stop going?"

"No. Can't. It's true. I hate them." *And him.* "I've heard what Daley, and the others, have to say. It isn't working. It couldn't work. You can't convert gang members to productive members of society with library cards and summer camps. But I can't let them say that I quit." Moore has his reasons for mistrusting Daley, besides his incompetence, but doesn't get into those. He shields her from certain unpleasantries. It's part of the way he cares for her.

"Well, what about the others? He's brought in a lot of different qualified people. Isn't there something there, with them?" She ignores the summer camp comment.

"His 'qualified people' are circuit court judges, human resource directors at the Board of Education and a dozen other parasite bureaucrats, " he says, skipping ministers. "Dr. King wanted to remove the barriers to...to life here in America. The next step is to lead them into that life. What people need and what Daley thinks—"

"Gangs, and Dr. King — Is the city's gang violence connected to Civil Rights?"

"Yes, of course. Civil Rights is just another term for equal opportunity. If you're not getting the opportunity, if you are stuck at the bottom, and your parents were, and their parents were, then you cut in line."

"Oh, right. Of course. Sorry, I interrupted. You were saying that Daley thinks...?"

"Not too well, he doesn't. He's running out of body bags. The murder of Dr. King sent a message; non-violence doesn't work. What's the alternative then? " They exchange looks. "Exactly."

Rolling her eyes and trying to bring him to-wards his own, and, hopefully, more pragmatic approach, she asks, "What could be done? What's your answer? Looking ahead, not back at history, but forward toward the problem." Charles sees that she doesn't want to, again, hear about his frustration over the opportunities lost. "It's massive and endemic to society, isn't it?"

"It's the South Side, Olivia. The core of the problem with gangs in Chicago is a South Side problem. Daley's got to arrest, and the feds, too, as many of those in power now as he can. That's going to happen. Okay, but for the next group, the young blacks coming of age, they need an alternative. Right now, there isn't one."

"It's more than the South Side, isn't it? It's affecting the West Side, too."

"Well, it's growing and if it keeps growing, it's going to affect everything, but its central core in the South Side. The old Black Belt comes up near Roosevelt Road. Moving out from that area gets you into the West Side. That's now the front lines. My church, our church, is in that path. As more black families move West toward us, and past us, there's just more ghetto. Those areas don't succeed. It's not going to stop with a block party where the Fire Department caps the fire hydrant so it's a giant sprinkler for the kiddies. " Charles, returning to his acrimonious language, catches Olivia's judgmental eye and nods his head in an apology, which she accepts.

"I know you are hurt and upset over black families trying to get a better life, and just ending up with a new address, and more debt. " Her last words hit the bullseye. The Federal Housing Authority, the FHA, covers the down payment for blacks meaning even though they couldn't save the money, they can get in the door. Realtors, seeing eager buyers, gouge them for extra profits. It helps even more if they panic the seller. To get the best deal, they buy low themselves, as 'speculators', and then sell high.

"Yes. The vultures. Blockbusters. Gougers. They..." He trails off leaving the something more he was going to say but thinks better not to. "For every immigrant, and that's what the blacks are. They immigrated to the city in droves, just like the Irish and other Europeans. For every group, race hasn't been an added layer of complexity. Stark differences like that breed hatred. Two races living together with a history of slavery between them is like trying to juggle bricks, gumballs and...and"

"Bwuhah!" The laugh spits out of her mouth. She quickly covers, hand over her mouth. Charles looks at her. He's encouraging it. "And cats? And suitcases? And...? " she offers, trying to finish it.

He suggests one for her, one that will really make her lose it. "And the widow Hendrick's breasts. I mean how, in heaven's name, is that configuration even possible? They have different zip codes." Olivia, eyes exploding, becomes hysterical with laughter to the point that she can't speak. She flaps a hand at him to stop. He takes it as asking for more. "Perhaps she has had two husbands, and each had a preference for a different breast? Or maybe she eats lying on one side and the nutrition slides down that one way. I just don't know."

They settle down. He'll returns to the point, but his frustration is gone. Talking with her always does that. "Anyway, if you mix fundamentally different natures, race or religion or cultures, world history shows us war. That's where we're at, war, again, and the whites win in a slaughter."

"You sound a bit like a segregationist with that statement." He just lifts his eyebrows quickly in lieu of an answer.

Calmly, with the voice of a man looking into the future and saddened by what's foretold, "For Daley, race and maintaining control is his go-to move, too. The great political machine is crumbling. Actually, no, it's already gone. When his tokenism doesn't work, he goes to violence, institutional violence. History shows that, too. There's been plenty of that against black people, to keep them in their place. And, I know that you know this better than I do. I'm preaching to the choir. "

Charles refers to her childhood. She grew up

in Birmingham, Alabama. Her father owned a small diner where he also cooked. He moved the family into a better neighborhood, a white neighborhood. The citizens were having none of that. Their house was bombed as were the homes of dozens of other black families trying the live there. It was so common the area was nicknamed Dynamite Hill. "The only thing that they know to do patronize, then attack."

"Attack? What do you think, exactly, he would do? Another shoot to kill order? " she asks referencing Daley's quote during last year's looting riots.

"Exactly, only, this time, I think it would be assassination style. They'll not just shoot anybody. They'll hit the leaders, a 'chop off the head and the body will surely die' approach. They know who the leaders are."

"Charles, where are we and what year is it, " Olivia says alluding to a past that should be gone? The implied answer chills her.

"Olivia, there's something I need to tell you. You've heard me talk many times, making the point there has to be a successful community of blacks in Chicago, living with whites. Austin, just 5 minutes West of us, will be the next neighborhood to go. That's where blacks are looking to buy. It's a nice neighborhood. Doesn't represent much uprooting to move there. The realtors are doing their block-busting thing, but I've learned about something else, something more dangerous. " He gathers himself. This is what he's been holding back. Reverend Moore has not shared this with anyone. "Austin is going to fold like a tent, anyway. I want to stop that. But I'm holding something back from them."

"What?"

He looks at Olivia and says, " I don't trust Daley."

"Please. Charles, you can skip the tremendously obvious, " suggests Olivia dropping her head like a teacher correcting a student.

He smiles and nods. "Okay. There's a realtor who has taken the next step and is colluding with black gang members to harass and intimidate. They organized a march through Austin recently. That kind of thing has the potential to turn into something disastrous, and it would set everyone and everything back. Plus, they're doing more than marching. And these realtors don't know who they're dealing with. Stick a dollar bill in front of them and they're blind to everything else. I have to do something. I am doing something. And it's not through Daley and the city. I am going to get in front of this thing." He looks at her to say that she has to understand. It's what he must do. He says nothing further. He can tell that he has frightened her. She had to be warned.

"I'd better get cracking on these dishes, if I'm

to get started on time," Olivia says, moving on from the subject. Charles has told her enough for now, for the time that they have this morning. She rises lifting stacks of dishes and coffee cups with each hand. Getting started time refers to her art studio and gallery. She rents a modest space in Bucktown. An accomplished artist, her work depicts images of blacks in American history from slavery to modern times in all manner of settings. Her art is more critically appreciated than sold.

Charles is, again and always, impressed with his wife's poise and intelligence. She doesn't avoid the problems, but she knows when a conversation is no longer productive. She understands that some things are best to slowly reveal. She has an elegance and tact that challenges him to also operate at that higher level.

The cleanup is quickly handled. She turns to the bedroom to change for work. His wife is also physically beautiful. He follows her in, moves to stand close behind her. She can feel his hardness behind her and can see the intention in his eyes through the dresser mirror.

CHAPTER 4

Micky hurtles up the stairs that lead to his second-floor apartment above Friendly Liquors on Chicago Avenue. He's a little excited, but that's his normal way to climb them.

"K-9? Yo. You here? " he bellows, opening the door and hoping to hear a response from his roommate, Edmund "K-9" Kannon.

With none forthcoming, he heads toward the small middle bedroom that he, long ago, converted into an office. Of sorts. At least it's where he keeps his work stuff. He drops off his backpack, which contains both his notes from the talk with the Alexanders and today's incoming mail for his boss, Jim Diamond. His large hand scoops out the four-inch thick stack of mail that he's bound with rubber bands. He cradles it against his rib football style and walks to the living room where a 20-inch fan resting on the floor and facing outward from the side of the television does its best to cool off the hot apartment.

The building enjoys no shade. The exterior brick heats under the sun and starts to permeate to the interior just about this time of day, late afternoon. The apartment doesn't cool on summer days until the outside temperature lowers to 65. It's too warm for him to work right now.

It's time for a rooftop session. Just beyond his back door and past the rear stairwell, he can access a series of flat roofs. The first of these covers the storage room for Friendly's, where, in his youth, he was known to, occasionally, borrow a case of beer. He's made up for it since, with over-tipping, now that he can enter the bar legally. He and K-9, jokingly, refer to this as The Veranda. Five consecutive flat rooftops connect everything from the alley to the Leamington, just across from his shop.

A Salvation Army sofa furnishes a small corner. Micky rips off the tarp and softly tosses the stack of cards and letters onto the middle cushion, plunking himself down next to it. First, he needs to do a sort. A 3-foot wide wooden spool that once held steel cable serves as the coffee table. He creates three separate stacks: Diamond needs to read this, I have a form letter to cover this, and this is pure junk.

He can handle this task pretty fast. The mail is mostly the same. There are invitations to be a speaker at certain events. They love for Diamond to tell some stories of the old and new criminals in the Outfit. There are thank-you cards, mostly for speaking. Rarely, has he done anything worthwhile, at least in a long time. Some are in the fashion of tips, things it's worthwhile for him to know. He's paid well and in-demand because of what he knows. He needs to feed a lot of carrier pigeons to get that knowledge.

One letter stands out. It's a request for help. He can't believe the words and re-reads it as he, unconsciously, sits up and moves to the edge of the couch. His brow furrows. There's a bit faster heartbeat.

Dear Mr. Diamond, I am the senior minister at the   Garfield Park Baptist Church. You may also know me from my previous work on Dr. Martin Luther King's Chicago Freedom Movement.

I am writing to ask you to investigate Avenue Realty, 4624 W. Chicago Avenue, for unethical, illegal and potentially dangerous actions regarding the selling of homes in the Austin neighborhood of Chicago's West Side. It is my hope that the investigation will provide sufficient evidence such that Avenue will be forced to conclude this relationship.

As you may know, the West side is on the verge of being integrated by black families. This has created an anxiety among many white owners enabling what realtors term a buyer's market. This panic is not something that I, nor the other spiritual leaders of the black community, whose members are interested in supporting the relocation of families for better schools, safer neighborhoods and nicer homes, want. However, exacerbating the problem of integration are those who may profit from quick, panic-driven sales.

Many realtors are buying the property themselves and then selling at an inappropriately higher price to blacks. The usual scare tactics involve lying to white owners that black families have moved in and that black youth are committing terrible crimes such as armed robbery and even rape. These crimes, it is said, are not being reported to the police due to the fact that owners want to either avoid public embarrassment and/or to help quickly sell their homes without any further loss of value resulting from the release of such news. These tactics, and those who commit them, known as blockbusters, are very disheartening. Yet I am writing because of efforts that go beyond even this.

During my work experiences in the community, including that previously mentioned in this letter, I have made many contacts with gang youths, including leaders. Through such contacts, it has come to my awareness that Avenue Realty has entered into an agreement, a collusion, with gang members in order to have them harass white neighborhoods within Austin. They drive through the streets at night, disturbing the peace, and, in some cases frightening young women. They vandalize properties and spray-paint threatening messages

. One example that this is, indeed, an organized and coordinated effort is the recent incident involving up to 100 youths marching down the street commanding the entire sidewalk. They had neither a permit nor a demonstrable intention. Such a provocation could only

be accomplished with some organizational effort and planning.

A situation like that march could be most danger-ous. I think that the integration of Austin is inevitable, but I desire to see it succeed in the way that other inte-gration efforts have not. If you would be willing to meet, I can provide you greater detail, though I must protect the anonymity of my contacts.

It's the march, Effie's march! Organized in collu-sion with a local realtor? Son-of-a-bitch!

The letter is signed Reverend Charles Moore, Senior Minister, Garfield Park Baptist Church. The name Avenue Realty is, maybe, familiar to him, but for what? He grabs a city phone book. There is an Avenue Realty. He remembers now; he knows the place. They even have an ad in the Central Stand-ard Times, a pretty big ad, comparatively. He didn't take the account himself, though and doesn't know them personally.

It's late, but realtors work evenings. He covers the mail with the tarp and walks inside to his kit-chen. He's moving fast, not thinking. He reaches for the wall phone and calls the number.

"Avenue Realty, Leslie Higgins speaking. How can I help you? " requests a man's voice.

"Yeah, hello. This is Greg Zarkoosis. I work for Walter Jacobson, Channel 2 News. He'd like to set up a time to interview you for an investigation he's doing on the West Side and integration." Micky has used the Jacobson gambit before, rather than possibly get himself in trouble. He waits for response.

"What about the West Side and integration? " asks Higgins, with a sharp rise in attitude.

"Well, Mr. Jacobson has received some reports. People say that realtors are, you know, scaring people, blockbusting." He clears his throat. "For example, recently, there was a march. Reportedly, a hundred or so young blacks. The intention seems to have been intimidation, you know, to panic the white owners. Such an event requires a good amount of organization. You know, the people, the logistics of it all." Higgins just listens. "Some people have suggested that this organization might be coming from realtors. It's just logical. They would have the motive, be the ones that would profit. " He's gone too far. "Uh, would you have any knowledge of that, of just any part of that?"

Micky doesn't know what he expects Higgins to say or do. He's not sure exactly why he called, but he's stuck right on the man's forehead now and has to live with it now. Thank God I didn't use my name or the name of the paper.

"Fuckin' bullshit!" starts Higgins with a boom. "That's what I have knowledge of, a lot of lumpy, creamy, multi-colored bullshit. You tell Jacobson that! And you tell him to call me himself, if that shrimp can reach the phone. You tell him one more thing. " His voice turns gravelly and threatening. "Tell him that he'd better be very careful putting my name or the name of Avenue Reality, into any published report. If he's got people that are naming us, and me, in particular, I'd like to talk to him, too, about who said what. I think someone might be trying to smear me with a lot of innuendo. That's slander. That's defamation of character. And there's motive for that, too! Excepting that and until that, and then, and when and if, tell him to go fuck himself and have a nice day."

His head jumps with the slam of the phone by Higgins. He slowly replaces his phone back in its cradle. Higgins' response seemed too tense. Wasn't he a bit defensive? He should have just laughed it off, right? On the other hand, maybe it was the right response because I basically accused him of serious illegal actions.

Micky knows that he called too quickly. He didn't prepare. He needs to slow down. What does he really know? There is an Avenue Realty and what? Maybe they're doing a little blockbusting? Big deal. Who isn't? That's hardly news. There's no corroboration of this collusion because he hasn't talked with Reverend Moore. I don't know what Moore can substantiate. I don't know jack-squat! That's where he needed to start. No. That comes after talking this over with the guy this letter is addressed to, Jim Diamond.

Returning to the Veranda and uncovering the couch, he finishes sorting the rest of the mail. He binds each pile with one of the large rubber band he uses for CST. Then he places his feet on the spool coffee table and crosses his legs. He stretches his arms up and clasps his hands behind his head. This is his best thinking position.

The neighborhood is under siege, next up on the hit parade known as integration. That's for sure. But that's one thing. No one knows exactly how that will play out. Now, you have gangs coming in harassing people, trying to push the timeline up and the conditions to their immediate favor? Local realtors who can't make the money fast enough willing to risk a major screw up with people getting hurt? That's another thing, quite a damn other thing.

The wooden back stairs creak under someone's weight. The pace sounds a person hiking two steps at a time. He recognizes the sound of his apartment door unlocking. It's K-9. "Yo," he yells, leaping off the couch and adding a wave. He wants to catch him before he enters.

"Hey, K-9, got a minute?"

No answer, but footsteps on the tar roof signal him coming closer. K-9, whose thick, coarse and already greying hair is still slightly wet from the shower he took after his sparring session at the gym, is walking his answer over.

K-9 is Micky's roommate and colleague at CST. He writes the sports column. He also works as a sparring partner for professional light heavyweights among whose ranks he once was himself. An inch taller than Micky, he is much leaner with the boxer's body.

Micky sits patiently watching as he takes a seat on the opposite end of the couch, an indication that he thinks this may require more than a minute's attention. "I guess. What's up?"

"Like to run something by you," he answers by way of an explanation.

"I guessed. The real one-minute things you usually just yell out, or maybe wait on. The it's-not-really-a-one-minute-one-minute-things take more time, include more than one question. That's why I walked over and got comfortable. Whaddyagot?"

"Okay. Here goes. There was this march of blacks with guys who are maybe in their late teens, from what I gather. They walked down Laramie, but on the sidewalk, not like a protest march all 'we shall overcome' and everything. This is more all tough and everything. They don't talk."

"Gotcha. Tough silent black guys on the sidewalk. How many?"

"Maybe a hundred." K-9's look turns a bit more serious.

"Anyway, little Effie Alexander—well, she's not that little anymore..."

"Who?"

"Neighborhood kid. Greek. Effie, I think, its short for Aphrodite."

"Oh, lord, " K-9 laughs. "And she doesn't like to go by that? How strange?"

"Yeah, right. Anyway, she gets a bead on one. He's particularly scary. She's not over it. Effie is not getting a lot of sleep."

"Poor kid. Just looked at her?"

"Yeah, but it gets better now. He's older than the other, maybe 25ish." His look to K-9 begs the question is maybe this one the leader. "He's got a tattoo like an arrowhead on his neck, a triangle, she says. Let's stop there. Ring a bell?"

"Triangle? Arrowhead? Hmmm. Maybe a pyramid?

"I guess."

"See, black guy with a pyramid would be, well, could be the Blackstone Rangers. They use the symbol. Their pyramid represents Egypt and black history or their ancestry, which was destroyed by the slave trade. Stones been building their own black nation of gangs. That's the Black P Stone Nation thing. It's like America. There's a centralized lead, like the federal government, that they all have to follow on certain things, but they're all individual gangs, too, like the states, with rights. Together, they're the Black P Stone nation. And the pyramid has building blocks. There's one block for each gang."

Micky knows that K-9 has some familiarity with Jeff Fort and Bull Hairston, the founders of this group. K-9's early life was a mess. He was sent to the St. Charles Juvenile Detention Center for robbery where he knew these two. It's, in fact, where he took his first straight step, boxing. K-9 was well-known at St. Charles for boxing. Fort and Hairston were well known, too, becoming gang leaders even at that time and at that age.

"Aha!" Micky starts, catching the theme he hopes for. "Okay. Here's the rest. First, read this." He shows K-9 the Moore letter and adds, "I talk to Effie.—Her mom called me.—Then I asked around. People are telling me that there are some other incidents of harassment that are happening in the neighborhood."

"What other incidents of harassment?"

"That's the second part. Like a little vandalism, like hawking women who are walking alone, like spilling garbage cans, AND, like writing Stones Run It on garages, like that. The pyramid thing works with that. I'm going to talk to Diamond about moving on this. We'll see what happens.

So, the tattoo is maybe saying Stones. The garage spray paint message is also saying Stones. Do you think the Blackstone Rangers could be the gang that Moore was talking about? And that they are doing this harassment?"

"Not exactly their modus operandi. They're interested in conquering the world and setting up their own country, you know, after the revolution, of course. But there's money in it, right? Second thought, I don't know. How much money's in it?"

"Don't really know. Have to find out more. What about the message "Stones Run It" on the garage?

"Only takes a can a paint. Most teenagers can spell those words." He's staying unconvinced.

"Yeah, but the march. That took something to pull together. Can you use your various and sundry contacts to see who this 25-year old with a maybe pyramid tattoo might be, or who organized this march?"

K-9 shrugs, which Micky accepts as a yes.

CHAPTER 5

Micky spends the morning digging through the Daily News archives. He finds a ton of stories on Reverend Moore, more that he can absorb, but his conclusion is that this guy is for real. About 4 years ago, Martin Luther King implemented a strategy for breaking Northern segregation by targeting jobs and housing for black in Chicago. He named the initiative the Chicago Freedom Movement. It had a good deal of success getting major concessions from the city.

Moore is not just a minister. He's also a lawyer and had worked on developing the policies and eliminating racist tenant covenants. A story of his brokering a truce between two warring gangs, one of which was the Blackstone Rangers, provides some credibility that he has the gang connections to make his assertions. Micky takes the letter back upstairs and place it in the top of the pile.

Early afternoon, and Jim Diamond, sits at his desk, begging a stale cup of coffee to work a minor miracle. His appearance has all the appeal of last winter's bowl of oatmeal. Micky picks up the letter and hands it to him, telling him this is one he wants to read, then watches his face sour as he does.

"I know this guy. And, Mulvihill, you think I should say yes, and have you leg out the details? Hmmm? Well, this is not the type of organized crime that interests me," he says, answering his own question and adding a cold look in Micky's direction, which says 'you should know that'.

"I know, but you are the one he wrote to and you do have the pull to make things happen, " he offers to defend himself. It's bolder than Micky normally is, almost like trying to give his boss an assignment. He adds something which is an insult, for sure. "And it's seems very serious and important." *This is important, more important than my taking notes on which mob guy is meeting with which mob guy that you don't do anything with. You just want to know so that when they need an expert for tv, or maybe a book, they might call you.*

"Does it? Well, I don't think so. Know why? The West Side is going to fall, along with half the city. In ten years, the city is going to be a black fucking jungle. " The Jamison lunch has left him a bit surly.

"Okay. But gangs speeding up the clock could be very dangerous. And if realtors start doing this type of 'collusion' it's, just, you know...bad. And this Moore guy, he checks out. I looked him up in our archives. He worked with King on the Chicago Freedom Movement. He's worked with black gangs, too, stopping the violence with a truce."

Diamond's not softening. In fact, his mood goes just the opposite way.

"Look up Moore, didja? Waste a few hours down in the archives? Hmm?"

"Yeah." *He's taunting me. Did I miss something?*

"Found all his wonderful history, right?" Micky shrugs a yes. *I did. Here it comes.*

"Bet the articles didn't mention that he was a member of the Vice Lords?"

"What? Moore? He's a minister and a lawyer—"

"And a gang member. He found Jesus and went holy. Oh, yes. He studied at, what is it?"

"The Chicago Baptist Institute and the University of Chicago Law school."

"Okay, and before that, he was in the Vice Lords. It was back when the black gangs first started, in the 50s, and they weren't what they are today. But they were still gangs. There was something going on. And, sure, you read about how he's negotiated truces with warring gangs, right? Well, that's because he was once one of them. That's how he could do that.

The Blackstone Rangers got into a war, one of their many. A rival gang, the Disciples, killed a Stones guy. He was walking where he shouldn't. In steps Reverend Moore. He gets a truce. Okay. Big hero. "

"Well, it was a truce. People stopped killing each other."

"Yeah. Now look a little closer. No, actually, not closer, but at the next thing, which is that both the Stones and the Disciples got federal program money. Pretty slick, well, at least it was, before they started screwing it up. Isn't that just the kind of thing a lawyer could help with?

"What are you saying? Moore showed the Stones and the others how to grab federal program money?"

"Well, how did they learn to do that? Jeff Fort? And the other guy, Bull Hairston? Barely can spell their own names. Somebody helped them, and our esteemed lawyer was right there. And didn't they take up, then, with a second minister with a, shall we say, checkered past? Yes, now they suddenly like ministers. Fancy that. The other guy — What's his name— Curtis Burrell, Reverend Burrell. Oh, they've been having a little riff the last couple months, just as the feds are looking to lock Fort up for their money scheme. The heat's closing in and they're looking to blame each other, dump each other, whatever. Yesterday, in fact, Burrell holds a conference, separating himself, criticizing the Stones, but he has been a key guy for them, a real golden boy." He stops a moment for emphasis. "AND, did you know that he's also an ex-con. Oh, yeah. Look that up! Gang guy, ex-con becomes minister and helps the Stones. He's a real charmer. Your guy, Moore? He's in the same bucket. Gangs and ministers. Ministers and gangs. He marched with King, and he played dirty games with gangs. Not everything is in the archives." He stops, delivering his decision, " You don't do anything with this on my time."

"Yeah. Okay, " Micky says, meaning the opposite.

You're less a reporter and more a gossip columnist wagging on about the mob guys, who are celebrities of sorts. You're a celebrity hopeful yourself, complete with the alcohol addiction. All you know is this one talked to that one, then this other thing happened. Yeah, you have the inside scoop on this one. It was right at the bottom of the bottle waiting for you.

◆ ◆ ◆

"Garfield Park Baptist Church. Hello. This is Rosemary. How may I direct your call?" The pleasant sound of a young female voice greets him.

"Hello. My name is Micky Mulvihill. I work for the Chicago Daily News. Reverend Moore sent a letter to the paper. I'm calling in response to that letter. Is he available?" Rosemary confirms Micky's information and asks him to hold.

"This is Reverend Charles Moore, " a voice says,

breaking the minute-long silence of Micky's wait. He's only identifying himself. He's cautious, which adds to Micky's nervousness.

"Reverend Moore, my name is Micky Mulvihill, Chicago Daily News. I work for Jim Diamond. He received your letter regarding Austin and the collusion between gangs and Avenue Realty. Mr. Diamond sympathizes with the situation that you described in your letter. However, he is extremely busy now with other investigations. Also, this isn't his type of work. He wonders why you haven't gone to the police and how it is you came to find out this information." He's trying to get Moore to admit that he needs help. That would make it easier to accept his own paper over the Daily News.

A long pause. "Jim Diamond took a request regarding a very serious, not to mention, very sensitive matter and asked his assistant to call me to say no thanks, how do I know, and to suggest that I am better served by contacting law enforcement? Is that what I am to understand? And I should just carelessly hand contact information to his assistant, so Mr. Diamond is not left uninformed even though he's not going to help. Is that why we are having this call?" His strategy didn't work. Micky breaks clean. He won't try to defend his question.

"No, sir, not entirely, sir. You see, in addition to being Mr. Diamond's, uh, assistant, I am also the publisher and owner of the Central Standard Times.

It's a weekly periodical distributed in Austin, the very neighborhood that you discuss. The Times has a circulation of about 6,000. While Mr. Diamond is not able to assist you, I..I would be...interested in this story for my paper."

Micky has startled Moore a bit startled with this revelation. Before he could get his next question out, Micky adds, "And Jim Diamond didn't ask me to call. I do work for him, but... There's a pretty much standard letter we would send out describing his inability to respond. A phone call isn't part of it. I am here because the issue you described matters to me and my readers."

Moore adjusts his tone. "There can't be a story where I reveal information that I would have shared with someone doing an investigation. I simply can't provide anything that would be printed in any story about this collusion for many reasons. However, there is another possibility. I would like to write an article in your paper about Austin about integration. I would like to illuminate that working-class people don't all have white skin. I'd like your readers to know that there are many families just looking for the same thing that they themselves were looking for when they moved to Austin." He stops, waiting for a reaction. It's now Moore's phone call and Micky's on the defensive.

Micky doesn't like it, but Moore is interested in the Central Standard Times. He's made an offer on what he's willing to do. Micky needs to get at this collusion. He has to be careful. Moore might want a pulpit, but that's not what he's after. "With all due respect, Reverend, preaching to my readers about the decent black people who want to be their neighbors won't stop incidents like the one that recently happened on Laramie last month that you noted in your letter. It won't stop the late-night harassments of young girls that have been occurring. It won't stop what you yourself called a situation that can be most dangerous."

"I'm very upset that Jim Diamond didn't think this worthy of his intention. And I won't be party to a reckless article. I'm afraid my offer—" Moore is going to bail. He thinks of a counterproposal.

"How about an interview instead? " Micky asks, cutting him off before his ultimatum. "In the interview, there will be opportunity to describe those blacks whom you wish to characterize. But there will also be questions as to your opinion about other, and previous, Chicago neighborhood integrations. And also, I'll ask questions about the Laramie march."

"What questions, " Moore asks?

"Nothing referring to your contacts or knowledge, just your thoughts, the way you see this from your perspective, what's happening." Micky has him back on the issue. He also knows enough about his business to tell him only the subject areas and not specific questions in advance of an interview.

"Black people in Chicago, who they are, their integration efforts to date and Laramie, then? Is that it, " Moore asks indicating that this compromise might be workable?

"Pretty much. No cheap shots." It's not an agreement to tell all he knows, but it's an agreement to at least talk about it in general terms. Then, maybe something can develop.

"Very well then. Come to my office, which is behind the church sanctuary, after service the last week of the month, Sunday, July 27th, say around 12:30. You have the address from the letter, " Moore offers, agreeing to the interview. He seems to be making one last check that Micky truly has the letter in his possession.

"It's a deal, Reverend Moore."

It's a beginning. Maybe he can build a little trust and Moore will work with him on an investigation?

With the call ended, he looks at the newsroom. It's crowded with legmen. Some are nose-deep into running down leads, checking details and coming up with sources. Some do the crossword puzzle waiting for the next breaking news to chase. He wants to tell them all that he's a newspaper publisher and owner, and he's got a story. He stops to think about that; this is the first time that he's developing the news story. He's, previously, either written or provided the facts, or he's given opinions on stories. This time it's different.

This story is not even in the news. This story with its hundreds of blacks, organized, colluding with a local realtor who has gone way beyond the usual panic-peddling to try to create a rush of sales would be an investigation. *If it's real.* He needs to move carefully.

His interviewee is smart and media-wise, more than any in of his previous interviews. That was quite a jousting match just to get him to agree to a generic talk about the subject. Moore could evade the issue. He needs to know a lot more about this. He's hoping K-9 can come through for him on this one. It's this guy with the pyramid tattoo. He's the key. If he pulled together a hundred guys, got them in place and made them disappear, someone must know about him.

CHAPTER 6

T wo tumbler glasses sit on the table, each half empty now as the men have toasted to their history of success. That celebration is not the purpose of their meeting, though.

"You need to sign this Declaration of Faith." The intention in Lewis Leonard's eyes adds that he is serious. Sammy Gallagher well knows men whose look is not a bluff. He is such a man himself. "You are my follower. I am guided by God. I work miracles in His name and destroy false gods and those who idolize them." Lewis adds for emphasis watching him ponder his options.

Sammy already knows what choice he will make. He knew it before they sat down. People who take for a living just keep taking. They have to, even though, eventually, they will take too much.

Sammy Gallagher is a black man born in Earle, Arkansas, just across the bridge from Memphis, in 1933. He picked cotton for white farmers from the time he could strap on a bag. The pennies he brought in could buy a potato or two to help the family eat. It's not enough, not for a boy who could see the movie posters and the newspapers and the magazines showing more of a life. Some will take the meager life that white folks here dole out forever. Not him.

It didn't take long before he began to steal, first from the church, then the general store and, finally, from white folks, right out of their homes. Word got out about the little gang of thieves soon enough. They weren't that bright about it and small towns like Earle don't hold their secrets well, especially if you live on the wrong side of the tracks.

He was lucky, people said, only to be beaten before being arrested. The reference for the people of Earle is always Elton Mitchell who made the mistake of refusing to work for free for a white man. Elton was disemboweled, and then hanged from a tree like a butchered hog. The hanging was a message on the way it is. That happened only fifteen years before Sammy was born.

Ricky Bob Eddy was the white sheriff who arrested Sammy the first time and the second. Ricky Bob wore a pearl-handled .38 on his hip as a signature. When it wasn't insufferably hot, he'd wear a white jacket, too. White for being a good guy. He went to the beauty parlor to get his sandy brown hair cut. The one town barber, trained in the Army, just wouldn't do.

Sammy improved his skill while he was in prison. Window locks are easier than door locks, and bedroom windows are often unlocked. Getting on roofs is easy and getting to a window from the roof is ballsy, but not hard. He learned where to steal, too. It's easier to steal in a big city than a small —let alone poor— town.

Chicago was the obvious choice. St. Louis was closer, both of them being straight North on I-55, but Chicago was so much bigger and Shakey Jake Harris, who was born in Earle, had become a bluesman star in Chicago. Everyone thought about that city first. All the black folks who left twenty years before he was born had gone there. There are lots of blacks in that city and lots of place to hide, and lots of places to rob.

He still wasn't bright about it. He expanded his options. The black gangs needed tough guys. That's where he met Lewis Leonard. They stole and extorted. Lewis was a good source for money. Sooner or later, though, he would end up back in the pen. It became a life he accepted.

Thieves need to stay tough. He lifted iron in prison until he was a beast. He raped men for sex, but it was really part of the power game. He knew, little by little, that the kind of professional thief he had become and the life he led would end early. It didn't matter. Better to have something for a while than live with nothing forever.

Sammy briefly had read Leonard's Declaration of Faith. He's not that great at reading, but he could tell that a simpleton maniac with grand delusions had just copied sections of what he thought must be the Bible and put himself in the place of some great prophet and miracle worker. Everyone used the Bible or some scripture to validate themselves. It's time to choose. He won't follow this maniac longer.

Only Sammy doesn't know it's already too late.

He looks out, but not focusing on anything. Rather, it's the small burning in his lower intestine that has his attention. It quickly erupts. He can't think. He turns to the kitchen sink to make himself vomit.

Lewis Leonard clubs him in the back of the neck. As he starts to slip away, there's a thought as to what happened and who did it. *Fool!* Leonard pulls a tarp and two plastic garbage ties from a lower cabinet and bundles him. The hydrochloric acid, odorless and tasteless in the vodka, eats him, but he'll live. Even in his unconscious state, he knows that he'll live long enough for Lewis to complete a planned ceremonial goodbye.

◆ ◆ ◆

It's late evening and the summer sun has,

finally, given way to the black of night. Lewis lays alone in his bed. An alley street lamp shines silvery light in through his window as the only illumination. He always leaves the apartment dark. The changing amounts of light create shadows. And that's when he hears the whispering voices. Some are outside walking by. Some are in the apartment with him.

A small black and white television with its antennae pointed toward the window sits on top of two wooden crates. He rises, reaches over and tugs on the power knob.

A voice appears before the picture does. "This is Walter Jacobson, channel 2 news. Yesterday's fire at the Mennonite Church on Chicago's Southwest Side is very suspicious to many. It comes on the heels of an extremely critical rebuke of the Blackstone Rangers by the minister of that church. We have John Burrows, live, to report from the Mennonite Church. John? " The image sharpens. An oval-faced man with curly hair and glasses is speaking. His delivery bounces, giving a heavier beat every few words.

"Thank you, Walter. I am standing in front of the Mennonite church on Chicago's Southwest Side." The television image switches to the closed doors of the burnt church. On the side of one door is the name of the church. When there is sufficient time to see the blackened wood and read the sign, the camera pans back down to the sidewalk where the reporter stands. "The church, just as you described, was essentially destroyed by fire, yesterday, one day after the minister, Reverend Curtis Burrell, held a press conference to denounce Jeff Fort, leader of the Black P Stone Nation. Reverend Burrell was highly critical of Jeff Fort, saying, at one point, emphatically that 'Stones don't run it', an obvious reference to the Blackstone Rangers slogan, 'Stones Run It.' Reverend Burrows called the press conference to address the damage that the Blackstone Rangers, in his opinion, are doing to South Side residents and businesses. He accused them of shakedowns for protection and extorting into joint ownerships. He said that their presence is pervasive and damaging to the South Side."

Lewis listens to the reporter detail the damages to the church. *The fire of God and its power shows to the people.* Burrows continues to reference Burrell's assertion of the growing problem of gangs, particularly the Black P Stone Nation, who are trying to control the black community. *Burrell was punished by the fire of God. I called to God to deliver the fire.*

Burrows continues. "Reverend Burrell's position is complicated, and not solely holding the Blackstone Rangers accountable. Here is what he had to say about the Black P Stone Nation or, familiarly, the Stones, just a few months ago." He stares motionless into the camera until the tape rolls. "The real power brokers are the white people who have empowered the Stones with their anti-poverty program money. It's white people behind the problem, causing the problem. They're feeding a fortune into the Stones' pockets knowing that they're going to buy guns and use those guns to extort and kill and commit all these crimes. It's the white people's way of destroying the black community without getting their hands dirty." Burrows recaps telling everyone what they just heard for themselves.

The broadcast returns to Jacobsen. "There is a real problem on the South Side with gangs and it's spreading to the West Side." He and co-anchor ensure viewers that they are not jumping to the conclusion of the Blackstone Rangers being guilty of arson, even though everyone has made that same assumption. Bill Kurtis, Jacobsen's co-anchor, offers how Channel 2 will be following the investigation of the fire closely and reporting on any of its developments.

Click. Lewis pushes the knob in to shut the television off. Static from the screen crackles from the touch of his shirt hem. The shadows quickly start to move about in the darkness. The voices mutter. Sitting up on the mattress with his knees, he listens closely.

"God has sent a message. Jeff Fort is going to be a preacher. He will lead everyone. He will use me. I am the messenger. White people have been the pawn brokers, but no more." Lewis speaks out loud back to the voices. He knows it's what they want to hear from him, that he understands. He uses a long sewing needle to etch a name into his stomach. Elijah.

◆ ◆ ◆

Lewis Leonard stands in his bathroom looking at himself in the mirror above the medicine cabinet. His clothing has grown heavier. It's now the wool or heavy linen or even the animal skins that provided protection when he first walked and did God's work. "The blessing is that which we receive. The revelation that guides us. The curse, the punishment, is the test of our belief in that revelation," he says out loud to his image in the mirror. "Reveal yourself to me. I will believe."

The razor and shaving soap sit unused on the white porcelain rim of the sink. The hot water has been running for 20 minutes now. His image looks back at him and commands his attention. He sees that the eyes look where his do not. It's beginning. The revelation comes. *Look at me. Look at me.* He sees the light skin that reminds him that his mother once washed him in bleach trying to clean the filth. As Lewis Leonard, he is the filth. As Elijah, he is the miracle worker of God. The reflection reads his thoughts and evaluates him. His every thought is transparent. From the corner of his eye, he sees that someone stands next to him. When he turns his head to look, he can tell that his image in the mirror does not. It continues to look straight ahead and watch him.

Jeff Fort! It's Jeff Fort who stands next to him. *That's good. The preacher, the angel, is here.* He feels the warmth. The steam rising from the sink touches his face, driving deep into his pores. He turns back to the mirror. And Jeff Fort is now there. The face he sees reflected, on his body, is not his, but Jeff Fort's.

He turns back to his one-time leader and asks, "Are you...with me?" he asks to confirm his understanding of this. Fort nods smiling, then he is gone. He feels safe, blessed. They are one right now. His own image returns, showing the tattoo on his neck. It's the symbol that signifies his allegiance to Fort. Today, it shows Fort is part of him.

Steam still rises from the bowl of the sink. It fogs the mirror in brief flashes. The small window in the wall just above the bathtub a few feet away is cracked open two inches. Air draws in lightly and clears the mirror. Then it fogs again. Over and over. Seeing the change surrounding the reflection of his face, he understands. It's a sign. Smoke. *My face is consumed by smoke. Of course. That's my weapon, from God. I am Elijah who can call fire from God.* Elijah emerged last year, during the riots after King's assassination. He looted. Then he set fires. The fires were the rage of God against the false Gods in these stores who robbed the people. The fires showed the power of God, who gives that power to Elijah to work miracles and rid the world of false gods. The fires were cleansing. He stares longer. *Reveal more to me.*

He can see the sides of his face, even the back of his head, although he only looks straight ahead, not moving. He's being watched. Someone else is with him now. Only someone else who is all-seeing could have these views. He feels the Presence, His Presence. It's presented to him through his own eyes to show him that He watches. *He is with me, too.*

◆ ◆ ◆

The apartment is empty when he returns. A glossy paper church bulletin is rolled up in his hand. He opens the narrow middle drawer in the dining room hutch and drops the paper onto it. Beneath it, a Xerox copy of a letter signed by Reverend Charles Moore that asks for help to stop the collusion of an Austin realtor with black gangs. *How false! What betrayal! He writes to the white pawn brokers to ask for help against his own and against the preacher who unites us. He doesn't even offer a prayer to God or mention God. He is false. The pawnbrokers are false.* His trip this Sunday has informed him as to how he can do what he needs to do. He is ready, or will be, as soon as he finishes one task.

The basement air is heavy with moisture from yesterday's rain. Inside a locked storage bin, a chloroformed Sammy Gallagher lays bound and gagged. Lewis drags him to the center and removes the tarp. The body, still alive, smells of urine and sweat. Slap! Slap! He smacks his face so that he can watch. A small 5-pound acetylene torch makes him squirm and wriggle against his ties and gag. Lewis listens to his muffled screams. "I'll sign. I'll sign."

"You are a priest to a false god, like Ba'al. You must be destroyed. It is His wish. I obey."

CHAPTER 7

Garfield Park Baptist church was erected in the late 1800s by black residents who wanted to a closer alternative than the South Side's more famous and historic Olivet Baptist Church. To Micky, the overall impression of the architecture of the church is slightly sinister. The red and brown brick of its 3-story façade has darkened over time. The stained-glass panes in the windows on the main level have been replaced by glass block, a concession to durability over beauty and inspiration. The sides of the building are a greyish brick where the mortar is thick and applied with less concern about appearances. In the rear is the two-bedroom minister's home that was added some decades later. There's an office inside the church behind the sanctuary, where he'll interview Reverend Charles Moore. Charles also uses an add-on enclosed back porch to his living spaces as a home office.

Micky arrives early, in time for the service. He wants to watch Moore preach. His appearance at an all-black church would not go unnoticed, which is what he'd prefer to be. He sneaks in. The greeters close the front doors from their propped open position. He moves near them. He hears them close the interior doors sealing the sanctuary off from its vestibule. That's his chance. Inside he spots a stairway leading up to a choir loft marked "Closed for Renovations". *Perfect.* He shoots up the steps quickly. Some of the loft's flooring has been uprooted. A few one-gallon cans, possibly wood stain, sit on top of a folded tarp. The seating is divided into two sections of pews, separated by an aisle of wood-covered steps. Sitting on a stair in the aisle, a few rows back from the railing, he is invisible to anyone who may look up from below.

The crowd quiets. Micky can't tell, but they are particularly excited and attentive this Sunday. Reverend Moore last week promised them a very special lesson. Moore enters. The choir, onstage and behind the pulpit, rises. As soon as he reaches his seat, the Musical Director cues them to begin a song and the service is underway. Micky waits, patiently, enduring more singing and announcements until Moore speaks.

The wooden pulpit is a two-step walk-up. Reverend Moore settles on its platform and announces, "Ushers please come forward and distribute the paper." Copies of a single sheet of paper with an image begin to pass. Members accept the paper, exchanging curious glances. An excitement over the image begins to fill the room. Moore continues, before everything is distributed.

"The paper you are about to receive is a Xerox copy of a photograph. The photograph is the subject of my lesson today." It's too far for Micky to see that the black and white picture shows a young man positioned close to the camera. He has a beaming smile displaying a bright and perfect set of teeth. Behind him in the photograph, back far enough to be able to see its full length, is a train car. Its exterior bulkhead carries a single word, a name, near the top and centered to the middle: Pullman.

"You are seeing the face of Ernest Johnson. He stands, and quite happily so, as you can attest, only a few steps in front of one of the famous Pullman train cars for which he was a porter." Moore slows his delivery to allow for the remaining distributions. "In his face, I see joy, almost laughter. That joy is born from faith, a faith in the future. This picture was taken in 1918.

"Ernest Johnson moved to Chicago in 1907, to escape the Jim Crow life of a small town in rural Southern Indiana, close to the Kentucky border. He had a 10th grade education, which helped him to get a job as a Pullman Porter. There were standards for porters in order to make white travelers comfortable." A slight rumble of laughter passes through the sanctuary. Micky grimaces slightly, glad not to be on the main floor among the membership.

"I ask you to notice the windows of this train, sparkling clear. Reflected in these windows you are able to see white clouds against a bright sky. Do you know what clouds symbolize? They symbolize dreams, yes, dreams. And purity. And intelligence. That their reflection is captured in the train itself is uncanny. For the dream that makes Ernest Johnson smile is also rooted in that train, in the industry it represents, and all that the position of a porter holds for him and his family."

There is an appreciation of the beauty in Charles' description. Micky is only vaguely familiar with the Pullman story despite having lived his entire life in Chicago. In any case, he wonders, what does this have to do with a Sunday sermon? *Shouldn't this all be from the Bible? What's being a porter got to do with anything?*

Moore tempers his lesson with dramatic pauses which allow the eloquence of his words to blanket the sanctuary and all in attendance. He then punches through the silence for dramatic effect. " I chose this picture because it represents a time of faith and a turning point in our history. Everything was rosy for Ernest that day, but it wouldn't last. It would be challenged. Yet our people were not dismayed by the challenge. Our people used their faith to attain strength to come back from devastation and to advance the journey." A few members shout 'Amen' and 'Truth'.

"I also chose this picture because it reminds you that you are a beautiful people with a history in this city, this very city, and that you belong here, have earned the right to live here and, inherently, are equal." Parishioners smile, loving this message.

"I chose this picture because I love Ernest Johnson. You see, he is my grandfather." He pauses a moment after this startling revelation. "And he is sitting right here with us today. Grandpa, would you please stand up for the people?" A black man of about 80 years rises gently and acknowledges the warmth and appreciation. His wife, Eleanor, sits next to him. "This is Ernest Johnson, father to my mother, and I have more of his story to tell, but, first, I want to ask you a question. What is becoming of the children in our city, this city where we have earned the right to live, anywhere? I will tell you. The children are not making it. And the prospect of them making it grows dimmer. The schools in black neighborhoods fail our children. And the neighborhoods that blacks move to for better schools, they only soon become like the slums that have been left. " Murmurs of sad agreement fill the room. Heads nod affirmatively.

"Gangs. The children look at the young black men, in the community, with money and clothes, with their flash and their fancy. All the riches here, with gangs. All the poverty and despair otherwise. They give loyalty to gangs and violence and crime, particularly since the assassination of Dr. King. The Mayor and his State's Attorney have declared war on young black street gangs. War! Yes! We have descended into a war in the city, have we not? Call it what it is.

"Now, I'll return to the story of my grandfather. This Sunday, July 27th, , marks 50 years to this exact day from the start of another war, the 1919 Chicago Race riots, that went on for a week spreading death and destruction throughout our community. And all of it no more than one year after that picture was taken, in all of its evident optimism. Five days later, 38 people had been killed Most, 23 to be exact, were black. Several hundred more were injured and an estimated one thousand black families lost their homes, burned to the ground or beyond use by whites. " The members are not aware of this horror.

"Grandpa is a survivor of those riots. His home was set on fire and burned while my mother, a baby, lie in her crib." A collective gasp. "His friends and neighbors, killed, were left lying in the street. Fire trucks and ambulances didn't come. They were photographed, like that, dead bodies, in the street, and the photos posted to the front page of the newspaper, where the children could see them. That was a message about the consequences of starting a war." There is total silence as they hang on his every word. Each small creak of a pew is heard throughout the sanctuary. "If something isn't done, we will see the corpses of blacks again, killed in the streets and in their homes." Members exchange horrified glances, nodding.

"How did that riot start? A white man killed a 14-year old black boy while he was floating on a raft. Hit him in the head with a rock, knocking him unconscious, where he drowned. Witnesses spoke up, but the white police would not make an arrest, not when it was only a black child." Some appear horrified and nauseous with these facts. Micky thinks this sounds more like a Blank Panther rally than a church sermon, but he, too, is riveted by these details.

Moore continues to fuel the emotions of his listeners. "The city had investigations, panels, committees, just like there are for black gang violence today, but nothing. No concrete actions, no charges, let alone convictions. These were things in control of the powerful. Well, here's the happy ending. Five or six years later, the Pullman Porters became the first all-black union in America, and that organization, and I tell you this from my personal experience in the movement, was a forerunner to the Civil Rights Movement. And Ernest Johnson, a union steward, was a leader in that development. He and other dedicated themselves to empowerment. Our people did not go away quietly. Today, we have a war declared on our children and we have had a killing, too, a murder of Dr. Martin Luther King. All that has been gained is threatened by the loss of Dr. King, again threatened. And again, we must again come together and advance ourselves."

His culminating point defines the action he wants from them. "To the West," he starts, his hand pointing to his right, "is the neighborhood of Austin. We will, together, organize to ensure that the upward mobility of black families not only works in that community, but that it becomes the standard across this great country and the forbearer of many such communities to come. I will call on you. Together and with God, we will make it work. Call on your own faith. That faith, I say to you, is faith in Jesus. For He is the way, the truth and the life."

Micky studies the room. People have been mesmerized by the sermon. The personal history, the living embodiment of that history in Ernest Johnson and the legacy that is passed on to his grandson has, today, made him their leader not just their spiritual leader.

The choir sings loud and full. Energized by Reverend Moore, they smile and even tear up. The church members rejoice, fully investing in the words and the emotion of the song. Charles, as he always does, moves to the back of the church, to greet the attending members as they exit. Another sound is present. Charles face changes. Micky, from the back position hears it. Sounds like someone screaming from the floor below.

"Fire!"

CHAPTER 8

"Keep everyone out of down here," Moore shouts to the greeters referring to the lower level where children attend Sunday school and where the fire is located. "Move them outside and away from the church, " He lifts the long purple vestment he's wearing and hurries downstairs as the children move past him hurriedly, exiting.

The boiler room is on his left. A glass pane in the top half of its door to the boiler room, shows him that's where the fire is. The room houses the church's hot water tank, furnace and an industrial sized washer and dryer and wooden clothes-drying racks. The racks, covered with linens, choir gowns and vestments, are on fire. The wooden table that the men's group built that's used for folding and ironing is on fire. Rags and old wood from the remodeling effort hiss, crackle and burn madly giving off tremendously high heat. Charles touches the glass pane in the door. Skillet hot. He fears opening the door to fight the fire would only cause air to rush in and fan the flames.

He tells the children to hurry, but not run. Be

careful. Quickly, everyone is out, except Charles. He pokes his head in to check classrooms, closets and —a wail goes off filling his ears! There's one girl. Five-year old Addie Mae Wesley, who was in the bathroom. "Come here. Come on. I've got you. I'll take you to mommy." She's been frightened by the rushing and yelling, everyone leaving her alone. Charles runs toward her. She knows him and rushes to meet his embrace. He has her up in one scoop.

As they scurry past the boiler room, the glass pane explodes with a fury, emitting a stream of fire, which gushes out across the hall like a hydrant, hitting Charles flush on the side of his face. His body shields Addie Mae, but she turns her head toward the sound and catches a glass shard in her eye. She cannot scream; the pain is too intense. Charles stumbles forward. His movement slows as he enters a state of shock. He lays Addie Mae down and peels off his burning purple vestment. His hands shake, scorched and peeling as he uses his suit jacket to smother the flames on Addie Mae's dress. Her hair has been badly singed.

Looking at the glass in her eye, he prays, "Jesus, guide me. Please, guide me." He pinches the end and pulls the glass from her eye. Hemorrhaging fills her eye to a deep and frightening red. "Can't stop. Got to keep going. Get you to help. It's okay. It's okay." He talks to himself as much as to Addie.

He staggers forward, carrying Addie Mae who

loses consciousness. The men, rushing back into the church moments after the sound of the explosion, meet Charles as he reaches the vestibule. They usher him hurriedly to safety.

Reverend Moore, holding Addie Mae, but assisted by the men, steps out onto the front steps of the church. Over two hundred people gasp and shriek in horror. Their appearance is ghastly. Charles' skin has melted giving a hideous and monstrous look. He gasps for air, his burnt skin slides on his face. Addie Mae is bleeding from her eye and not moving. Her hair is singed and smoldering. Where it has been burnt off, the openness reveals her deeply blackened scalp.

A commanding voice sharply bellows, "Take the child from him. Carry them both. Follow me. All of you, carry them! Now!" Charles is aware that Jennifer Harrison she is a nurse, but the others, regardless of what they know, immediately obey. She speaks to the child's limp body. "It's okay, Addie Mae. It's going to be all right. You keep listening to my voice and it will all be okay." Jennifer's eyes bulge with tears at this child, bleeding and burned.

"I need clean white cloths and towels soaked in cold water as fast as you can possibly get them. " She motions where to lay them.

"There's a faucet on the side of the church with a hose. " It's a young choir boy.

"Ain't no white cloths and towels. Anyone wearing a white shirt, take it off. That's the white cloths now. And your undershirts. They're the towels". It's a senior member speaking. Everyone follows.

Charles hears Jennifer's voice begging. "Where is the Fire Department. We need that ambulance!"

He is conscious, bewildered, trying to orient himself. He stares at a strange white face. "Who are you, " he asks, pointing? It's Micky. This white man is out of place.

"Yeah! Who are you? You don't belong here," demands one member. Others begin to crowd Micky.

"I'm Micky Mulvihill, a reporter. I came to interview Moore, Reverend Moore."

"I don't know you. " Moore stares at him shaking his head and alarming the others.

"Where'd you come from?" shouts one member.

As he answers, another shouts, "I ain't never seen you and I'm a greeter. I see everybody." Micky looks down at the man, thinking about whether he should say that he snuck in. His silence and size threaten unintentionally.

"I just was here, came here this once, to interview Reverend Moore."

"We never met. I don't know you." Charles words incite the men.

"Micky Mulvihill, Reverend Moore. It's Micky Mulvihill." Nothing. Micky turns to the men, trying to explain. "Look. He's in shock. He doesn't remember. I'm a reporter. We only spoke on the phone" No one listens. They're enraged. He's just what they needed to see.

Those further back who come closer and add to the emotions, can't hear too much even, anyway. They misunderstand what's happening. It's a mob, Micky thinks, backing away, getting ready to run. This is a sure signal of his guilt to suspicious and frantic church members.

"You ain't goin' nowhere," says one man grabbing him. Moore is fading again. Another and another. Their arms bind him like a straitjacket. He twists anxiously to break free. He loosens the grip of some, but more grab on to make up for it. A punch is thrown to stop his resistance. Everyone wants to let out their anger. An avalanche of fists and boots follow and continue even as he falls to the ground. He becomes motionless taking the kicks like a bag of sand.

"Hold up. Stop! Stop. That's enough," one of them yells. Micky lays on the ground with minimal and, possibly, only involuntary movement like a small animal that's been run over. His lungs won't expand enough.

The thunderous and deafening roar of a fire

truck, mercifully, powers down the street. Police sirens follow. The firefighters leap off their truck as it rolls up to the front of the church. At a near-running speed they charge into the setup. Hoses unreel and are pulled up to the hydrants. Once fastened, the call of 'ready' goes out like a steer-roper lifting his hands to show he's finished. In seconds the hoses flex rock-hard with pressure, ready to deliver. Police direct people out of their way.

Police see Micky lying on the ground. Most everyone around Micky moves away when they approach.

"He was asked who he was, and he started to run. When he was stopped, he started to fight, " offers one of the black men. Micky cannot answer for himself.

"Who did he hit?" the cop asks.

"It was over when I arrived."

"Then who told you they were hit. "

"He's gone. In all the excitement, I don't remember the face. He-he just told me." Unimpressed with these responses, the cop signals to the emergency staff to attend Micky. The ambulance staff rushes Charles, Addie Mae and Micky off to emergency care.

The initial explosion ruptured the protection over the gas flames for the furnace and hot water tank. Energized by this fuel, the fire then scampered up the wall like a cat chasing its live food eager to kill. The church acted as a pyre of varnish-covered wooden floors, wooden pews and flammable paint.

Members move from shrieking horror to a somber resignation. The black smoke billowing out the doors and windows tells them that the wooden frame between the outer brick exterior and the inner drywall, is being defeated.

A total of 83 firefighters battle for 90 minutes to get the fire under control and ensure its containment. By the time they do, the story has broken of a bombing at a black church following a civil rights leader's offer to lead a new initiative on integration.

CHAPTER 8

M icky opened his eyes to a slit. Or he thought he did. Then he realizes he's seeing from only one eye. But he doesn't know why. He's very light, near weightless. It's not unpleasant. Nor is the smell of fresh bedsheets. The motion of his head turning toward the window to see the sky fading from dark blue to black garners K-9's notice.

Speaking softly, but with his ever-present sarcasm, K-9 says, "As a fighter, you're a good newsman. I think a chick in a high-waisted print dress took you out. I'm sure she was tough. I mean she did have a matching jacket and handbag." *Who had a dress?* He's too confused to understand, and he wonders why this seems to make it all the better for K-9. "I think it's an improvement for you." *What is?*

"Listen, Mick, bein' serious, you're in Cook County, the hospital, not the jail. You're beaten pretty bad, but x-rays say nothing is broken. The whole CST gang has been here. Your family was here. The whole crazy Mulvihill clan descended on County, and they wanted answers." *I'm in the hospital. Nothing got broken. That's probably good.* He sees the painting on the wall breathing in and out. He thinks that must be what hospital paintings do. It helps people.

"Your father, his ambulance siren voice shrieking at nurses, was not appeased by the 'we have to wait' prognosis as they looked at your x-rays. He's not a patient man. By the way, does he have his rabies shots? 'Cause I thought he just might bite someone. And your sister, Kathleen. I thought she was the nice one. She was, seriously, up in that doctor's grill. He was behind the thing —where the nurses go, with the counter —not nearly enough. He could have hit the men's room. Hell, he could have gone into surgery. She wanted some answers. I think Whitey was going to let her go for it. He was backup in case security came. Anyway, I had a great time with it all and, well, everyone got word that you're hurting, but you're okay. — Visiting hours, incidentally, closed, hmm, maybe 2 ago. "

The painting no longer moves. He's dying of thirst. K-9 sees his face and guesses right. He pours a glass and aims the straw into his mouth. Micky grabs the cup.

K-9 stiffens a little. "The church, Michael, " he begins, calling him by his Christian name. "What do you remember?"

Micky tries to think. *The church. On fire. People screaming.* "Mob scene. Mob scene is what I remember. Black everywhere. Pulled down from behind.

Don't want to hit church people. Wait! Reverend Charles? The kid?" He moves his head an inch toward K-9 with the questions still on his face.

"It's not good, but haven't heard much more, " K-9 responds. "I wanted to be here when you woke up. Just to mess with you. You know, doin' my job. But you need to rest. You're drugged up for pain, but I want to tell you this much. This is getting carried. Radio has been on it all day, not just here, across the country. In fact, might be on now." He looks at his watch. "Should be on now."

There is a radio on the bedside table that K-9 brought to the room. He turns it on and tunes to a station he knows will have news in a few minutes. "Figured being the news-freak you are, you might want a radio. Or maybe it would annoy you? Either way, sounded like a good idea to me. Here. Now. It should be coming now," he says looking at the time display on the face of the radio, eight minutes after the hour. News on the Eights.

"A breaking story. We've been reporting throughout the day that Civil rights leader and minister, Reverend Charles Moore, remains in critical condition after an explosion in his all-black church, the Garfield Park Baptist Church, while announcing during his sermon that he would start a new initiative for integration into the Austin neighborhood. Cook County Hospital physician, Dr. Morris Anderson, told WJLO radio that Reverend

Moore has burns over 75% of his body and that they are fighting infection and severe dehydration. Today, the day he chose to make his announcement, is the anniversary of the 1919 Chicago race riot, the deadliest in the city's history. Leaders in the black community question this bombing and the timing of Reverend Moore's announcement. Reverend Jesse Jackson had this to say "

Reverend Jackson's voice can be heard in a small sound bite. "The most important thing is the safety of Reverend Charles Moore and Addie Mae Wesley. Our entire community and the community of Chicago offer their prayers for them and for their family. When that objective is reached, there will be time to ask what happened and to look at all surrounding circumstances."

The announcer's voice returns and drops a half-octave for dramatic effect. "Five-year old Addie Mae Wesley, attending Sunday school class in the church basement, was also severely injured. She is not only suffering from extensive burns, but the explosion damaged her right eye. We'll keep you apprised of her condition and any news as soon as it comes, regarding that situation." Back to the normal voice. "Vietnam veteran, Michael Mulvihill, was injured trying to flee the scene. Mulvihill is not a member of the church and members of the congregation were not familiar with him. Police are investigating the unexpected appearance of Mulvihill at the scene of the deadly explosion."

"That's enough," says K-9 switching the radio off. "And, yeah, you are the suspicious Vietnam veteran, who was not supposed to be there and must have been hiding 'cause no one saw you until you tried to run away. Did you know it was the anniversary of this big race riot? —Oh, wait. Before that, I dropped a dime on your boss. I guess he understood. He didn't seem too happy, or too concerned, about you catching a beating. It's like he thought about how this might limit his use of you. Nice guy. Definitely King of the Sweetheart Dance. And the police do want to talk to you, even though they've at least been told that you're a news guy who was going to interview Moore. When they say you're a Vietnam veteran, on the radio and tv, crazy is implied, I think. One guy started talking about you, and the serial bomber, Frank Kulak. You know, bombings-Kulak-veteran-crazy and bombing-Mulvihill-veteran-must-be-crazy." Micky's face is contorted taking it all in. "Again, that's probably enough, too much, for now. So, don't say anything and go back to sleep. Whole thing kinda went from zero to whacko in 5 minutes, from glory be to gory be, from..." The 3rd one is always hard.

"This was not an accident," Micky rasps out. "Burrell turned against the Stones publicly and his church was set on fire. Moore writes to media outlets about gangs in collusion with realtors and his church is set on fire." Micky, eyes momentarily lucid, looks at K-9 with conviction.

❖ ❖ ❖

"Will she be blind in her right eye?" asks Carolyn Wesley. She knows the answer, but she wants the attending physician to tell her. Her husband, Womack, who goes by "Mack", holds her hand.

"It's too early to address that, " he says in response. He's hiding it from me, she thinks. *He knows that she almost certainly will, but he wants us to focus on the good news for the moment.* "She's stabilizing and responding to the antibiotics. We're very optimistic." He describes the burns, by location, and includes the loss of hair, which may not return. Carolyn's thoughts drift to her daughter's future: will she go the high school prom, how will she be limited studying with one good eye, will she be mocked. She knows that she should take it one step at a time, but she can't.

She thinks how the news somberly characterizes her daughter's condition. She is almost numb with the thought of the suffering that their child has endured and will endure. Everyone feels sorry for her. Her daughter is something to pity. Proud. Beautiful. Intelligent. An inspiration to others with the life she leads. All that her daughter is, and would be, are gone in one moment. Charles Moore is the big story. He is the reason for the story. "Mack, this is because of Reverend Charles. He had to be a civic leader, not just a spiritual one. He put the

whole church in the crosshairs of the racial integration of Austin. Our daughter, and all the children,
should not have been put on the front lines."

Before he can answer, the physician takes his
cue. It's time for him to leave. This is a family discussion, not a medical one.

"Let's also remember Charles shielded her,
smothered her burning skin and carried her to
where others could help, while he was burned alive.
He saved her life." This is hard for her to accept. He
saved her life, but he's the one that put her in danger
in the first place.

"But why did he have to? Why did he have
to tie all of this to the riot from 50 years ago?
Was it because of Civil Rights? Or was it because
of his grandfather? Was he trying to make amends
for that, and, by doing so, put all of us, the whole
church, at risk?"

◆ ◆ ◆

"Let's call it. Time of death, 1:32 am on July
28th. Cause, sepsis, rampant infection due to exces-
sive loss of skin from a fire. The family is here,
right?" Dr. Anderson, informed that they are, braces
himself for the next task.

Charles' mother, Esther "Blue Feather" Moore
sitting in the intensive care waiting room can feel

it's happened. Her son is dead. She is part Pot-awatami Indian on her mother's side, but only she has the sight. Her father, Ernest Johnson and her mother, Eleanor, sit somber and quiet. Hope is still in their mind. She then sees Charles' spirit enter the room. His look is peaceful, but he's sorry, sorry that she must suffer his loss. She lets him know that she understands.

The face of Dr. Anderson walking towards them confirms what she knows. She watches her husband, Henry, explodes in tearful anger when the news is revealed. He threatens that 'they' won't get away with this. She thinks of first meeting Henry, the writer. When he was younger, he wrote for the Defender. His sense of civic responsibility was passed on to his son. He yells, "My son was the target of arson, just as the Mennonite church was a target of arson."

He is a good man, this doctor, but there is nothing that he can say that would matter. She waits for trail of death to be revealed. *Am I too old? Has it been too long? Why can't I hear them?* Then it starts. The sound is first. In another moment, she glimpses the sight of the ashen horse. Charles will not be left to wander. He will be taken to his place of rest.

Her daughter-in-law, Olivia, doubles over. The knife-like pain of her loss presses into her. Henry weeps now, his anger replaced with sorrow. She reads him. He thinks of Charles as a boy, a student, a soldier and all the things that have happened in his life. His pride in Charles is so great that it hurts him. She knows that he has a desire to ensure Charles death is avenged, but right now he can only think now of his loss.

"Please, everyone, hold hands. We will pray together for my son." They follow Esther's request. Henry has one of her hands. Emmeline, her daughter, has the other. "Dearest God/Spirit lift Charles into your arms. Forgive him all that might trouble you. Let him come to us in thoughts and dreams and show us that he is all right. Let our continuing love be known to him. Protect and love him always. " They don't let go as she finishes, rather staying focused on her words and, silently, offering prayers of their own. "Now is not the day for questions of why or how. Now is not the time for oaths of revenge. Now is only for thoughts of our love for Charles, so that he may enter the afterworld glowing with its spirit."

The next few days the news reports that there was a bomb, even though no evidence to support this exists. The 1919 riots are revisited. Ernest Johnson's name and photo are highly publicized. Everyone looks for a connection to the Blackstone Rangers and the burning of the Mennonite church. Olivia and Micky have both reported the letter from Moore that would establish that connection, but the police have not made it public.

CHAPTER 9

Ernest Johnson, wearing the same black suit and tie that he wore to Charles funeral, looks over the gathering for today's hastily organized press conference. The Southern Christian Leadership Conference (SCLC) suggested its occurrence to Olivia. The purpose, they said, would be to move the focus of attention away from the inflammatory rhetoric that has surrounded the fire at the Garfield Park Baptist Church and toward the immediate, and more community-strengthening need, rebuilding the church. She said yes, of course, but it's too much too soon for her to attend. She asked Ernest to fill her role.

Ernest thinks that the real purpose is so that the SCLC put themselves in the lead position when it comes to all things Civil Rights. They want to take the helm on any, and all, initiatives that result from this tragedy. Reverend Ralph David Abernathy, succeeding Martin Luther King as President of the SCLC, hasn't yet have developed anywhere near the same support among the various black Civil Rights groups. They loved Charles, but they need this.

Ernest doesn't care about their personal agenda. He is going to focus the attention all right, and on the right thing. Today.

He sees Reverend Jesse Jackson, a very close associate of Dr. King, a personal friend of Charles and also a member of the SCLC. Reverend Jackson has been asked to provide brief comments. Abernathy supporters bristle at the prospect. Jackson is a very charismatic and quotable speaker. His remarks and his delivery draw attention to himself. If the light shines brighter on Jackson, it, by comparison, is dimmer on Abernathy.

However, this is Jackson's home city and, it would create more of a public tongue-wagging if he didn't' speak. Why didn't he speak, they'd say? He knew Reverend Moore, was a close friend of Reverend Moore, they'd say. The pictures of the two of them working together in Chicago would surface. Not helpful. Ernest sees this. His work with the Pullman Porter's Union sharpened him to the political aspects of large organizations and leadership issues.

He keeps the smiles to himself as he views the presence of other black organizations which are too controversial and, definitely not non-violent. The Nation of Islam is headquartered here in Chicago. Their presence on the front in the struggle of blacks for equality has exploded in the last few years with the membership of the world's most famous athlete, Muhammed Ali and both the emergence and the subsequent assassination of Malcolm X.

The latter has left the heir apparent to leader Elijah Muhammed as Louis Farrakhan. Their doctrine for the strict separation of the races is directly opposed to SCLC and Dr. King's philosophy. But they're here. Members, sharply dressed despite the nature of the event, wear the unmistakable green or brown suits with red bow ties. He thinks maybe some Nation pamphlets have made their way around the crowd. He wonders if the newsmen will ask them to comment? Everyone looks when they're on camera.

The Black Panther Party for Self-Defense has opened only its second chapter, right here in the city. Its leader, Fred Hampton, lives on the West Side. He also keeps the Panther offices there. This year they've expanded to social programs, like children's free breakfasts that coincide with SCLC ideals, but fighting is right in their name. Their number one goal has been to fight back against police brutality in the neighborhoods. Ernest thinks of the irony, of how when he was young, it was the Irish gangs that patrolled the neighborhoods, and not to defend against brutality, but to commit it themselves.

The activities in and around the funeral, not surprisingly, have been anything but a unified front. Black leaders, those living in the city and those from all areas of the states, all chose to make their own press statements. News cycles, especially radio talk, have fed off these statements and heightened anger over the death of Reverend Moore and the loss of an eye for Addie Mae Wesley. Some pundits go as far as to say 'an eye for an eye' implying an unnamed violent restitution for Addie Mae's injury. A lot of noise, he thinks, but the action isn't focused on finding a killer. They will be, though. *Wait and see.*

Camera crews, reporters and analysts wait, positioned both at the Chicago Civic Center, where the conference has been staged for a dramatic effect, and in their station studios. Copies of statements from the various speakers have been distributed to the media to avoid misquotes.

The red lights come on. Each channel pans the key attendees before switching to the podium where the senior minister at Olivet Baptist asks to lead all in a few prayers, particularly mentioning Addie Mae and Charles Moore. No one prays for Micky. When he finishes, he introduces Ernest.

Ernest has become a celebrity due to Charles' last sermon. His story, as told by his grandson on his last day alive, has been repeated over and over by the media. The picture of him that was passed out at that service has received national exposure.

He clears his throat. The cameras scrutinize

his face, hoping to capture for their audiences a display of emotions he has for his dead grandson. "The families of Charles Moore, my grandson, and Addie Mae Wesley, early this morning, received an official report from the Chicago Fire Department on the fire at the Garfield Park Baptist Church." SCLC leaders snap their heads toward him. Television directors know what's happening; Ernest is going off script!

"This here report states that the fire that took my grandson's life and so badly hurt that sweet little angel...". The pain of this memory is real. He fights to keep his voice. "just happened by itself. They are calling it 'spontaneous combustion'. " He looks down at the letter, which he holds in his hand. His contempt visibly evident, he looks out at the gathering. "No. I say that is not what happened, and I won't stand for it. I've seen cover-ups before." He used the word. He's charging a cover-up by the city! "The hurtfulness of this proclamation, that it 'just happened...that the church...," he rages now to refute the assertion in this official letter, "I say that church has been around for forty-five years and ain't never been no spontaneous combustion fire ever started there before. Everything they do in the boiler room where the fire started, is what they always do. They don't want to listen to the people who takes care of the church because they is telling them that things were moved by someone." Ernest knows that this remark, evidence of an intention to start a fire will last, no matter what the official report. "And I know, sure as I'm standing here, I know, that something ain't right." Cameras zoomed to his face, exploding with the pain of his loss and the whitewash of the truth. He raises the side of his right fist to his lips, bracing. Lowering it, he starts, "My grandson and Addie Mae…"

He can't continue any further and walks back to his seat. He's fought injustice for fifty years, organizing and empowering. He's taught his daughter and his grandson these principles. There is a hellfire burning in his stomach. He knows that Charles was murdered, and this was arson.

There is an eruption of questions, but Charles has returned to his seat. The minister from Olivet comes forward, but he looks toward others for signs on how to continue. He hopes to quell the reaction a bit. The faces he sees, though, are clearly at a loss as to what direction to provide. Finally, he stumbles to an offer that the coalition of ministers which have formed to help in this troubled time will obtain and distribute copies of the report to members of the press. There will be discussions among them, he says, to determine the next steps. No one is appeased. They want to know more about the charge of arson. He then introduces Jesse Jackson, essentially, tossing the ball to him.

Reverend Jackson shows resolve on his face. He lets this expression reassert a control over the audience before he speaks. His opening, now changed, moves to a familiar note. "This tragedy affects us all. We all feel the suffering that Ernest Johnson has exhibited today. I, myself, have felt the suffering of a white government controlling our lives." Jackson continues, "Just 9 years ago, I was put in jail for trying to use a library in South Carolina. Many of my front-line brothers are no longer here with us to help. Their deaths went without justice. Justice failed Medgar Evers. Justice failed Malcolm X. We cannot allow this continued failure." Jackson, catalyzed by Ernest Johnson's speech, has galvanized the crowd.

He decides to go no further. It's wiser to wait for the full set of facts to be discovered. Masterfully, he takes it back to the original purpose. "This tragedy affects us all, " he repeats, but this time using it to return to the message of help. " and we must do all that we can to assist the Garfield Park Baptist Church and the families of Reverend Moore and Addie Mae Wesley. We have lost a great man, a man that I knew personally, a man that devoted his life to helping his people reach equality as he did, calling for action in his last words, when he said, 'the children are not making it'. We must pray that this child, Addie Mae, makes it. We must all come together and pray for this child and then take the actions for all our children." He refers to the others who will follow to provide details on ways to help the two families and the church.

Jackson closes offering one additional next

action, given the news from Ernest Johnson. "We must also call for the mayor to provide a full investigation into this matter of the cause of the fire. That investigation must report to a panel of civic and religious leaders. Why did this happen? There must be an accounting. There must be an accounting."

Reporters yell more questions, but they hit his back as he returns to his chair. Are you saying it was arson? Do you think it is arson? Will you be on the panel? Who do you think would have motive for such a thing? Can you read the letter to us from CFD? Only the last question receives a response. The Olivet minister looks at Ernest with a questioning face. Ernest comes forward and pulls the envelope from his pocket. These are the very actions he wanted to trigger. He'll compose himself and read the hollow words in the letter.

Dear Olivia Moore and family,

Please accept our condolences on your loss. The following report, compiled after a thorough investigation, represents the professional opinion of forensic investigators specializing in fires who are acting on behalf of the Chicago Fire Department, which accepts their conclusions.

Spontaneous combustion occurs when any combustible material is heated to its ignition temperature through a chemical reaction that involves the oxygen in the air that surrounds the combustible material. In the case of the Garfield Park Baptist Church fire on July 27th, 1969, the oil from the rags used by workers repairing the church, oxidized the surrounding air and generated additional heat into a closed and already overly warm area, commonly referred to as the boiler room.

Additionally, the boiler room is known to have higher temperatures than the rest of the church throughout the year. The Sunday of the fire, occurring mid-summer, the south-facing wall of the boiler room would have provided additional heat energy sufficient to ignite the flammable material, the oily rags.

Fragments of cotton rags found in the room confirm the presence of combustible oil-based paints likely from the painting, staining and cleaning work that is going on in the loft of the church.

When the fire started, it was further fed by wood that had likely been removed for replacement from the loft. This fire, in an enclosed area, caused the temperature and, subsequently, the pressure in the room to rise dramatically, which shattered the glass window pane of the door to the boiler room. Once the fire escaped the room it was further fed by paints and varnishes incorporated into the structure of the church and then by the wood pews within the sanctuary of the church.

The explosion was caused by pressure overcoming the resistance of the glass pane in the boiler room door and was not caused by a bomb or other explosive device.

No evidence of any explosive device was found by fire investigators.

Ernest reads the words slowly and includes reading the signature from the Chicago Fire Department Commissioner. He'd already gone over it many times. The minister serving as facilitator of the press conference asks for calm in order to continue and assures all, again, that this report will be made public.

Evelyn Walker, the Director of Youth services at Garfield, clearly shaken and upset, steps to the microphone to report on the medical condition of Addie Mae. She will be drowned out by questions. Speaking over them she announces that Addie Mae is receiving the best possible care and bravely fights against infection and for recovery. She has been to surgery twice. There is no prognosis to release at this time.

She finishes, repeating, "The best doctors in the country are offering their help. "

"Do you think it was arson," a reporter shouts ignoring the details of Addie Mae's health?

"Do you think that Micky Mulvihill was, in any way, involved," questions another.

The questions produce a startling amount of guilt on her face. She cannot bear the thought that someone purposely hurt this child and, that in her role, she didn't protect her.

Ernest Johnson stares at the camera, which gladly accepts this connection to show his reactions. It's not the grieving elderly grandfather viewers see. It's the will and determination of a fighter, with total conviction in his eyes. He hears the questions being shouted but addresses none. Ernest has said exactly what needed to be said. He'll not embellish or redefine them.

Ernest now stares into the camera to focus in his mind on one person, one television viewer, in particular, as he stares into the camera, one person that he wants to see his face, Olivia Moore.

He accepted her request to speak on behalf of the Moore family. He knows that she must be watching on tv. And she is. In his head he hears her words. *Dear God, Ernest, help me.*

He then thinks of one other person that he wants to know that this incident will not be buried, the murderer.

CHAPTER 10

T he brick frame of the church remains, but the structural integrity of the interior is beyond repair. The minister's quarters are not badly damaged, but they've not been deemed habitable either. Still, Olivia takes the risk and suggests to Ernest that it's the best place for them to meet because they'll be alone.

She opens the door to let him in. Dinner is almost ready, and the aroma overcomes the faint traces of smoke. His wife, Eleanor did not accompany him. It's just the two of them. She can see how anxious he is to get to the matter at hand. Too anxious. A formidable presence in the family and a great influence over Charles, he is now 80 years of age, she worries about the emotional toll on him. She offers him a glass of wine to relax. He doesn't want one, but accepts, anyway. He'll only take a sip.

"Fried chicken?" he guesses.

"Yes. Southern fried chicken —a family recipe going way back in my Alabama roots, and green beans with bacon and a dill potato salad. It's a real Southern style dinner. "

"Well, you know, I'm originally from Sellersburg, Indiana. Chicago folks think Indiana is Northern, but our home weren't but ten miles from Louisville, and walking distance to the Kentucky border. A Southern meal sounds just great."

While they eat, Olivia keeps the conversation light until she believes they've reached the comfort level that she hoped a shared meal would attain. Ernest, she's sure, has understood this and abided her. They've never had this much time to talk, just the two of them. He is more than she had imagined. There is a power both from his intellect and his character that she had not previously noticed.

When they finish, she briefly debates him about who will clear the dishes. His argument of being family, and not a guest, wins. They'll do it together, all of it. He won't settle for just clearing. Everything gets cleaned and stored.

Olivia has never had a truly serious talk with her husband's grandfather. It's been the usual family fare of church, kids, homes, holidays and the like. This time, she knows, he wants to truly reach her. She settles in to let him begin.

"I want to tell you some things about that riot Charles spoke of, something that he didn't mention, but that you should know. He might have spoken of this, if he'd had more time."

He places his hand over hers. She knows that he wants to respect her feelings with that comment. She, in turn, understands his own grief, as well. "I should never have had to see him die. Shouldn't have had to go to the funeral of my own grandson."

"Ernest, " she says moving him away from the possibility of reliving it. "There's something that you wanted to tell me. I'm listening. I'm here and I'm listening."

Weakly smiling, he accepts her nudge. "I was at the beach that day, when the young black boy was killed." It's quite a revealing statement to Olivia. "I saw it all. I was part of it."

She looks at him and thinks of him on that day. The image of the young man whose face was captured in the photo helps her. She sees that face, rather than the man she only knows as a gentle grandfather. That's the man sitting at her kitchen table now. The man who was starting a family and had plans and dreams. What did he think now, remembering himself looking to the future, now that it's his past?

"Alone?" she asks.

"Yes. I'd worked all night, and for almost 24 hours straight. I'd had some sleep, though, and needed mostly to unwind. Ain't nobody I know that really sleeps well in the day time. After we pulled in, I changed and headed to the beach, our beach. " She looks at him, a question on her face.

"The 25th street was the colored beach. That's where we had to go." *Of course, that's OUR beach.* "Everywhere, it was just sizzling and airless. I was hoping that there might be a breath of cooler air down by the lake. And there was. All of it, sitting there, was just grand. The term lake just don't seem to fit. Lake Michigan stretches out like an ocean, fading away into the horizon. There ain't no seeing the other side. Of course, there's only small waves rolling to shore. It's nice, gentle-like and calming, just like I needed. A little further out. the water was just quivering with energy. Each tiny surge would catch the sun's light for a second. It was like a thousand camera flashes. Like, I guess, the fish was taking our pictures." She smiles at his intentionally humorous description.

"I'd have that Sunday and the following day off. Just going to take a little time by the water, watch the kids play and relax."

"Did you witness what happened?"

"Yes, I seen it…many times." A deep breath, repeating. "Seen it many times. He—name was Eugene Williams. I didn't know him or nothing.— he was dragged out of the water with grappling hooks. Was just fourteen. I seen that and I guess I always will." She worries again. He has quickly moved past the pleasant memories.

"Go on. I'm listening., " she said, placing down coffee for them both. She grabbed a 'broken glass cake' made with whip cream and Jello. "Ernest, did you...on that day...were you one of the...with the rioting—"

"No, once hell broke loose, I went home, took out my gun and got ready 'cause I knew what was coming. I was a brand-new father. I thought only about protecting my child. And my wife. The men that went crazy had children who were older. They could imagine it was their son killed like that." He lifts his head to look at her. "We took a lot to get a little in those days, but you can't just kill our children in front of us." His eyes, heavy, looking at her and into her soul ," I saw it starting."

"What do you mean?" *I thought it was just a rock thrown at a young boy.*

"I mean it was the children. The neighborhoods were ovens, smokehouses. And it was Sunday. Everyone went to the beach that day. And everyone had to fit on the colored beach, which was small. Naturally, the children started asking their parents if they could go where there was room. They wanted to cross the line. Now there wasn't any line, you know. It was just understood. The parents said no. I saw them shaking their heads, but then I saw them change.

"They saw something in their children's faces.

It was like their children were learning that their mommies and daddies weren't as good as the white mommies and daddies. And that's why they couldn't go. And so, then, neither were they. Just not as good. A man, a grown man, he puts up with a lot, but it's for his family. That's why he does it. He can't take his family taking less, hanging their heads down. So, they said yes. And they went.

"The children went, and the parents went with them. And that didn't sit well. So, some jawing started, and more folks came over. Ain't neither side backing down. One was thinking that you can't let these Negroes take what's ours. They don't understand. Got to wait their turn. The other was thinking I ain't waiting. I ain't telling my child he has to wait. We free. Been waiting a long time already."

"That's how it started? And then what about the boy?"

"He was on a raft. Looked like old logs and railroad ties once I saw it close. They must have made it. He was with 4 other boys. All about the same age. They came drifting South on the lake current. It pulls South. Fool kids staring up at the sky, the summer sky. The day is wonderful and it ain't never going to end. But crossing that barrier, that imaginary line at 29th, is like them opening a door to the wrong room at the wrong time in a place they should never be. Only they backing in. They can't see nobody, but they're seen. They don't hear nothing either, likely. Maybe the kids screaming as they play, but nothing to make them aware. They don't hear the words getting ugly. No entry for your kind here, boy, not now, not ever." Ernest burns with frustration.

"Try a little, " she says meaning the cake. She wants to slow him down. "Everyone loves it. Broken Glass, they call it because of the Jello bits. It's sweet and creamy and goes well with coffee." He tastes it and nods an approval.

After a long minute, he can speak easily again. "I went in after that boy, try to find him. He was unconscious. His lungs took water just like a balloon off a hose. And he sank like an anchor. Finally, the fished him out. It was cold to the heart to see that. He was like debris they cleaned off.

"I seen dead men before. When I was a boy in Indiana a black man looked at a white woman. Maybe looked at how pretty she was. White men seen him looking. They beat him to death and stuck him on the fence in front of his own house. They lived outside of town. We heard and went to look. He was there for two days, on his own fence. But a drowned child..." She shudders at the thought.

"I'm sorry to go on, but what I do want you to know is that the police had witnesses on the beach and did nothing. I was one of them. I seen who threw it. He weren't hiding himself. I told a cop, Callahan was his name, Daniel Callahan. A lot of us told him. Cop wouldn't do nothing. It went on for hours, just talk.

"No one was losing their courage. No one was leaving. They stayed because of what happened. Well, not entirely. Some left, but they went to spread the word and others did come to help. The numbers kept growing even as the sun moved off the beach, too low to clear the buildings in the South Loop, until maybe was a thousand black people all wanting something to be done. One had a gun. More than one, I expect. But this one—I learned his name was James Crawford.

He pulled that trigger and it was like the starting gun. The police fired back and killed him. We all scattered. Black men took to the streets looking for whites to beat. I ran home. Didn't even take the trolley. Couldn't wait. During those days, the Irish gangs patrolled the area, keeping us in our place. When the Irish gangs took their revenge, the cops wouldn't do nothing neither.

"And then, when it was over? Then it all got covered up. That's why so many at Garfield Park don't even know. Folks know about George Halas and the Chicago Bears from back then, but not the worst race riot in history, and in their own city."

The Irish gangs? Olivia wants to hear it all. She'll come back to this.

"I know how that feels, Ernest. We had a bomb blow up on our front lawn. It blew out the front windows and set the living room on fire. It was Klan. And the city did nothing. It was common. They just let them terrorize us, like it was our fault for wanting to move. "

"Okay. You know. Then know this. Olivia, they doin' that now. It ain't changed. The city, they don't want no dead black Civil Rights leader and minister to be a murder. Could be a lot of trouble. They don't want it. You can't expect them to help. Not at all. That's part of what I want you to know." She nods.

Maybe she knew before, but her history is back when she was a child. Ernest is making her see that, right now, she can't count on the city officials.

Olivia wants to ask him about the fire at his home, and Charles' mother. "Charles, when you got home. Was your house on fire then?"

"No. It wasn't until the middle of the night, almost morning. Me and Eleanor slept sitting up in chairs in the kitchen. The gun was loaded and sitting on the table. Any man come through that door, I would have killed him. I ain't never killed more than a deer, but I would have killed then. We would wake up, sometimes from falling out of the chair, sometimes it was the gangs with their war-whoops and other times it was people screaming." He hangs his head. "I couldn't leave my family. Couldn't help nobody."

She sees how the memory hurts him. "Do you want to just sit in the other room for a while?"

He shakes his head. "We heard voices. They was coming closer. I picked up the gun. Whispering. Then it was fainter. And the footsteps. They was running but running away. Then, well, Eleanor smelled it first. She screamed 'Fire. Oh, my God, my baby.' Like lightning hit me. They'd stacked, oh, anything that would burn. They soaked rags in gasoline and poured gasoline over everything. The corner of the building was going up like a skewer on a barbecue.

"The water pressure was low. Summertime always is. Lots of other fires, too, on that night. Kitchen sinks used a pump then. I pumped it for all I was worth. A few tried to help, but there were other fires on the block, from firebombs, 'Molotov cocktails.

"The Fire Department?"

"No."

"And police neither?" He shakes his head.

"When it was finally out and wouldn't start again, sun was up, there was a hole in the corner of our place clean through to the outside. Eleanor sat by the crib shooing flies off my child. The burnt smell made her wail. My baby girl, Charles mother, wailing from the sting. I patched it, but like Charles said, I knew how this happened.

"Whites had all the power. It's not a matter of proving yourself. It wasn't going to be inching your way up to something better. It's about getting power. I was going to do everything I could to get that power. That is why I worked to build the union and became a union steward afterwards. He was right about the connection with the Porter's Union and Civil Rights. We showed how being organized got things done. Power in numbers. Brotherhood."

"Ernest, I'm so sorry you went through that. And I am grateful for the work you did with the union. There is one thing you said, the Irish gangs? What do you mean?"

"That's another thing I want to tell you. I mean the Irish gangs that were nearby from Bridgeport and Canaryville. They called themselves "Social and Athletic Clubs". First, I want you to know that the Mayor was a member. Not, only was he a member of those gangs, but they elected him President a couple years later. You think he was a member who didn't go out beating and burning, but they made him President?"

"The mayor? Richard J. Daley, the mayor we have right now?"

"Oh, yes, ma'am. That's the one. Ain't nobody

knows that. I know that. And it's a fact! Don't trust the city, but especially with that son of a bitch running it! Excuse me."

He leans closer. " And, Olivia, there were two brothers who led the clubs at the time. Those Bridgeport clubs, all of them, was the breeding ground for the city's politicians. They led it, these brothers, but they weren't members. They were both older than the members. They paid the rent on the clubhouse with the kickback money from aldermen who got it from contractors that got nice city contracts. The brothers kept it all going so the new members always understood what had to be. Their name was Mulvihill. They from Bridgeport. That reporter fella whose paper didn't want nothin' to do with the story, but he sure did. He wanted to be here, didn't he? He's a Mulvihill. He's from Bridgeport. It ain't that common a name, Olivia. It ain't that common a name."

Olivia is startled at this. "Ernest, I understand what you're saying about Micky Mulvihill. I'll look into that. But I want you to know, that I think it was arson, too." He nods, satisfied.

"What was done in that boiler room was done on purpose. I know it. You know it. And they know it. They killed my grandson and they trying to hush it up just like they done fifty years ago." Ernest's eyes are filled with tears. He trembles with rage. Olivia goes to him. They hold each other. She loves him deeper than she ever has.

"I go to Olivet, even though Charles ministers at Garfield. But I talked to Clarence after the fire."

"The handyman?" *That's who you meant by 'the people who take care of the church.'* Clarence Wilson is a recovering alcoholic. The church allows an AA group to meet on Tuesday evenings. Clarence, a member of that group, ended up being hired by the church.

"Yes. He said they ain't no way those oily rags was in the boiler room. Nor that old wood. He told the police. Nobody believes him, or nobody wants to. He's a drunk. Easy to dismiss him. He's covering for himself and all. He's confused. Lots of ways to see it, if you want to, if you need to."

Olivia had not been aware of Clarence being interviewed let alone his account being dismissed or discredited.

CHAPTER 11

T his is the heart of C-Note territory. The Patch. K-9 just wants to see it before he has to return, on foot, as instructed, later. He drives up Western Avenue from his South Side gym and cuts left at Grand Avenue to go past his meeting spot, Smith Park.

The C-Notes are an Italian street gang with a strong connection to the Outfit, going back twenty years to the early fifties. Joey "The Clown" Lombardo, jewel thief, loan shark and Outfit boss, grew up here, smack in the middle of the Patch. K-9 has made a connection through Joe Mandacini, who once owned a piece of his boxing contract. Mandacini is Outfit and hangs at the Taylor Street Social and Athletic Club (SAC).

◆ ◆ ◆

A little dinner, eaten while standing in front of the fridge, and K-9's back out the door to hop a city bus. At the corner of Chicago and Campbell, the shrill hiss of air brakes announces his exit. It's a short walk to Smith Park. He's looking for a C-Note leader named Richie. A last name was not provided. Richie's reputation is that he knows everything, gang or crime related, that happens on the streets of the West Side. You make a high-level move on one of the businesses, Richie knows. You make a heist or even boost something, Richie knows. You beat someone or so much as steal a bike, Richie knows. Let's hope so, thinks K-9.

Heads turn seeing K-9 on the sidewalk. Their faces ask who you are and what's your business here. He knows how to act. Look like you know exactly where you're going, not like you're looking for something. Observers and random dope buyers are dangerous.

He reaches the park and the designated meeting spot. No Richie in sight. A dark-green wooden bench seems like a good place to wait, if there even were such a thing here. He moves to the top of the highest cross-beam that forms the back of the bench. His feet rest down on the seat. It provides a good view. He can see over the hedges.

There's someone, but it's not likely his connect. It's trouble. A large muscular kid who's maybe a year or two younger than him, around 22 years old, looks over. Maybe he's suspicious of anyone he doesn't know? Maybe he just wants an excuse to fight? His face is scarred from acne. His hair is fine and dark brown and probably once was combed to be a pompadour, but if it ever succeeded, now it has clearly failed. It's overgrown, but not evenly, more like weeds and bushes in an empty lot where a house once stood. The look reminds him of the London East End kids in To Sir With Love, only mangier. A sleeveless t-shirt reveals large taut biceps. They're tan, an effect that must have taken a concerted effort and a lot of free time in Chicago weather. A C-Note tattoo is fully readable in the width on one of his arms. K-9 pegs him as the type he calls 'too tough to think'. This is not unpredictable in this neighborhood. If you cut through backyards in the city, you're likely to find one with a guard dog who neither welcomes nor ignores strangers. Too-Tough, even more irked by K-9 looking back at him, decides to approach.

"...the fuck are you? " he asks to ensure things start off poorly. K-9 knows that his answer, regardless, will be not be good enough. He also knows that vague and indirect will not fly. There's no escape.

"I'm just waiting for someone." He stands to face Too-Tough but leans back. He elevates his right foot and rests it against the seat of the bench. He appears relaxed and non-confrontational. Actually, he's positioned to launch.

"Oh, yeah? Who? Maybe I know them? 'Cause I sure as fuck don't know you." Introductions are over, K-9 thinks. The bell has rung. He pushes off the bench too fast for anyone to defend, delivering a kick straight to the jaw. A stagger then falling to a knee, he fights to hang on. He wants to show that he's not done. But he is. K-9 lets him climb to a stand, just watching. He is a punching bag now, just waiting to be hit. A spinning back kick to the stomach buckles him forward. Motionless, like he's floating in spaces, a right hook deep to the hinge of his already swelling jaw ends the discussion. He drops.

"Taylor Street?" a voice behind K-9 asks. He turns and acknowledges silently to the voice, which belongs to a not-tall, 30-something with a shaved head and dark, maybe Sicilian, skin tone. THAT's Richie. His men's store Italian knit contrasts with Oshkosh blue cotton working man's pants, cuffed once for style. He motions K-9 closer while the East End Kid groans.

"Take a walk down Huron. I'll catch up. You're little dance has drawn some interest that I need to address." He's funny. K-9 likes him right off. A small stampede of loyalists come running over.

"Taylor Street," he explains to them. "I'll handle this. Tell HIM when he gets up." He looks down frowning to provide a judgement on Too-Tough's poor choice and bad fighting skills. Richie's words manage to assuage everyone. This isn't a threat. It's just a misunderstanding. Too-Tough gets helped to the nearby green bench.

"Hold up," Richie calls out to K-9 to slow up. When he reaches him, he says, "Outfit guys don't usually walk into the park and they don't come alone. You didn't look right. That could have been bad for you." He just nods. Obviously, it could have been bad for someone else, and was. He's both grateful he didn't have further trouble and that he steered himself away from this life. There, but for the grace of boxing, go I, he says to himself.

Richie veers off the sidewalk and out into the street, grabbing the door handle of a red '67 Dodge Charger. "Nice ride. What's under the hood?" K-9 doesn't really know about cars. It just seems right to ask. It's polite.

"It's got a 440 magnum. Came out in '67. Three hundred and seventy-five horse. But with a lot of nice inside features. Mean, but sweet, too." K-9 lacks a good way to respond.

"Nice." He gives himself away.

"We'll get out of the neighborhood. There's a beef stand on Cicero Avenue just South of Chicago. Five minutes." The Charger roars down the streets. It's a greeting. Everyone is familiar with this car and with Richie. Nods. Smiles. They appreciate the gesture.

Richie turns right at Cicero, heading down a block to the beef stand. He picked the right spot, not surprisingly. The area is dead except for this tiny food shack advertising Italian beef sandwiches and hot dogs. The main road, Cicero Avenue, a truck route, is mostly cleared for the day. One dive beer joint on the other side of the Cicero illuminates a dirty Old Style sign. It's open. Maybe it has a few customers? Anyway, the lights are on. The cross street, Race, covers the side of the huge Gonnella bread company, which is currently closed. Prime time for bread is two am. When they get going, you can smell it baking from a mile away. Right now, though, it's just a very quiet place leaving a half-block long empty parking lot.

Inside the small shack, the air is hot, thick and hazy from grease. The smell is a combination of sweet and peppery spices that the beef simmers in. Fries boil in wire mesh baskets. Sausages sizzle on the grill. Customers can handle a few minutes in front of the counter. The cooks in back look as if they've been sentenced to hell.

"Two beefs, juicy, sweet, hot. To go" Richie gives his order in succinct terms that they both understand and prefer. "That's for me," he adds, to avoid confusion.

"Same for me." Adds K-9 even though he's eaten. The food is part of the ritual. Declining would be a faux pas.

They move to a picnic table outside the stand and maybe fifty feet from the shack. Alone now, as other customers drive away, choosing not to eat on an ancient wooden table with peeling paint in the middle of a gravel lot. Once seated, an envelope of money passes between them. They can begin.

K-9 begins. "I relayed the main question ahead of time. And it's my understanding that you wouldn't be here if you didn't have something." He looks for a confirmation, but Richie only stares. He continues. "Here the thing. Somebody organized a march of young black guys down Laramie in an, as yet, all-white stretch of blocks in Austin. It seems like it's a little message. Get out! We're looking at our next homes. These guys are 17-20. One was maybe 25 and he maybe had a pyramid tattoo on his neck, like the Blackstone Rangers. Who is that guy is the big question? And, ultimately, who is behind the march? That's what I'm looking for. "

Richie swallows another bite, wipes his mouth and settles in to speak when K-9 interrupts, adding, "Maybe there's realtors getting a little ahead of themselves. They're maybe involved, connecting with these guys. Who is the leader, who is running that show, is what I want to know?"

Richie waits to see if any other additions are coming. They're not. "First, Rangers don't give a fuck about Austin. At all. If you were 95 with a broke dick that hasn't worked since WWII, you can't give LESS of a fuck than they do about what happens in Austin home sales. A white realtor?" There's a nod.

"Puh-fucking-lease! Look. The neighborhoods will take care of themselves, but it's not even about turf anymore. It's about money, big money and moving into areas that will continue to feed, not one-time sales. They extort. They deal. They have been looking to expand in other ways, with the feds, for example, the programs to help the poor that they can scam, and even connecting out of country to offer enforcement here. Of course, right now the heat is on them something fierce. Stupid. Everybody is Woodlawn is stupid.

"Yeah. I think it's a zoning law requirement for moving in." K-9's cute response is met with a blank face.

"Anyway, they're not sending their soldiers to Laramie to intimidate white people who are leaving any fucking way. And that is not why you're here. So, to be clear; I'm here to get paid twice. Once from that envelope and once from you telling me more. I like to know more." K-9 studies him and accepts the requirement to exchange information. This is part of why this guy knows everything.

"The fire at Garfield Park Baptist church. The minister who died maybe had information on who was organizing the march. He was going to the newspapers, saying it's a 'collusion', " he emphasizes the word., " asking for some help to look into it, to investigate. Now he's dead in a suspicious fire. Maybe that's very convenient for somebody? " That should be enough to get this exchange going.

"I like it. It makes sense. It fits what I know. I like when things fit. Yeah. Okay. And you're right. I didn't come because I don't know something." He perks up. "There was a guy looking to get people to do a quick walk in Austin. He's got like a half-dozen guys with him. They pull other guys together. The half-dozen he's got are ex-cons whose future is either violent death or lifetime in prison. They know this. That makes them very dangerous. Also, they're persuasive, especially if you're dealing with kids. The recruits, mostly, they're from the high schools, not the gangs. Went back as early as May during the school strike when kids were on the street. Kids thought this guy was sent directly from Jeff Fort himself with that tattoo – yeah, on the neck - and being older. That's him. Those kids were 16-17 mostly. His name is Elijah. And he's who's running the show."

K-9 repeats it to get confirmation, which he does. "Thanks. I'm good," he add, as he rises.

"Look around the schools. Seems lots of them seen him. Slender guy. Tall. Goatee. Maybe 30? That tattoo. Drives a '64 Riv. with the driver's seat broken and a muffler with a hole in it. Thinks he's bad, I guess, with that muffler. Anyway, easy to spot that piece of junk. Driver seat is propped up with a tire from the back seat."

K-9 tries to remember everything. Elijah. West Side high schools. He put the sandwich back in the bag with two bites taken out. "Thanks. Appreciate it. That's what I needed. I can get back from here."

◆ ◆ ◆

He changes when he gets home. Micky is not here. He'll go for a run. This news has given him lots of energy. K-9 thinks to write everything down so he can tell him. He heads out the door and turns East on Chicago Avenue. *Is there really an Elijah? Did Richie lead him on?*

He needs to get information from around the schools. A flurry of questions flood his thoughts as to the next steps. *Crap. No one will talk to me there. Need a black guy. A black guy? Why don't I know more black guys? Wait. I do know black guys. At the gym, there might be someone. Okay. Hmm, send a pug onto high school campuses asking questions about an intimidation march? What could go wrong? Everything. Do we go to the cops?*

He runs down Chicago to Central and turns North. It's not his usual route. He's working through this. He thinks about the young high school students. They wouldn't have cars. This was trucks, maybe 6-8 medium size trucks each dropping people off spread apart. And that means 6-8 drivers – the half-dozen dead-beat guys - maybe rentals? It would only take a minute to coordinate an inconspicuous set of drops. They maybe didn't have designated pick-up. Once you get South, spread out and get home.

Over the railroad tracks at Bloomingdale

down to Fullerton, looping back to Laramie, he finishes a 7-mile run. Micky is still not home. It's nearly 10 o'clock. The phone rings a minute after he enters. He takes a startling message for Micky, whom he must find. Now. This can't wait until tomorrow. He showers, dresses and walks over to the print shop for the Central Standard Times where he finds him, working.

"Hey. Got something."

"What?" Micky gives a slight glancing look but continues to work. The next issue is ten minutes from being ready to roll. He needs another hour to deal with his meager accounts receivable and doesn't want to be slowed down.

"Oh, just the name of a guy who fits the description—you know, the pyramid tattoo, and was recruiting high school kids, from West Side high schools, to do a little intimidation walk on Laramie. Just that."

Micky abruptly stops. "A name! You've got a name?"

"Yeah. First name. Elijah." Micky is deliriously happy. Then he stops. "Are you in danger now? If you have a way to connect to this guy, does he have a way to connect to you?"

"Not likely, but maybe I'll have to get somebody at the gym, someone who is black to look further it. Or maybe not? Maybe you know someone? How many blacks do you know that you could ask because I was wondering. " A frown from Micky makes him happy. It encourages him. He slips into his way of joking.

"Just what, exactly—"

K-9 steps on his question. "Anyway, it's kids from high schools that were recruited, thinking that they were helping the brothers from the Blackstone Rangers. Look. I'm black and here's a tattoo. That must make it real. Plus, you're a stupid high school kid. So just go with it." Micky's eyes narrow. *Can't stop myself.*

"Anyway, once we start asking around there, then it could be a little dangerous."

"Let me finish rolling out tomorrow's CST. Then I want to hear everything that was said."

Kathleen Noonan hears what's been said. "I can finish if you want to talk."

"No. Thanks. That's okay"

"There's a little bit more," K-9 adds with his impish humor beginning in full swing, "You got a phone a call. A woman. Let's see. Hard to remember. Who was that? Let's try the process of elimination. How many women would actually call you? Your mom. No, wasn't her. Forty-Eight? No, she's here with you – Hi, Kath - because she works for you. Hmm. Not Mary either. The list is pretty short after that. Yeah, it was someone new and... Oh, yeah! It had something to do with this, the story."

"You're a strange man, Kannon, a strange and perverse man," Micky answers understanding that this is another one of K-9's slow delivery games. "And holding back on me is not wise. If you're feeling safe because you're a boxer and karate guy and all that, remember I'm a combat trained and experienced Marine. Now, to the point. Do you mean the story about blacks marching through the neighborhood to intimidate homeowners that led you to a name or do you mean the story about the fire at the church? Was the call from Mrs. Alexander? Effie?"

"It's Jiu Jitsu, well, and kickboxing, and you're close, very close. I mean if close was standing next to you, you couldn't tell the difference, because you are close. If God said, 'Let there be close.' It would be you. If a scientist, " Micky waits. He knows the rule of 3. "wanted to make synthetic close, you would be better because you are close."

Micky can either choke him or guess. Guessing is less work. He searches for the answer. "It's the fire. There was a call for me from a woman about the death of Reverend Moore and the burning of the Garfield Park Baptist Church." K-9 smiles at his response.

"Olivia Moore called." K-9 put up his hand as Micky's mouth opens to fire off a hundred questions, "She wouldn't talk to me. She left this number. It's her gallery number. It's best to call her there, tomorrow, for a private conversation. "

"Right. Got it. Wait. What? Gallery?"

CHAPTER 12

If Olivia had any confidence in the city authorities to investigate the fire, it was diminished by the CFD report and then, completely eroded by her interactions with Detective Peter Wagner. He hadn't thought it necessary to even speak with her. She called him multiple times. He was adamant in his positioned that there wasn't any 'evidence' of a crime.

The letter to the Daily News, of which he was now aware, and which put Charles at risk, proved nothing. Her account that Charles had a plan and maybe some of his contacts knew about it was dismissed as speculation. On a final call with new potential evidence, he tacitly implied that she was a grieving widow who, in her desperation, was ready to fabricate such items.

That's when she called Micky. He was her last best hope, but she also had to deal with the connection that Ernest brought to her attention. Despite the warning, she's going to meet with him. It's early evening, but the sun is still high this time of year.

The single metal bell swings out as he opens

the door and returns to its place giving a familiar jingle. Peering through the curtain that separates that back room and her work space from the gallery, she sees Micky. The tiny head shot of him which appeared in recent newspapers did not indicate that he would have such a formidable presence. *He's well over 6 feet and must weigh 225 pounds or more, all of which appears to be located in admirable places.*

"Be right there, Mr. Mulvihill," she offers pulling back the curtain. Eye contact. Smile. She reaches up to hang her smock on a hook revealing a gun holster under her blouse. Walking briskly toward him she, again, flashes a full and warm smile, which he doesn't return. Instead, he stands immobile, staring. She realizes why.

"Call me, Micky, please. No one calls me Mr. Mulvihill." His tone is flat, obviously still concerned by the pistol.

"Mr. Mulvihill, " she begins, ignoring the request. "it would be more comfortable to talk at the corner restaurant, the Coffee And, but before we go, there is something that I wanted to show you. " Wrong words, his response quickly tells her. She closes her eyes for a second and shakes her head to erase the comment. "I mean...well, someone has been in here, after I've closed. It's happened on more than one occasion. They don't take anything. I don't know what they want, but I think it's related to Charles' death."

Surprised, he asks, "Are you sure? If nothing is missing, how do you know?"

"At first, I noticed that the paints were moved, " she begins referring to the cans and tubes she uses for her art. "It might not look like this in any order, but I know where I'm at in the creation of any piece. I am working with certain colors. The mixing, well, it's hard to explain, but it's like my tools and I know where they need to be to finish the stage."

"At first, you said?"

"Yes, then the drawers were slightly rifled."

"When? Did you call the police?"

"The first time was the day after Charles sent the letter. And, yes, I told Charles and the police. The police told us to change the locks, put in a dead bolt and put a bracket with a lock on the windows. I suppose there was no reason for them to be concerned. I'm not sure that they thought it was true, and they take action only when needed. They're not very prevention-oriented. Charles, though, was concerned. I told the police a second time after the fire. Again, it meant little to them. Then, because there was something else, something more, I called a third time. They came, looked and added it to a report. That's it."

"Could you back up a little. The first time?

What did your husband say?"

"It worried him, but it was an odd reaction. He was worried about something, but he wouldn't tell me. Trying to protect me from worrying too much, I think."

"I see. You mentioned something more?"

Olivia takes a small uncomfortable breath. "Mr. Mulvihill, " she begins. "I'm a woman, black, who didn't grow up here. I'm easy to disregard. The police, also, don't want this to be a story. Charles death made national news. If that death is a homicide, if this is arson, it could be a big problem for them to handle."

Her eyes stare straight back into his to reinforce her opinion of the police behavior. She navigates over to a work of art that is leaning against both the wall and the counter. "This piece, " she begins, holding up a medium size painting of an apartment building. "It's not a historic portrait, obviously, as many of the others. It's a glimpse of the current state of the blacks living in Chicago. The figures —as you see, they're all bugs- represent people in different emotional situations, dealing with drugs, gangs, abuse, parenting, religion and other aspects of life from the perspective of a black person living in an apartment in the city. All of them collected into a single building. The viewer's perspective is through windows of that building." She checks. He follows, more or less.

"What made, er, inspired you to depict them this way, as bugs?"

"The idea came to me while riding the Lake street "L" train. The train rides so close to the buildings. I can see into the apartments along that street. Most are not living spaces. The ones that are, these, as I'm sure you know, are low income city apartments where blacks live. The train comes so close at times as to invade their privacy. And in the Loop, of course, they're even closer. I'm sure I could reach out and touch the buildings. These folks don't really seem to be experiencing the city. They live here, but so do the ants and cockroaches live in the city, surviving on crumbs. I have drawn them in bug-like fashion for that reason. An artist, or anyone, could easily imagine the life that is, and always has been, in those apartments."

"Mrs. Moore—" She know he wants to her get to the point. She didn't mean to explain so much.

"Here. " She points to a lower corner, seeing that he needs her to get to a point. "I didn't paint this figure. The police, as I said, have seen it. Apparently, their rationale is that I'm an artist, I want a stalker so that I can have an investigation, which won't lead to anything, of course, since there's nothing to lead to. Or so they hope. They imply that, well, they seem to think the figure is mine. I needed something more to garner their attention. Now I have it. Convenient for me. That's when I called you, after I found your number in the phone book. I'm exasperated with the police." She watches him as he looks more closely. "I didn't paint it, " she emphasizes. The figures in this work were, indeed, all drawn in bug-like fashion. This one figure barely approaches that look. Micky can see that it has clearly been completed in a crude copy on the style. They must have thought she did that on purpose to make it look like it wasn't hers. It also appears to have...yes, he sees it. A goatee!

"Do you have a magnifying glass?" She answers yes with a question in her voice, but retrieves one, anyway. She hands him an odd one with a foot-long and very decorative silver handle. The glass is 3-4 inches in diameter. Micky examines the figure. There is something else. It appears that this figure has something on its neck. It has the four lines and squared base like a pyramid.

"Mrs. Moore, did you see this?"

She looks through the glass. "No. What does it mean?"

"I have a description of a person that was in the march, the one your husband wrote about in his letter to the Daily News, a very unique description of someone older than the other marchers. That description is of a black man with a goatee and a pyramid tattoo on the neck. This figure...It's like this one. Can I use your phone? I want the police to know." Her eyes widen.

"You're right. It's very small. It has a construct like a pyramid, a transparent pyramid. She leads him to an area by the counter where a phone is attached to the wall. "Wait, " she moves toward a desk drawer to retrieve a business card. "This is the detective assigned to the fire, the one who thinks it's an open-and-shut case. His name is Detective Peter Wagner."

Micky takes the card he'd received. He dials the number, but there's no answer. Ultimately, he must leave a message with the person who answers the main number where the detective is stationed. "Please tell Detective Wagner that the figure Mrs. Moore showed him — the one she didn't paint — matches a witness description of someone in the march that Reverend Moore wrote about." It takes a few minutes to clarify the message. He then begs a second call, which he uses to reach K-9 and give him the news. Olivia listens. She hears him say that the witness— he, purposely, avoids using a witness name — description of the marcher and the description of the guy who has visited high school campuses to recruit marchers and the image he sees in this painting in Moore's gallery are all the same right down to the pyramid tattoo. She knows that Micky believes her and, even more importantly, there is a lead.

"We'll see what Wagner says now." She nods, looking gratefully at him. Micky really looks at her now for the first time. She is beautiful with long straight hair, shining and parted in the middle, more like an artist than a preacher's wife. Her skin is dark, rich and smooth. She leaves her eyebrows full, which gives her a sense of strength.

"We should go now, to the restaurant, " she says to break his gazing. Her looks always draw attention from men.

"Of course, " he answers, slightly embarrassed. "That piece. You mentioned that it's not a historical portrait, " he adds looking for an explanation. Olivia makes a slight sweeping move with her hand at her other paintings.

"I create images that show blacks in all manner of occupations and family life to provide a fuller view of the history of their life in America. They are from different eras and parts of the country. These works give a historically accurate view, and one that's not well known. There are many portraits of famous black Americans. Here is one of a black man who is a champion racecar driver." The plate reads Wendell Scott, NASCAR, Grand National Winner Speedway Park, 1961. "Another is of Rebecca Lee Crumpler, physician, who received a medical degree from Boston University School of Medicine in 1864 to become the first black female to do so. There is, also, a Robert Henry Lawrence, astronaut, 1967. Not many know about a black astronaut. " He shrugs an agreement.

"Some identify classic American roles that we, the public haven't been exposed to, like black cowboys." She senses his question is why. "I'm an art and architecture historian. That piece, as I mentioned, uses bug-like figures because it seemed to me that many blacks live in the city, but aren't allowed to be fully a part of it, like the way bugs live in your house, but it's not their house. These others... Well, many blacks, and, perhaps, especially so in Northern cities, have little knowledge of their own history. " She sees he's trying to be an appreciative student, but he doesn't want a history lesson, especially on the poor plight of blacks. It's part of her work, though, to export this knowledge. She continues, anyway.

"Chicago, for example, is interesting in that regard. During the early 20th century, a massive migration began from the Southern states to big cities and, in particular, this one. There was opportunity here. That is to say, there were jobs. Manufacturing, stockyards and, of course, like for Charles own grandfather, transportation, the railroad. Still, they were forced to live, sequestered really, in the "Black Belt" section. Bugs have to hide in certain sequestered areas lest they be killed." Her look to him is intended to pause on the word killed and convey that being killed was a possibility for any black who might violate the border. "I have recently created a picture from the photograph that was Xeroxed for distribution during Charles last sermon. You know, to have any surviving photographs from that era is a treasure, let alone of people, and in particular black people, happy, employed and dreaming of the future." They exchanged glances. She's done. The matter at hand is what's important

"I'd like to hear everything you've learned. I heard mention of some recruiting...and I'll share with you anything that may be germane." He nods. She turns to grab her purse. "Mr. Mulvihill? " She waits for him to turn. "Thank you. As I said, I can be easy to disregard. You didn't." His embarrassment at such a compliment is obvious and charming.

Micky turns again to the door. She walks behind him to lock up. She sees him looking at the deadbolt. Newly installed from the inside of the door. This is not simply a thin slide, screwed onto the outside. This is a solid circular three-quarter inch steel bar. To install this, you have to drill into the door itself so that it can slide directly into the opposing door jamb.

The police suggested the deadbolt, but they never came back to check. Had they done so, they might have noticed that she not only took their advice, but that this is not likely the kind one adds as a pretense. It has the serious intention to prevent entry. "Put the deadbolt in. The brackets on the two back windows as well, secured with a lock. Called you, and no; no visits since that deadbolt was installed, in two days," she offers anticipating his question.

"Right. By the way, what do you call that piece, your painting, the one with the bugs that's been changed?"

"Black Silhouette on White Background."

"It's a nicer title than Black Bugs Living in Your House, " he offers to be amusing, but instead makes it awkward. She can see that he's clearly not used to this type of art. She senses a hint of disdain. Maybe his thinking would be something like there could, likewise, be a painting of white people, similarly struggling. Struggle is expected. Everyone must climb up from their circumstances. No one feels sorry for you it's your turn. She doesn't have to solve that debate. She has someone to help her. And, though young, he's a good man.

◆ ◆ ◆

The coffees arrive, fresh and hot, even though it's late in the day. She chooses a booth against the wall near the front, by the windows and away from the kitchen. The Coffee And serves a full dinner menu but have a large selection of bakery as well. It's past dinner time and their customers now mostly have take-out orders. The room smells of a mix of sugar, stale bakery and hot cooking oil. The floor has a light film. It might get cleaned daily, but it isn't enough. The waitstaff sneak looks at

Olivia, whom they know and this stranger, whom they think they now recognize as the suspicious white man who was at the fire. They're sure to talk amongst themselves about this.

"So. You've got a stalker who wants to be part of your art work. I've got a marcher who scared a witness. And K-9 has someone calling themselves Elijah who hires people to march. All three have the same description right down to the pyramid tattoo." The name gives her noticeable pause. *Elijah and fire.*

"Excuse me? Elijah?"

"Yes. Through some contacts at my paper, we found that a person calling themselves Elijah with this tattoo recruited high school kids on the premise that they would not only be helping blacks get into a better neighborhood but also helping the Blackstone Rangers directly." Olivia looks, in amazement, at Micky. *He's already found someone? The police won't even budge on this!*

"That's amazing. It's a real breakthrough. There is also Clarence, the handyman at Garfield Baptist, who told Charles father-in-law that the oily rags and the old wood from the remodeling were not put in the boiler room. He told this to the police. Supposedly. "*Did he say K-9?*

"Clarence? The handyman?" To Micky it has a rhythm that reminds him of Clarence the crossed-eyed lion. Olivia nods and tells him that Clarence is a recovering alcoholic. A disqualifier, if you're looking for one, as a credible witness. And maybe they were?

"Let's take the path that leads us to an intentional fire."

"Okay." Olivia likes him. He's helping. He's working. And he's honest, not exploitive. After all he is a newsman. She gives him leeway. She also wants to ask, 'are you ex-military or did you play football'?

"To make this look like an accident, he's got to put the flammable materials in the boiler room, and, he's got to know, first, that there are flammable materials in the church for him to use." Her eyes widen. "He's been in the church at least twice. Finding the materials and then he must have been there hours before it happened on Sunday to move things into place." She shudders a bit at the thought that she might have been next to him the first time.

"It would not have been harder for him to access the church when it was empty," Micky offers seeing her dismay.

"The last person out locks it, " she says, then shakes her head, looking at him. "That wouldn't present a problem, especially for someone able to enter the gallery."

"Wait. Could you draw a photo of him?"

"Of course. And we could use it at the church?" Or, we could—"

"Let's finish guessing things about him. It looks like an accident. So, he doesn't want much of an investigation. Instead, he's trying to send a message to someone who will know to read it."

She says the words with him. "He's an arsonist."

Micky adds 'A professional. Somebody like that might have a history where a few people would know him."

"Really? I mean who knows professional arsonists? K-9? I mean, you said...Is that a person?"

"Yes. He's my partner, Edmund "K-9" Kannon. Partner, and best friend. We can get you hooked up with the witness to add details for the drawing. Then, let's see how the police respond. And talk to them about everything we know. Also, are there other means to help us? Know your enemy, and his strength, as well as your own before you battle. Church leaders? Civil Rights groups?" He's very... tactical, she thinks. Definitely, ex-military.

"The SCLC..." His brow furrows, unfamiliar. "The Southern Christian Leadership Conference, for which Martin Luther King was President, thinks the best action is to petition the mayor for a special investigation. They're ready to demand it, even organize protests if it's not done and done correctly. I think the mayor has ways of stalling, and he wants to stand behind his Fire Department. The NAACP is ready to litigate the matter in any, and all, ways possible. That takes years. The other print media, like your boss, did not respond before and are not interested now. There are television talk shows, but they want to spin this story to the bigger issues of gang violence because that's what people will want to watch. We're talking about a criminal act. Crime trails grow cold quickly. Inflammatory rhetoric is what sells well on tv."

"Okay. You, me and my CST staff, all of whom have never done anything like this."

"Mr. Mulvihill, we're talking about an arsonist, whose evil acts kills and debilitates. We're—"

"I'll let the others know." She looks on, appreciatively. He wants to get this killer, too. "There is one thing that we have to solve first."

"Yes?"

"Can you stop calling me, Mr. Mulvihill? We're in this...the work requires...I mean—"

"Yes, Micky. I can do that." This is the opportunity to ask him about his name. She hesitates.

CHAPTER 13

Detective Wagner, on being informed that there is yet more corroborating evidence for him to review, agrees to come to Olivia's studio. Micky eyes Wagtrner's face as he completes his evaluation. He's skeptical, Micky thinks. No, he's more annoyed to be even asked, like someone who has, regrettably, answered the door to a salesman and is courteously, but impatiently, waiting for the opportunity to decline. It took two days before he could, or was willing, to find time to come and see and hear this evidence.

"We have a witness description of a marcher with this tattoo, same as is in this painting. " He points out the obvious.

"Right. A hundred black guys walk past thousands of people. One of them comes up with a description which, coincidentally, matches the bug figure in Mrs. Moore's painting. You found this out after Mrs. Moore brought you here. And she brought you here to help, by generating some publicity. Isn't that correct, Mrs. Moore."

"Except for the skeptical sarcasm." Micky answers for her.

"It is ludicrous, Inspector—" Olivia begins.

"Detective." Wagner corrects her.

"Detective, " a smile with anything but a pleasant intention. "ludicrous that I would fabricate a portion of a painting and then convince Mr. Mulvihill to go along with that just for publicity."

"Mrs. Moore, you showed me this painting before. At that time, you didn't mention the tattoo on this figure, correct? There wasn't any tattoo or goatee, as far as you knew. Now, with Mr. Mulvihill involved, there is."

"It's very small. Micky knew to look for it from the witness description." She's visibly upset by the implication in his words. Micky steps in.

"Let's talk about this over coffee, like we agreed. Because insulting the credibility of Mrs. Moore and me is not a very good way to proceed. Let's meet K-9 as planned and just talk." He's got Wager by five inches, twenty years and more than fifty pounds, which he tries to impress upon him. Whether it was that or just the idea of calmer heads, Wagner, begrudgingly, it seems to Micky, agrees to complete the brief conference at the corner restaurant, as planned.

K-9, arriving earlier, greets them. Micky glances at the waitstaff as the seat themselves. They are ever more fascinated by these meetings.

"Mrs. Moore, as I was saying, you didn't notice the tattoo on this figure earlier when you showed me?"

"And as I responded, it's tiny. You need a magnifying glass to really see it. Micky knew to look for it."

"Uh-huh. And you, Mr. Mulvihill, when did you find the witness who has the matching description to someone who marched past their house, but did nothing illegal?"

Micky folds his arms across his chest, forearms tighten like ropes stretching against a load. "The description," he begins, avoiding the question," which ties the person stalking Mrs. Moore to the march, which is tied to her husband's letter alleging a dangerous collusion, matches the description of the guy who was recruiting marchers, and hangs with some pretty bad hombres. And the answer to your question is weeks ago when I received a phone call from...them." He stopped himself from saying anything to define Effie.

"Uh-huh. And that information about recruiting marchers, which came from you, " he says turning to K-9, " is coming from a member of the C-Notes, a street-gang who hustle for the Outfit. And did they ask for money to give this information?"

"Uh-huh, " answers K-9, with his expression as flat as he can make it, "and was the fire at the Mennonite church, which occurred this week, an accident or a figment of everyone's imagination, too?" he adds, jumping to both the CFD report and, presumably, the heart of Wagner's skepticism.

"I'm not on that investigation, Mr. uh Nine is it, K-a-y Nine?" A stare-down contest. Micky thinks K-9's look says, 'I'm could smack you so hard, you'd slide to the floor like so much goop out of a broken lava lamp.' *He's not likely far off.* Wagner just holds.

"Gentlemen. Please. We have a serious matter. " Olivia interjects to break the animosity. She looks at Wagner, holding the gaze for a long time to get him under control. "A brawl would make a fine story for the Daily News," she finishes sarcastically. With a quick glance to Micky. "I am going to draw a picture based on the witnesses' description particularly, and which is in concert with all of the other circumstantial evidence, which will be published in the Central Standard Times. The story will ask for people who recognize the individual to come forward."

"I wouldn't advise you to do that, Mrs. Moore." Wagner says head tilting, implying the danger.

"The story will contain the connections to Mrs. Moore and the statement of Mr. Clarence Williams that were provided to the police. " Micky's statement rattles Wagner as intended.

"Revealing details of an ongoing investigation

—" Wagner starts a threat.

"What investigation?" All three of them blurt, in unison. Wagner looks like he just walked into a door.

"Why did you dismiss the testimony of Mr. Williams?" Olivia asks Wagner.

"I...it wasn't testimony. It was a statement and it's in direct contradiction to the fact that the rags and wood were in the room. Besides which, until the pyramid bug guy showed up, there was no evidence of a person who might do that."

"That's not true. You had Charles' letter to give you motive." Wagner is getting stumped. "A fire. A death. A motive. And a STATEMENT that indicates a person involved. I mean, if you were on the other investigation, the other church, and you found something, you wouldn't ignore it. You have motive with the gangs. If you found any evidence, you'd follow up on it. Why aren't you willing to do that now?" The waitstaff have all stopped what they're doing. The customers, too, stare. Micky thinks the cooler heads theory is not working.

"I...look...Mrs. Moore, I appreciate that this is a very emotional matter for you—" He doesn't get past that.

"I'm a Master's-prepared professional artist and business woman who is the wife of a senior minister at Garfield Park Baptist church. I know how to conduct myself. So, let's stick to the facts and stop the innuendo which isn't helping." Micky makes eye contact with K-9. *Definitely not working.*

Everyone waits. "I would like to speak to this witness, " Wagner, finally, begins again.

"Sorry, I have to protect my source and, as you said, they did nothing illegal." Micky is firm.

"If you are alleging a crime, this is hiding a potential material witness, which is not what you want to do. Besides, I could offer protection."

"We're not identifying the witness in any way." He isn't sure about the legal footing now, but he's not letting this idiot talk to a fourteen-year old kid.

"I understand. Still, police protection is a good safety measure, if you really believe you have... well, this potential felon." That makes sense. Cops might make Effie and Electra feel safer, too.

Without looking at Olivia, he accepts, "Okay, but you have to keep the witness name and any other identifying information out of police reports. Otherwise, no deal." Wagner shakes his head in agreement. "I need to hear you say that."

"I will not enter the witness' name or other identifying information into any police report." Wagner squeezes this out between gritted teeth. Micky is happy.

K-9 speaks. "I'm going to be scouting the West Side for someone who knows Elijah, or an arsonist with a pyramid tattoo. It would be beneficial, I think, if the police who work that area could be on the lookout." Wagner looks ready to explode, which gives Micky some satisfaction as he has grown annoyed with the man. Wagner takes a deep breath which, to all, looks like he's calming himself. "Just sayin," K-9 slips in, not helping matters.

"Thank you. I'm sure your—what is it, your sparring experience? —has sharpened your sense of details for police procedure. Thanks."

K-9, first seethes then simmers. Micky thinks that maybe he should rub his jaw because he walked right into that one.

"Okay. Touch base here in a week?" Micky's question unsettles Wagner who isn't completely sold on any working arrangement. He had only offered to view the new evidence.

"Well, we'll see. I'll let you know." Wagner rises and quickly exits.

"Micky, can I talk with you alone about something?" Before he can inquire as to the need for it, K-9 is out of his chair and moving.

He can't imagine what she might say, but he can tell this isn't easy for her. "Whatever it is, just go ahead."

"Ernest Johnson is Charles' grandfather, " she stops to see if she has to explain. Micky nods. He remembers who Ernest is. Everyone, in fact, knows. "He told me that there were two brothers named Mulvihill, from Bridgeport." Brow down low to show his confusion, he yet nods again so that she may continue. Gingerly now, she says, "They, apparently, ran the social and athletic clubs, the SACs. These SACs, they were the ones, their members, that roamed the neighborhoods during the 1919 riots seeking fights. They set the fires. They were the ones taking revenge."

"Your grandfather, or rather, Charles' grandfather thinks my family burned his house? Is that it? And then, so, what does that mean? I must have burned the church?"

"Hr might think that. I don't. I DON'T, " she emphasizes. "But there shouldn't be any...it's just that if there's some history, I'd like to know what it is. It's best if it's out. I don't mean out. I mean if we all know what it is." He recognizes that she is considerate of his feelings, unlike she was with Wagner just moments ago.

"I have a lot of family from Bridgeport. My dad's family came here in like 1850. They're cops, cab drivers, truck drivers...my father is, or was, a freight checker for the Santa Fe, then Consolidated Freight. There's lots of brothers and lots that live in

Bridgeport." He thinks about his grandfather, who had clout with the city, and his great-uncle mostly, but doesn't add that to his response. "I don't know anything about rioting. We've always lived in Austin. The first I heard that there even was a riot in 1919 was from your husband on July 27th, the anniversary. That's all I know. I don't hate black people. I'm not trying to burn your church to stop anything in Austin. I'm trying to stop a dangerous collusion that maybe has led to a homicide."

"Yes, of course..."

Micky thinks maybe she wants to add 'not you, your family' but wisely does not. He then looks away, catching the cashier who is getting all of this heated exchange. Upset with the listening in, he glowers at the eavesdropper. "You want to pull up a chair? Be easier for you to hear all of this? We're customers. We bought stuff. Now we're talking. Just us. Hadn't really invited you." He sits upright to be intimidating and ready to take this wherever it needs to go. The restaurant is only partially filled, but every table hears this and watches. The cashier turns immediately away, and he turns back to Olivia. "I'll ask my dad about it next time I see him. Okay?" He asks in such a way that demands an answer. She nods, eyes at startle. Long moments pass with neither of them saying anything, digesting what happened. It was a private conversation.

He returns to her point. "How could anything my family might have been involved in during those riots have any bearing on what happened, " he asks, referring to the fire?

"I just want to know, maybe to comfort Ernest. I just think that there's some connection. Better for us to know first than anybody else." This strikes a chord with him. He agrees. "You should ask your father, for your own understanding as well as mine. There's some connection."

◆ ◆ ◆

A middle-aged black man, distinguishingly dresses waits on the sidewalk by her door as she returns from speaking with Micky. He smiles as she approaches, as if he recognizes her.

"Good afternoon. Are you Mrs. Olivia Moore, the owner of this gallery?"

Olivia smiles, hiding her nerves. "Yes, I am. Can I help you?"

"I'm Harrison Kellum, senior editor for the Chicago Daily Defender." He offers a business card. "It's come to our attention that we have a recent letter written by your husband."

CHAPTER 14

O livia, shocked by his words, does a quick scan to take in all of him. *Is he serious?* If his clothes are any indication, Harrison Kellum is not only a serious man, but one who attends to meticulous detail.

He's overdressed for Chicago's short, but frying-pan hot summer, wearing a dark blue pinstripe suit, white designer dress shirt and narrow black tie with a thin gold stripe. His black wing tips are well worn, but polished though likely not by him. The handkerchief in his breast pocket compliments not only his extended cuffs, but a thin stripe of white in his tie. Apparently confident in his handsome features, he doesn't try to embellish them with either product or styles.

She has two quick thoughts; it just doesn't seem that a ruthless killer would have such tastes, and what socks would he be wearing? She decides to trust the first, dismiss the second, and invite him to explain himself inside of her gallery.

Checking the business card once more reassures her. She is very well aware of the Defender.

It's been an enormous resource for her in studying black history that she can depict in her art. The Defender has been a force in that black history. They influenced the Great Migration, encouraging blacks to move away from the South to Northern cities. Possibly, she thinks, it even influenced Ernest Johnson and, in that way, has affected her own life.

She drops her hands to her side, looks directly at Kellum and blinks a few times with a semi-smile. Please get to the point is the message. "First, let me say, Mrs. Moore, that I am deeply sorry for your recent loss." She offers a silent, but somewhat cool acknowledgement. His politeness is understandable, but not necessary. She's looking for answers not sympathy.

"Thank you, but, I'm sorry, uh, Mr. Kellum, " she again refers for a moment back to the card to ensure that she has said his name correctly. "My husband wrote a letter? What kind of letter? What did it say? Do you have it with you? May I see it?"

"I do. Yes, of course. I do have it. I'm sorry. Suddenly showing up at your door with this news must provide quite a start. It's just that I just couldn't imagine this conversation as a phone call. Is there somewhere that we can talk? I'd like to explain a few things, to tell you everything that I know. Perhaps, you could fill in some answers for me, as well? "

"I'm afraid there isn't another more private

place to go to, not right now, Mr. Kellum. I've just returned to the shop, for one. And there are some pressing matters." She indicates to him a slight annoyance at his delays.

"Yes. Of course. I understand." They stand awkwardly facing each other in the center of the gallery. He appears to be nervous, and fidgets slightly trying to get comfortable. Unconsciously, her eyes widen, and she takes a deep slow breath watching him pull an envelope from his inside breast pocket. He hangs on to it for a moment longer, seeming to need to preface the content. He's making her nervous. *Why does he delay?*

"Mrs. Moore, I worked with your husband a number of times over the years. We even collaborated, occasionally, on articles for the Defender. His father, as you may know, once worked for the Defender. Charles and I, well, mostly, it was quite some years back when his involvement with the Chicago Freedom Movement was just in development." Olivia lets him continue without comment of expression.

"Reverend Moore, had, this past Spring, asked to review our archives. He was researching the 1919 race riots." Charles hadn't mentioned this activity to her. "The Defender writes on a broad array of subjects: the city's government, black churches and black nationalist organizations and, to a lesser extent, black gangs to name a few. "

"I'm an art and architecture historian, Mr. Kellum. Specifically, my focus is black culture in America. I'm very familiar with the work of the Defender. It's perfectly logical that Charles would want to use your archives and leverage any past relationship." She hopes that gets him to the point.

"I see, " he says, but only continues in the same explanatory manner, "Well, Charles wanted to look at all that had been written on the latter of those and on the riots themselves. The archives are like snapshots in time. What was written on the first day, a week later etc. It gave him a deeper understanding, a feel for how the issues developed day to day. That, it was my feeling, was what he wanted. Who and how was the message controlled the message, how did different parties go about managing —what— the situation, learning how people were responding to any single headline or incident? " Now, the point catches her interest and sparks a question.

"I'm sorry, Mr. Kellum. Charles wanted to understand how the reporting was handled?" The rise in her voice indicates her surprise.

"Yes. All I know...He informed us that he intended to develop a speech for the Garfield Baptist church that would coincide with the 50th anniversary of the riots. It was something like 'Here's Where We Were and Where Are We Now'. Or at least that was our take. Knowing what was said by him in his last speech, I guess that he always intended this research to inform him on, leading his own initiative, from a historical perspective."

"But he'd been a leader for some time."

"Certainly. But the Chicago Freedom Movement and every strategy involved, was Dr. King. Charles was a great asset, but it's different being a key player, a star player, from creating your own game plan." Olivia remains expressionless, but she accepts it logically. "We, of course, said yes...to his request for access. Then, just before his passing, we received this." He points to the envelope in her hand.

Finally. Before Olivia opens it, she notices the postmark, July 14th, just two weeks before his death. It's addressed directly to Harrison Kellum, Editor, Chicago Defender.

Dear Harrison,

Per our recent conversations, I wanted to let you and the Defender know that I have been pursuing the movement to successfully integrate the Austin community on Chicago's West Side. As a result of this pursuit, some disturbing details have become known to me.

In order to expedite the exit of the remaining white owners, Avenue Realty is collaborating with black gang members using intimidation and harassment tactics. Their methods are as dangerous as the people who use them. To take advantage of this, the realtors act under the guise of real estate "speculators", which are people or entities who buy low with the hopes of selling high. In this case, they're assisting themselves, facilitating it all with their collusion.

On Sunday July 27th, the anniversary of the 1919 Race Riots in Chicago, I will present a lesson to the Garfield Park membership that will be a call to action. I have investigated other area realtors, particularly, Burke-O'Malley Realty. Though their motivations and perspective are different than mine, they are not interested in the destruction of Austin for quick profits. I believe that we can find fair prices for incoming black families without introducing the tidal wave that washes the community away for yet another stretch of ghetto.

As part of my effort, I'd like to work with the Defender on a series of articles: one piece would define these speculators and the ways to identify them. Others would focus on not losing any of the value of the neighborhood that they wish to enter. This will be led through my church and other black congregations.

I hope that we can establish a time soon after July 27th to discuss the possibility of this series.

The salutation was typical of Charles, listing his title with the church. When Olivia finishes reading, she scans the letter again confirming the details, looking for some clue. It's mostly facts that are known to her, but now there was a new name, Burke-O'Malley realty. And *there is the mention of the lesson, specifically, to be on July 27th. Curious details to add.*

"Mrs. Moore, One thing I want to bring to your attention." This, it seems to her, could be what he has been so nervous about. And so careful. "Charles could call us anytime. It's unusual that he would write. It's as if he wanted this information in writing, as a matter of record."

Olivia looks sharply into his eyes. "Whatever for, Mr. Kellum?" Kellum shrugs. He doesn't want to offer speculation, yet he wants to introduce that. *Odd. Tell me what you are thinking.*

"I need to take action in light of...I've had a certified copy that will be delivered to the police as it alludes to a possible danger in which Charles was placing himself. I wanted to inform you before doing so."

She understands that, but the content itself and some message that Kellum is trying to convey without saying. "To your earlier point about Charles writing to you versus calling, you think that Charles wanted this as part of a documented record, possibly, because he knew that he was at risk for harm. And you think that maybe that risk has been realized? You think he wanted this writing in the hands of an old friend who was part of an organization that has been a public advocate for the black community, even going back to the riots of which he spoke on his last day?"

Harrison Kellum appears surprised by her directness yet perhaps relieved that she has understood his point without further awkward and gentle hints. He nods.

"Yes. Well, documenting the risk… That's one reason, possibly. I mean, to that end, he didn't need to drop names like this in a letter that might get into the hands of others at the Defender. And, he didn't need to define real estate speculators to us. As I mentioned, as you know, we're intimately involved in all the affairs affecting the community, especially in Chicago. We know what a speculator is. He knew that." *Charles was definitely talking to someone else through this letter. In case something happened?*

An icicle of fear stabs up into her heart. *Charles was in danger. He wanted a full record with someone he could trust, the Defender. If only he'd completely confided in me and didn't try to shield me from worry.* Her instinct about Charles' death was becoming more likely with every revelation. Any action by her would put her into the same danger as her husband had faced. She couldn't help, but wonder if she was making herself bait and if she was ready for that? Did this killer already have her in the crosshairs? Is the figure in the painting just a sadistic way of terrorizing her? Maybe this killer might believe that Charles had confided in her, that she also had some evidence of collusion. *Was he just trying to scare her? Is that how Charles knew of the danger? Was he stalked?*

"Mr. Harrison, I am working with the publisher of a local paper in Austin. We are going public with a letter, similar to this, that was written to the Daily News. That letter mentions a march as evidence of an organized effort of intimidation. This intimidation was conducted by black youths. That is an indication of a collusion with black gangs, which is part of that letter as well. There also will be a witness description of one person who participated in that march. The description matches an image of a figure, right down to a revealing tattoo, that has been painted onto one of my pieces in the gallery, by an intruder." Responding to Kellum's obvious shock, "I'll show you."

The painting sits on an easel in the back room where it was viewed by Detective Wagner. He seems to think I am colluding with the publisher, a Mr. Mulvihill, to generate public notice and pressure, which is, absolutely, false." Harrison, she thinks, believes her. She senses his trust. Possibly, because he must have fought many times against such reluctance from the police and other authorities. Possibly, he just trusts the wife of his friend? Possibly, the prospect of pure greed turning men violent or to collaborate on violence surely isn't unfamiliar to him?

"Is there anything that I can do to assist."

Thank goodness! The help of such a man would be invaluable. Neither she nor Micky has any experience in tricky investigations.

"Yes. In fact, I was hoping you'd offer. I'd like to ask you not to publish this letter or reveal its contents to anyone else. I will confide in you as to why, and as to where we are in investigating Charles' death. The individual we seek uses the name Elijah. We don't want any public distractions looking for him. The mention of the other realtor, Burke-O'Malley, would create exactly that. We want this focused on one thing, and one thing only, finding Elijah." She expected that her forcefulness, coming from a woman, an artist no less, would surprise him and take him aback, as it does so many. It hasn't. Mr. Kellum, obviously, looks past such things, focusing on succeeding, which she sure that he very often does.

"I can't be certain whose eyes might have seen this letter to date. I mentioned that Charles was almost flagrant in making sure it was noticed. However, from this point on, and excepting the police, I don't see a need to reveal it further. " Harrison Kellum had quickly become an ally.

"One more thing, Mr. Kellum."

"Yes, Mrs. Moore."

"You're giving this letter to me? That is correct, isn't it?"

"Yes."

"This is a Xerox copy. I'd like to have the original."

"That's what we received, a Xerox. We don't have the original." She stares at him to understand. His face says he doesn't know why.

CHAPTER 15

Who Is Elijah? screams the front-page of the Central Standard Times. Reverend Moore's letter alleging a collusion is front and center. The march, alluded to in the letter, is validated by comments from Laramie residents. Micky and Olivia chose to redact the name of Avenue Realty. They want to work leads to find Elijah. If any of it goes back to Avenue, then fine. They have their evidence. Otherwise, the unsubstantiated allegation would only detract from their goal.

A column titled Reverend Moore's Widow Stalked quotes Olivia stating that someone has broken into her shop on multiple occasions, leaving telltale signs including the image on her work. A photograph of Olivia's altered painting and overlaid with a blowup to show the goatee and the pyramid tattoo sits next to her artist's rendering of Elijah, stated as "drawn from witness descriptions."

The information includes the CST research describing a reliable source who identified a person who fits the description from the witness and was recruiting marchers.

The last piece, an accompanying article, shows the CFD report on spontaneous combustion and the contrasting statements of Clarence Wilson that there were no oily rags or other flammable materials in the boiler room.

Micky wanted to write an editorial on the police to point out their reluctance to really investigate Moore's death. He wanted to say that Moore never could have gotten help from them in the first place because the conventional thinking is that Austin is going down and no one is going to get their hands dirty trying to do anything about it, except Moore, and that's why he's dead. He doesn't act on any of this for the same as going after the realtors. The big goal is to find this killer and stop him. Accountability for the realtors and cops can wait.

The story erupts in the city and is picked up nationally with major news outlets salivating at the prospect of an assassinated Civil Rights leader. Mayor Daley makes no comment and refers reporters to his police superintendent, who gives a resounding support to all in his police force. National Black leaders, queried for a response, contact Mrs. Moore. She keeps them at arms distance waiting for the article to generate the desired tips.

◆ ◆ ◆

"Hello, Mr. Mulvihill. I'm John Wolford." A smiling man about forty years of age extends his hand to Micky. "We'll get set up in a minute. Are you ready to go?" Micky has granted a live interview to WJLO TV, Channel 7. Their news truck arrives in front of his CST spaces and within minutes a crowd of neighbors gathers to watch.

"Let's go over this. What kind of questions are you going to ask?" Micky doesn't want an ambush.

"Mostly just reiterations of things that are in your publications. Not everybody reads that paper." Presumably, that was a dig, Micky thinks. Maybe, too, it was a dodge? He'll need to be careful.

The camera is off to his right while Wolford stands back and to the left. He knows the drill. Wolford's questions will be removed from the version that airs. It will look like Micky is just talking into the camera.

"We're here with Vietnam veteran, Michael Mulvihill, who has, explosively, published allegations of a collusion between realtors and black gangs that was written by Reverend Charles Moore who perished trying to save a 5-year old child in a church fire that the Chicago Fire Department, after completing a full forensic study, has ruled an accident." He and the camera turn on him. "Mr. Mulvihill, what evidence do you have of this collusion?"

Stay calm. Don't get mad on camera. Micky puts a serious, but rational face on, as best he can. " The first evidence of a collusion is the march of a hundred black youths witnessed by neighbors for blocks on end. You simply can't get a hundred blacks transported into a neighborhood for a march without some organization." He's interrupted.

"How do you know that they were marching or demonstrating or doing anything except walking down the street?" *Because I'm not a moron!*

"No organization has come forward to the police, who've investigated, or to the Central Standard Times, to explain the appearance of one hundred blacks walking down the sidewalk in an all-white neighborhood."

"I see. Please continue."

Don't smile. Just reset. "The next evidence of collusion is the corroboration of that march as a quote, show of force, unquote by Reverend Moore." Again, he's interrupted.

"Mr. Mulvihill, How do you know that Reverend Moore was referring to the march on Laramie. Austin is the largest neighborhood in the West Side. Could there have been another march to which he was referring?" *Go on the offensive or you'll get jabbed to death.*

"Would that, Mr. Wolford, be another march that has a specifically identified marcher who also appears in a painting by Reverend Moore's wife and has been identified by Central Standard Times sources as recruiting high schoolers to march? Is that the other hypothetical march to which you are referring?" All delivered with innocence. He's getting good. He needs to be.

"Cut." A smiling we've-just-had-a-misunderstanding expression precedes, "I'm just trying to illuminate the facts one at a time." Micky thinks he's buying time to gather himself.

The red light comes on again. Micky, this time, connects this march to Reverend Moore. Then he goes further. "Mr. Clarence Williams has spoken as to the conditions of the boiler room that don't fit what the fired department found. This clearly identifies the possibility that someone entered that room, placed those articles, knowing that the conditions would cause a fire. And...and..."

"Mr. Mulvihill, can we return to the march?"

"And the fire likely just occurred too soon. It was perhaps like the fire at the Mennonite church where the intention was to destroy not kill."

Wolford smiles falsely. Micky returns the same, knowing that Woolford now understands that he is not the rube he'd hoped for. He got the connection to Burrell's church in. "Detective Peter Wagner, lead investigator, notes that Mrs. Moore did not show him the figure in her painting, until after you were contacted, and you had this description." The question is implicit. *Don't bite.*

"Mrs. Moore was unable to interest the police in a full examination of her painting. The neck marking is very small. I knew to look for it. I'm interested in keeping Austin safe. Integration may be inevitable. It may not work well. Certainly, that's what Reverend Moore's interest was. But the march and other intimidation actions that have been documented by the Central Standard Times led me to action. Would you like to speak to residents, in order to corroborate the likelihood that this was an organized action of intimidation, that Reverend Moore knew about, before the unprecedented fire that killed him and scarred that precious child." Micky's sorry to drag Addie Mae into this, but that will surely back this reporter off. If Woolford runs all the questions, he's going to have to talk to other residents.

"Do you have any leads as a result of your story?"

"Not yet."

"Will you take further actions without that?"

"We will continue to work all aspects of the case until this individual can be identified and found." On Wolford's signal, the overhead flood light goes out and the red light vanishes. Micky is very proud of himself. He stayed cool, got the name out there on multiple times and even used the word "case", which pressures the police to respond or say

that there isn't one despite these facts and a suspicious death.

CHAPTER 16

Lewis Leonard moves restlessly between sitting on the couch, lying on his bed and standing in front of the mirror in his dining room. Newspapers, strewn about the apartment, scream of the horror of the fire that burned the church, the minister and the child. They question the link between this fire and the one at the Mennonite church, both of which circle around the Blackstone Rangers. Both tie to immediate retribution for calling out gang actions.

Lewis thinks that he delivered as he should have, that he was guided. His sense of purpose is mixed with a sense that it is unfinished.

"Who Am I? I am the worker of miracles. The Reverend Charles Moore has been rightly punished for placing himself above me. The Lord works through Elijah not through Moore. He was smitten for his attempts to lead." He asks more than tells.

His reflection stares back at him. Then its arms open. " *A sign.* "And Burrell, did he not do the same? Did he not attempt to lead? Did he not decry the name of Jeff Fort, leader of the Black P Stone

Nation? And he, too, was punished. Are these not the works of the One who is all-powerful, l done through me?" The reflection places its right hand over its heart. The right-hand slides over. Both hands are on its chest. *Me. It's me. It's who I am and was always intended to be.*

All that has happened to him in life, the very reason for his life, was to bring him to this moment. How else could it be possible that this happened on the anniversary of the sacrilege, and that this man, Mulvihill, was there. And now Mulvihill rises to challenge and oppose him publicly. *I was brought to the minister and now to him. He is the false one, not me!*

He stands waiting for more. He can't move. Hours pass. Visions and sounds of his life visit him. He hears his grandfather call him the filth. He remembers how his grandfather stole him and tried to hide him away forever. His mother turned on him, too, and came to hate him. His life burdened her. Every simple need enraged her. *Why was I so worthless? How do I ever clean off the filth? This is how. These acts I must complete.*

The answer finally reveals itself to him. "I am evolving. Mulvihill asks who am I? I shall show him who I am."

◆ ◆ ◆

Lewis Leonard waits for the others in the basement of his apartment building an area which holds laundry machines and storage bins for the tenants. Only the occasional sound of a door closing or the creaking of floor boards above him breaks the silence of the late evening. The apartments are mostly not occupied, not now and hardly ever. The few residents he might encounter stay away once they meet him.

There is only one entry, a five-step walkdown from the backyard. Sitting at a table at the far end of the basement which residents use to read or play cards while their laundry finishes, he acknowledges each of the three men silently. An uncovered low-wattage light bulb above the table makes his skin appear yellow and leaves dark shadows covering his eyes and under the bridge of his nose. They are followers, signed to the Declaration. They do his bidding. *They have accepted me as Elijah.*

He tosses the CST onto the table. "Mulvihill asks who I am? Tomorrow night he will receive an answer. And he will ask questions no more, ever. " They understand his words. "The address to his office and his home are here in the paper." The news accounts also detail his habits and, that as a result of both his publishing and working for the Daily News, he goes to his office late in the evening. "I have been on that block myself. It's is far enough away from Chicago Avenue to be dark. It will be easy to remain unseen. Cover his body with a paint tarp. Take him to the Des Plaines river. Slice him into unrecognizable parts. Cut off his face to bring to me. Dump the rest of him and burn the tarp. Understood?" They do and acknowledge this.

"Where's Sammy?" one asks and then, instantly regrets his question.

A kitchen chair sits in the corner covered by a dark green camping tarp. Elijah slides his chair over to it and pulls the blanket away. "He's here with us, too."

It takes them a few moments to recognize him. The top half of his face is blackened, the result of skin burnt by a blowtorch. The flame was held near, but not on his skin so that features would remain recognizable. He was cooked.

His eyes and mouth are fully open. The lips of the mouth are unnaturally receded. The look is, startingly, lurid as if pain to the point of insanity had been captured in a charred sculpture. An eruption of lumped material by the nose and right temple show a dispersion of brain matter that had boiled over.

"Sammy did not believe." There were no further questions.

CHAPTER 17

M icky lumbers down Leamington with an uneven gait as if one side of him weighs more than the other. He longs for bed, still sometimes thinking of it as the 'rack' from his Marine days, along with the saying 'The old rack is going to feel good tonight.'

He, along with his staff, have been constantly answering inquiries and relaying them to the police. He's carefully managed the onslaught from other media. The national news is of no interest to him, except where it raises awareness locally.

As he walks, the streetlamps stream through the tree branches leaving a spider web of shadows on the side of the building. The light breeze moves the shadows back and forth.

Something else and different unsettles his peaceful walk. A shadow moves differently than those driven by the wind. It registers as wrong, but only subconsciously. Behind him, faint and rushed footsteps like the scamper of small animals raise his awareness to alarm level. He realizes what's happening.

He spins around and raises his right arm to block a blow from a blackjack. Despite the sharp pain and fear response, he fires off a straight left to hit the attacker flush on the nose with the heavily-boned heel of his open left hand. The attacker's head snaps back. A sound of pain and anger emerges. The attacker's eyes water from the sting. Micky follows quickly with a chop to the throat, the middle knuckles of his left-hand spearing into throat cartilage. The man, gagging, steps backward.

Before he can finish off the attacker, two other men come from the shadows. Both are large and powerful. Each of them grabs an arm and locks it down. Together the pull him backwards.

"Get him! Here!" one yells loudly. The first man recovers and comes forward to deliver blows while he's being held.

Micky grabs the shirt of the two assailants who hold him. He leverages the lock they have on his arms to lift himself up and deliver a kick to the chin of the man straight in front of him. The man falls backward two steps, letting out a yelp of anger. He touches his mouth. Bleeding. His teeth are numb.

Enraged, he lunges forward and fires off blows with a fury. Micky twists and moves his head trying to diminish the impact, but too many punches land. He weakens. Summoning his strength, he drives the heel from his left foot into the side of the knee of the man holding his left arm. The man slumps, his knee buckling. His hold loosens for a moment. Micky wrestles free on that side and fends off their attack. He's too weak and won't last.

Someone launches a flying tackle into the mid-section of the man who's been hitting him. It knocks him to the ground and takes the wind from his lungs. The tackler grabs the man's head and drives it into the cement, repeatedly, screaming obscenities at him. Micky knows the voice. *Eight-ball! It's Eight-ball.* The shouting from Eight-ball causes a disturbance. Lights come on in the nearby houses.

While Eight-ball pounds on the man that he tackled, a thunderous drop kick sends the other attacker to the ground. This time it's K-9. He turns and follows with a spinning back-kick to the stomach of the man who had dropped to one knee and now stands again. He folds and hits the ground.

K-9 pounces throwing hooks with either hand. The sound of each hit is a muffled cracking. He's hitting where the bone is near the skin, which is tearing.

The first attacker tries to run. He's met head on. A child's bat ends his escape. It's old man Doheny. In all the years, that Irishman's only has shown two emotions: rage and depression. Micky's glad tonight was the former.

The homes on half the block show lights. Neighbors emerge with clubs, pipes and service revolver 45s. One has an M-1 rifle. Someone's in trouble. They heard the yelling and then the sound of fighting. They don't stay out of trouble, not on this block. They'll call the police once they take care of it.

Mr. Jennings, whose name is certainly not Jennings, and seems to have no job and keeps very odd hours walks forward with a 38 snub-nose held straight down pointing at the ground. He stands calmly surveying the scene as if watching children wrestle. He turns his head to look for other danger while everyone excitedly tries to learn what happened.

"I saw the fight. I said I know that guy. I know that guy." Eight-ball spitting out an explanation to Micky as to why he entered with his tackle.

Micky, face swelling, slaps him on the shoulder and, sloppily adds, "And that's an acquaintance I'm glad to have." Eight-ball can only go by Micky's smile. He has the mind of a child ever since he was beaten badly with an eight-ball over a pool game. He has a metal plate bolstering the side of his head.

In a few minutes, the police swarm, lights blaring, coming from both Chicago Avenue and the wrong way down the one-way street.

"Friends of yours, Mick?" asks K-9.

A slight relieved laugh. "And where'd you come from?"

"I'm on our back roof, the Veranda. I thought maybe you're taking dance lessons in the dark, especially when I heard the sounds of pain. You're stepping on your partner, I figure."

"Thought you'd cut in, didja? Maybe save her toes?"

"Exactly. Well, that and save you from a law suit for assault. Toe-stomping could get you time." His smile is so big it's nearly a laugh. K-9 is rarely happier than when he's punched someone.

"Who the hell are these guys, Mick?" the question comes from the Doheny in his always clipped manner of speaking as if "the hell" is enough. You know what I mean.

"Don't know, Mr. Dohoney. Guess the polices will id them and have to figure their problem."

"It's the story, isn't it? Elijah fella, isn't it?" He receives his confirmation from Micky's look. The rest all return home thinking that their boy is now a star, and maybe he's just caught a killer.

◆ ◆ ◆

After the charges have been filed, statements completed, Micky and K-9 go back home. Sitting on the Veranda sofa, K-9 says, "Those guys aren't saying anything yet, but I'll bet my lungs, they're career criminals, career and often-convicted criminals. So often convicted, they've got squatter's rights in some pen. That one guy? He smells like the joint. By the way, I'm fond of my lungs. So, you know I'm confident in this assertion." Micky studies his partner but gives no response. He's thinking the same thing.

"That one guy was a moose. Tattoos and giant biceps, that's a yard-bird. He didn't have a pyramid tattoo, though, not anything else that said Stones either. How about those guys that Richie said worked FOR Elijah? Their career guys, right?" Micky asks.

"What do you want to do? " K-9 says, conceding the point and his face dropping to serious. He wants to know how Micky will protect yourself.

"If I stay with anyone else, I endanger them. You, my friend, could make a visit to someone. They're aiming for me."

"Right, but then, you know, your next dance partner needs her toes protected."

Micky didn't expect that K-9 was going to take the suggestion, but he needed to offer it. "I've got the .45, which I'll keep near and loaded. We'll rig the doors with bells or something. I don't know what to do about the windows."

"Get some 1-inch dowels and wedge them on

top of the bottom window so they can't be raised, even if someone slips the lock open, which you cover in Play-Doh. Comes on and off, but someone trying to slip a window lock with that junk covering will need more time and make more noise. "

Micky nods, appreciatively. "You have Play-Doh, don't you? It's what you really do when I'm not around."

"Yeah? And? What's your point?"

Micky doesn't answer and stops talking altogether. After a while K-9 leaves him. Just weeks ago, he was thinking his future was some opportunity at the Daily News. That thought always led him to think of getting a big case to follow. He would use that, somehow, to build another newspaper. He didn't want to be a columnist. A paper is a business. There's a lot of work that is just numbers, market strategies, sales. It was always the stories that he wanted. The business was what was necessary. Now he's investigating. He likes driving to the truth, finding the bad guy, but it's too close. He's in danger. Worse, his presence puts those around him in danger.

CHAPTER 18

M icky has two staff besides Forty-Eight: John "Preacher" Stevens and Mary Lee.

Preacher, a 20-year old student with two years of education at the teacher's college, Concordia University, in nearby River Forest knows many things he doesn't want to be, but none that he does. He is well-versed in the Bible, though he hardly had a choice in the matter. His father is the minister of the tiny Southern Baptist church which, conveniently, is just two doors down from the CST shop on Leamington.

Their church building is so small, so old and so plain that people have walked by it for years without realizing what they were passing. The tiny wood-sided house provided to the minister and family is only one door down, in-between the building housing CST and the church. This location leaves Preacher right next door and very available to cover on days when the snow and ice are deep, and residents, again, make promises to move away from Chicago, all of which they'll forget in the spring thaw.

Mary Lee is the 21-year old staff photographer. She thinks that she might stay with photography a career. The chance to be creative, to maybe travel and to learn tug at her. On the other hand, so does the idea of being a mom. She might want to have lots of kids and make photography a hobby. Already married, she took her husband's last name, changing from Kosinski. Her married surname is so short and runs together with her first that no one hears it right the first time. She repeats it without frustration and jokes 'my husband made me an adverb'.

Then his rock, Forty-Eight, the diminutive Kathleen Noonan. She's brilliant and underutilized. Born in November, she would have finished high school a bit young at seventeen. Instead she took a heavy load and went to classes in the summer to finish high school at sixteen. Hard for Micky to tell if Kathleen was just eager to get her career started or she can't help herself from maximum achievement.

Completing a fiction novel by graduation about a father raising a deaf daughter who is sexually molested called <u>She Can't Tell</u>, earned her a partial scholarship at Northwestern. No one, Micky thinks, could have written that story based solely on research and imagination. Kathleen offers no explanation. He doesn't pry. Ultimately, she had to drop out of school. The eldest of five children, she took on the role of mom of the house when cancer took her mother. The paper is her way of staying in the game.

At 23, she's learned every aspect of his business. Micky is sure that she'll write more novels. Or become President. He tells her, "One day, I'll say I knew her when."

They were supposed to all take turns staffing the phone to ensure that they don't miss a message. Last night's events changed that. They're more like family than his staff. He worries for their safety now. He'll cover as much as he can, pleading a little time off from the Daily News. He'd never get over any of these folks getting beaten or worse. K-9 though, who would never get over anything happening to Micky, insists on staying with him.

The two of them sit in the CST office. Neither talks. He thinks of the people that came to help him. That's how he got into this whole thing; them, the people who live in this neighborhood and have lived in his life. They're why he writes and has the paper. In small type below the name, Central Standard Times, are the words 'aimed at the interests and concerns of the working man'. The same is certainly written on his heart.

Earlier in the day, the phone rang every few minutes. Now it's slowed down. All messages are documented in the same notebook. Mostly it's people with questions and opinions on the publication. They want more. Other print news outlets continue to call as well. They, too, are just looking for additional information, and not providing any. He repeats the basic facts to them, avoiding any speculation. No one who has called the Central Standard Times has offered a reliable answer to the question, 'Who Is Elijah?'.

Micky pulls a drawer out from one of the nearby file cabinets and lofts his feet up and onto it then slides down low into the all-wooden office chair. He is bone-weary. The article, as yet unproductive, is nonetheless, exhausting because of the amount of attention it has received.

"K-9, tell me something good, man," he breaks the silence eager for something a bit more uplifting than recent events.

"Okay. Here's one. I wouldn't say it's good, but it's new. I've got something for the Blotter that just came my way."

"Shoot." The Blotter is the CST column that covers crime. Usually, it's a copy of the neighborhood crime report from the police at the 15th precinct. Mostly, it's bland. What, he wonders, could his curious friend have, and where did he obtain it?

"Ronnie Gamboni is dead, beaten to death," K-9's delivery is breezy and jaunty despite the grisly nature of the content. Not entirely surprising. Gamboni is one of many exaggerated, if tragic, characters that inhabit the West Side and, in whose existence, he finds amusement.

"What? It's a joke, right? " he asks, even though he suspects it isn't.

"Nope." K-9 responds as if the word were spelled starting with 4 Ns. He reveals nothing more.

"Give, man. What? Where? How?" He is a rush of questions. Even though he's pushing, he knows that he will, most likely, need to wade through a slow and tormenting game before he can obtain any real information. This kind of torment is one of K-9's favorite things to do.

"Don't know. They haven't found the body yet." Micky is sure that's the line he wants to deliver. What fun! "But you can bet the farm on it."

"Okay. Cut the crap. What's the story? " Mickey snaps at him, hoping to at least expedite the charade.

"Well, you know that Gamboni is greased all the time, right," K-9 questions. Micky acknowledges this fact with a slight nod. It's commonly known that Gamboni is a barbiturate addict. "Well, one greasy day not long ago, he gets the idea to go down to Michigan Avenue and visit a jeweler. He asks to see some diamond rings. He questions the quality, the size, like that. They're chatting. It's all quite splendid, I'm sure.

"Then, in a very clever moment, he tries to get the jeweler to look away. Likely this is a tactic he learned from some criminal masterminds. Perhaps the Three Stooges? Anyway, he gulps down a ring on the momentary head turn. Where is it? What? The ring? Me? I don't have it? Search me. Honest Injun. The jeweler now, being above the age of 10 and, possibly, suspecting that Ronnie's slur is not caused by a neuromuscular disease, he calls the cops. Gamboni goes to jail and, shall we say..." he stops and plays a drum roll on the desk. "...things pass." Micky waits silently knowing that K-9 would like this to play out like an Abbot and Costello routine.

"And they have their evidence?" Micky asks. K-9 beams to indicate yes.

"Beaten to death is not funny—which, I understand, is where this ends up— and it shouldn't be laughed at out loud." A straight shooter, he hopes to make an appeal regarding the serious nature of this talk. It doesn't help.

"Now. This is grand theft, " he continues, unphased. "That ring is like 2 thousand. Grease boy is going to jail. It's not 30 days in County. This is Joliet, Pontiac, like that and 3 to 5. No! Wait. What's this?! He walks? He's not bailed out, mind you. He's walking." K-9 stands and takes a few choppy steps for the unnecessary visual example of walking. "Our story now shifts to Tony Pirelli, who fences for a lot of guys whose first names are Reputed." A smile. He's enjoying this more than Micky is. "Tony gets raided a couple days after Gamboni's unexpected exit from jail where he should be facing a felony rap. Now Tony's not that big a secret, but the cops don't know, least ways not any cop who would do anything about it. First, nobody would want to give up a fence. That's an asset to the neighborhood, like public transportation, like 3 fire hydrants to a block, like..." He needs a third example to continue. It's the rule.

"Like a drug store that sells condoms to guys who aren't 18 because it's better to keep everyone safe," Micky offers to close the point.

"No, something more valuable." Since he offered, K-9 now wants him to come up with the third example. He gestures, implying 'try again'.

"Like a lady who buys cookies for the neighborhood kids who just have to knock on her door?" He is thinking of Mrs. Murray, who is uncanny for her preparedness with available cookies.

"More adult. "

"Like an Outfit boss, whose presence deters the opportunist burglar."

"Yes! That's it. Where was I? Oh, yes. The Reputed brothers will lose money if Tony goes to jail. They would rather lose their sisters than lose money. And they really love their sisters. It didn't take long for facts to be revealed and to surmise that Gamboni gave up Pirelli so he could walk. It's a nice bust, a really nice bust. As you are aware, Gamboni does not travel, that is to say, move about, inconspicuously. He is recognizable by his, mmm, shall we say, eccentric gait." The "g" lurches out of his mouth from deep in his throat. "He kind of navigates his way around using his arms for balance. It's like he's swimming, only there's no water. What I'm saying here is that the Aquaman impression provides a noticeable, uh, am-bu-la-tion." Micky purses his lips in an acceptable response, acknowledging that Gamboni is always stoned to the point of staggering. "He was spotted being escorted into the back of the SAC club on Taylor in Little Italy by some kids playing softball in the alley. That was 2 days ago. He wasn't seen coming out. No one has seen the grease spot since. And when they do, it is certain that he will not be able to discuss his recent whereabouts. He will not be shot. He will not be stabbed. He will just...not be...anymore, beaten to death." He's probably right. A gruesome death will be accepted because he violated a code of ethics. He snitched.

"Do the kids know who it was that escorted him in?"

"Nope. Nobody sees those guys." Another example of the code.

The shrill ring of the office phone announces the end of their talk before Micky can reiterate what K-9 assuredly knows; he can't use one word of that story.

Micky grabs the receiver answering, "Central Standard Times. Micky Mulvihill speaking." He does his best not to sound like he's uninterested in yet another person seeking more than was published.

"Yeah. Hello, Micky Mulvihill." The greeting sounds sinister, like an evil smirk. "I live on Kilpatrick near Lake Street." A pause. It extends. *Still there?* He's patient, sensing that speaking is giving this caller trouble "It's greed. It's like Reverend Burrell said, they're the pawnbrokers. The gangs are just the pawns." Micky feels a chill. Maybe there had been a thought that HE might call, but it was far in the back of his mind, where he didn't need to address it. A stark serious look alerts K-9 that this call might be important. K-9 leans forward in his chair until he's resting his arms on his knees.

"Yes, sir. Is that why you called, to express how terrible this is, and who's really at fault?"

"I think, yeah, well, that, but I think that maybe I saw him, Elijah, on that day, the day of the march." He hears a soft chuckle.

"Really? Uh, yes, sir. Please tell me what you saw and where you saw it." He grabs the pencil, moving the notebook in front of him.

"Your description is accurate. The pyramid

tattoo on the left side of his neck. It's the symbol for the Black P Stone Nation. The girl, she was sharp to pick that up. "

There's no mention of a girl in the paper. This is him! Micky doesn't respond to the assumption, not at first. Then he thinks to offers a dismissal. "I think the police have the description from more than one witness.

"She was in the wrong place." The voice condemns.

"What exactly did you see, sir? And who are you?" He drops the courtesy, wanting him to make an admission.

"They came down Lake. They was walking, spread out. It's just that there were too many. " He avoids the question.

"Too many for what? What do you mean?"

"Not to get noticed. You don't want people to pay attention. But if you live there, you know what looks right and what don't. - I work nights. I was just getting up and walking over to the grocery story on Cicero. They're all passing by as I'm heading back to the crib, " he explains using a slang for where he lives. "Then they all climbed the stairs to get on the "L" going East. And a lot of them were already on the train, like maybe they got on at Laramie 'cause they didn't want to all get on at the same stop. It looks real normal to see kids that age on the "L" anytime in the afternoon even in the summer, like that day. "

"And this is where you saw Elijah."

"He kept walking. He didn't want to be with the kids."

Micky tries again to get a response to his name question . "What did you say your name is — did you watch Elijah further? Did he get in a car, maybe? Did he talk with anybody, anybody not walking away from Laramie?"

"I watch Elijah. Yes. I can see him now."

"What do you mean?"

"I can see his image. He did meet someone. There was this other cat down the street, white guy, waiting, leaning on the trunk of his car, pacing around a bit. The car was green, a Ford. Yes, a green Ford Fairlane, a '58."

"That's great. Did you see the license? And your name please, sir?"

"I'm just shopping. That's all. Is there a reward? I mean the girl must be in line for something." He asks again, indicating that he's looking to confirm the witness is a girl.

"I don't know who you mean, but let me get your full name, address and phone number. The police will want to speak with you. This is all very helpful."

There was another too-long pause. Just before Micky asks again, he hears, "Tell the police what I said. They'll want to know exactly what I said."

"Well, let me ask a few more questions, like height, weight, clothing. Just anything to further describe Elijah."

Gone. Micky hears the phone go dead. A syringe of adrenaline straight to the heart. He looks down to review his notes. "Okay. He referred to a 'white guy'. He's not white. He mentioned Burrell. He twice asked about a girl. He's Elijah."

K-9 is standing. "What else did he say?"

"He lied. He said he saw black kids on the "L". You can't see inside the "L" which runs two stories above ground, from standing anywhere on Cicero and Lake. And there's no grocery store on that corner. I know the corner of Cicero and Lake very well. I hung around there for years starting when I was a kid, shining shoes in the bars all along that street. He lied that he lives there."

"And playing pool, Mick. You were shining shoes and playing pool." It's true. That's how Micky learned to play. No one cares if a shine boy shoots at a few leftover balls when the game finishes. Over time, still a kid, he began to play in those games. He got good enough where some of the regulars told him to lay low, don't play his best. They'll get him into a game, they said. He'll make more than he would with that shine box.

"Yeah. Guys would be like, 'hey, me and the shoeshine kid will take on you and your partner. My job was to make one now and again, if needed, but more importantly to snooker them when I missed, leaving them nothing to shoot at. It's more like billiards than pool. I learned to look very disappointed at my perfect misses. Wait." He jolts back to the moment. "Let me dial Wagner." He leaves a message with the desk sergeant. "Let's go. Elijah, saying it was a girl, fishing...because he knows it was Effie!"

Micky's '67 Chevelle SS is parked on the other side of Chicago Avenue by the Catholic grade school. He explodes out the door and flies over to Preacher's house to tells him to staff the phone. Now! He and K-9 run to the Chevy.

The tires screech turning onto Chicago Avenue and again down Laramie. They spot an unmarked police car sitting across the street and down a few doors watching. Breathing only slightly easier, they cut back and head over to the 15th precinct.

That call needs to be traced. Rushing to follow up, he doesn't know that Elijah still has his hand on the phone he's just used, in the Alexander house.

CHAPTER 19

It's late morning, on one of Chicago's dog-days. People don't pay much attention. They've seen this day too much. Endured like a jail sentence, all but the young wish to be paroled into the cooler Fall. Indian summer, many will say, longing for the cold, which they'll, subsequently, and quickly, start to hate. Parents, having reached wit's end with the twenty-four-hour management of their children over the summer, are thankful classes have started.

Elijah knows exactly where to go to get a vantage point. He scoots down the quiet side streets. He gently touches the accelerator to avoid causing any excitement until he coasts up to the curb on Huron just south of the Alexander house. He parks under the shade of an oak. The leaves, just beginning to turn their color away from green, are a natural camouflage. He's drawn no interest from nearby apartment windows. A passing car will be rare on Huron. Most will use streets where the traffic lights keep them moving. His car sits on the side of a six-unit orange brick apartment building, Hogan's building, where foot traffic will be light.

Who am I? And, where am I? Where you would never look, right under your noses?

The Alexander house is about half a block away and across the street from where he's parked. He can see the front porch. Now he climbs over the seat to wait in the back of the car. He sits low should anyone happen to walk by or look out. A small pair of binoculars makes him feel so close, like he's hiding right on her porch, but in the dark where he can't be seen. There. He sees something.

Driving past him is a 1968 Plymouth Belvedere, very plain, but with the tell-tale flood light on the driver's side. It parks directly in front of Effie's home. Two men emerge wearing poorly-matched pants and suitcoats. He spies a glimpse of white socks as they stride. *Cops.* In a matter of minutes, they return. After leaving the Alexander home, the Plymouth does a U-turn in the middle of the block and parks a few doors away on his side of Laramie. It adds up; that's a detective car and these are plainclothes cops who've perched themselves in a watch position. This is just the indicator that he is looking for. *Whom are you watching, and why? Have you been news report drawn you to guard her? Perhaps you enter for follow-up questions? Maybe you want to show her some pictures of known felons for possible identification? Or maybe it is a visit just to re-mind her that she'll be protected? She won't be.*

With careful and deliberate movements, he

mutes the sounds of the door both when he opens and closes it. No one flashes in front of a window or peeks around a corner to inspect. He's on the street and, as yet, safe and unnoticed. Calmly, he walks to, and then down, the alley. If school were not in session, the children would be out playing soft-ball, hopscotch, pinners and various other games. Today, without them, the alley is empty.

The backyard of the house next door, with its overgrown grass, offers opportunity for an entry. The yard receives little attention. Anyone who should enter it enjoys the same. A small fruit tree braced against the wire fence along the property line assists for a quick hop over. A 3-foot high hedge behind the Alexander's coach-house garage hides him from view. He stops to listen for sound in the house.

It's only a short while before a car pulls up the alley and parks parallel to the large bay door on the cement apron in front of the garage. Too late and not a good spot. From their position, they could see someone walking or driving up, but not someone who is in the yard already.

There she is! That's her. He's certain its Effie he sees walking by one of the windows. But only her, no one else. Electra is still at the dry cleaners. Young Paul is in school. Effie's school won't start for another week. This little one has the whole house to herself. How lucky for her, he laughs to himself.

Elijah marks his luck as more Divine providence.

Two ground-level windows, each perhaps two-feet in height, provide access to the basement. Each is overlaid by a storm window. Binoculars show that the storm windows are affixed with thumb-screws. Just a twist on each and the window can be removed. Looking through the storm window glass, he sees that the inside house window is not flush. They leave it ajar. The frame is overpainted. If it were forced fully closed, it might never open. Un-closed is unlocked.

Elijah crawls down the walk. The hedge hides him. He removes the storm window and, carefully, pushes and wiggles the house window to loosen it noiselessly. It gives. He crawls through and reaches back to bring the storm window in behind him.

The basement has a washer and dryer, a clothes-drying rack and shelves of old carpentry tools. An older washer with a hand-wringer on top sits in the corner, obviously past its time. A natural gas furnace with forced air provides heat now for this old Victorian, but remnants of the former heating system remain. A tiny and totally dark room filled nearly wall-to-wall with two large drums for heating oil. The drums, no longer in use, are not completely empty, not at the very bottom. The oil inside and thinly smeared on the cap is a pudding-like sludge.

He waits just a little longer, going over what

he'll do and how he'll do it. The blood courses through him, warming him. The Bible verse, vengeance is mine, sayeth the Lord, comforts him. *I will repay. Elijah calls to the power of God and receives.* He has taken retribution many times, but this time, it is directly against Mulvihill. God has guided him to this moment. His excitement is evident. He is erect.

The police have assured Effie. News of the attack on Micky has exploded through the neighborhood. They tell her what she has desperately hoped for; that whoever he is, he can't harm her and is, probably, on the run now. The police will run down the contacts and previous whereabouts of those he sent to attack Micky, and now reside at Cook County Jail at 26th and California. It's just a matter of time. *Yes, it is exactly that.*

Most of the others who know Lewis Leonard will not speak to the police on general principle, but someone will. It only takes one. It'll be soon enough. His time will be short. He knows that. Her time will be shorter.

It's her last day alive and all the feeling-good days of her life won't make up for the terror and pain that she will endure today. She will lose control of her bowels. Her horror will be so shocking that she'll feel she has lost herself. He will look at her virgin blood and think it to be perfect; the only man this bitch was ever with was Elijah, not the filth, but God's avenger. He's ready.

◆ ◆ ◆

Effie jumps two inches as black fingers curl around her mouth and nose like a giant tarantula. She can't breathe causing panic. He yanks her force-fully to the ground where a powerful blow stuns her. A second renders her semi-conscious. He duct-tapes her mouth and delivers a warning. "If you try to scream through this, you will die and so will your family."

She is a good daughter and a good big sister. She loves them. He sees that she feels resigned, that she has no choice, but to put faith in his words. That's what she does or tries to as best she can; her sounds of terror are muted and can only be heard by him. He relishes them through his release.

Elijah has thoughts of burning the whole place, but then, no. It's too much attention while he's still here. Just her. The small room in the basement with the old oil tanks is perfect for him. There is enough burnable residue in the tanks for his needs. It's been placed there for him by Him. The heating for this old Victorian has been updated many times, from wood-burning furnaces, to coal, to oil and now to natural gas. There is no other reason for these tanks to still be there, except to wait for him.

Elijah quickly bounds up the stairs to the first-floor apartment. He finds the thermostat and turns on the heat as Effie lays on the cold cement floor of the basement with her body, black, smeared with oil. She is slightly conscious. It's better for her to hear the furnace ignite and see her torn clothing stretched and leading into the furnace like a wick.

"It's just that you were there, right there in that moment when our eyes met, and my tattoo could be seen. You shouldn't have been there. None of you should still be here. This is not your home, any more. But you stayed too long. I was summoned. "

Elijah thinks it's justice. God must have maneuvered him so that he may exact a revenge, in both nature and kind, through the very act that made him the filth. It's merciful as she will not need to raise the product of that filth where she and the child would both be hated for the act. *It's all perfect.* God punishes with fire. Fire cleanses the darkest of sins. *Fire is Elijah's gift of power from God.*

Elijah draws the back end of a claw hammer and drives it deep into Effie's throat. Her mouth is covered. She gags and convulses but is unable to make any other sound. He swipes the blood on her neck with his index and middle fingers to write on the floor next to her body. The fire reaches her.

He walks up the stairs and calls the Central Standard Times to play the cat and mouse game with Micky. So delicious to tip him now when it's too late.

❖ ❖ ❖

Electra rushes down Laramie. The phone call from Mrs. O'Reilly, saying that Paul is with her and he can't get into the house, has alarmed her. She told Electra that the door is locked, and Effie doesn't answer. Electra knows something is wrong. Effie is supposed to be at home when Paul's schoolday ends. And she always has been. She retrieves Paul, who is standing with Eileen O'Reilly in front of her home, right next door.

"Thank you, Eileen. I no know what happen, but I find out." Inside the house, both she and Paul call out Effie's name. That awful burnt smell.

Mrs. O'Reilly is barely back in her own house when a shriek of terror and a repugnance, pierces her ear, freezing her. Electra! She runs back to the house. She panics to the point that it slows her ability to move. The door is not locked. She works her way through the house and toward Electra. Her legs are shaking from fright. She moves to the basement. Halfway down the stairs, she can see Electra thrashing about in a convulsion. Paul, his face white with a horrified expression, screams insanely and paws at anything that is near.

There's something else. Someone...lying on the floor. Her heart thunders in her chest. It's a body, but no longer a someone. She can barely climb the stairs to reach the phone on the kitchen wall.

"Operator, " she sobs. "Get me the police. For the love of God, get me the police."

CHAPTER 20

Olivia, through a tearful heaving, endures the ghastly details when the police tell her what has happened. They're checking and warning her, too. Things have escalated. This was neither an accident nor a pretense. There has been a homicide that's tied to news article, which tie to her. Her name stands out in those news article as being stalked by this predator. Her only thoughts, though, are to get to Micky as soon as possible. She calls him, but there's no answer.

She locks up the gallery as the cab pulls up to the front door. It's an emergency, she says, but avoids anything more specific. A glance back at her face in the mirror, and the driver believes it. He's off quickly. Traffic begins to clog. The travel time is excruciatingly slow for her. Using a series of deft shortcuts, they, finally, pop out onto Laramie near Chicago Avenue.

"Can't go further. It's blocked off. " A blue and white squad car, light flashing, sits perpendicular to the road, blocking traffic. Two police officers standing straight, thumbs hooked inside their belts, watch cars approach and direct them to alternate routes.

"Just let me out." He pulls over. She drops a bill on the seat to cover the charge without looking back. Her exit receives a scornful look from the police.

As many as a dozen police squad cars, arriving from all directions and parking at all angles, blanket the street in front of the Alexander home. Their red and blue lights flash, careening off nearby buildings to alert any, and all, to stay away. Hundreds of neighbors have walked out of their houses and stand around staring at the sight of it all, waiting. They can't help themselves. It's the potential to see Effie's body that keeps everyone watching.

Police forensic staff somberly attend to their tasks. The media wasted no time. Three news trucks sit parked further down, waiting. They'll report live from the front of the Alexander house for the evening news shows and replay those films for the ten o'clock news.

Inside, after sufficient photos and evidence have been gathered, they cover Effie's body and carefully move to the ambulance. Police surround the gurney to block views. Olivia watches, thinking of the young boy that Charles and Ernest spoke of, Eugene Williams. He was just about Effie's age when his body was dragged to shore with grappling hooks. And on that day, the authorities, just hoped to 'clean up' and get everyone back to their business. People wouldn't stand for it then and erupted into a riot. *What will happen now?*

Olivia leaves the scene. Moving beyond the barricades she navigate her way to the spaces at CST, which are dark. *Maybe he is at home or with the police?* She leans in and focuses through the window. Her back to the street, she becomes self-conscious and nervous. She's black in an all-white neighborhood where a horrible crime has just occurred, committed by a black man. No one will doubt that this tragedy was caused by the one calling himself Elijah.

Two doors down, she sees some people entering the church where Preacher's father is the minister. And then she sees a few more. Moving closer, she watches them enter. The church doors are open. She's just following instinct, unaware that the crowd was too big for CST and Preacher had made a suggestion to the church, where they could more easily meet.

The church building is well over a hundred old. Its grape-jelly brick exterior, mottled from age, is, nonetheless, original and unpatched. She thinks that these bricklayers must have known their craft. A century ago, the church was a carriage house for the estate on the corner. Now that land holds the large apartment building where Micky rents a space for the Central Standard Times. The rear of the church has wooden doors that reach nine feet high, one on each side of a brick pillar that separates them. When it was converted to a church, the loft area was made into a sanctuary. The main floor, which once held horses and their carriages, is storage and the minister's office.

The stairs, long and steep with no landing and slumping slightly in the middle greet her just a few feet inside the doors. The second floor is higher than a normal requiring perhaps twenty steps. She hears Micky's voice emitting from up in the loft asking people to have a seat. At the top of the stairs outside the sanctuary doors, she hesitates and decides not to enter.

Micky stands in front of the first pew, but not up on the platform. He waits for everyone to settle in. K-9 stands off to his side. Two uniformed cops are in the back and off to the corner, only observing.

"A lot of you know Effie Alexander, a high school student who lives in this neighborhood with her brother and mother. " He chokes on the next words. "She's been killed." The news is not news to anyone. Hearing what has happened either through the media or from other neighbors, is why they're here. They came to get answers. Why, and how? Everyone connects the incident to the recently published articles.

Micky's face shows that he's in pain, but he is determined to be open and honest with them, no matter how difficult. "The police were guarding front and back, but he, the killer, he got in, anyway. Effie's brother, Paul and her mother, Electra were not harmed, but the shock overwhelmed them. They were taken to St. Anne's, I'm told." He can't bring himself to say they're okay.

"Look, I swear to you that I don't know how," he just breaks into a defense. "The article we recently published to identify Elijah did not use a name, age, gender, address – nothing that would tell someone to go to Effie's house. And it mentioned the word descriptions, plural, as in many witnesses. Outside of me and the police, no one knew our witness' name or even that it was one witness. And I swear to you that I haven't said that name to anyone else, not anyone." He hides the fact that Olivia had to meet with her for the artist rendering. He's sure that doesn't matter. Even then, a name and address wasn't used. "Look, we did everything we—"

One of the neighbors stands and yells, "You mean you knew it was her that gave the police the description. It had to be either the police or you that let the cat out of the bag. Ain't that right? "

Micky repeats, "No name or anything was given by me or anyone at the CST. This guy had something else. She saw him. Maybe he saw her? " He stops. He realizes that's it. It's been right there in front of his face the whole time. The sudden guilt on his face creates an explosion of accusations.

"You knew he saw her, didn't you? You printed her story anyway! Here's a witness. How could you do that! She was just a kid! My God, they're saying she was set on fire! On goddamn fire!"

The women start to cry. The men grimace in pain. That's why Effie was so frightened. He should have known. His head drops.

Preacher speaks up, "I think it was me who screwed up. There were phone calls we took yesterday, looking for tips. One guy says, he says...he says, "she", when he's making a comment. I didn't think about it, didn't deny it. I didn't know who it was. I knew it was a female, but that's all. I didn't catch it. It didn't mean anything to me. We were trying to catch a killer. Didn't you read? He's the guy who killed Reverend Moore and burned that little girl"

It not only doesn't excuse their actions, not to these neighbors, but it makes matters worse. "And so, to catch a killer, with this story, you put Effie's life on the line, too? Like bait, is it?" asks one man who stands. The question is repeated in shouts.

"No." A loud clear female voice booms from the back. Heads shift toward the sound in unison. It's Olivia. "Not her, but I put myself in danger." The sudden appearance of a black woman jolts them. "I understand the pain, anger and grief that you are all feeling. My name is Mrs. Olivia Moore. Reverend Charles Moore was my husband. He is dead. A little girl, a member of our church, is scarred and blinded by a man that the police weren't too eager to look for. The police were the first to be brought into this." The two officers in the back shift uncomfortably. "The account in the CST talks about the person who repeatedly broke into my gallery. The police said, 'Bolt the door'. That's it! The coverage shows a person who inserted his own image onto a painting, a sinister and threatening move. Again, the police ignored it. They thought that perhaps Mr. Mulvihill and I invented the story and changed the painting for publicity. All of it was to catch someone who had already killed and was stalking and threatening again. That story is not responsible for the death of this poor girl. Elijah is. He kills." She stops, her voice shredding. *Remember those words. He kills.* "Mr. Mulvihill, and his staff, trying to protect you, investigated and were able to find out that a person fitting this description did indeed recruit young men for a march of intimidation, to frighten you more quickly away from your homes. Still the police scoffed at the idea and wouldn't look for him. Elijah knew who she was and had his own reasons for wanting to kill her and, I'm sure, nothing gives him more delight than to have you attack Mr. Mulvihill, the one who uncovered him. He wants you to blame Mr. Mulvihill. He is evil. " Her voice trembles with rage at the last word. She calms herself.

The women stare at every detail of Olivia, at her look and powerful educated manner. At her blackness. The men listen, shocked at what they're hearing and who is saying it. She repeats. "He knew who she was and where she lived. He was just toying with the staff on those phone calls, probably to better blame them. But he already knew and was going to kill her anyway, even with no article." Olivia is almost sick at the rawness of her statement. To speak that way of someone's child makes her nauseous, but she continues. "He is a killer, a predator. And he's been here, like a predator, in this neighborhood and on your street." These words horrify the crowd. "Mr. Mulvihill was trying to catch him, to protect you. And Elijah knows it!"

The crowd is much more subdued, if not completely convinced. Olivia's presence possibly more than her words has them off. She wishes that she could talk more to them, to tell them what her husband was like, to let them know that her husband believed in the potential of black and white living together in Austin, not only peacefully, but without harm or loss of value to the community, but this was not the moment to make those points. This is not an issue of race relations. This is a madman.

These words appear to end it. The neighbors look at each other with a question, then drag themselves to a stand and turn to exit. As the crowd files out from the church, sounds of discontent and anger begin to grow anew, one bolstered by another. All of Olivia's points were being diminished. What resonated was that if the CST hadn't run that story, Effie would still be alive.

By late evening, the detailed news connecting all of this would be out in the city and nationwide. Effie's burnt body had been recovered from the basement of her Laramie Avenue home. The sexual assault will, eventually, be included as a detail. The written message remains guarded with a few.

◆ ◆ ◆

After the crowd is gone, they've moved back to the CST offices. Micky is despondent, as is Preacher. The guilt overwhelms them. Olivia, Micky, K-9 and Preacher are joined by Kathy and Mary who came as soon as they could. Mary has the radio on, but the reports only restate the horror that everyone knows, and not anything new. The repeated facts hammer their souls. She makes some tea and forces it on them all.

Micky speaks. "You see, you think you're fighting for the right thing. It's the way you've been brought up. Then someone says you're not. You're actually part of the problem." They all understand that he's crossing today's events over to the war.

"Micky, I meant what I said. He had his own reason for killing Effie and he knew about her and where she lived already. The story didn't get her killed. I also meant it when I said that I understand all the feelings. Don't you think I feel guilty for not having done more? I knew Charles was in danger, that he was worried. I've second-guessed myself on everything I said and did."In the end, no one knows what the perfect tactic is, but it's Elijah that kills, not you, not me, not the story."

Micky face says that he understands her point but doesn't accept it. Excuses don't change results. Would Effie be dead without the story? Maybe he remembered who she was, but did he need to kill her?

"Why did he kill her?" Kathy questions Olivia.

Not letting Olivia answer, Micky asks her his own question. "Why did you react to his name, Elijah, back when I first told you? " She has something that he hasn't told her.

Olivia has been hesitant to mention thoughts that she has about Elijah, thoughts garnered the moment she heard his unusual name. Now, maybe it's not such a far-fetched notion, after all.

"When you first said his name, I thought of the Elijah that is in the Hebrew Bible because he is famous for calling down God's fire." She looks at their blank faces.

"I get it, " Preacher quickly chimes in. "Been thinking the same thing in the back of my mind." They stare at him. " Elijah, in the book of Kings, wants to rid Israel of a false idol and to discredit the priests who are proffering this idol to the people.

Ba'al. The idol was named Ba'al. He sets up a challenge to the priests. They'll both be ready to sacrifice a bull, but each will ask their God to light the fire, the sacrificial fire. Whoever can call upon their God to light their individual sacrifice has the true God. He who cannot, is worshipping an idol. Elijah's sacrifice, even after he requests water be poured on the wood, is lit on fire. The sacrifice of the priests is not set on fire. Baal is proven to be just an idol and the priests are discredited. " He takes a breath. They're not following.

"That's right. That's what I found. Biblical Elijah calls to God to start fire. It proves that he's connected to God, that he has God's approval. But it seemed, well, it just couldn't be. Remember the danger started with a real estate gambit. I think that, maybe, our Elijah is a zealot and an arsonist. Avenue Realty might have hired someone to harass people that they can't control. The Blackstone Rangers might have used the same arsonist to payback Reverend Burrell. Charles, like Burrell, was getting in the way, poking around Avenue Realty and their gang connection. Elijah was maybe paid to send a message like with Burrell. Elijah is, likely, not his real name."

Olivia Moore looks at Micky and all of them. The next point has only recently occurred to her. "Fire, also, is commonly associated with revenge and it's also, usually, not a healthy mind." She looks down at the floor. "To answer your question Kathy,

Effie was the only witness, the only person who could have identified him as the man in the march from a lineup. He removed the witness." Turning to Micky, she adds, "And he would have done that just to be safe, whether there was a story or not."

"The call I took, " he begins, moving past her point, "the police should let us know about the phone trace. Another day or so, they'll know whether anyone local owns a green 1958 Ford Fairlane." Then it comes back to him. " Olivia... "

She cuts him off, "The police station a car by my house and the gallery. I have a signal to give them if anything is wrong. I can't identify him. I'm no different than anyone who has seen the image from the painting." He doesn't respond indicating that her words don't reassure him. And they don't. This has become personal.

CHAPTER 21

The phone rings every few minutes until he unplugs it. He's not talking to any press. They'd have him tear his soul apart, and on camera, if possible. His knows that his family must have heard the news. He calls them. His father answers. Usually, it's his mother. Dad wants to talk with him. Micky wants the same. Please come over tonight. Have dinner. Stay with us. He'll eat with them, but that's it.

The doorbell rings. A window no more than six inches show him the hat that Wagner wears. He asks to come in and hopes that K-9 is not home. He has something very private to show him. Okay. If it's important to the case. It's the only thing that he has energy for.

"Mr. Mulvihill. " That's, definitely, not a good start. "I have a polaroid of the victim as she was found, in the house." His eyes narrow. " *What the hell do I need to see that for?* "The killer left behind a signature of sorts, and a message, in a very grisly fashion. It's not easy to look at." Wagner's attempt to help him brace for the impact only making it worse. "The message is to you. I think you should see it, not just hear about it. It's…"

"Let's just see it." *Get on with it, already!* He faces indicates that the tip-toeing effort should end. Wagner agrees. He was only trying to help, but he's not good at this.

It's a series of polaroid pictures, all taken from different angles. The first one hits him flush in the face. He sees the message. He bends forward from the hurt. He's alone now. Wagner doesn't exist, nor the world. Wagner wanted this to be a warning, a sign to be careful. It's a call to battle.

◆ ◆ ◆

Micky knows that his parents are waiting. He barely has the energy to comfort them with assurances that he's okay, but he's going to try. He parks and walks toward the now familiar brick bungalow that is their home.

Martin, tow-headed like Micky is known to friends as "Whitey". Mary, grand as any name can be, always ran the house in typical Irish matriarchal fashion. She paid the bills, decided on the schools and established the house rules, unless something was wrong. Then Whitey would take care of it. His reputation for letting his fists fly goes back to school days.

They're both different now. Age has mellowed

Whitey. Mary appreciates the man who changed his life and his health working in labor for so many years to care for all of them.

The Mulvihills haven't been in Berwyn that long, but those who live around them already know who they are now. Micky's glad that they'll wait inside the door to avoid a show for neighbors, who would doubtless ogle every second of it, given his new notoriety.

Micky and his siblings were raised in apartments. It wasn't until a little money fell his parents' way that they were able to buy a house. One bundle was an inheritance from his father's dear, but childless, Aunt Helen. The other was an insurance settlement from accident on the job last year. His dad almost lost two fingers, pinky and ring, on his right hand trying to help a forklift driver get a pallet of goods in the right spot. They sewed the fingers back on in emergency surgery that night. Six months later, the fingers are a little weaker, but they work well enough. The bonus was early retirement, which he was desperate for, anyway.

His father spent more than three decades moving freight between trains and trucks. He was a Teamster, and proud of it. The family has always been part of unions and organized labor, leading these groups, in fact. It's like the mob and the military smushed into one. Dedication. Commitment. Victories, but lots of dirty work and violence.

Despite Micky's best effort to conceal it all, he can tell that his father knows that he has been through the ringer from both sides. He stands straight wearing his dutiful I'm-okay-face, but as an actor, he doesn't make local theater grade. Micky has always tried to live by a set of high ethics. He's held himself accountable for any failure in that area and rarely, if ever, repeated. The guilt over Effie with the articles and all, makes him ill. It's like a poison inside him. He rages at the pain into exhaustion. Then, he recovers a bit, but it comes back again. He needs some way to release it. Maybe, he hopes, he can get a little peace tonight.

"Hi. C'mon in, son. Mom's made some dinner for you," his father says over Mary's shoulder, while she provides a crushing hug. "We all ate, but that don't matter. We'll be with you for your supper. It's waiting for you in the kitchen." Micky nods and steps that way.

Then his brother, Patrick, and his four sisters: Diane, Kathleen, Eileen and Florence, intercept him and attempt to hug him back to health right there in the hallway. Each of them changed whatever they had planned and came as soon as they knew he would be there. They don't want to let him go, ever. He's trying to show that he understands and appreciates what they're doing, but the lump in his throat leaves him only able to nod.

Mom, who never intended for him to eat in the

kitchen, not with all her children over, amends the plan. "Let's just go to the dining room so we all can sit more comfortably."

Comfortably is a relative term. This house is bigger than the apartments they were all raised in, but this simple brick bungalow, new to them, but fifteen years old, isn't built to host a family of seven in the kitchen.

The dining room table, oversized to accommodate just such gatherings, crowds the room. The kids each suck in their stomachs, passing between the backs of the chairs and walls. Reaching their seat, they shoehorn their way in. Mary has kept the oven warm and popped in his food as soon as she spotted him.

The warming plate is an aluminum foil dish that once held a pie crust she purchased from the Jewel. Long ago, she used it for a pie she made. Since then it's joined other tins to be warming plates. Micky's had many meals heated out of these aluminum plates. His father used one every night for years working the second and, sometimes, third shifts. The porcelain dinner plate that she'll have him eat from, as well as utensils, napkin and all the rest lie at the ready. The food will be piping hot in a just few minutes.

His father sits down next to him holding two cans of Old Style, already popped open. He places one in front of him. The others can serve themselves if they wish to join. They don't feel the least bit slighted by the difference in treatment tonight. Patrick checks eyes with his sisters to see who would like to join them. He gets cans for himself and Diane. Mom places dinner in front of Micky. He knows that, hungry or not, it's his job to eat while seven sets of eyes watch. No one is sure how to begin, but Martin opens.

"It's a terrible thing, this, with that poor girl. Dat son of a bitch will burn in hell, and the sooner he gets there, the better, " the screeching voice is back.

"Yeah, and I'm going to put him there," is the somber, even and unsettling response. It's a promise.

"Now Micky, let the police..." his mother advises, but only says that much. It's not, advice that he'll be taking. His face change, contorting into anger and frightening his mother

"Oh, no. Not them! The police? They didn't want to get involved. They knew way early, but just didn't want to get involved. This is too black a thing. Can't risk the trouble. They would provide protection for her, even though she wasn't identified in any way, they said. Not good enough, was it? He'd already killed her by the time the doughnut break had finished. Plus, he'd already burned another kid. Burned, mom! How many charred children does it take to get their attention? The hell with them. A lot more bad things will happen if I wait for them." He knows that they are concerned with his rage, but he just stares downward at the table. "Me and the police, we were the only ones that knew exactly who the witness was and where she was. For all I know, the police think I did it. I was at the church fire. I was in the neighborhood when Effie was murdered. Calling them could be my attempt to throw them off the trail. No, I can't count on them." He almost growls the last of it. "There's an animal loose, a predator, among the children. It needs to be killed."

His father comments hoping to temper his mood. "Mick, easy, son. I know..."

"You don't know." His voice booms, near a yell. Martin squints at him. Micky puts down his fork and knife and leans back in his chair. He's going to tell them what was in the polaroids.

"There was a message written next to her... body." He chokes out the words. Martin's eyes widen. "It was written...in blood, her blood. It was...written...to...me." He tightens a fist in front of his mouth, eyes ballooning with water. He's barely hanging on. He envisions each word, and always will. " It said, 'Who the people say I am, Michael Mulvihill?' It's taken from something Jesus said, I guess. The police say so, anyway. Olivia, she thinks he's acting out this guy Elijah from the Bible or something. "

His head weighs a hundred pounds. He is wet, tired and trying to move through mud. Chains bind his chest laboring his breathing. Silence as the moments pass.

Dad braves a comment, a rationale to dismiss the message. The phrase sounds Old Testament to him. "Well, he's a religious nut, Mick."

"He's a fucking fake." Micky knows his language shocks them. He never says that word to his parents. They're very worried about him. They all wait. He adds, "But it would be good if he were a believer, 'cause when I get my hands on him, he will meet his God, that very day. As I live and breathe, that...very...day." His voice slightly breaks on the last few words.

This wasn't some tough-guy brag. He meant it. Martin takes a breath, not knowing what will come out to help his son. Micky cuts it off. He's going to explode.

"It was an answer to my question in the paper. His answer to me. He...wrote...my name...next to that child's body...her burnt and raped body." Eyes flaring, he grits his teeth. "MY...NAME!" He screams like he's being gored. It doesn't stop. It's acid, poured on his face.

Martin jumps up, lifts Micky up, wraps his arms around him saying, "No. No. No." He grabs his son's face, his own tears running down his cheeks. He kisses him, saying softly now, "No...no...no." Again, and again. That something hurts his son this much crushes him. Micky hugs back fiercely trying to let some of the pain leave him.

Mom and the siblings converge. It's a phalanx, everyone protecting a little bit of someone else. No one moves. Everyone is shattered, but they hold on together.

CHAPTER 22

The family understands that something has to happen that is only between father and son. They have, finally and reluctantly, either gone home or gone to bed. Micky is not the oldest among them, but his role in the family has always been as if he was. He was the one that went out shining shoes before he even knew his multiplication tables. Then he brought home that money, and enough pool money, to really help. A lot of other kids wouldn't have.

They all burst with pride seeing him in his Marine uniform. He sent a good chunk of his paycheck home. His sister Diane doesn't get through college without it. He extended this to everyone in the neighborhood. They'd asked him for favors, too, and he never refused.

Martin walks from the kitchen with his Old Style. Micky declines. Now, it's just he and his son. He notices his son staring a bit too long at the front door, which is open to let the cool fresh evening air enter the house. *He's on guard.* He wants to break his thoughts.

"We hate Winter and aren't too fond of Summer, but Fall is great, the best." He smiles and nods toward Micky, looking for a friendly agreement. It doesn't really help. Best just to get on with it.

"Last month, with Moore and his sermon, the last one, his final one?

"Yeah, I guess that's where I wanted to ask you a question, too."

"Well, we remember the story a little different." By we, he means white people.

"How do we remember it?" he asks, jokingly. "I don't know much about any of it. Did you know about the anniversary?"

"No. I mean, yes, I know the dates, if I think about it, but I don't. Ever. It was a half-century ago. I was 12 or 13 at the time. Moore, he wants to make some connection between then and now with him in the middle. But it's not the same now."

"With Daley's war on gangs, it could be. Way I know it, the blacks started the riot, and the whites, with a lot of city looking the other way, finished it. Moore's wife, Olivia, she says that her husband figured that Daley thought it was time to go head-hunting. Take out the top guys, anyone not getting locked up, and maybe even then."

"Well, I don't want to rehash his view. Let me say what I need to say, starting with my father,

Leo, and his brother, James Joseph, "JJ". The family was living in Bridgeport and Canaryville back then. They were in their late twenties at the time. My dad, of course, had been out hustling early in his life. By that time, he'd done a lot of favors in terms of turning out the vote for the city. And the city had reciprocated with some trucking contracts to his friends. He was a go-between who could get things done." He stops a moment to sip his beer, but he really wants to eyeball Micky for a reaction to this kind of thing. Nothing. "He also helped smooth things out when unions got into beefs with the city. The both of them had a kind of oversight for the SACs in those neighborhoods. Those members were the guys who patrolled the boundaries making sure no blacks crossed the line." Micky winces slightly. Martin quickly defends. "People was protecting what was theirs. The blacks could have built things for themselves, same as everybody else. They didn't, not then and not now. Look at integration, the whole thing that Moore was talking about. He admits it hasn't worked. He admits that everywhere the blacks go just becomes more ghetto. Whose fault it that?" Mick shakes his head as an acknowledgement. "Anyway, when the riots started, and like you said, it was the blacks that started looking for whites to beat first, Grandpa and his brother were protectors. "

"They beat blacks? Grandpa and Uncle JJ beat blacks?" Micky asks.

He shrugs. "Yeah. Some. Well, JJ, for sure. My father was an organizer type." He sees that this unsettles Micky.

"And the Black Belt, overcrowded and with dilapidated buildings that they were overcharged for, is where blacks were forced to live? I always thought it was just the black neighborhood, where the blacks all lived like Bridgeport was where the Irish all lived."

"Well, everybody was forced to live with their own kind when they first come. You come here from down South during the war years? You was trying to get away from those crazy crackers. There wasn't room. And there wasn't no welcoming committee. Why would there be? They took jobs from whites by workin' for less! Every group that comes here is leaving something bad. You can't be giving your job away to the next ones. Anyway, here's what I want to say. Our name, Mulvihill, and them riots, are linked for any that know.

"That's what I need to know. How are they linked?"

Martin looks down at his beer before he finishes the can. "Here's what I know. I was— let's see —like I said, maybe 13 and due to start high school. When the riots ended, all the men—Hell! Men! They were only teenagers, just a few years older than me. —They met at the SAC. I snuck down to listen, and

I got an earful." Micky sits forward in the sofa chair to listen closely.

"How come I never heard? Why am I just hearing this now?"

"Mick. I guess I never had a reason to tell you. That's different than keeping something from you. It was 50 years ago, and things were different. You don't survive in a big city, not back then, without spilling some blood. Otherwise, your family would starve, and you'd be out on the street begging. I guess I didn't think I needed to tell you about how it was when it wasn't that way, anymore." He sees his son's eyes bracing for what is to come.

"Okay. Just let me hear it."

"Yeah. Well, my dad is holding court, leading the discussion. All of them are there to hear what he has to say. My uncle, he's kind of in the background, trying to stay in the dark. I seen why later, when they started to leave. His face looked like a bobcat clawed it. He'd definitely had been out there himself.

"Anyway, my dad brings in this veteran. Name's Finnegan. He starts, saying most of you don't know me. I've been away, he says, fighting in the war, me and half the world. I remember that. 'Me and half the world.'

"Anyway, he talks about the war; saw men die, fired his gun and heard men whimper getting hit.

He says, at times, he went so long without a decent meal that when he finally got one, he threw it up. But he lived and he's grateful for it and not complaining. Everyone listens, real quiet. I mean he's got their attention with that; a man talking about war. Then he gets to the point.

"When he came back, some colored who works for less has his job. That one didn't fight, he says. I didn't see no darkies at all on the front lines. " Micky makes a skeptical face. Martin understands. He knows now that they were there. "Then Finnegan says they're not a people like us. They don't work and build. They take. His own family came here from Ireland long ago with nothing. They took what jobs were open. They cleaned stables, chimneys, barns. They didn't steal no other man's job.

"Then he talks about the boy who drowned. And here now, he says. One of theirs gets hurt, killed. He didn't stay with his own and moved onto a white beach. Sure. It's terrible. He was a young lad who made a mistake and paid for it with his very life. So, is he the first to die unwarranted? Did many an Irishman not die being in the wrong place. It's like that. He puts it in that perspective, a comparison of the Irish to the blacks.

"That, and what they did then, that's his big point, but he adds something first that went right through me. He says, I'm telling you, they'd be in here now after your own mothers and sisters if you didn't protect like you done. He says the Irish didn't go around killing people in a rage. We organized, got political power and all. That's how a civilized people do it. And then he adds, whatever happened, it was like you was in a war, too. Soldiers mostly keep things that happen to themselves. You'd be wise to do the same."

"Okay. I see his point, fighting for what's yours. And they were looking at it like the blacks started the fighting. But what about burning homes?" He doesn't know that Micky has a particular home burning in mind, but he wants him to understand that it was a different time.

"Everything was crazy, Mick. There were lots of lies about what happened. Neighborhood wags said it was a white man that got killed. White gangs were the way things got done. There were Ragen's Colts, the Sparkler Club, the Hamburgers, even the White Club. They were all young and believing everything in print, and the papers were making it out to be a planned race war. There was a black guy, named Mose Thomas, who was just shooting whites as they drove down the street. That's the truth. He was caught. That's how I know his name. There was a lot of talk about old Mose. It fueled people's hatred. "

"Right. They're beating, stabbing and shooting. They started it. So burn them out?"

"They thought it was a war, a real war. That's

probably why Finnegan was brought in. Anyway, you know, when this happens, some fight from a sense of protection, or to maintain the proper order of things. The way they figure the proper order of things." He adds seeing Micky's disapproval. He sighs, but what he has to add is worse. "Others come to fight because they love the violence." He collects his emotions. "That was your great-uncle, JJ. My dad was about the order of things, protecting. JJ just loved to hurt. " He watches Micky, who is more braced now. He must be expecting that there's a lot he doesn't know and he's ready for it. "Over the next couple of years, there were guys that talked to me, to tell me what he did. Yeah, he burned houses. And that line from Finnegan about mothers and sisters...that, too." He drops his head in disgust. Micky opens his mouth and looks up at the ceiling.

Martin tries to finish. "My dad spoke after Finnegan. He said whatever's been done to them has been done to us, too, here and in the old country. Only, remember, he says, that was our land. The Irish are the niggers of Europe he says. Them that came here before us built a life here in the city for their children. And then their children, a little better off, built a life for the next. He talked about how all the Europeans worked together, no matter the country, but it's different with the blacks. He said that there'd be investigations and probes and not to worry about any of it. Just don't talk about none of it to no one, any more and forever, not even amongst yourselves, nothin' nowhere. And it really isn't that well known today. So, I guess everyone pretty much did. Moore knew about it from his grandfather, that Ernest Johnson guy."

"Yeah, that's for sure. " His son is somewhere between shocked and disgusted, trying to digest it all.

"Mick, it's like that song the kids were singing this Summer, 'freedom's just another word for nothing left to lose'. That's who comes to cities. People looking for freedom who've got nothing left to lose. Well, that and the big rollers, the entrepreneurial types like Sears, Goldblatt, Montgomery Ward and all them. I don't know. If you need to build a big factory or a big store, you go to a big city, especially one that has transportation, you know, trains, trucks and now planes. And it's got a have a nice big work force, nice and ready to abuse 'cause they're desperate, nothin' left to lose." He stopped. They sit not speaking for some time.

"Okay. That answers a lot. Mrs. Moore, the minister's widow, she and I, as you know, are working this, together, as an investigation. Her father-in-law is Ernest Johnson."

"Yeah. I've seen him. On tv. He's the first guy charging arson."

"Yeah. He lived in the Black Belt. His house was

burned. He's one of those that know, you know, about our name being linked, like you said. He knows our name. So, maybe he's right? For all I know, Uncle JJ burned his house. " It hurts him. It's the first time that his son isn't proud of the family.

"Micky, there ain't nobody that didn't do something wrong. But whatever happened then, in that time and place, is not your fault." His son acknowledges the logic, but he can tell that it doesn't change his feeling. He's connected.

"I'm going out to the garage, dad. Then I'm going home. " Micky uses his parents' garage for weight-lifting and fight-training, things he learned in the Marines and some moves from K-9. He rises from the chair. They hug each other. He adds, "Thanks, dad. Thanks to mom, too. " Whitey will pass that on. He wants to say more, but they understand each other as far as it went, and it was enough.

His father tries weakly to get him to spend the night. He doesn't like the idea of him sleeping so close to where this brutal murder occurred with the killer still on the loose and with that horrible personal message and all. "I'll be all right, " he answers meaning it's not easy to get in and I have a service 45 loaded and eager to meet this snake.

***

Martin looks out from the upstairs bedroom window at his garage. Micky has placed a towel on each of the two windows that face the house, so the light doesn't bother anyone. Maybe he wants the privacy, too? Martin slides a chair over. He places his chin on his forearms and rests on the sill in front of the open window. Shadows. Micky's movement. Now the shadow is more rhythmic. He's hitting the heavy bag, which swings under the force of his blows.

"Marty, come to bed, " his wife urges.

"In a bit, " he answers. "It's cool here."

He lies, but he knows that he doesn't fool her. She'll let it be. A muffled metallic sound tells him that Micky is dead-lifting with a lot of plates. He remembers what his son said at dinner. Looking up to the sky, he prays. *Don't let him. Please, dear God, don't let him.*

CHAPTER 23

"**C**hicago was already a powder keg of racial tensions. The brutal murder of Effie Alexander just lit the wick. We'll be right back with our special report to tell you about it," John Wolford announces on his television broadcast. Micky's heart sinks. He's been increasingly worried in the last several days waiting for this report to air. Adding to the pressure is a full house. K-9 and the entire CST staff have joined him at his parents' Berwyn home. His family is all there, too. He received word that.

The station deliver their in-depth report on the murder of Aphrodite Alexander. Now is its effect on the neighborhood which will include his interview and interviews with the Alexander landlord and neighbors

He's nervous. He imagines people reexamining every detail showing him to be careless, costing the life of a child. The timeline of events will be cold and omit the sense of urgency, that Elijah had burned a church full of people and was tormenting Olivia. His choice to go public will make him look overzealous at best, and worst is too much for him to consider. He told Wolford to talk to the neighbors. He'll have to see their faces blaming him.

The dark circles under his eyes worry everyone. He hasn't slept more than two hours at a time for a week. When he does, he dreams of Elijah attacking Effie. He can't get to her. He's running down the street, trying to reach their house, but he can't find it. They moved it, he thinks. The neighborhood is changing, and they moved the house. Another time, she's not in the house. They're at Preacher's church because it will be empty during the week. Preacher's not home. He can't get in. He'll have to climb the side stairs and try to come in from the roof. He can't move up the stairs. He's calling out to alarm everyone. "He's in there. Elijah is —" He wakes up saying "in there." They're all the same; he fails each time.

Salerno's pizza boxes are piled high in the kitchen. Empty Cokes and Old Styles overflow the garbage can in the alley. Mary and the sisters have everything cleaned up. Micky stands in the back. He won't take a seat. It's better to be ready to move to a private area.

After the commercials, anchor Joel Albertson manages the lead-in to the report by questioning Wolford, who sits in the studio with him. The actual report is on film.

"John, when you mention the powder keg, are you referring to the escalating gang violence in the city? "

"Yes, Joel, that, the mayor's war on gangs, the new grand jury initiated to evaluate gang crimes and efforts, some say, by gang members who are under scrutiny to influence the grand jury and scare witnesses. All of this contributes to anxieties, especially in Austin as black families and black gangs, separately, of course, move closer. The residents are fearful of loss. The publication by Central Standard Times of a connection between the fire at Garfield Park Baptist Church and harassment by black gangs in their own neighborhood shocked the people living there and prefaced this homicide. Let's see what they say."

A copy of the Central Standard Times blaring the question Who Is Elijah covers the screen. A police captain answers, verbally. "Who is he? He's a madman, a demented, sick madman." A neighbor, Mr. Lacont, an Austin resident, is on screen answering. "He's a killer. A sick killer."

Then the report show a serious looking Wolford walking by the Alexander house. He asks the camera, "Was it wise to post this question, to taunt a madman?"

The screen changes back to the police captain. "We advised against it. There was an ongoing investigation." Micky feels gut-punched. The film cuts to Olivia. A caption tells everyone who she is.

"There wasn't any ongoing investigation. The

police didn't do one thing. They were advised of the break-in at my gallery. They were shown the painting. They were shown matching descriptions of the killer from multiple sources and ignored them. They were given statements by the custodian that the flammable materials were not in the boiler room. Someone sinister put them there. And they ignored it all. They were dragging their feet, afraid to say a black Civil Rights leader had been murdered. And it cost another life. They didn't do their job." Mrs. Olivia Moore, elegant as she is beautiful skewers the police effort. Micky stares at his unlikely friend. He's grateful, but he also admires her. It was her courage and pure strength of will that got this going.

Another voice speaks in deep resonant tones. "Mrs. Moore enlisted this young publisher, who was going to interview her husband, because he cared about Austin. After the fire, he wanted to catch Reverend Moore's killer and the man who blinded Addie Mae Wesley. The police were not interested." It's Reverend Artemis Simpson, senior vice-President of the Southern Christian Leadership Conference. The film changes again.

Micky's on camera for a minute reiterating how they corroborated facts, how it's connected to the Mennonite church fire and how they still weren't able to interest the police, despite evidence.

Wolford is back on, walking down the Leamington sidewalk speaking into the camera. "The gruesome attack and murder of a white girl by a man presumed to be the black and associated with gangs has caused an eruption of incidents across the West Side. The city has ramped up protection. Police moved from three shifts to two twelve-hour shifts to ensure additional resources. The mayor, though, will not issue a curfew." Wolford pauses a second to let his face show frustration with that effort, but he says nothing. "Finally, the National Guard were called to get the dangerous fighting under control. What, though, did the people closest to the murder feel? Are they safe? Do they blame Michael Mulvihill, publisher of the Central Standard Times?" Micky, hands in his pockets, involuntarily, forms two fists.

"You're damn right they didn't do nothing. And you're damn right that my boy was trying to help, to catch a killer. He'd killed before, and if they'd listened to him, that girl would be alive. " It's Mr. Lacont again, and he's taking no prisoners. The room erupts. They're slapping Micky on the back. He looks like the world just came off his shoulders. Another resident speaks.

Another neighbor speaks. "This is my home. I'm not afraid. I raised my daughters here. The Alexanders were family to me. Yes, family we were. If Elijah makes the mistake of returning, I'll blow that— fool's head clear off." It's Mr. Williams, Electra's landlord. A tiny blip in the film indicates that he had another adjective in front of the word fool. "And that boy, Micky? I've known him since he was in 5th grade. He was working, bringing home what he earned when he was half as tall as a bar stool. Anybody, and that includes you, Wolford, shouldn't bad mouth him in front of me, lest they want to eat without your natural teeth the rest of their life." The house roars with laughter. Everyone now mimics the blip.

K-9 beats Whitey to the best line. "I love that guy. And I'm not ashamed of it. I...love...that...guy. If he's got grandkids, I'll give 'em free boxing lessons." Whitey laughs with the rest of them.

A parade of short comments starts. One neighbor after another, including those who were blaming him at the church, all tell the camera that they don't blame Micky and he's a stand-up guy. He is too emotional and turns to get out to a place alone. His brother, Patrick blocks hm.

"Not even. First, you need to hear all of this. Second, you think I'm missing a chance for you to cry publicly. Not even." The others come. They pull him to the center of the room.

It's Hogan now. His brogue is thicker than normal. Possibly that's because he's excited. Possibly, he likes to sound that way with a big audience. "What are ya? Daft? That boy, and remember kindly that he works two jobs, was out on foot canvassing soon as he heard that the little girl was scared, BEFORE there was the fire at the church. BEFORE, mind ya. He's a United States Marine, whose served his country on the front lines. And he can knock most fellas blocks off, but I never seen or heard tell of him fighting except to defend. He's as good as they come. And the police? They're the finest police force in the country. It's just the one. The one who had the led on the investigation. You'd better talk to him. Wagner. Peter Wagner."

The name dries Micky's eyes instantly. Sure, he blames Wagner, too, but to call his name out on television. He feels for him.

"Mick, I know what you're thinking, but they threw your name out there. They need to assign the accountability here. " K-9 reads his buddy right.

The report ends, and the coverage returns to the studio. Albertson asks, "What's next?"

"Well, Joel. There's been a lot of conjecture about how Elijah targeted this young girl, Effie Alexander. Some of that conjecture includes information that may have been supplied or confirmed, even accidentally, by staff working for Micky Mulvihill at the Central Standard Times newspaper. Our staff have confirmed with police that the phone call that was made to the newspaper at the time of death was from INSIDE the Alexander home. A second phone call, made earlier, was from a phone booth at Central Park and Lake street. Elijah could be close to there, but it's also a train stop and a place he could easily have travelled to and from anywhere in the city. The police have intensified the search all along Lake Street"

"Startling information, John. To phone from the home tells us the depth of depravity of this killer. And it may provide some relief of guilt to the staff at the newspaper who took that call. For the family, though, the results remain."

"Indeed. The Chicago Police Department has initiated a full homicide investigation into the Alexander murder. Additionally, the three men who attacked Mulvihill are being interrogated for information. There is an ongoing negotiation to get them to identify Elijah. They know. Their story doesn't check out any other way. The main stumbling block there is that they don't feel pressured to take what is offered as they are not overly concerned by the threat of jail. It's more of a home to them than anywhere else. Also, Joel, Mulvihill has helped to raise $5,000-dollar reward for information leading to the capture of Effie Alexander's killer." The report ends.

"That son of a bitch was already there, Mick. He knew. There's no way he gets into her house without already knowing who she is." His father booms this truth. The others remain silent.

"Yeah. Yeah, dad." Those present see the tremendous relief in him. He looks over at Preacher, who still wonders about the call he handled earlier.

"You think that phone booth will check out?" his father asks.

"Maybe? K-9 here, " he points a thumb at his friend, "has posted flyers at Marshall High School, too." With the report concluded, folks begin to leave. They congratulate Micky one more time, thank Mrs. Mulvihill for everything and leave.

"C'mon, Mick." K-9 sneaks a question in. "How about we go over to Fitzgerald's for a few. I think I could use it, but I know you could use it. I'm right out front." Micky agrees.

◆ ◆ ◆

Maggie is tending bar at Fitzgerald's tonight. She knows these boys and she knows that they need these drinks, but the pace is concerning. "Slow down. Have a Coke. On the house. " They look at each other, then bust up laughing.

"You got any diet? I already had two sarsaparillas earlier. Got to watch the calories. I train for a living, ya know." K-9 finishes with a silly smile.

"Yeah. Thanks," adds Micky. "Probably not. Stuff's bad for your teeth. " She gets it, goes with it and walks away, but she'll drag her feet a little bringing the next pitcher. Micky watches her walk away, admiringly.

"Yeah? And?" K-9 is encouraging him to act.

"I think she had a crush on me in seventh grade, but I was too embarrassed to acknowledge it."

"And now? Still feel the same way?"

"She's probably over it. That's ten years ago."

"She's not. Why do you think we're here?" Micky whips his head over at K-9, startled.

"I was in here a little while back. How's Micky? Still at the Daily News? You all still living above Friendly's? Micky, Micky and a little more Micky. Think about your answer. I have to hit the John. " He mulls this over, excitedly for some minutes before he realizes that K-9 isn't coming back. His message sinks in. K-9 drove. He needs a ride. He settles his doubts, rises and walks toward her.

"K-9...he...well." She's cleaning glasses as he stands at the near-empty bar.

"Deserted you?" She saw him leave. She guessed why, too. But Micky has to step up.

He looks at her sly smile. He loves that smile.

He loves her. And has since the seventh-grade. She's the most beautiful girl and the nicest person.

"I could use, that is, I need a ride home. When do you...I can wait. If you're willing. I mean, to give me a ride"

"Yeah. Michael Mulvihill. I'll give you a ride. " He looks her in the eye at that line and reads her thinking as 'I thought that'd do it.' It did.

◆ ◆ ◆

Two other people had watched tonight's news report. Their reactions are dissimilar and unlike anyone at the Mulvihill house. Electra Alexander, watches from her cousin's house where she's staying. She can never live in the Laramie house again. She may go back to Greece where she can be as far from all of this life as possible. She's lost twenty pounds. She tries to sleep, hoping that Effie will come to her there. She sometimes does. Micky's story keeps her awake. She asks God to give her the strength and courage to forgive him.

Peter Wagner watched. Every time someone said 'police', he heard his name. He lives alone, never married and no children. Johnny Walker, chilled on the rocks, gives him something to feel.

The brass had told him how to handle this. It came from downtown, on the fifth floor, they said.

CFD has this as an accident. That's what it is. He had the job of protection. The job is to protect. It's written right on the side of the patrol cars, to serve and protect. He didn't take it seriously, didn't think anyone would be so bold. Did he expect this crazy to just stroll up to the front door, or walk pretty-as-you-please down the alley up to the blue-and-white?

The bosses didn't want him stirring the pot. Where are they now? Turning on him. He doesn't have much and never did in this life. But he had the job. At least there was that.

CHAPTER 24

M argaret "Maggie" Zamorski slips out of the covers. He's not there. She grabs a robe and moves through the apartment lightly calling his name. There's no sign of him, not even a note. *He wouldn't have.* She notices that her keys are missing. A few minutes later, while the coffee percolates her first and highly anticipated cup, she hears the door on the first-floor main entrance giving its familiar creak. It's a sound she knows well. The foyer is large. Its marble floor and walls create a distinct echo chamber for any sound.

Micky slips back in to Maggie's third-floor apartment hoping that he won't wake her, only to find her standing right in front of him. Arms folded, she asks, "Where've you—running?" It's obvious. "You went for a jog?" *At this time of the morning, after drinking?*

Sheepishly, and soaked, he explains, "Six, seven miles. Just to my apartment and back." He stops short on the explanation. A small backpack corroborates his words. Motioning toward the shower, "Gonna...just...right back." She knows he's always been a very physical person. Even when they were in seventh grade, he was on the football team plus lifting weights. She remembers hearing him tell friends that he had received a Ted Williams 110-pound weight set for his birthday. How impressive that seemed to her, at eleven years old, even though she had no idea who Ted Williams was. She also then knew, and never forgot, when was his birthday.

She doesn't know that he's on a serious work-out regimen right now and that he sticks to it rain, shine or beer. She's just glad, reassured, that he wasn't going to just leave, which she didn't really think he would do. She's also glad he didn't simply return to say goodbye in the sweat-soaked clothing he wore yesterday.

Last night was a monumental shift for him. Her, too. She's pretty sure that he hasn't really dated since before he went into the Marines. Certainly, it wasn't the time when he entered the military. After his discharge, it was school, job and starting a business. He used the GI Bill to get an associate degree in journalism. He then obtained a business loan again using his veteran benefits start the Times. Many didn't seem to notice. He might still be the kid who shined shoes and played pool to them, but not her. She sees all the work he's put in to become a certain kind of man.

Maggie meets guys all the time, but the bar isn't maybe the best venue to initiate a relationship. Micky comes in with friends from time to time. She drops enough hints to let him know how she feels. He smiles. That's it. Well, that and the looks. She can tell that he's been checking her out, but until last night, he never did anything about it. Maybe it was because K-9 forced the issue, for his own good? He needed a push in the right direction. Maybe it wasn't that? There are cabs, walking, and, as proven, he could run. Maybe something is different?

She lives south of Roosevelt in Berwyn. It's just a few miles to his West Side apartment, but it might as well be two counties away. Her neighborhood is still heavily Polish and Czechoslovakian. Any breech there will be Hispanics moving west out of Pilsen. Austin, as Micky knew it, is ending. The military and Vietnam, for better or for worse, is behind him. Maybe he's just seeing this and making changes? *Hope so.*

He emerges from the shower minutes later, jeans on, but no shirt, still cooling off. She wants him to know. "We had the Channel 7 report on the tv at Fitzgerald's last night." A quick glance. She sees that he's not had time to think who else might have watched. A little shrug serves as his response. She didn't expect more. *That's Micky.*

He is standing, stripped to the waist and in broad daylight. *Is he bigger? It's probably been two months since he's been in the bar. And he IS bigger.*

Shoulder, arms and legs, all of him. "You training for something, Mick?" As soon as she says it, she freezes, knowing the answer.

The story of the attack swept quickly through the neighborhood, but especially the bars. *Marine kicks thugs' asses* is a story that goes well with beers. After the revelry, the thinking was that it was this Elijah guy. She's worried, as anyone who cares about him would be.

"Yeah, you know. I always work out. Once in a while, I kick it up a level." She stares at his face but doesn't want to challenge him further. He adds, "How 'bout you? You're running, right?"

Yes, but she ignores the question. "Everyone's behind you." It's not easy to tell him, even though she's known him most of her life. They've just been two people who know each other until now. Embarrassed, she turns toward the kitchen, quietly saying, "Me, too, Mick...me, too." Louder, she adds, "How 'bout some eggs?"

He pulls himself into a faded red sweatshirt and moves toward her. He responds to the unimportant question first. "Thanks, but I'll eat while I'm working. Too far behind to hang around. " He places a hand gently on each of her shoulders, looks her square in the eye, adding, "Maggie, I'd thank every one of them, personally, from the bottom of my heart...starting with you. I just...just...yeah." He kisses her, then wraps her and kisses her again. It's not lust. It's passion. Her eyes glisten.

God, this lug is finally seeing me.

She watches him from her window as he walks to his car. The sidewalk on the entire block is covered with small children in uniform walking toward the Catholic school. Some look eager; they'll learn, play and have fun the whole time. Others drag themselves onward with the look of those returning to the cell after their free time in the prison yard.

A man steps quickly out of the car down the street. He's walking toward Micky, hurriedly, and hailing him with his hand. Micky recognizes him, but she doesn't. Who? How? And here?

"How on earth?" Micky asks. He wants to know how Wagner knew where to find him. The car, he supposes, gave away that he was still there. *And he waited? That's not protocol.* Then he decides he'd rather get to the why and leave the how alone.

"Spare me." He wants to get to whatever it was that drove Wagner to chase him down. *It couldn't be that urgent or he would have come to Maggie's door. This guy's been through a lot. Maybe it's knocked a screw loose? Or two?*

"What's happened? Spill." His demeanor with the detective has changed, and not for the better.

They both feel it. Normally, he honors the job cops have to do. It's dangerous and not that well-paid, but mostly, the respect comes from the fact that he identifies with their mission. Now his curtness indicates a certain amount of contempt.

"Nothing has happened. Well...Look. This won't take long. You might want to hear it. It's...um...about doing something." Standing curbside, next to his Chevelle, Micky leans back against the car to listen. His palms rest on the top of the door near the window. His face says that he's out of patience and would sooner break Wagner's jaw than anything else. Seeing this, Wagner nods, puts up a palm and pumps it lightly. He's trying to say take it easy, message received. The expression doesn't change.

"I didn't do my job." His voice falls. He barely has the breath to complete the sentence. "Twenty-one years and that's the first time I'm saying that. But I'm saying it. Yeah, bosses didn't want this story. CFD is the cover. There's no real evidence. We didn't need speculation fueling citizen outrage. We didn't need a blowup in front of the whole country." This is the hardest part to say. "And, I didn't trust you or her, " he says, meaning Olivia. Despite a drop of sympathy, Micky's losing patience. *Let's not rehash things, just to say sorry.* He continues, "I had the protection. That shift, even, was mine. I wasn't there early enough. It wasn't directed well enough. I think...if I really thought that there was a guy..."

He can't say it. "The one thing I can do now is catch this bastard. " *Great. Big make-up play.*

"What does that change?"

"Could be others. It changes things for other people. Maybe others will get hurt if I don't, if we don't stay with it. " Micky stirs. He doesn't want anyone else hurt. He thinks about that possibility. *Hurt because I was sulking.* If Wagner was really on their side, it would be a big help.

"I'm listening."

"All right. First. Again, there's no way you could have known what this guy was capable of, and, it was me that was supposed to provide protection. The girl, too–" Micky shoots him an exasperated look for making dismissive sounding reference a second time. "Okay, the woman...lady–"

"Olivia Moore. It's not that hard. And that lady has more brains in her little finger than you do in your whole Sears-back-to-school-special-suit-covered body. " Wagner takes the hit silently. Micky thinks about Olivia's words on the WJLO report.

"Look, Mulvihill, you got to come in off the ledge. You're not going to help me. You're not going to help yourself. And you're not going to nail Elijah just being ready to blow all the time."

"Go ahead," Micky says, calming himself. He

knows Wagner is right. " You were telling me how great I was."

After a soft laugh, and feeling a little more relaxed, he continues. "Yeah, that's the thing. K-9, who picked up good information, works for you. Mrs. Moore reached out to you, trusts you, is kind of partners with you. The people in the neighborhood...thing is, to use all those folks together, I need you. I'm willing to, and asking if, we can collaborate on getting this guy." Before Micky can speak, he adds, "Despite what happened in the past, what could have been. You have to decide what you want to do about it. Punch the wall or get to work."

Reluctantly, he sees this is his best option. "How's this go?"

"We share information. We've got people on the street getting information on the three goons that jumped you. I'll get feedback from those contacts. I'll share it. It won't be long. But he's likely moving around. You get information. You share. I mean we really share, talk over the importance of any detail, look at options. That's how it goes."

"Olivia figures out what we should be doing. She shares. " Micky adds.

A smile. "Exactly. We meet weekly or as key information turns up. "

"One thing. Any action that there is to take, I take. Neither you nor any of your friends can go in guns blazing or fists flying. I'm authorized. It could cost you a prison sentence if you don't."

"Right." He's not really committing to this part. "Okay. Let me get back to work. We can talk tomorrow about how and when to meet."

◆ ◆ ◆

Micky arrives at CST, ready to work having first stopped across the street at Leamington Foods. With two bananas, an apple, a package of ham big enough for at least two sandwiches, a loaf of Pepperidge Farm Rye and a quart of Twin Oaks milk, he's ready to fortify and catch up on the next edition.

No one else is there. He decides to shove a tall file cabinet in front of his desk, shielding himself from a direct street view. Even in daylight, the room is shadowy. Now, with the cabinet blocking light, it's more so. He uses a small pen light to work. He's distracted by thoughts of Wagner. He looks years older and very tired. He knows that the guilt is eating him alive.

On his desk, two news items, both developed by Forty-Eight, are staggering to him. "It's like they're living separate realities," he says out loud. He often talks to the walls when he's there alone. This is a building that has seen many lives, many generations of lives, and over so much time, he's determined that it must have ghosts. He likes to think it's good if they know how he feels. He nods at his own words, assuming that the ghosts nod, too, agreeing with him.

One item touts the desire by the Organization for a Better Austin (OBA) to have a brand-new middle school approved at Harrison and Laramie. It'll take three years to build. These parents are white. He thinks that they won't be living in Austin three years from now. It'll be Stone and Disciples turf then. The lack of awareness or denial is astonishing.

The other item is about parents also. A petition by one hundred Austin High School parents asks the Regional School District to allow their children to transfer to Steinmetz High School. And they want their kids to get paid bus fare. These parents have charged that their children have been molested and beaten by blacks. Kathleen spoke with an Austin High teacher whom allowed her name and the quote that "Austin High is now 87 percent black." Micky's part of Austin isn't black at all.

Austin as a neighborhood, the article states, is the largest in the entire West Side. The superintendent of District 4, which encompasses both Austin and Steinmetz, explains why Austin High is mostly black, yet only the far west and south parts of the Austin community have black residents.

"Many of the white residents have placed their children in parochial schools." That would not only be true of the high schools like Weber, St. Mel's and St. Pat's, but also include the grade schools, like the Catholic school, Our Lady Help of Christians (HOC) and the Plato Greek School that Effie went to and Paul still attends.

"You could be living in an all-white part of Austin, keep your kids in private school and avoid having to deal with blacks. Other parents, who maybe can't afford the private schools, want their kids to have the option to go somewhere else in the District." The ghosts understand.

A third item garners his attention. Page six shows ads for both Burke-O'Malley and Avenue Realties. He looks back at the article regarding the petition to leave Austin High. "One of you put a move on, added some pressure, right here, in the still all-white part of Austin. That's why the march was on Laramie. That's why the harassments are right here." He thinks something like this was inevitable.

Micky moves on to the Blotter. He finishes a draft reads it back to himself. He's stuck on one item, wishing he could say more.

The deceased body found recently by police in the vicinity of Paulina and Flournoy has been identified as Austin resident Richard Joseph Gamboni, age 19. Autopsy results show a high concentration of the barbiturate, secanol also known as seco-

barbital. Police continue to investigate the circum-stances of his death.

Yeah. Gamboni doubtless had a belly full of reds, but that's not what killed him. And the police know it. He's sure of that. They have no will to look further into 'the circumstances of his death'. The wake will likely draw hundreds, but very few mourners. It'll be more of a social opportunity. Ricky's life was a laugh riot. It was inevitable that he would cross a line in the street.

He was accountable for those actions. Everyone accepts that. But, ironically, what he did was only what every citizen should be doing, reporting criminal activity. Another thought comes to hm; the parents have to read this report. He removes the line about the autopsy report.

"The way of things has always been accepted. By me, too. I never thought much about it, not until recently. As long as there are rules and codes, then this kind of killing doesn't bother anybody."

"Talking it out with Casper and the boys, are ya?" It's Forty-Eight standing behind him.

CHAPTER 25

Micky's return to the Daily News has produced an uncomfortable celebrity. A buzz goes around that he'll get his own by-line. "Not going to happen. I'm just a grunt, " he tells them when it's brought to his face. He's getting mail that's addressed to him, not Jim Diamond. A lot of the mail are thank-you cards for trying to catch a killer, for caring. The same thing has happened with the CST mail. He's also getting calls to be on other television shows.

"Jim Diamond's desk. This is Micky Mulvihill speaking. Can I help you?"

"Yeah. Hi, Micky. This is John Wolford. Did you watch two days ago?"

"I did. "

"And?"

"Well, it was good. I was relieved and very grateful to my neighbors and Mrs. Moore for standing up for me."

"Great. Well, as you know then, we're staying with it. It's ongoing reporting. We think that we can help you, well, help each other. This guy's been loose too long. The police leads aren't working. We'd like to ask you to come on the show, tell us what you know, and give us the neighborhood angle. We'll also include the police work, anything that's released publicly. All of it will help awareness and maybe catch a good tip on this guy. What do you think?"

Holy crap! That's what I think. "Well, I don't know. I'm just—"

"You're a newsman, just like me. This is a collaboration between news sources. Can't hurt your circulation any. "

True, and the point is still to find Elijah. But this is a big step. "Give me a day. No, make that the end of the week. I'll give you an answer on Friday. Is that okay? Can you do that?"

Silence. Possibly, he's covering the phone and speaking with someone else. "Okay. Friday. I'll call you in the morning. Just want to remind you. You saw that we played it straight. We're reporting and investigating by talking to people. No cheap shots."

"Yeah. Thanks. I...understand. Just have to be careful." When he hangs up, he thinks it's not just me. I'm going to let some people know this time. He grabs the receiver and calls Forty-Eight.

"Hello, little great one. I want you and

Preacher, and Mary, if she can, to pull a flyer together announcing a meeting on Thursday. Post it and go door-to-door with it. Where? Try Preacher's church. If not, I'll ask at HOC. What? No. Don't try to get it into CST. The meeting is to discuss a critical next step to nail Elijah. Well, don't say that, exactly. You know what to say. Yeah. Here's the thing. WJLO TV wants me to go on their news. I need everybody on board. Yeah. "

Diamond walks in. Angry? Can't tell. He squints at Micky. It's not that different than his usual and obligatory show of contempt because a legman is nothing.

More calls come in. He sneaks nervous looks at Diamond as they are all for him. He has other offers. He grabs the phone, hand getting tired. "This is Detective Holder, Mr. Mulvihill. I'm the lead investigator on the Alexander murder. "

"Hello. Wait! You are? What about Detective Wagner?"

"Well, he was investigating a church fire involving a death that's still categorized as being the result of an accidental fire. His report has been filed. He, too...well, frankly, he's on paid administrative leave. " *Shoot. Wagner's getting slammed for the Channel 7 report. He wants to collaborate, but he's out of it.*

"I see. Is he still around? In town?"

"I'm leading a murder investigation, not

watching Detective Wagner's movements."

"Right. Okay. So, what is it you want to know?"

"Confirmation of the facts as I know them. I've read your statements as well as the pertinent documents such as the letter from Moore to the media. I've spoken with Detective Wagner. Essentially, is it fair to say you intercepted a letter from Reverend Moore where he alleged a real-estate scam involving a collusion between unnamed black gangs and Avenue Realty?

"Yes. Fair."

"You contacted Moore and set up an interview, which never happened because a fire broke out resulting in the death of Reverend Charles Moore. A child named Addie Mae Wesley received third degree burns and lost an eye. You continued to investigate and, essentially, the information that you published is what you found: a similarly described person who was identified in the march and recruiting individuals for the march and shown in a figure in a painting at the gallery of Moore's widow. Good?"

"Good."

"Okay. So, you go public asking about Elijah, and it blows up. Another dead body."

"The police were to provide protection."

"Which they did, but we also advised not to do it at all."

"She was a witness that he already knew."

"You don't know that."

"I do. No identifying information was provided. He already knew where she lived and, when he called me, he was already in her house. If the police take this seriously when it's first reported by Mrs. Moore, and they drop the ridiculous 'accidental' from their report, then...well, then things are different." *Great. Another political staller.*

Silence, then, "Well, let's not get on that merry-go-round. So? What else don't I know?" Micky decides that he'll tell him about WJLO if it happens, and not before. He knows Holder's response already.

"Do you know about Curtis Burrell, Reverend Burrell, who spoke out against the Rangers. His church was burned the next day, also burned. Seems you want to look at the fires together."

"Currently, not part of this investigation."

"Are you kidding me? This is the kind of stall we got from Wagner and why he blew the coverage. " Micky is yelling at Holder.

"Let me ask about motive. He kills the girl so she can't identify him as a guy who walked down the street?

"Detective, he kills Effie so she can't identify him as a guy whose linked to a fire and homicide. He kills because he kills. He sets fires. He writes messages in blood. He's a religious fanatic. The whole Elijah thing is like a delusion. It's from the Bible. When you find this guy, that's' not going to be his name. But the thing is, now, he wants me. "

"Why is that? Why is he interested in you?" Holder asks, wanting to be a little intimidating. He's mashing his words together suddenly. Whyzat? Whyzhe ? He's a tough guy.

"I'm not sure, but it's something like what happened in the Bible, where Elijah was killing those who follow false Gods, which is like anybody, but him. You call him out. You must be a false God follower. I called him out. But he was an arson and killer before that."

"How do you know this?" *Christ!*

"The name and the message to me at the murder site. It's a Biblical quote."

"Right. Okay. We'll have police officers watching your back." *Comforting.* "One more thing. I'm going to find this guy, and pretty quick. We have prints, hair. It's rape and murder one. Your guy will be caught, but we're not tying this into Moore, Burrell and the history of race in America. Listen. I've been to Olivia Moore's gallery. And I've seen what she paints. We have a murder. We're catching a murderer. I don't want to see any more grandstand plays like you made with the paper. Capisce?"

"I'm a newsman. I cover the news. It's in the Constitution. You just do your job, and better than it's been done so far. " Slam. He looks up. The whole office looks back at him. No one has missed a word. A small round of sarcastic applause provides their comment. Then everyone returns to work.

Micky's going to cooperate with Holder, but he's going to still work with Wagner, IF he's still willing to work. He has a call to make. The phone rings a hundred times before the answer.

"Hello. Pete Wagner." Micky tells him what just happened. He wants to know where Wagner stands. "I don't care about the leave status. I can still get things done. It's not like they post that somewhere. Most people don't know. I am going to nail this SOB. Me! He's my new life mission."

◆ ◆ ◆

Walking out of the Daily News building, the clear sky allows the late afternoon sun to project long shadows from the tall buildings. His head is down. One giant shadow suddenly is not from the side. It's directly in front and covering him. He looks up to see the face of a man with short curly hair, a leather jacket that reaches his knees and shoulders the width of a Volkswagen. He recognizes the face. This is a Chicago Outfit enforcer.

"Mulvihill? In the car." He doesn't move. "Don't worry kid. No one's gonna hurt you." A 4-door Blue 1969 Oldsmobile Cutlass Town Sedan rolls up on queue. The rear door is pushed open by the driver. He goes with it. The Volkswagen follows him, closes the door and takes the shotgun seat.

There is someone in the back seat. He's still wears summer clothing; a white shirt with a straight hem stopping at the waist is open one more button than it should be, a pair of yellow gaberdine pants perfectly creased lead down to caramel-colored Italian leather weave shoes. A snub-nosed .38 caliber pistol strapped to an ankle is exposed past the pant leg, slightly hiked from sitting. It's a calling card. Micky waits for him to speak first.

"Where you goin', home? The "L"?" He is. "We'll take you. Give him your address." He motions his head toward the driver. He does.

"Nice car. This year, I mean, and the Cutlass Town in blue."

"Nassau Blue, " he clarifies. "You're the Marine, right? Yeah, we know ya. You're a good kid. Austin is changing. That's not news to anybody. But this guy you're chasing, he's an insult as well as a danger. He's in that bug paining? Right?" Micky nods. " You need an exterminator to take care of bugs." Everyone laughs. Micky goes with it. "This Elijah fuckwad...Whadyagot?"

He decides to tell him. Maybe it'll help? He knows that criminals don't like kid-killers, much less kid-rapists. "Not much more than is printed. He's got a delusion about himself as a Biblical figure who kills believers of false Gods. Apparently, I fall into that category because I wrote the articles to ask for information." The passenger still waits. "And there's a new cop lead, a Detective Holder. He's no help. Looking to get the cops out of the doghouse is all. But they do have three likely accomplices that they're trying to squeeze." No response.

The driver takes Washington Boulevard heading East toward his apartment. The passenger remarks on the near-West neighborhoods they past. "Look at all this? What's this, Garfield, right? That's where the minister's church is, was. It's all coons and it's a piece of crap." Micky stiffens. "The architecture is beautiful. The park, Garfield is one sweet park —it's got a little beach on a man-made pond. — one sweet park to have in the middle of a ghetto, what now is a ghetto. " He waves a disgusted hand at it all. They talk about the Cubs, the mayor, the war, and any general things, but no more about Elijah. Micky is now right in front of his house. "I think there's a lot of people that are watching, that want this guy. Yeah, police are embarrassed. Other people, " he shoots a sideways glance at Micky to tell him more than he's speaking. "are embarrassed. That embarrassment has got to be dealt with." He smiles. "Everyone's chasing him. He's, maybe, chasing you." He laughs. It's sinister and smirky. "Good talking to you, Micky. We'll be in touch." He never mentions his name.

Everyone is behind him. Everyone wants to help him. But he's the one on point. Wagner, WJLO, Outfit, everyone looks to him. He can't make a mistake.

CHAPTER 26

M oving her head to look through the middle of the windshield, Olivia peers down the short white stripes of the lane divider in the hopes of seeing any open road ahead. Instead she sees only the long stream of cars moving along the road, inch by inch. Openings? The formation's tight as a marching band and going about the same speed. Exhaust fumes wave in the air around the cars, a reminder that she's not only stuck, but it's toxic.

Her mind moves from the congestion to her home, which soon won't be hers. The church has been kind to her, but she is no longer the minister's wife. They have someone new who has already led the service. He and his wife need this space. The sooner she goes, the better for all.

Before she goes, and everything is all packed together, she needs to look into Charles' office. There are questions she has, things that she doesn't understand about all that's happened in the last two months. She needs answers. Some must lurk in there, even though the police have never raised an interest. It's daunting. For her, a ghost is in there, one that she has to confront. And the time has come.

Home at last. Opening the door, her arms hang straight down. She's twice as tired as when she left work. The drive drained her. She boils water for some oolong tea. She needs to get her energy level up. Tonight, they'll be here. It's their first chance to work together since the terrible incident. Then, after they leave, she'll go in there.

◆ ◆ ◆

She jumps at the first ring of the phone. She answers by the second. It's Micky. "I'll be there in maybe 30 minutes. K-9 is with me. Whatever we come up with, we share with Wagner." He explains no further.

"Right. I've also invited Harrison Kellum, from the Defender." It's a reminder. She told him before. While K-9 can get information second hand, Harrison is an expert with first-hand knowledge on black gangs in Chicago. He has covered their development for years. They have an archive of valuable material.

Micky knows Austin, the people, the businesses and the way it all works. Harrison knows the gangs and they both know the city government. The coordination with police is a valuable asset, even though Wagner is a personal reminder of callous inaction. She approaches this the same as she would an academic project. The team has all the right experts and resources. Olivia believes that she can get to the answers quickest by thoughtful analysis. Micky trusts her way.

"Olivia, there's something else I need to say. And it's probably best, certainly easiest, if I just tell you without the others.

"Okay, Micky. I'm listening." *What now?* She braces herself.

"It turns out my great-uncle was quite a performer in the 1919 riots. My grandfather, his brother, was kind of a General type, leading, but not doing. It wasn't about the fighting for him. It was controlling, really, maintaining the status quo." She thinks that Micky must hate to admit his family supported a status quo of brutal segregation, but it was also the norm then. "My great-uncle, well, he was kind of a...I, guess, you say—he set fires. Ernest Johnson was right. I'm sure that he isn't going to trust me, but honestly, I...I just..."

"Thank you, Micky. I can speak with him about it. I'm sure you're probably right. He wouldn't trust you and he definitely doesn't trust Daley. But I trust you." She does, completely. She's never known a more honest and open soul.

Olivia has changed into a good pair of jeans and a light black mock-turtle neck sweater. She's decided to hold the meeting in her kitchen. Some things here will be last to be packed. She's kept four teacups out along with an assortment of tea that she keeps in an 8-inch tin.

Harrison arrives first, by a good ten minutes. Not unexpected, of course, and nattily dressed. Not only does he wear a suit, but the tie is right up to his Adam's apple. *He probably sleeps in pajamas that look like a pin-stripe suit.* Micky and K-9 ring the bell. Harrison declines the tea, but Micky and K-9 accept, selecting black tea, because it sounds closest to coffee.

She has often been the only woman in a working group, whether in art, architecture or history, and even when she is leading. These three men are, perhaps, a little challenging and intimidating, all large with two of them white having a decidedly non-academic background. Nonetheless, she's quite prepared.

"Motive. It starts with profit, quick and easy, " she begins. "That's the realtor, at least initially. Then they're found out, and there's a need to send a different message to protect their interests." It's extremely hard for her to discuss this without emotions, but she must in order to get to the truth. And she wants to get to that fast. "The lead gang member involved in the intimidation and the fire-setting, and the murder, is Elijah. Charles warned me that the realtors didn't know whom they were dealing with."

"Okay. Hold up," Micky interrupts, wanting

to take logical steps carefully. "Let's go slowly and be careful with our assumptions. Someone wants to burn Garfield like Mennonite, they have to pay for it. That's—" he stops to check with K-9 for confirmation, " maybe ten-grand? More if it's going through a gang? The more people it touches, the more cuts that need to be made. That's quite a bit just to scare someone off a real estate deal that's coming their way anyway. It's not worth it, especially if the torch is someone he doesn't know well." K-9's shrug indicates the dollar amount is a reasonable estimate.

"Then what?"

"There is no collusion at the gang level. This is a one-on-one connect. Less money. And the realtor doesn't necessarily know there's no gang. Elijah covers himself with the Stones story. It's scarier. I'm not the Lone Ranger. I'm the Blackstone Ranger. Same as he did to recruit for the march."

"Go on." Olivia thinks that Micky's obviously put some thought into this. This is his expertise. He has some insight into how these kinds of people think.

"It's all working then Elijah gets wind of Charles' allegations. Maybe he's got a connection at one of the media outlets that received the letter. Myself, I wanted to do something about this issue. Maybe someone else did, too, only from the other side?" She must put up with these casual references to the willful destruction of the church that cost

Charles his life.

"I would tend to agree," Harrison Kellum's smooth voice interrupts to offer concurrence. It's late. "The gangs have too much to worry about from the city's grand jury and the federal probes. And they're into much bigger pots. This is a someone leveraging the fear that the name the Blackstone Rangers evokes."

Olivia looks to K-9 for his thoughts. "It makes sense and it goes with what my connect said. It's Elijah by himself, and let's remember, he's unstable. Now let's find him. On the one side, you've got twenty thousand guys, easy, that are black or mixed–'cause that skin's pretty light — that might fit this MO, a torch who is cuckoo bird. —and who might take less. —On the other hand, I can count on one hand the number of realtors that would likely benefit from this. An easier number to sort out. I want to spike everybody's anxiety. They're coming to me, or one of the other top guys for real estate. I've got the listings. Soon I'll get the buyer's direct. I want that piece, too. I want this all to pass through my hands where I get commissions on both ends to boot. To find Elijah, you find the realtor. Avenue has been questioned. Maybe that part is wrong or maybe they didn't look too hard? Start there, with the short list of realtors, one I can count on one hand." *Genius.*

"Nice. I knew there was a reason I hung

around with you. I'd say it's only the first two fingers. Avenue and Burke-O'Malley. I mean, it's not Austin, exactly. It's this one special part, targeted, because there is a holdout of white families. We need a trail of real evidence, not just logic. I'll ask Wagner or—Okay. I need to tell you something. They put Wagner on leave, but he's not stopping. A Detective Holder is leading the investigation of Effie's murder. One of those two realtors is talking to the wrong person. I'll get either Wagner or Holder to do the work, to check phone records, appointment books and listings. Let's do this. I'll tell Wagner, give him a day. Then I'll tell Holder. One of them will have people to comb through the connections. I'll also talk to the neighbors nearby for any eyeballing they might have done. Seeing a black guy that fits this description going into the office, especially late." Micky's face lights up. "And the letter. Trace where else that letter has been. The letter...I can...actually...Mr. Kellum—"

"Harrison is fine. Please," he corrects Micky. Olivia smiles, both that he offered and because she remembered Micky offering the same, which she, initially, declined.

"Harrison, is it possible for you to check with the main newspapers to see if they received a copy of the letter? Your name will get a better response than mine."

"We can do that. Has Olivia shared with you yet, knowledge of the other letter, the one we received?" Several exchanged quizzical looks.

"In all the commotion, I didn't think of it. Also, it didn't seem that important at the time.

"What didn't, Olivia? Harrison?"

Harrison answers. "The letter to the Defender, similar to the one you received at the Daily News, includes a recommendation to use Burke-O'Malley." They stop to digest this.

"Okay, " Micky begins slowly. "It could be Burke-O'Malley is the realtor and they get to Reverend Moore with the tip. They're like 'Oh, these other guys. Go stop them. We'll help."

Olivia adds, "Or it's still Avenue, and Burke-O'Malley is offering in good faith. Charles wasn't gullible."

Olivia looks at Micky first, then the others. They all shrug.

"We don't need to sort that out. It's those two. What else is in the letter?" Micky asks.

That's the big difference. He also mentions, actually, defines, speculators. He says he's ready to kick off a call to action with the Garfield Park Baptist church members on July 27th. The reference causes Olivia to shudder slightly and they move on.

As the evening winds down, Micky takes an initiative and starts grabbing the empty tea cups. The others all help. It's a sign of how well it went.

They begin the goodbyes and that they'll be in touch when Harrison starts again. "Let me go back to the statement on Detective Wagner. He's officially not working the case?"

"That's correct."

"Then why don't we just leave Wagner be. He wasn't helpful before."

Heads turn to Micky waiting for his answer. "Okay...okay. There are a couple reasons. One is because this guy is gut-shot. He screwed up and I don't want to leave him to bleed to death. He's a good cop who made a bad mistake." Olivia is impressed with his ability to empathize and to forgive. "And the other is that he's now on board. Holder is back at the save-the-rep. sign. It'd be like going back to square one with Wagner, the old Wagner."

"Let's be very careful with that. We don't really know this dynamic. Working with a suspended police officer. " He doesn't add the consequence, but everyone gets it.

"Agreed." Micky says firmly.

They stand by the door. Olivia says, "It would be good to know who tipped Charles and how Elijah got connected to a realtor in Austin. There could be more here than we realize. "

"Won't that just all come out once we capture Elijah, and do so before he goes off again?" Micky asks her.

"It's more than a curiosity, than an academic point. There could be someone else we're fighting and don't know about. Know your enemy before the battle." She smiles, using his own words.

CHAPTER 27

T he silence of the apartment yells at her; alone. He's gone. She's no longer married to him. He'd been his happiest when he was busiest. He needed to prepare the next lesson or the next meeting of the church Board. He needed to study and read, including the news. Maybe especially the news? He had to stay current. He would say, "Reading the newspaper is like reading a thermometer, taking someone's temperature. Is it normal or are they feverish?" He'd been very positive about progress, the 'normal', until the King assassination. Then, it changed.

The Freedom Movement had produced results. Now King was gone. He became very frustrated with what he could do with the city. *What did he tell me earlier this summer? 'I am doing something. And it's not through Daley and the city. I am going to get in front of this thing.' It was the desperation that families had for a better life for their children that he wanted to get in front of. He stepped in front of it, and it ran him over.*

Tonight. She must look in his office tonight

before she moves, and these boxes get mixed in with all the rest. She stops in front of the door. The side facing the kitchen has a painting of hers hanging on a nail. It's a construction more than just a painting. She built a small light window frame, attached a sill and placed a painting against the back of it. Looking from the front, the viewer sees their block, on a sunny day, with people, young and old alike, filling the walks. It's idyllic. It was so funny to look at this painting when they actual street was buried in snow and ice.

The wooden door is solid and heavy. Once, this wall was the back of the minister's residence and the door led outside. Now it leads to an enclosed back porch that Charles converted into an office because the one in the church isn't directly accessible from their living spaces. Charles wasn't going to walk outside, back and forth, each night to work. Not in Chicago weather, he wasn't. The area is fully insulated, but the temperature is never right. It's both too hot in the summer and too cold in the winter. He was always reluctant to leave this door open and take heat from the house when it was cold. He'd rather suffer in the office than have her be cold. The old lock has a skeleton key. *Do I still have that key?* Like something is going to jump out at her, she slowly pulls it open.

Entering, arms folded under her chest, she's apprehensive, protecting herself. It's just a feeling; she can be hurt here. Gingerly, she inches her way to the center of the room, almost like she's testing the floor strength. Many items cover his desk. A framed pair of pictures that are hinged together triggers her memories. The photos are not more than 3 inches tall, but the moments are gigantic in their lives.

One was taken in Ansbach, Germany, where they met and fell in love. Charles was stationed there, part of his military service. She was visiting, having taken the train up from Nuremburg where she attended a special art school for those with historical interests. She had decided to visit Ansbach to see the Benedictine monastery.

Charles' handsome looks immediately captured her attention, but he was so much more. He was brilliant and passionate. A minister who joined the military for the veterans' benefits which he intended to use to attend law school back in Chicago. And he did. Charles was very diligent about follow-through. He'd set a plan and then put it to work.

She also, ironically, lived in Chicago. The American Friends Service Committee, a Quaker organization that moved academically qualified black high school students from the segregated schools of the South, the underperforming non-competitive high schools, to progressive integrated schools in Northern cities, gave her an opportunity. She applied for, and received, a scholarship.

Then the opportunity to study in German came. It was funny to both of them that they lived so close to each other and yet did not meet until they travelled thousands of miles away.

Charles' character was strong. She knew his history, that he was tempted for a while, but, ultimately, he refused a gang way of life. After all the hatred and violence that she'd lived through, the way he talked of the future inspired her. And she knew that she inspired him, too. Her art, the ability to capture and create images that represented human struggles gave him ideas on how to reach people. She helped shaped his thinking. How proud she was. How perfect it was.

The other photo in the set was taken during a December trip to Yosemite in California when they were not yet married. They stayed in a tiny town just outside of the park, Fish Camp, California. It was very friendly to their budget. He rented a small house that was part of a lodge. They called it the Bird's Nest. It was right in the center of town, which you could walk through, leisurely, in five minutes.

Besides the lodge, you'd see a bar, and a general store. Across the road was a frozen pond. Not even a gas station. The nights there were very special. The wonderful smells of the forest, which teemed with animal life. The residents, so calm and content, living in this world, just radiated a warmth. Their second night the pipes froze in the Bird's Nest. They were moved to the only equal or better accommodations which was a much larger log cabin. That night they made love there for the first time.

After a dinner that she made, they decided to take their wine and enjoy it on the floor in front of the fire sitting on a thick shag rug that varied between a dark navy color and white. They sat apart, each with their back supported by an opposing couch. The fire was hot. Neither of them minded. She removed her sweater and smiled at him. A signal. Tonight. She had no experience in lovemaking, certainly not with a grown man. He crawled forward on his hands and knees. Stopping two inches from her face, he placed his hand on her stomach and kissed her. His hand continued to rise, the buttons on her blouse yielded willingly. Her nervousness complicated her feelings. *Was she doing it right?* Too much thinking. Then she saw that the fullness of her had completely excited him, giving her more confidence. She slid down to the rug reaching her arm back over her head to place the wine glass on the flat stone hearth in front of the fireplace. Lastly, she removed her bra and remaining clothes.

Later that evening they went to the bar, starving. The kitchen was closed, but they had chocolate crème pie to serve. The bought the whole tin and ordered cokes. Afterwards, they had the bartender take their picture, this picture. Olivia looks at her face next to Charles. Completely in love. Charles exudes a joy that has always made her proud and been precious to her. It was his love for her that gave him that joy. She puts the photo set down carefully. A dear love that is no more.

She returns to the present. "Help me, Charles. Help me., " she pleads out loud. "Why did you have to die?" She tries to answer her own question. "You found something or someone that told you there was a collusion between black gang members and Avenue Realty. And they found out about you, that you knew. And came to..." She stops, then continues, "but it wasn't black gang members, was it? It was one person...who is not with a gang...one person who enlisted high school kids. Why did you think that there was collusion with a gang?" *Was Charles fooled? Wouldn't he have checked?*

The china cabinet he bought at a consignment store and then converted to a bookcase contains thick volumes of notes. Charles' work was to constantly investigate Christianity, the Bible and the forces that have oppressed his people for so long. He told her how the Baptist church was first established on the East coast. *Was it in the 1600s?* Then it moved to the South. It was only natural that so many blacks would become part of that church, having been enslaved there.

His keeps his in 3-ring binders. He used the first pages as a sort of table of contents to what notes and references are contained in that particular volume. Quick referencing is important. A minister's sermons more revisit than discover anew, but each visit can offer something new.

There is a natural and repeated timing to the liturgical calendar based on Scripture and the calendar. Summer is a low tide mark. Members travel for vacations or to visit family in other areas. There are summer Bible camps and Bible studies, sometimes spiritual trips are organized for members, even sabbaticals. It's also a time of planning for the church Board toward the year ahead. This year, though, he wanted to start in July to time things to the anniversary date.

Olivia carefully selects the binder with notes on his initiative for integration. His last initiative. She spreads out the various copies of news articles and notes. The photographs are haltingly brutal with bodies of dead black men lie in the street. The words of one story read, *At 38ᵗʰ and Ashland, Nicholas Kleinmark and a gang of whites boarded a street car and attacked three black stockyard workers. One of the blacks pulled a knife and killed Steinmark.* One articles from the Defender cries out in anger, "The black worm has turned. " Not all of the stories cover white brutality. It's clear that the white-owned newspapers reported one way and the black-owned newspapers reported another. It's also clear to her that the papers on both sides, white and black, were reporting rumors. There is a copy of the Herald Examiner from July 28, 1919 with the headline Negroes Have Arms that details how the blacks broke into the Armory. Its premise is that the riot is the planned beginning of a war. It is a completely false article.

One story is from the Daily News and written by Carl Sandburg, just one month prior to the riots. Sandburg surveyed the Black Belt, from housing to churches to labor. He called Chicago a "receiving station" and noted a "campaign of agitation" to drive blacks from the South up to Chicago. So many blacks were led to believe that they could expect more. She smiles at the thought of Daley's comment regarding channeling blacks into recreational activities as a solution to gangs.

His notes have lines drawn to show his intended parallels. He ties this infamous anniversary to his own personal story with Ernest. He ties the killing of blacks and the burning of their homes in the 1919 riots to Daley's war on gangs. Certainly, she thinks, as the grandson of a survivor, and with his own stellar Civil Rights background, he would be perfect to lead this new initiative. This gives her a thought. *This could even make Charles a national leader if it worked. Leadership! Taking the lead! If the initiative succeeds and the integration of Austin goes well, if he leads this and it is all tied to his personal history, then that might place him in a bigger role, a position from which to become the national leader. Did Charles want or expect to become a national leader? Was it more than Austin? More than Chicago? Is that why he tied this to Ernest and, in doing so, to himself.* The thoughts of a larger agenda are disturbing.

The slender center drawer of his desk against the other wall catches her eye. She pulls its two metal handles. Locked. This would have to be a very small key. She knows it's not part of the key ring that he carried with him, nor is it in the junk drawer where they keep extra copies of keys. She shakes a small vase sitting on the desk that holds a few pencils and pens. Something rattles at the bottom. There. She tries in, and it works.

Inside is a manila folder stuffed with other notes. It's odd she thinks that it's here and this drawer is locked. She slides the band off, being careful not to release it too quickly. Maybe something will stand out? Nothing. The dates, the metaphor with the clouds, more about Daley and his personal background. It's nothing that informs her of the connection to a gang or a person who's pretending to represent a gang.

Then she does it a second time. A list catches her eye. *Because, it's a list* of actions with dates...for the march, the letter to the Daily News and to the Defender and his last, fateful sermon to announce the initiative. *Why is the date of the march captured in the list of actions?* The dates of the march and the letter are written with the same pen. The spacing is like the writer knows what's being written next, not like adding it after something happens. *It looks like...he knew about the march before it happened! This is not just a list. It's a plan!*

She clears her mind. Only one conclusion comes to her. She rejects it again and again, looking for something else. She, ultimately, tells herself that she doesn't know enough. That there are more clues yet to find. That, she thinks, is the best thing to do; look for more information.

Her attention lands on some numbers. They're phone numbers. She recognizes a few of them. The Central Standard Times is very familiar. Others, with abbreviations, appear to be other news outlets. That one might be the Defender. It's close to the one she knows. One is unmarked by any abbreviation but has the same exchange as Micky's paper. It must be close by. Who could that be, she wonders? Only one way for he to tell.

Hands-shaking, she dials. On the third ring, the answerer says, "Burke-O'Malley Realty. How may I help you?"

CHAPTER 28

M rs. Moore sits in the church office with the interim minister, Jay Goodman, and the President of the Garfield Park Baptist Church Board, Thomas Tillman and Treasurer, Dorothy Jones.

"It's a total of $14,237 dollars. The discrepancy between all our revenue and donation sources minus all our expenses, planned and emergent over the past twelve months is exactly that and has been checked many times." They all stare at her for an answer.

"I assure you all that I don't have that money, nor do I know why that discrepancy exists." She has a good idea, though, one she's not yet sharing. "I'm willing to show you our bank records and personal bookkeeping for that period and beyond. You know that I have a business. Charles and I both had occasional speaking engagements, though none in quite some time. Probably none in that timeframe. "

"These dollars are cash. No interaction with a bank would be required to utilize them. Did Charles ever express a need or urgency related to money, not having enough money? A minister's salary does not provide for wealth. " Thomas Tillman didn't need to add that last sentence.

"Yes, of course. We talked about children, a house of our own and all the things that any couple would want. Charles did everything right his whole life, sacrificing for his community." Her turn to add the unnecessary. "Sacrifice leaves a person, well, short on personal gain. He accepted this reality." It enters her mind that this money may have been needed to make his plan work.

"He was responsible for these figures. " Dorothy wants to ensure everyone knows it wasn't her. No one has that thought. "He signed off every month on the accounting. He made the deposits. He authorized every expense. " They accept these statements without questions.

"And no one knew that those figures were discrepant until he passed, and we moved to an interim minister." Thomas Tillman narrows the possibilities. Reverend Goodman decides that nothing needs to be added. He shifts his eyes nervously.

"I understand the implication, but I'm not privy to any part of it. I just have no information on the $14,237. You can see that our living area has not changed. We've not taken vacations that are different than we've ever taken. Our bank accounts are easily supported by our incomes. " She's buying time, time she desperately needs to have.

"The full Board has been advised. We will soon have to make an announcement. That will not only shock the church. It will lead to publicity, a public scandal." How different they are now, treating her this way.

It's she who has lost the life of a loved one. It's the Wesley family who deals with the blindness of a young child. This is just the money. The church has received enormous attention and, with that, significant donations. They will be able to re-build and improve the church. She thought she knew them. She thought she knew Charles

CHAPTER 29

Micky has been here countless times. The lady of the house is a legend on Leamington, and beyond. She stocks her cupboard with cookies. Uncannily, it's always enough to parcel out to the small near daily band of children who flock to her door like so many birds trained to the timed release of bread crumbs. They're store-bought. No one minds. No one abuses the privilege either, like going every day or more than once in a single day.

He was one of those kids himself at one time. She would beam a joyous smile much handing out those cookies. It must make her happy, he'd thought. *What luck is that?* Today, though, is not such a visit. The Murray house is almost directly behind the Alexander house, just across the alley. And, as he found out years later, she is much more than a cookie lady.

Micky interviewed her for the Central Standard Times not long ago. Dolly grew up in an Italian family. At birth she was Yolanda Imbroda, the youngest of four. Her parents were both Italian immigrants. Their marriage had been arranged.

She was born in 1912 in Austin, no more than a mile from where she's been living with her husband, Jack, all these years. Her father was a carpenter by trade, but he moved into general contracting for homes. As a teenager, she wanted to go to college. She was more than capable, academically. Her father had informed her of the family's intention for her to do so.

Then the Depression came. Her father sold off the development land he owned and managed to keep the family house. It was no small feat, but it was too much of a luxury to send a girl to college under those conditions and in that era. There was just a hint of disappointment as she spoke of it, even years later and being very successful and happy.

Maybe because of her father, he'd thought? When dad told her that they would send her to college, he talked about what that would do for her. He said that such women were cultured, refined and understood the world better. He'd said that their minds developed more. She wanted to be that and never got a chance. Would she never be all those things, in his eyes? Maybe, too, she just wanted to show that she could do it, which, he thought was doubtless true.

After she married Jack Murray, she took a part-time job in a local dress shop on Chicago Avenue. Then she moved into full-time work at the very fashionable Madigan's Department store, selling cosmetics. To get to work she would take the bus to Madison and Pulaski. Eventually, she received a perk, the prestigious Estee Lauder line. Most years, there was a training event for that line. It would be 2-3 days in length and occur at one of the downtown hotels, like the Palmer House. The purpose was to show the sales ladies all about the new year's cosmetic products. It was every possible thing one could learn about those products. The women who would buy Lauder would need to know, would want to know. She met Estee Lauder at these events on 2 occasions. Mrs. Murray showed Micky postcards that she had received from her over the years, but at the same time she dismissed them. "Probably gave them to everyone. Maybe didn't even write them." The handwriting all looked the same.

Madigan's opened new stores and placed her in charge of the cosmetics for all of them. Women bought cosmetics from her for years. Over time they came in with daughters as they reached an age for makeup. Once when she was hospitalized with phlebitis, her room was filled with stuffed animals, flowers and small gifts from her many devoted customers.

The story of this woman, who was born before women even had the right to vote and to a typically patriarchal Italian family, was a big hit. Not only did she have a wonderful career, but she invested in safe blue-chip stocks and squirreled away a tidy sum. Smart, out in the world and with her own money, CST's female readers were avid to read about her. She had no children. Therefore, no one criticized her for working.

The Murrays have been married for thirty-seven years. Mr. Murray, who was considerably older, has long since been slowly losing his faculties. The highly-intelligent Dolly Murray is ever vigilant in protecting him. On summer and early fall afternoons Jack sits on the back porch yelling at the WGN radio broadcasts of the Cubs' games. The Cubs are the only ball club still playing all their home games during the day. Beyond question, he's been crushed this past summer. This was a great year for them until this last month where they dropped like a steam iron in the bathtub giving way and are hopelessly behind the New York Mets for the Division title and what would have been their first playoff in twenty-five years.

And Dolly, Micky remembers, was sharp as a thumb tack. That's why Micky would now see her. Dolly takes care of her husband herself. When his condition worsened, she cashed in on her Madigan's pension and gave him full-time care. If he so much as coughs on that back porch, she knows. She is like air traffic control watching all radar screens and weather indicators. Too much sun for him, rain coming, kids running into the yard to retrieve a ball, any sound that wasn't supposed to be there;

she watches, listens and keeps him safe.

Dolly stays back from the door. There's a screen darkening his image. Her eyes must adjust and focus on who has rung her doorbell.

"Oh, hi, Micky, " she says, delighted to see him. "Not here for a cookie, are you?"

"No ma'am. I'm afraid it's a bit more serious." He's sure that she is aware of recent events and probably watched the Channel 7 report or heard all about it. She seems to have decided not to offer any comments. He came to see her. It's important. He can see her thinking through it all while she releases the hook-and-eye lock that secures her screen door. She gestures him into the living room.

"How aware are you, Mrs. Murray?" The interior of the home is immaculate, though the furniture is like from a history museum. *Does no one buy furniture in this neighborhood? Ever?* "Of course, you know, you're aware, I'm sure, of the recent tragedy in the neighborhood and the terrible fate of Effie Alexander?" A somber nod answers him yes.

"Hope you're not here to tell me I should consider moving, that it's not safe." He shakes his head no, vehemently. "Because we could never leave this house, for better or for worse. The change would be too much trauma for Jack. We'll live there for all of his days."

"Yes, ma'am. Not that. This killer – he uses the

name Elijah - I think that this Elijah has been here, in the neighborhood, before, maybe many times. He marched down Laramie. I think he might have been right here on Leamington, too. There's evidence, or information, that he's working with a local realtor, just as Reverend Charles Moore had said in his letter before he was killed, killed in a fire that gets more suspicious every day." He is trying to be careful, to not revisit too much, before getting to the point. Dolly would not easily revisit the abhorrent details of any of these deaths. She's nodded a few times. This is all familiar ground.

"Here's the question, Mrs. Murray. You're close to the Alexander house. Is there something that…well, I thought you might have noticed someone, either on that day or another, on more than one occasion. Looking for someone who is black that you didn't know, that maybe had a goatee beard." He looks at her hoping, and gently pleading. *Please still be the Mrs. Murray that I knew.*

"I remember the march," she begins as if walking through it in order. "It was late in the afternoon. The Cubs game was over. Jack was back inside. I'd start dinner soon. I went out to feed the birds." Mrs. Murray, like many others, would scatter bits of bread into the back yard and watch the birds flutter in for a feeding. The neighborhood is lavish with crows, robins and sparrows, mostly, along with some morning-doves and the occasional cardinal. "You know, next door they took down that old garage and made a cement car port. Then they built a new garage. It's further to the side. That opens the view through to the back of the Alexander's long yard and further onto Laramie." He'd walked through there, tracing the steps that Elijah must have taken including the basement window. He's looked at that alley but didn't notice anything at the time. Now, yes, that's new. "I think it was the sound that made me look, the shuffling, like marching, but distant and faint. The window was open. I was stunned and walked out to the alley to get a closer look. When it was over, it was like it didn't happen. It couldn't have. Why would something like that happen?" Her head drops, and she shudders. She allows herself a moment, looks down at her hands. Is she thinking about the change that's coming?

"The march is for intimidation, to scare people out of their houses and into quick sales," He tells her. She smiles at him benevolently. It's like she's saying 'Of course, precious child. That's not what I mean.' It's a way of gently correcting him. He thinks better and understands her question now. It's who, what kind of people, try something like that. What happened? What went wrong in their lives that this is how they are?

"I heard them, Micky, the screams." He's startled. She's tracking through it. His heart beats faster. "I guess it was Electra's screams at first. I went to the porch. Maybe someone was hurt? Then I saw Mrs.

O'Reilly running. Never saw her so scared in all my life. And she was screaming, too. I knew it must be terrible. I told Jack I had to go, and I'd be right back. I didn't give him a chance to ask a question. He'd want to go, too." The thoughts hurt her. "I helped her with Electra, but I left as soon as I saw the police cars racing up." Unable to avoid reliving this moment, her eyes fill with tears. She excuses herself to get tissues, but walking away says, "I didn't see anyone or hear anything before that. I'm sorry." Micky nods, trying to mask his disappointment. When she returns, in the distance, the Laramie Avenue bus can be heard accelerating on its diesel engine. She stops crying instantly. Her mouth opens. She closes it and her expression intensifies into a realization. "It's a Riviera, a burgundy Riviera. Yes. That's what it is!"

Micky's eyes open wide as he stands and moves close to her. "Mrs. Murray, what do you mean? It's a Riviera. What's a Riviera?"

"There's a car. It's driven through the block slowly before, sometimes at night. Once I saw it park. I watched it like a hawk. When another car would come down the street with the lights on, I could see it. Eventually, I got it, a Buick Riviera. I read the name on the side, you know, the model name in chrome, just a little bit, but enough. It's a burgundy color. I'm sure it was 'Riviera' that I saw. That car has a real growl of a sound when it accelerates. It's like a lion, with the deep low purr coming at first, when it senses something. And then loud and threatening when is going to take action. When the driver steps on the gas hard, that car is very loud and very distinctive. Micky, " she says turning her face to his. "I heard that sound on that horrible afternoon. It was odd to hear it before dark. That's when it's normally around. That burgundy Riviera was somewhere near to Laramie, within earshot, and not long before it happened. I didn't think about it before. That sound was an hour or so before the screams. I just forgot about it with everything that happened, until now. I have reported that car to the police on more than one occasion."

"Mrs. Murray, did you ever see a license plate number?"

"Yes, I did, well part of one. I saw it and I wrote it down. I don't remember it, but ages ago, I gave that to the police. Ages ago."

Micky was ready to jump out of his skin, but he remembers to ask further questions. Was there anything else she remembered? No. How many people were in the car? Just the one. Dolly went over every detail that she remembered. It didn't lead to any further understanding. That car had frightened her. How far would he go? What does he want? The girls who might be out. What about them? Everyone, females, elderly, even kids, were not afraid to walk these streets after dark. He thinks that may never be true again.

"Mrs. Murray, this is the best cookie I could

ever have had." He stands, wanting to quickly say goodbye and leave. "Wait. Mrs. Murray, there's a five-thousand-dollar reward." Micky thinks that there might be a boat-load of items that she wants to buy to help with her husband's care.

"If this leads to the capture of that horrible beast, and I'm due a reward, give it to Mrs. Alexander. She has to change her life now and money will come in handy. "

He looks at her. "Mrs. Murray, you…well, you not only are an accomplished person, but you have the highest quality of the refined human being, compassion. Everyone could learn from your view of the world." Whether she understands the reference or not, he can't tell. But he knows that she believes him when he says it. Micky's sincerity has never been a question.

She waves him toward the door. "Go. I know you need to tell the police. Go."

"I'm going. I don't know what the police did with your plate number before, but I know what they're going to do now. We're going to find him. Now we have a way to track that to a name and address." He thanks her one more time and flies out of the house running to his office where he rips the phone of its base to call Detective Wagner. This time, thankfully, he answers. The list of Rivieras registered to an address on the West Side, maybe near Lake Street and Central Park that have that same partial plate number could not be that big. And it will doubtless match with an owner who has a pyramid tattoo. Wagner would have an answer by tomorrow, if they didn't have one already that they just never did anything about. *Holder!* Wagner will know how to handle telling him.

CHAPTER 30

"Mulvihill? Yeah. Officer O'Leary. Detective Wagner asked me to call you. Elijah's name is Lewis Leonard."

"What? Say that again please. Are you sure?" It's three days since he informed Wagner about the burgundy Riviera,

"Lewis Leonard, and it's a lock. The Riviera, the artist's rendering, pyramid tattoo on the left side of his neck, a long rap sheet that includes charges for arson, and blood type. He's AB pos, not very common, almost the least common. Also, he's suddenly missing. Detective Holder and police crime lab techs have been to his West Side apartment. That, by the way, adds further circumstantial evidence. Detective Wagner and two police officers are headed there now. Detective Wagner said to tell you, and, if you wear your Daily News credential, he'll see that you get let into the apartment. It's on Laflin by Carrol." He reads the address. Micky, sitting in the Daily News newsroom, writes the address on the back of his hand and heads out. He doesn't look to see if Diamond notices. He doesn't care if he did.

Micky jumps at the chance. It isn't a face-to-face with Elijah, but it is a step in the right direction. Something in that apartment will lead him to the next step.

Laflin street by Carrol is Near West Side and only maybe two blocks away from Lake Street. The surrounding area is mostly filled with small manufacturing plants for various motorized parts, car parts, electrical parts, radio parts, and general machinist type work for building molds. Micky knows nearby Union Park, always a rallying point for political actions, ones that are generated from unions. The entire area is lousy with labor union offices: Teamsters, Electrical Workers and many others. Union park also has concerts. Famously, Tommy Dorsey and Ramsey Lewis have performed there.

That's all North of Lake. Train tracks change everything. On the south end, it's not densely populated. The plants are mostly series of single-story brick buildings. Some have windows that angle open for desperately needed ventilation. Others are a little more protective. If they have windows, they're high and intentionally too small for a grown man to crawl through. A few buildings, where small factories failed, have been converted into homes. Rarer still are apartments. The 5-story faded brick and heavily graffiti-laden building that is home for Lewis Leonard is an exception.

He drives south on Ashland to Carrol and cuts over, passing the Egyptian King bar, and parking across from the Leonard address. A few mid-day drinkers, smoking in front of the lounge, spot him. They're eyes follow. It's probably just curiosity. It's not safe here, but it's daytime, and mostly, the danger would be opportunists. A white guy is either looking to score drugs, meet a hooker or he's a cop. The Chevelle SS doesn't say cop. When he parks and emerges, he doesn't present an easy-looking target.

On the top floor with the corner apartment, Micky sees the police officers standing guard outside the Lewis Leonard's door. They have his name. His press credential hangs around his neck. "Use the gloves and shoe covers, " he's told. The cop points to a box of rubber gloves and paper-like shoe coverings for his feet. The lab folks have had their run, but it needs to remain it clean in case there are questions or a need to return. It isn't a crime scene, exactly.

"Look, don't touch without asking. I almost invited the girl since she's got a bead on him." Wagner's comment gets Micky's eyes rolling, but not so that Wagner can see. "Here." He points to a photo. "That's Lewis Leonard in a prison file photo." Now he has a real image on which to focus his hate.

He quickly steps through the rooms, staying in the open space areas of the floor. He stops in the bathroom and looks at himself in the mirror. He can feel the evil presence strongest in this room. An old-fashioned claw-foot porcelain tub is positioned near the window. He's read a little about delusional people ever since Olivia profiled Elijah that way.

"Detective?"

"Yeah?" Wagner walks to the bathroom wondering what Micky has.

"Were there any knives or razor blades with blood on them found here?"

"A razor. And, yes, with blood. It's Lewis Leonard's blood type."

"They hurt themselves. Cut themselves. Carve words in their own skin. I don't really understand what it means, but they do it. It fits the MO." He sees that the Detective doesn't care for details that are not leads, but anything could be a lead.

The bedroom has no dresser, but several mirrors have been positioned on the floor and leaning into the walls. *Images? Imagery? Maybe.* The television, hosted on wooden crates, is not more than seventeen inches and close to the end of the bed A two-drawer nightstand in the closet is completely empty except for a few books. The clothes that are hanging don't cover half the space. Presumably, he grabbed the rest. *And where did you go? Where could you go?*

"Let me look at these. I've got the gloves on."

He points to the books.

"Okay. They have the photo of where it was. And, by the way, leave it as you find it."

One book is a collection of famous fires. Each chapter describes the investigations. Methods that were used by arsons are part of the narrative. The book is old and from the Chicago Public Library. One chapter covers a catastrophic fire in the Ohio Penitentiary. Certain words or phrases are underlined, such as 'the cause is still debated', 'wood scaffolding' and 'construction project'. The pages indicate that the scaffolding, burned furiously and hot enough to start the building on fire. *This is to learn what to do and what they look for, so you can hide yourself better.* The fire killed over 300 inmates. The deaths are not underlined.

He picks up another. This one every single Chicagoan knows, the 1958 fire at Our Lady of Angels school. It's only been eleven years. No one can speak or read those words without dropping their eyes. Grown men stop talking so that they're voice doesn't break. Many will make the sign of the Cross and say a quick prayer. Over ninety died, almost all children. A lot of them were the same age as Micky had been. Those school children who survived were enrolled temporarily into other Catholic schools, including his, Our Lady Help of Christians. Some were even in his class. Elijah's highlights give him a chill; the fire began in the basement and the smoldering went undetected until it was too late.

He spots a small glossy paper flyer, the Baptist Bulletin. The date says that it's from the services on July 6th at Garfield Park Baptist church, three weeks before the fire lay on the floor wedged between the nightstand and the baseboard. *This is when you cased the place for your return visit. You didn't choose to break in. Why? Do you want to know the faces that belong to the church you're going to burn? Sadist. Whatever made you what you are, you're no longer human.*

"Ready to look at the basement?" The comment brings a question to his face. "There's more from this little sweetheart down there. " They head down the stairs. The basement is cordoned off to prevent entry. "This is not a matter of gathering evidence for another crime. This, itself, is a crime scene. Change, over here." He indicates that they should don a new pair of gloves and paper booties. Micky complies. "That chair in the corner? We found that it contained human blood. Figures to match one Sammy Gallagher. He was a partner with the goons that wanted your head. And he's nowhere to be found." The sarcasm in the final words indicate that he means 'We haven't found the dead body yet'.

"Too bad they can only fry you once."

"Mulvihill, these are the real guys that inhabit the city. They kill for money. They torture. It's a business. It's a game. A way of life. I don't know. But that's why I said before, and I'm reminding you now...you can't go hero on me. This is what I get paid to do. It's my job." No response is offered.

A wooden storage area, one of many lined up in a row, is marked with Lewis Leonard's apartment number. The lock has been removed. With permission, Micky lifts the lid from a metal Pepsi Cola cooler to reveal several jars of liquids. He sniffs near them. The chemistry kit: oily liquids, varnishes, stains, alcohol and gasoline permeate to the point of robbing his air.

Wagner acts like the tour guide. "Upstairs is the home of a seriously disturbed mind. It's a workshop for degenerates. He meets with the goons down here. They work and plan. He killed somebody down here or he dragged the body here later for entertainment value. " Over the next twenty minutes, he continues to examine everything, but he doesn't know what he's looking for. He can feel his presence again. The blood in the chair is where he tortured someone, delighting in it to send another message like the one he sent to him.

They move outside and talk in front of Lewis Leonard's apartment building. The uniformed police have left. Wagner leans against his 1968 Plymouth Belvedere. "Some of the reports are in. I took a glance. Sad story. Like I said, I don't care. What do we have here? Well, he did some research on his craft, maybe some modeling, but where the hell is he? Is there any clue here that leads us to him? Well, we do have the start of a trail. There were paper pay-stubs from the Sears Warehouse on Homan Avenue. There was a bank book. His account had been almost fully withdrawn. Almost. Maybe by leaving $35 dollars in it, he figures that there would be less conversation and no special paperwork to make his withdrawal visit either memorable or lengthy. He has, at least, $752 dollars. And he's definitely on the run.

"Anything on the '64 Riv.?"

"Like where is it? No, and with the all-points-bulletin on him which includes that description, plus the fact that thing moves about as indiscreetly as 'hey, the circus is in town', I'm thinking its tucked away not to be easily found. He could have left town without it." Before Micky can speak, he adds. "Yes, we're going to follow up on every lead from that apartment and everywhere. His file names his family." Micky nods.

"Can I have a copy of the police reports, the inventory and any lab stuff? I want to piece it all together. Somewhere in there is the clue that leads us to him. I know you're going to look at everything, but it may be something small. Two sets of eyes, ya know?"

"Yeah. Sure. Come by tomorrow. Just call first," he adds unnecessarily.

"What about Holder?" He just wants to keep this square.

"He's got everything. He has been here already."

"And everything he gets has your fingerprints on it." A smile. That doesn't require a response.

"I am meeting with Olivia and K-9 tomorrow. And Harrison Kellum. You should join us." The last name doesn't ring a bell. He gets a look. "Kellum is senior editor at the Defender. He got a letter like the one that came to the Daily News. He's smart, connected and was a friend of Reverend Moore." He sees its enough.

They stand awkwardly, not sure if that's it. Micky starts. "One more thing. Well, two. WJLO wants me on TV. I'm going to get some level of okay from the people in Austin. I'll have a meeting, maybe at the church, on Thursday. You should know that, too. " Wagner can't offer protection this time. And it would sound hollow, given his last effort. He offers nothing on it.

"And the mob wants Elijah. I got a special-favor-I-didn't-ask-for ride home, wanting to know what I know. Citizens interested in saving the tax-payers on court costs, I think."

"Yeah. Mayor wants this guy found, and NOW. I want that. You want that. The whole city, and now the Outfit, wants that. If he stays, he'll be found. His specific future depends on who finds him." They lock eyes. Each of them wants badly to be that particular 'who'.

CHAPTER 31

Gladys Johnson heard the Chicago Tribune hit the front steps while she was still in bed more than thirty minutes ago. Now she is up and dressed. The coffee's on. She'll retrieve the paper and settle into a long hour of coffee, toast and jelly, and reading the news.

She slides off the chain lock and turns the key, which always sits in the door lock, on the inside. A tremendous jolt hits her in the chest knocking her to the floor the instant she opens the door. A man's hand covers her mouth. She makes eye contact in sheer terror.

"Any sound at all, and I will kill you. Otherwise, if you do as I say, then no harm will come to you." He uses his foot to push the door closed but remains on top of her on the cold linoleum floor of her enclosed front porch. She feels his weight, dominating, pressing against her, but he only holds the position, nothing more, until she nods in agreement. No sound at all.

A thousand times she will torment herself with what else she might have done in those moments that would have avoided her capture. Why didn't she look? She never does. She's not afraid to walk out of her own front door. But just a look...

He uncovers her mouth. His eyes control her. She risks a question. "What do you want? I don't have much money. You can have it. Take it. Take anything."

"What I want is to rest in your home, to eat your food and to wait until I am called again." He is calm. Too calm. It frightens her. He's not a desperate thief, afraid the police will come at any moment. *Until I am called? What does that mean?* The possibility paralyzes her.

"I...just...there's not much. I could give you money to get food and to get far away."

"Listen to me. I am staying. But I have no calling to harm you." He smirks delivering his next comment. "No one will miss you, will they?" She thinks about what he has said and knows he's right.

Mrs. Gladys Johnson, a widow whom the neighbors, from children up to adults, unanimously view as both bitter and mean, doesn't have one person in the world who would be checking in on her. Her house is not far from Lewis's apartment, but the value of her land is very different.

She lives close to the new college. It's all being converted to accommodate the new University of Illinois at Chicago campus, the "Circle", named after a configuration of the nearby highway. She could easily have rented out to students and herself, lived elsewhere. Or she could have sold the house to others who would do that. Simple enough. Not for her. She doesn't like change. It's too much trouble to deal with it all. The hell with them, anyway. She doesn't care about the money. She doesn't care about anything or anyone. And no one cares about her.

Her husband died many years ago, but she will always be Mrs. Gladys Johnson. Her sister, whose husband was killed in the war, moved in for a period. Then she was gone. Neighbors say that Gladys is just too mean to die. How perfect she is a for him to take as a captive.

She never goes out, except to deposit monthly checks. She has neither friends nor family that come around. Lewis knows that she makes calls, as needed, to Lexington Grocers and tells Tony, or one of the other two brothers who own the store, what she needs to be delivered. That's how he knows her. One summer long ago, he delivered those groceries. She doesn't remember him. She never looks delivery boys in the face. No tips either.

"You could take my car," she suggests. *Too much! I said too much.* She hopes she hasn't given him an idea, that he could escape in her car, which wouldn't be reported as missing because she'd be dead.

He ignores the offer. "I'm not leaving because I'm not done yet. I need to lay down, to rest and then plan the final challenge to the rapin' white boy and all that are related to him. It's what I'm being guided to do." *Guided? Raping white boy?* She can't help herself and starts to cry. He pulls her to the bedroom, rips up some of her clothing and ties her hands. Grabbing yesterday's paper from the floor near the back door, he wads it into a ball and stuffs it into her mouth. With strips of clothing he secures the paper so that she can't talk or spit it out. He tosses her to the bed and ties her hands to the headboard, then lies down next to her.

Too frightened, Gladys Johnson begins to urinate slightly before she can contain herself. The smell reaches him. Her heart is pounding. "You will clean yourself and change. I will watch you, to be safe. " She does as she is told, trembling and humiliated. He watches without a sign of emotion.

They both enter the bed. He ties her again. "I told you that I'm not going to harm you. If I killed you, you couldn't call the store to deliver food for us. You couldn't cash your pension checks for me. When I'm ready, I'll just go. The police already know who I am and what I've done. I have no fear of you as a witness. I don't care. There's no reason for me to bother to kill you, even at the end. When I've finished what I need to do, I will be taken into heaven. I'll be free. It's why I'm guided. I needed to complete the will of God." *Who I am and what I've done? What does that mean by that? Oh, God, help me! This...must...be—I'm lying next to the man who brutally killed that high school girl and set fire to a church filled with people. He is Elijah!*

Trembling and nauseous, she does not sleep. The hours pass. Dehydration caused by the constant sweating increases her heart beat, which makes her warm, which leads to more sweating and further dehydration. She feels herself slipping away. Her heart, she thinks, won't take much more. This can't be real. Torture.

When he awakens, he moves her to the kitchen. He finds a tin of leftover chicken, mashed potatoes and peas in the fridge. When he finishes, he places bread and cheese in front of her and unties her hands. He plops down a half-gallon of milk that's mostly filled. "You must do everything I say. Now eat." She forces herself to comply.

◆ ◆ ◆

Three weeks have passed since his invasion. No harm has come to her. The fear, now, is living with him. *He has no reason to harm me, but how long will he stay? Maybe months or even years...forever?*

His talk is delusional. His mannerisms are ritualistic, masochistic. He's positioned the mirrors so that he can see himself all the time. He stares. He talks to himself. He's cut the name Elijah into his chest. He's burnt the skin on his face blistering the scars that were already there. His look is frightening. She can't just wait it out.

The delivery boy rings the bell. As before, she wears a robe and pretends to not be fully dressed. "Just leave them inside on the floor." The boy obliges. He walks back out. She pushes the door mostly closed while he grabs the tab from his shirt pocket. She pays the store at the beginning of each month when her pensions arrive. The door is open just enough for him to pass the bill through. She signs and pushes it back to him.

"Thank you," she says curtly and closes the door quickly.

"I'll put these away." She must do something to hide her nerves. *Please God, help me.*

"Hold it. Don't move a muscle. " She freezes at his command, almost dropping the bags. Her heart hammers against her chest wall. Elijah peeks from the side of the window. He watches the delivery boy. A blue AMC Rebel station wagon sits double-parked. He hops in, dropping down onto the seat like it was a trampoline, and speeds off. Lewis is careful to notice that the boy never looked back. Satisfied that he's gone without incident, he says. "Okay. That was good. Go ahead."

He watches her put the groceries away. She's nervous, but not more than she has been and not for the reason he might think. She's trying to concentrate on what she's doing, but just keeps praying that it goes a little longer. If it does, it just might work. She knows that her captor doesn't suspect, not yet. She must not change her behaviors. *Hold yourself as always.* She wants to scream. She doesn't know if it will work, or if it does, when. And when it does, how it will happen. All she knows is that she did it. She signed the tab ELIJAH HERE!

CHAPTER 32

"Detective Wagner, Chicago Police Department. Ma'am, like to speak with you about your son, Lewis Leonard." He knew two things as soon as she opened the door; the badge frightened her, and Detective Holder had not been here.

The first was understandable. Mikala Leonard has done nothing wrong, leastwise nothing criminally wrong. It's just that, her whole life she's been told that everything she does is wrong. And he was a white cop. The second? Maybe he understood that one, too? It's cleaner for Holder to keep her name out of his record. That way, we stay out of any discussions about the city and its systems that way.

The Riviera led to his driver's license which led to his social security number which led to birth records and, ultimately, led him here, to the Cabrini-Green housing projects just west of downtown. Mikala Leonard lives in the most dangerous neighborhood in the city. It's different than Woodlawn, on the South Side, where the Stones and other gangs prevail with a ruthless and self-serving manner.

Cabrini-Green is just desperation. It's more jungle than war zone. Predators are everywhere. There's no plan, no vision of the future, not even a perverse one. The idea is survival, not revolution. Even that doesn't matter too much.

He might have been shot coming here just because he's a cop. He took the risk because he hopes she can lead him to her son, Lewis Leonard. He doesn't care if it's messy, or ruffles feathers in the city. This cop will find Lewis or die trying. Right now, he doesn't look like he would mind the latter option.

"I'm trying to get to sleep. I work the night shift, the overnight shift, at the J&R café on Halsted." He tries to look at her kindly, sensing that she feels she must tell him that she has a job. It's like all white people are the police, the ones you must answer to.

"Yes, ma'am. I can appreciate that. This is very important and won't take long. There's a homicide involved." She lets him in and walks to the couch, dropping on it in a near collapse, apparently exhausted.

"I don't know nothin'. If he kilt somebody, I don't know nothing about it. I ain't seen him in a long time, a month, two months." *If he killed somebody? Does that mean she knows why I'm here or that she doesn't, and just presumes he killed someone? This is a city-wide manhunt for her son.*

"Is this your son?" He hands her the picture he carries, taken at Pontiac prison. A bottle of beer sits sweating on the end table. She's trying not to stare, lest he see her. He smelled it, or one of the empties, walking in.

Her face cracks in emotion then stiffens. "Funny question. Is this convict your son? Did you raise a convict? Ain't you got nothing to show me from his school? Or church?" He starts to speak, but she continues. "Is he mine? And, well, whose child am I? That's the real question. 'Cause he's the son of the daughter that's the filth. So, he's the filth, too." *Lewis Leonard did not fall far from the tree.*

"Mrs. Leonard? Are you okay?" He waits for an answer. She half-gives one with her face. She might like to ask, do I look okay, poor and living in the worst projects? He gets back to the point, but tries, poorly, to offer help, if she wants it. " I'm trying to locate your son. I just want to make sure we're talking about the same person. I could...I mean, if you need...if you're not well, perhaps I can get some help?" Her face indicates that the most important thing to her is for him to get on with it and leave.

"That's my son. Told you. I ain't seen him. Try his grandmother. He likes her." She looks over at him, imploring. Her eyes sneak a glance at the beer. Wagner pretends not to notice. "I don't know where Lewis is, who his friends are, where he works or nothin'. Lewis and me don't see each other. It's how they say with families, estranged." She sits up straight on the edge of the couch, with a new and sarcastic attitude emerging. "It's just a terrible shame." A smile bends her mouth slightly. She's delighted to be estranged. She's laughing at the good fortune of it.

"Has your son every had any treatment for mental illness or had any type of psychiatric care?" He surprises himself. Normally, only the where is what's important. The why is meaningless. Her look tells him that she knows he's seen the reports on her son from his times in prison. Schizophrenic. Delusional. A history of child abuse from his mother. He wants to hear about it from her own mouth.

"He hurts himself, you know. Everyone thinks it's me, but that boy cuts himself, carves letters and names and symbols into himself. It's him, and well, his grandfather, my father. He tried to send him away forever. But he don't do that no more. Can't. " She stops short.

Mr. Washington? Elmer? What do you mean he can't?"

"They say he 'passed on'. I'd say he went down, way down where God wants his kind. And good riddance. A stroke took him just a few months ago. I didn't go to his funeral." She stops quickly, like she doesn't want to explain. Her look convinces him he doesn't need to ask why. His guess would be good.

"I bet he did kill someone. Lewis." She's different again. A fiendish and angry look comes over her. "Last year, there was a lot of shooting, here in Cabrini. During the riots. Folks just sniping. He told me that. He's got a lot of that in him. Me, too. Although I don't set no fires." She's triumphant, better than him. She wants to hurt him now. "He kilt a boy that was in the Disciples. Yeah, that boy was in the wrong place. But, thing was, Lewis didn't understand. Jeff Fort's got a lot of connections there, in the Disciples. And Jeff, he likes black gangs to work together, not kill each other. They call him Angel." Wagner looks at her with a question. "Jeff Fort. Not Lewis. He don't really have a name. His grandfather just wouldn't let him or me be alive hardly. We was ghosts, there, but he wouldn't use our name, ever. Just didn't accept me. Called me the filth. " Wagner knows all the horror stories. He's just not able to dismiss it this time. He has to understand everything about why Effie had to die. "So, anything come from me, like him, don't really exist either. Never accepted him. He's the filth, too. I ain't no filth. Just ain't" Her face transforms to a sneer. The she releases an evil laugh. "He is, though, ain't he? That's why you're here. Catch the filth." She laughs. "And clean him. I couldn't. I tried." Wagner knows what this reference means from Leonard's file.

"Mr. Leonard, your husband?"

"He ran off. Probably California. His father

lives there, I think. "

"When was that?"

"About three…no…must be five years ago."

She gives Wagner the address that she remembers as well as the phone number to Irene Washington, her mother, Lewis's grandmother. He mutters a quick thanks. Locking the door behind him, she heads for the beer.

Wagner unfastens the leather snap on his holster and covers the handle with his palm after he leaves her apartment. The mother has been documented as abusive. He's read the reports. She cleaned him, he remembers, contemptuously. *With bleach!* But the trail leads to the grandfather. *Sounds like he was a real pip.* His next stop is to find out exactly that.

◆ ◆ ◆

Irene Washington ambles toward the door. "Coming." It takes her some time to get across the house. She lets Detective Wagner in. When he tells her who he is and what he wants, there is an instant pain. She expected it might come to her, and what she would do if it did. Questions about Lewis make her sad, but she never quits. "Follow me to the kitchen. I'm cooking. Got to get back to it.

"Yes ma'am. Certainly. " A mirror that sits on top of a dresser in the hallway to store blankets and linens. She tries to ignore it, but today, with a stranger in the house, she can't. She's 74, but the mirror reflects an age much beyond that. Wagner takes a seat, as instructed near the corner of the kitchen table, which has chrome legs and a blue Formica top. The chairs match the table. The seats are upholstered in vinyl.

"This is my own soup, my own. It's a bit like a minestrone, but I make it different. I don't use the beans." She shakes her head to tell him that beans aren't good for her. "And I add a Portuguese sausage that Tilde brings. Tilde Almeida, well Matilde, but she doesn't go by that with folks who know her. She's from Portugal. We're good friends. She gets it. And I love it." She leans toward him. This is something important and she much be close so that he hears it clearly. "This is good soup."

"Yes, ma'am. It smells wonderful. I'm sure it is good, great." She can tell he means it.

"Yeah, well, a lot of what you're smelling is that sausage. I just finished frying it. That will get a body ready to eat. It's a wonderful sausage."

She sits at the head of the table across from him and nearest the stove. She's not afraid, but it's not going to be easy.

"Mrs. Washington, do you know where Lewis is or might be?"

"Might be? Most anywhere. I don't know

where he is, though."

"Did he have some friends that you knew?"

"Elmer, my late husband, he didn't like Lewis. He wouldn't come around much, only a few times when he knew that Elmer wasn't here. And then he just stopped. He says he's not mine or Mikala's. But he is. He sure is."

"I understand that it was difficult at times with Mr. Washington. I spoke with Mikala." Her eyes changed. She is a mother who loves her daughter, but can't help her, never could, and it is killing her.

"At times, all right. All the times, that what times it was. Elmer hated her from the minute he knew I was pregnant. And, even when that poor innocent child was born, he didn't change. How a body can hate a baby, I'll never know."

"Yeah. I...don't...well, really the question is —"

"Would you like some tea?" Coffee is too heavy, now, not long before dinner." She cuts him off. She has something to let out and they need to take it slow, so she can do it. She's never been able let it out, but now she will. Someone should know and understand Lewis. *This time it's the end.*

"Uh, yes. That would be fine."

"I'll tell you about Lewis, why he is the way he is. But I have to tell you my story to get to Mikala's story to get to Lewis. "

"Sure. Ultimately, I am just looking to get to where Lewis might be." She purses her lips. *This man is going to listen to me.*

She starts slowly. "Everything didn't stop because there was a riot going on. The trouble was mostly going on around our neighborhood, Bronzeville, between there and Bridgeport and all. " She appreciates that he's trying to listen and not be in a hurry to get through his list of questions. Her eyes keep telling him 'this is what you really want to know.'

"The riot that you're talking about was in 1919? It's the riot that Reverend Moore talked about?

"Yes, that very same one. I went to work, in Oak Park. I took the trolley down Dearborn and got on the train. The white folks I did laundry and housekeeping for wouldn't care about a riot. If I didn't make it, they'd find someone else and tell me never mind, ever again never mind."

"Must have been dangerous, to go outside."

"Dangerous? That day changed my life, created Mikala and her problems and Lewis and his problems." He lowers his brow, waiting, trying to understand.

"Coming home now, it was 5:30 pm —the

drivers would carry these big watches that were inside of a leather case. The case had a loop that they could use to hang on the end of the handrail. They kept their time, the time for their stops, by eyeing that big watch. Every stop has a certain time. I saw it, leaving. 5:30. — I stood up from my seat, which was very near the front. I could. The Dearborn trolley was pretty near empty. I peered out, twisting and bending my head to see if anyone was lurking on the street. There's plenty of light at 5:30 on July 29th. Satisfied that there weren't nobody to threaten me, I step off, letting the trolley continue its route, keep pace with that big watch. " This is a memory she hates, but it's been in her too long. Hard. Pain.

"Maybe you should take it easy for a while?" Wagner's concern would normally make her smile. She can't.

"When I turn the corner onto 31st, I see 4 white men carrying baseball bats and chains and all, just in front of me. Were they watching for the trolley? Did they leave themselves just out of sight knowing someone might step off, a working woman might step off? That trolley driver was white. Did he…" She's pained by the thought. "Did he see them and know? Were they there before? Were there other women?" She leaves the questions hang unanswered. She adds nothing. Wagner offers nothing. Time just stops until she's ready. "I froze for a moment, everything going through my head. I was hoping that there was some place to go to be safe. There wasn't. I turned to get away. I know, before it happens, I know, I'm not going to escape. When they catch me, I start fighting with every ounce of strength that I can muster. They're hitting me, grabbing me. My own fear is fighting me, defeating me, but I'm fighting it and all of them." Tears run down her cheeks. She pulls a handkerchief out of her apron.

"Take your time, ma'am."

"They pull me into the alley," she continues, pushing through to the end. "One is holding my hands. And two more...my legs. " She looks up at him, a strength comes to her, a dignity. "You, Detective Wagner, will never know. And no one who hasn't had it done to them, will ever know, what it is like to have men pull you open like you were a can of tuna. They were smiling, excited...they were happy for...you know, I think, mostly they were happy to be able to do this to me. To be in control and humiliate me, that was their biggest excitement, the power."

There is no argument from Wagner. He doesn't try to tell her that he can empathize. He'll never know. He has no wife and no daughter to try to feel it that way.

"I screamed. I lunged forward to where my head could bite the right arm of one holding me.

Got him right in the fleshy part of the forearm. He loosens his grip. I pull my arm free and take a vicious swipe at the face of the man mounting me, digging my nails in like we were breaking ground for a new house. He was my age, that man. A lot of the rioters were in their teens. I was 24. He was that, at least. He came back and hit me, " she touches her left cheekbone remembering. "I was nearly knocked unconscious. My eyes was filled with tears. I had no more fight left. " Her voice trails softly. "He smiled. The more I cried no, but couldn't do anything, the more he smiled. He taunted me, said things I'm not going to repeat, and he hit me again and again."

"Please take a break. I'm listening. Anything you want to tell me. I'm listening." He is a kind man. She past the moment of it. She waits together with him in silence.

"I tried to hide it from Elmer, but in no time my face looked like an eggplant. I told him that they beat me, but I jumped on a trolley to get away. He didn't believe me much. Over the days, the marks were a shameful reminder to Elmer, that I'd been attacked. He didn't protect me. See, that's how he saw it. He thought that I had been raped. I would have kept that to myself to my dying day. But soon enough, there weren't no hiding. He knew that he was right. I couldn't pretend any longer.

"The seed of that hateful white man had found its way to my egg and was stimulating growth. A life. That was Mikala. The name means gift from God. All children are gifts. That's why I chose it. She had nothing to do with that man. Elmer? No. This was not a gift, not to him. God didn't do this, he'd say. The baby is the filth of that rapin' white boy. That's what he'd say. He'd say it right now if he was standing here. That's the way he treated her, all her life. And Lewis, too, when he came along." The look returns to her eyes. This is what has been killing her each day since Mikala was born.

"It wasn't long before he knew who it was that did it. Galled him. He wanted to kill him. I think he tried, more than once, but it never worked, and they saw his face. If he shot him now, he'd have been killed right back. And Lord knows what would happen to us? That man, the one who done it, he was protected. He was a brother of an important man to the city. He was a Mulvihill."

She sees that the name triggers a response from Wagner. "Mulvihill?" he asks.

"Yes. Mean something to you?"

"No. Just trying to get it right." He lies. "Surprised, too, that you would know the name."

"Mulvihills ran the SAC, the Social and Athletic Club, in a lot of places. People did things for them. They got favors from the city. He doesn't do that anymore, though. But that one, he was different. Wherever he started with his evil desires in life, he was like a country dog that, once it has killed its first chicken, always looks for further opportunity to feast.' Not no more, no sir. A man like that, he makes a lot of enemies. One of them stopped him." *Forgive me for the joy I feel that this man was punished, Lord. Forgive me.*

"I know they gonna kill Lewis. " She looks down. "When they do, well, when they do, it's gonna kill part of me, too. And, I can only imagine what it's gonna do to Mikala. She's learned to hate. But when it's over, it's going to be different. She'll remember the baby, just that innocent baby. Because they all innocent. And he's gone. Elmer, I mean. The hate's gone from this house."

"He ain't left. That's one reason why I'm telling you all this, partly. He's here and he's going after that white boy. That child, he's got to kill that white boy, Mulvihill, even if it costs his life. His life don't mean more than getting back at that family. That's the same hate that destroyed Elmer. It's the same hate from Elmer."

She gives him what she had that might lead to finding Lewis. Mostly old numbers and names of people she knew he'd been with. "I'll look through these, check them out. I'm grateful to you." He stops. He knows she wants to say more.

"I lived. I tried to be the best mother I could. My other child, Ronnie, is okay. Mikala is going to make it one day, too. Elmer, the man I married, he's gone now. I knew he was not going to live that much longer. The Lord took him so that I can help Mikala. And they'll just be my love and not his hate. Won't be none of that. My love is very strong. She will make it. We'll all be together. I lived." Wagner looks at her and can only believe.

He didn't drive more than a block. *Lewis Leonard is the son of a woman whose birth was from a rape by someone in Mulvihill's family? And that makes Elijah...and Micky?"*

CHAPTER 33

Micky, first to arrive, gently lowers himself into the chair, careful not to spill his coffee. He's taken their usual table. Back to the wall, as is his preference, he can tell that the Coffee And staff are, again, excited at the prospect of hosting a meeting with him and the others. They began to buzz as soon as they saw him. K-9 walks in next. He orders a large orange juice and an egg sandwich before joining. He's still apologizing for not mentioning the car, even before he even sits.

"I didn't think much about it. No one had a plate or a partial. But I should have told you about the model, the Riv., the night that Richie told me. I was excited about the name and, frankly, that Olivia called. Sorry, man."

"Forget it. I told you a million times. I heard it from Hogan even before the fire. We write news. This investigating stuff is all new. But we're better now. Not even bad, actually." That earns a smile.

By the time he gets his refill, Olivia and Wagner have joined them. "Thanks, everyone, for coming. Okay. The meeting is seven o'clock tonight at Preacher's church. Kathy and Preacher have been door-to-door with flyers. It's all went out right around the epicenter, from Laramie to Cicero and from Augusta to Lake. That's the area that's really been targeted. That's where the march was, where both realtors both are, where the other intimidation acts happened. " he hesitates not wanting to say it's where Effie lived. "Etcetera." The main point for tonight is Channel 7. If I go on there, it's about heightening the search. "

"How would this work? What exactly, would be the kind of thing that you would say on TV. " Olivia wants him to be very clear. He needs to be able to present that clarity tonight.

"Reports are already hitting the street in written articles. Lewis Leonard's past is coming to light for the public. I, we, will have the police report. Well, Detective Wagner, are there any problems with my using that information."

"Yes, " he answers, emphatically. "The criminal part is fine but stay away from the medical information. It's just gratuitous. The public wants those details, but—"

"Well, let's think this through. The more we give them that they like, the more they watch. It's their eyes we want. The WJLO reporter, Wolford, wants his station to own the tips. They're better staffed and have better equipment. Look, no one knows that I get it from you. To my grave, no one knows. " Wagner has already widened his boundaries extensively. He thinks about this. Micky tries to cover his concern. "I can claim that I have sources from the Daily News as well as other unnamed individuals. "

He's nodding, then breaks into, "Yeah, but nothing too technical, that would require a medical person. Be general."

K-9 chimes in. "First things first, Mick. The meeting. What do you want the people to really say?"

"I don't know. I just have to tell them. I have to hear them."

"How much risk do you think there is?"

"I think that he's focused on me. That's the number one risk. Those closest to me are next. You, Olivia, are part of this. You're at risk, too."

Olivia answers, "I don't have the same address anymore. The shop is being watched already. I have a gun and I know how to use it. I'm from Alabama. You learn how to handle a gun about the same time you learn to write in cursive." She looks at each of them, one at a time.

Wagner jumps in. "Can you get a push from the black leaders, the SCLC or whoever, to the mayor's office to increase cops in Austin."

"I can try, Detective. And I think I can do it. If Daley says no, the SCLC can say that they need to go public. He's not going to want that. But it's a limited timeframe. We have to get results fast."

"That's a key." Micky says. " I could tell them tonight that the reports are for, what, two weeks. Give 'em an end date. Okay. Good points, all. I'll be prepared to talk about these safety measures. Okay. What else? What doesn't everybody know?"

"I've been thinking about why he came to my gallery, after the fire? Why did he, gallingly, draw his own image onto my painting, to include the tell-tale mark, " she asks? "Of course," she continues, answering her own question. "he wasn't thinking about Effie, and didn't know that she had provided a description, that there would be anyway to link him to the march and to Reverend Moore. It was a mistake, but why is he doing such a thing in the first place?"

"This is a mind that is not rational." Wagner doesn't want this to be an academic lesson in behavior. "Look. We have the results of some tests he took from time he's spent in jail, in juve. On the one hand, he has the ability to develop skills, like he did to become an arsonist, maybe other things as well. On the other hand, he's, actually, far below normal in intelligence. Not below average, mind you. He's below NORMAL, below the minimum for normal intelligence. We talked to the psychologists, too, the doctors that specialize in criminal and abnormal psychology. They have used the term "maladaptive behaviors". It's like some type of coping. Instead of adjusting your behavior to the societal norms, this guy adjusts to his needs, or his delusion." He gestures toward Olivia emphasizing this last word, adding, " But that's just not a rabbit hole that I think we want to go down. I mean, maybe he has this religious delusion, and his, uh, mental state, allows him to cope with the fact that he is the son of the product of a rape, a rape that occurred in a racial war."

"Whoa. You're going too fast. What rape?" She says. All of them have suddenly furrowed brows with questions on their face, all except Micky.

Wagner starts to explain, awkwardly. "I... uh...spoke with Lewis Leonard's mother, and his grandmother. The grandmother, Irene Washington, was raped during the riots that your husband talked about. She got pregnant from that rape and named the kid Mikala, which means 'gift from God', apparently. She wants to disconnect the kid from the rapist. This is an innocent baby. They're all gifts from God. Okay. Great. The husband is Elmer Washington. This is not his viewpoint. He hates the kid. Calls her the 'filth'. Anyway, Lewis Leonard, Elijah, is the child of Mikala and Irene's grandson. Elmer, who is president of the Father of the Year club hates him, the grandkid, too. Maybe more because he's a male? That really reminds him of the rapist."

Micky shifts his weight, uncomfortably, at the discussion of the rape. He avoids any eye contact Wagner, who appears to be doing the same. Then he speaks.

"Okay, " he says. "Mulvihill was a prominent name back then in that neighborhood. This fool knows the name. That's his vengeance. Anything and everything that happened is their fault." He stops, then adds, "My fault." Everyone tells him that whatever happened, it's not his fault. Wagner goes no further in relaying Irene's descriptions, leaving Micky a little breathing room.

"Okay. Back to the why he comes to the gallery. His delusion is to be Elijah, a prophet of God who is also the wrath of God for the Israelites who follow a false God. Yes, he might have started this delusion because he has a terrible guilt over his own existence and his low intelligence might let him arrive at some 'maladaptive behavior'.—"

"And one other thing." Wagner interrupts her.

"Elijah might have been a torch for the Stones, but they had a break. His mother says he killed a Disciple. Not what Fort wanted. There's a break. It fits our theory."

"Fine, " says Micky. He shrugs his shoulders to indicate 'and so what'. Micky keeps eye contact to get Wagner to see that now he's the one adding things that don't move them to the goal; get Elijah.

"He uses the name Elijah," breaks in Olivia to get them moving, " which, as we know, is a Biblical character that uses fire to defeat enemies, but not by destroying them with it. He discredits them first in a challenge. Then he kills them. Maybe his grotesque message next to Effie was the first part." She looks at Micky. Here it is. "He's going to contact you, and there's going to be a challenge. "

"And I'll call you." He looks at Wagner, sarcastically. "Well, just a minute after I break his neck. " Wagner expands his lungs ready for a blast. "Just kidding." Wagner says nothing, but eyes him suspiciously.

"We've got you phones tapped, at work and at the Daily News, if he tries to call, " Wagner states, reminding them.

"And there's something else, that I was getting to before, in the scriptural story of Elijah. He is also sent, by God, to the home of a widow. He performs miracles for her. She is without food. He, through God, performs a miracle like the one with Jesus and the fishes and loaves so that she and her son have food. Without that, they would have died." Olivia takes a breath, looking at each of them. No one is looking away. "His image in the painting, perhaps, is seen by him as, in some way, living here with me, a widow, as in the story. He was already entering the gallery, but the image appears after Charles' death. I'm not likely a priority target."

K-9 takes Wagner's view, trying to get this to a point where he can take action. "He wants to call Mick out. Mick would like nothing better. Whatever." K-9, keeping his head motionless, shoots his eyes over toward Micky for a reaction. He adds, "This discredit part. Let's remember that It doesn't work. The public opinion of Micky now is changing or has changed. The WJLO TV report on him. Mulvihill, the good guy, the guy trying to break up a real estate scam. He's got a long and good rep. The tide is turning. It could be that this fire-setting, child-killing rapist sees Mick as the target, a target he can't ignore." Micky shrugs. He's said all that he needs to on this.

His own protection plan is to be prepared for a deadly battle. He makes regular visits to his parents' garage where he trains. He is dead-lifting 400 pounds and punishing a heavy bag with both his hands and feet. He practices moves to overpower and incapacitate a foe. His sharpness in these areas is back at a level that he hasn't had in 2 years. He carries a saw-toothed jet pilot's survival knife with in a leather holster hooked onto his belt. He's never been readier.

"Mrs. Moore, " begins Micky, still being very formal to show his respect in front of others. "Anything to indicate where or how he might go about coming my way, creating this 'contest', like in the Bible, " Micky asks.

Olivia doesn't know how or when, except soon. Her biggest point to make today is to not let their guard down. He's coming for Micky and it won't be long. "I'll keep looking for a link, but now. It would figure to involve some type of sacrifice with fire, I would say. That's the script. "

K-9 speaks up. "The realtors. The strategy is to start with them. Anything with that yet?"

"Holder's talked with them. Nothing. Frankly, I doubt he cares if there's a collusion or not. I'll do my own follow-up." Wagner's style would be to gather information first. He wants to go into the face-to-face meetings ready to catch a lie.

◆ ◆ ◆

Jay Stevens, Preacher's father, alternates between astonished and delighted. It's standing room only four rows deep, and they're still coming. He opens, thanking all and offering two prayers. Micky thinks it's good. It settles everyone down and puts them into a mood of low emotions and peaceful feelings. He mentions that there is a donation box on a stand at the back of the church, and anything would be appreciated. Micky starts by repeating the same thing, adding that this meeting benefits them all. After a slight pause, he begins in earnest.

"WJLO, Channel 7 would like me to join their live broadcasts. It's just 2 minutes, but every day at six o'clock. If I do it, it would be to heighten aware-ness, to give us three million sets of eyes and ears so that we can capture Elijah before anything else happens." He just blurted it out, went straight to the heart of the matter. He tells himself slow down. If he goes by the pace of his heart, he'll be done in thirty seconds.

"Let me stop and introduce the others who are here. Mrs. Olivia Moore. Edmund Kannon and Detective Peter Wagner. And, of course you know John Stevens." From the back another voice calls out.

"And I'm Detective Dave Holder, lead inves-tigator for the murder of Aphrodite Alexander." Micky, surprised, spots him, wearing a gray suit, standing about his height, stocky, but not fit. He looks more like he used to be fit but has given up any serious practice. Holder's presence throws him for a moment. Then he continues.

"So, anyway. On TV, I would recap what the police have found, keeping it all in front of people. I'd continue to identify ways to find this guy. Either someone's hiding him, or maybe he's kidnapped somebody or killed somebody, and is living in their home. Who's missing? Who's not around? Whose acting funny? Now these are questions for people in Woodlawn and other areas. Neither he, nor anyone that might hide him is here.

"What about the extra safety, Micky?" It's

Olivia prompting him.

"Oh, yeah. Olivia Moore will contact the Southern Christian Leadership Conference and ask them to talk to the may or about additional protection here. There are some specific targets, like me, my family and Mrs. Moore. We have precautions for that, too. And we'll run it only for two weeks." " He whispers to her. 'That's it, right?' A vigorous nod.

"Stay out of it, is my advice." Holder bellows and walks forward until he meets Micky eye-to-eye. Then he turns out to the others. "Extra police? That's taking police away from somewhere else. And frighten everyone? We have police and informants looking. We have accomplices that we're interviewing. We'll nail this guy quick without any further agitation risking his revenge."

"Is that really true?" Wagner challenges. Holder narrows his eyes. His dislike is evident. The neighbors try to interpret an argument between two cops. "You said the same thing three week ago. Your best chance was the first forty-eight hours. Isn't that true?"

"It doesn't always work so neatly, as you know. —

"Aw, hell. I'm with you, Micky. They still haven't found the guy that burnt the Mennonite church, which could be this guy. Every day is another chance for him to kill." It's Mr. Williams.

Then in seconds, it's Saturday night at the Long Branch saloon. People stand and yell back and forth. Micky can't be heard over the sound. A pounding on the floor starts. It gets louder as it comes closer to him. Slowly, they all stop to look. Everyone is dead silent. Standing in the center aisle, commanding their attention is Electra Alexander, wasted down to nothing, and using a cane for balance. And now to pound the floor.

She looks at everyone, but points to Wagner. She starts to jab her finger in the air at him, repeatedly. Her voice is weak, but a whisper could be heard now. She turns to Wagner, pointing. "You. You no protect. You let him. You let him." Using her cane, she swivels toward Holder. "You do nothing. You protect police. No one else." Finally, she turns to Micky, imploring, "Find him, Micky. Please. Find the thing that hurt my Effie. Find THE THING!" Her voice strains to release her rage. He moves to her and gently takes her in his arms, saying nothing. No one speaks. No one is match for the mother of a dead child.

Voice croaking, Micky, finally says, "I'll tell WJLO it's a go."

CHAPTER 34

J oe Burke is the owner of Burke-O'Malley Realty, the realtor that Reverend Moore's letter to the Defender identified as the go-to place for blacks wanting to get a fair deal. O'Malley died some years back and Burke bought the business from the family.

It's evening and he sits by the office phone, as is common in the working day of a realtor. Customers often call late. He has to be available when their workday is finished. A space heater on the floor warms him but dries his skin. The feeling reminds him how his mother, in bitterly cold weather, would put a pot of water on the radiator to help the dry heat it produced. Did he ever think then that this is where he would end up? Did he think that this is the man he would become? He looks over at the Chicago Tribune which lays near him on the desk. An answer stares at him from the pages, the page announcing that Michael Mulvihill will appear on WJLO.

He hears the light crunching of the gravel surface coming from the tight 2-space parking behind his office. He listens for further sound, but there is nothing. *Should I look?* No car doors open. No running motor can be heard. He shouldn't just dismiss it, but he does.

The clock moves past eight. Another nothing day, but at least it's finished. He closes up the desk, grabs his jacket and proceeds to exit through the back. With bloodshot and dry eyes, his thoughts go to the next hour and what lies ahead for him. A dinner will be sitting on the stove in a pie-baking pan that's covered in tin foil. His wife will come and sit with him while he eats. He looks forward to it. Only them. The food is as much a sign of care as nourishment.

The alley light nearest his parking area isn't on. No matter; he can make his way, even in the dark. He plops down in the driver's seat. The muzzle of a gun touches high on the back of his head, followed by the cold, threatening command of the gunman. "Get out...slowly. " It immediately panics him.

He knows what this is; it's not a robbery. It's much worse. He does as he is instructed. Another gunman emerges from somewhere outside the car and points to the back-seat door. "In the back." *This is it. There's no escape, nothing that I can say.*

Joe Burke vomits as he enters the rear seat of his car. The first gunman, disgusted, clubs him unconscious. Then he is tied, gagged and thrown in the trunk. "T'row-up all you want in there, you fuckin' asshole. You believe this shit!" he exclaims, turning to his partner.

◆ ◆ ◆

Only lies need more time. Detective Wagner shows up at Burke-O'Malley Realty, as is his habit, without prior notice. He parks halfway down the block so that the first sight of him is when he's walk-ing in the door. His presence, as he steps into the office, immediately makes Joe Burke uncomfort-able.

"Mr. Burke," Wagner begins, without even a hello. He palms a badge toward his face. "A caller to the Central Standard Times, just before the mur-der of Effie Alexander, offered that he saw "Elijah" on the day of the march at Cicero and Lake. He further identified a white man with a 1958 green Ford Fairlane, which, of course matches the car that you own. "Also, as you know, this murder and the fire at the Garfield Baptist Church are, possibly tied to some real estate dealings as alleged by the late Reverend Charles Moore." He pulls his head back to lock eyes with Burke. "He stated that there was a dangerous collusion between an Austin realtor and black gangs. " Now he hits him with it. "That was the call that came from the Alexander home at the time that Effie Alexander was murdered. That caller was Lewis Leonard, the one who calls himself Eli-jah." Burke is practiced at deception, but not well enough, not when murder is mentioned. There's a tiny breech in his defense.

"Detective?"

"Detective Wagner. "

"Yes, well, won't you sit down." He's stalling to collect himself.

"Terrible thing, this murder. Poor child. I don't know what it's all coming to."

"It's coming to the car, right now, a car that matches yours, identified by Elijah. How do you explain that?" He doesn't wait for an answer. "Can you tell me where you were on the afternoon of June 30, between 3:00-5:00 pm?" The question is unimportant, but Wagner needs a place to start poking around.

"Let me look." Joe Burke thumbs nervously through the calendar in his organizer until he finds the date. "My last appointment was 2:00. I would have come back here to check messages, make calls, you know, work. "

"Sure. And where that last appointment?"

"Mr., uh, well, 942 Kilpatrick." He has a habit of not dropping names.

"Kilpatrick, and, basically, Augusta. Really, Cicero and Augusta. That's not far from where this car, the green Fairlane like yours, was reportedly sighted. Did you happen to go in that direction, a little out of your way, for something before coming back here? Anything you remember?"

"I don't think so. Look, I wasn't on Lake talking to any Elijah or Lewis Leonard." Wagner waits silently, just to make Burke nervous. And Burke is. "You just said the name. I remembered it. I've read it," he adds by way of explaining something that doesn't need explaining. They always add more.

"Good memory, " responds Wagner wanting to make sure to leave a hint of suspicious at remembering the name. Sometimes he would want to do the opposite, to leave someone relax, give them plenty of rope as it were. Now, he wants to force a mistake. "Did anyone see you here? Can someone confirm that you were here in the afternoon? " He looks dead at Burke. "Probably phone records," he says before Burke can answer, then adding, "Don't worry. I'll get that."

"I suppose. As you may know, despite the name, I'm the sole owner. On a Monday, late in the afternoon – I park in the back and come in that way. I don't know if Anne was here or not. It's not a busy day for us. We work more on weekends" He's talking too much.

Burke was not the outraged interviewee that maybe a totally innocent person would be. Now was the time to change it up. He spots an opportunity. "You look a little beat up. What happened?" That was the question Burke didn't want to hear. He had been telling people that he got jumped, but he never reported it, and he didn't think much about developing the details of a fake story. He could just say that he didn't want to talk about it, but not to a police detective investigating murder.

"I was jumped." Wagner takes in a breath ready to ask questions. "I didn't report it. Don't really want to get into it now, you know, as a crime. " Wagner sees this for exactly what it is, an excuse for not having details, for maybe having conflicting details. "Just put it behind me. Not sure I remember everything, anyway." Wagner doesn't pursue any one point to the end. Someone has a better chance of inventing when it's a single thread. He likes to bounce around.

"Mr. Burke, why was Reverend Moore calling you this past Spring, into May?" Wagner's question causes Burke's face to drop again with just the tiniest quiver.

"Reverend Moore, uh, well, I think that those were just general conversations. We're acquaintances. He was probably checking on me and how sales were going to blacks."

Wagner sees that Burke is not confident in his own answer. He's lying. "He didn't call other realtors." The question is implied.

"He, uh, trusted me. He probably didn't call Avenue 'cause that's a place he didn't trust, I guess.

I mean that's what he said, uh, what he wrote. Just going to get lies there. Maybe he thought that?" Burke is melting down. He clearly is in over his head.

"Where were you jumped?"

"Uh. Just out back, getting into my car."

"And was anything taken?

"My wallet. I tossed it at them, and they split. I'm lucky"

"They hit you over and over. And then you pulled out your wallet and tossed it at them? And then they split. Is that it?"

"Well, I tried to fight. Then I thought this isn't worth it."

"When was this?"

"Two nights ago."

"And you have a new wallet already?"

"Yes. They sell them at Olson Brothers, right over here." Wagner's question led him to lie on the spot."

"Can I see it?"

"Well, this is my old one. They dropped it, just took the money."

"You bought a new one, even though they dropped your old one." Burke's face goes blank.

Wagner lets him think it's over.

"Yes. Well, thank you, Mr. Burke. Hope you feel better soon with the face and all. " As he starts to leave, hoping the inevitable one more thing could crack Burke, he adds, "Probably, shouldn't tell you this, but if you know his name, you likely know that this Leonard guy is a few turns short of tight. What we found on him would freak a lot of people. Or it should, anyway. He torches building with people inside and he sadistically murders. We have recovered and identified the body of one Sammy Gallagher. The gentleman was an associate of our dear boy. He blowtorched his face...slowly. Like a cub scout firing up a marshmallow. Black on the outside. All soft and gooey on the inside." Burke looks sick. "We know that Elijah was the caller and that he called from Effie Alexander's home. And, having just committed horrible murder, he calmly drops a description that fits your car. This guy's way more than anyone bargained for. Maybe he just happened to pick your car 'cause he's seen it somewhere." He tugs on his tie to straighten it. "If you do think of something, learn something, call me. It might help capture him quicker and before he does whatever evil thing that he is planning next." Wagner feigns like he's leaving, but he stops and looks back. It's what he hoped for. Burke's face is the color of his drab-white walls. "Hey, Joe, s'matter? You look like you just saw the ghost of Jacob Marley."

Joe Burke, elbow on his desk raises his hand

palm open. It's a gesture like 'Enough' and like he's ready to speak. "Please sit down, Detective." He grazes his fingers across his brow thinking what he should say. "You're looking for a killer. I'm not a killer. There are other people who are also looking for that same killer. People who talk, well, with their hands. You know what I mean?" He looks at Wagner for help.

"Do you have something you want to say?"

"I want to see a killer found. I don't want to talk to people who talk with their hands. Like I said, I'm not part of this thing. So maybe I could give you my thoughts as a hypothetical. " Burke is offering information but wants immunity.

"Yes. I'm looking for a killer, " agrees Wagner. "I'm a homicide detective. If you want to express something, hypothetically, or otherwise, about a killer, this killer, I can listen. You're out of it until you're in it. I'm not here to audit your real estate practices, but you're familiar with the term "accessory before the fact"? " He waits for Burke's queasy acceptance that, while it's better for him to talk, there are no deals.

Burke begins carefully. "I don't think Avenue, or any other Austin realtor would be able to collude with any black gang members. A guy like Leslie Higgins, for example, he might know black leaders. I know them from the Chicago Freedom Movement. I mentioned that Reverend Moore and I are acquaintances. That's how we met, the Freedom Movement. Higgins or another realtor might not have a connection like that, like I do, with gangs, no, not likely. Those connections...you know, it's funny, Reverend Moore mentioned in his letter to the Daily News that he, himself, had those connections." Burke stopped. Wagner touched his nose lightly digesting this 'coincidence'.

"Why? Why would Moore collude with gangs to harass whites out of Austin? Where's the juice for him?"

"I'm sure I don't know, but anyone who helps make the juice has a right to drink it? Wagner looks at Burke. The smirk indicates he wants them to be smart, make a deal after all.

With a thud, both of his hands suddenly grab a hunk of Burke's shirt, lapel high. Wagner slams him to the floor and slaps him. Again. He places a hand around his throat, squeezing, Burke's voice is a gurgle. "What? What're you doing? "

Reaching to the back of his belt, under his jacket, he pulls a revolver and places it on Burke's forehead. "This is a Korean War sidearm, model M1917. It's not registered to me. We come across interesting pieces from time to time." He's mocking Burke's smirk. "You don't have me on an appointment calendar. You didn't tell anyone I was coming 'cause you didn't know. No one knows I was here. "
His face is that of a man whose guilt has prevented

a full night's sleep for a long time. A tiny whiff of his whiskey breath is evident when they're this close. Desperation. "You're going to tell me everything you know or I'm going to blow your goddamn brains all over the floor. The likely motive will be mob-related gambling debts."

Joe Burke's deal is over.

CHAPTER 35

"**M**ulvihill, " he barks. "Think you can take some time away from being a movie star to do some work?" Micky thinks that Jim Diamond really likes him but feels tradition requires Diamond to treat him badly.

"Yes. Sure. Of course. It's them. They—"

"Save it. Take a dime from the coffee money and call someone who gives a crap." Micky just waits for him to continue, leaving the point alone.

"Jackey 'The Lackey' Cerone is, more or less, the head of the Chicago Outfit; more, because Tony Accardo is semi-retired and less because, Accardo is still Joe Batters, Big Tuna, the guy who expanded the Outfit into Las Vegas and is so damn smart he has never spent a single night in jail. And, as long as he's breathing, any new guy will be less. Follow Cerone. Get all the details. It's legwork. You remember that, don't you? Here's a file. " He opens a drawer to a file cabinet and lifts an empty manila folder with 'Jackie Cerone' written on the tab. "Fill it. Don't wait until it's all done. Fill it as you get it. "

"I'm all over it." It's a good excuse to get away from the office buzzards who want to pick at his carcass over WJLO, the search for Elijah, and any opportunities at the Daily News. It's more than getting information, too. He's the rising star. Some found a new desire to be nice to him.

"Wait." Micky stops and turns back. "Honestly, where are you intending on starting?"

"I didn't know. I thought I'd develop some leads."

"Chrissake! Have we met? Have you been here for —what! — a year! Do you take my calls with people asking for me as the expert on the Outfit? "

"Yeah, but you asked me. So, I guess I thought you didn't, you know, know."

"I'M where you develop the leads. Take this. Just take this. It's names and numbers of some cops that have files on him themselves. Tell them that you work for me. Well, if they don't already know, obviously. And ask them what they've got. Then let me know who told you what so that I can provide the customary compensation. To THEM. You're on the payroll." He never lets Micky forget how it is. And the implication is that, if he doesn't like it, lump it. He can always find another legman. But he can't. *Not like me.* "And, don't come back with their information only. I can get that from them directly. Follow him. What's happening NOW? NE-OW!"

"Right." He takes the paper.

◆ ◆ ◆

He had to hand-write the information from the police. They won't let him make a Xerox. He's not a steno. He's not good at anything quickly hand-written. His notes look like they were written by a blind man with mittens on. He hopes that he remembers what the hieroglyphics mean later. He has Cerone's home address and follow him from there in the morning.

Micky has been all over the West Side, Elmwood Park and River Forest, which is where Accardo lives. He hangs around. He follows. He takes pictures. He stays far enough back to avoid confrontation, but he's been spotted, and he knows it. When they want to be left alone, they look at him and throw out a thumb in a take-a-hike motion. He obliges.

Cerone is now at Horwath's restaurant on Harlem Avenue, just across the Chicago border into Elmwood Park. Both the restaurant and the suburb are favorite Outfit haunts. A few mid-level guys are having lunch with him, including one of the captains, Joe "Joe Gags" Gagliano. After they enter, Micky has a little time. He hustles over to Sears two blocks away, uses a pay phone that's near the store entrance from the parking lot side. He calls into the paper. K-9 has left a message: "Important. Call me.

Realtors". He's left his gym number.

Micky waits on the phone for ten minutes, while K-9 is summoned. He hears the pounding of gloves, the whip of jump ropes and the snort of boxers as they punch. He catches some in-your-face coaching to the boxers who are training. Much of it is yelling to work harder or throw a certain punch or combination mixed with encouragement. Mick can box some. The Marines had some 'smokers' bouts where he tested himself. He put everything into it, but he's never professionally trained to box. As he's wondering if he could and how they must work, specifically, to attack one fighter's style, his thoughts are jarred.

"Mick?!" K-9 exclaims. There's an exasperation in his voice. His waiting for a return call has been like Micky is late for Christmas dinner.

"Yeah. I'm on the job. What's up?" Trying to explain to the perception.

"Joe Burke. He's up. Well, now. He was down for a bit." Micky knows that almost anything can send K-9 on a tangent, searching for the joke. "And something went down, and it might have something to do with the whole Elijah and Moore thing."

"Spill, man."

"Okay. Burke got rousted by a couple of guys who may have been working for Joe Gags. He's a…"

"Yeah, I know, a loan shark." *And he's two blocks away eating at Horwath's*

"Right. So, that would imply that Burke owes the worst people to owe. Loan shark guys will cut your eye out and eat it like a grape in front of your mother. When we were kids, like 14 or 15, there was a guy, Action Jackson. Well, William was his real name, but outside of his mother, probably everybody called him Action. Cops found him naked hanging on a meat hook that was stuck up his ass. His kneecaps were smashed. They used an electric cattle prod on his dick. They...wait...wait – he was the collector, but he got whacked – technically, tortured. They left him alive. He hung there for like 3 days. That must have been nice. Reflect a bit, you know. You know, a Catholic can do his own confession like, if you're gonna die. I suppose anyone can, but Catholics know about it, and maybe everyone else doesn't? See the advantage? – Anyway, they tortured him because they thought he snitched. That's different. Okay. Cranial sorbet and we get back on track. De Stefano, Sam "Mad-man" De Stefano, he hopes you don't pay. He wants to torture you. His letter every year to Santa asks please let people..."

"I get it. I get it. They tortured Burke. And?"

"And that's the thing. They didn't really torture him. Burke still has both eyes. He's not behind. Can't be. It's strange. They must have wanted something. He gave it to them."

"What did he give them?"

"They only want two things, money and information. As we surmise, it wasn't money. What might this realtor know that they would want? Elijah. Burke is the guy that Moore identifies, the guy all the blacks should use to buy their home."

"They don't know that. "

"You're kidding, right? They know that. Knowing things is job one. Are you listening when we're talking? I've been talking about this stuff for years. If you're not listening, I'd like some compensation. Find me some years."

"K-9, I'm on the job. Let's negotiate later."

"So, let it be written. So, let it be done." *Lord, almighty. What I put up with...*

"What makes you think that they want Elijah? And what does that mean to you?"

"Well, you do, for one. They didn't give you a ride because of your curly blond hair, right. Certain people, remember, are embarrassed. Get me?"

"Okay. Good enough. They want information on Elijah, and they ask Burke. "

"Well, not quite ask. They smacked him around, but just to get his attention. Works wonders. Anyway, what if Avenue isn't the biggest snake? What if Burke forces or tricks Moore to get him on his side? Or something?"

"Yeah. Good, I think. No, not really. Go over it again, slowly, su-low-ly and without the many colorful examples." Micky guesses that if your business is having people throw punches at your head and stomach who are perhaps better at head-beating and gut-pounding than you are, you might be a little excited during those moments. Then, add to that the fact that you have something you think is really important. He needs to settle K-9 down.

"Joe Burke got a slight beating—"

"Okay but wait. First. Deep breath. More rhythmic." K-9 follows, literally.

"The neighborhood has a killer loose. Mob guys keep their neighborhood clean, except for what they do. When something goes down, they will squeeze somebody that they think knows something. Joe Burke got squeezed. He knew something, and he's the flip side of this realtor collusion thing. It's them. Him. Burke."

"Okay. Got it that time. Talk to you later." It's coming together.

He dashes back to Horwath's. They're still inside. He mulls over the details. Avenue. Why did Moore finger Avenue? He ponders the reasons, when he spots a recognizable car turning in off Harlem and swinging sharply dead center into a spot. It's a Cutlass Town Sedan, brand new and blue. Nassau

Blue. *Yes. It's definitely coming together.*

CHAPTER 36

Olivia, somewhat settled in her new apartment, is a ball of nerves in anticipation of meeting with Micky and the others. She'll have to tell them what she's learned. Everyone, eventually, will know that Charles developed a plan that backfired. The thought of the damage to his reputation hurts her. And what, she wonders, this will do to the reputation of any other Civil Rights minister, or the movement in general. How much damage will this cause?

At some point the news about the discrepancy in church funds will become public. On top of the horror, now it's a scandal and soon will be a national joke. *Our whole world is disintegrating. If it weren't for this one curse; racism. What do they say in Alabama? Curses, like chickens always come home to roost.*

The bell rings. She inquires, guessing who's there before opening the door, "Hello, Harrison?" Right she is. Harrison Kellum has changed though, literally. He's not wearing a suit. It jolts her speechless.

"May I come in?" He smiles, knowingly, at her surprised look. "It's just a sweater."

"Of course. I've just never...I'm sorry. Please come in."

"A cobalt blue ribbed Irish Fisherman's sweater, to be exact." *Of course.* They laugh together. "And yes, jeans. They're Italian. Very good quality. But it's all comfortable." He looks great, but it will take some getting used to.

A knock instead of a ring must be Micky. It is. "Nice place. And very convenient." He refers to the apartment being so close to her gallery. She thanks him. Micky, walking past her, is stopped in his tracks at the sight of Harrison as well.

"I do own clothes other than pin-stripe suits." He gives an expression of mock indignation. Micky catches it, as does K-9.

Wagner rings the bell. He only says hello. His clothing is unchanged, not unchanged in style, just unchanged. And not cleaned. Nor are his shoes shined. Nor is his hair washed. He settles into one of her living room chairs. The kitchen here is too small for all of them.

Harrison, sitting next to Olivia after they've all found a spot, opens with a question to Olivia. "If you don't mind, I'll start with what I've found. I think it's important." She doesn't mind. "The letter that was sent to the Defender with Charles signature is, quite possibly, well, likely, almost certainly, a fake. You mentioned, and we had noted before, that it was a Xerox. Why was that? We didn't wonder at the time? We noticed, and of course, it was odd, but all this had not happened." He adds a shrug to suggest that there was no need to further think about it.

Olivia is shocked and concerned, along with the others, except Wagner, who takes the information in calmly. She sees his lack of expression. "You knew about this, Detective?" she asks. She leans back a fraction, getting a better view of him.

"Yes. Well, I've learned some things since we last spoke. The letter is a fake. Joe Burke, owner of the Burke-O'Malley Realty, did it." He rubs his brow, appearing very tired. He's completely depleted. He continues to talk, with his hand on his forehead. "It was never Avenue Realty. This whole time it was Burke-O'Malley. Joe Burke and Moore..." He stops to correct himself. "Reverend Moore. They knew each other from the Freedom thing with King a few years back. It was about tenant agreements. Lawyers and realtors, you know, in legal stuff about renting." In his exhaustion, he's forgotten that neither Olivia nor any of them need the Chicago Freedom Movement explained at this point. Wagner realizes this now. "Anyway, Burke tells it that...Charles...Reverend Moore, comes to him. With Avenue having, say, a cloud over their head, placed there by the Reverend, Burke-O'Malley is going to be the main beneficiary. Charles will get a cut." His cop way of spitting out the facts hit her like punches.

"And then why fake the letter?" Her voice is too high, but she's not going to lose control, not in front of these men.

"Well, Charles, " he doesn't bother to correct this time, " thought word of mouth and that fact that Burke-O'Malley is the main other realtor, it'll work. Maybe, too he thinks a letter like that is a little obvious, in addition to being unnecessary. He wants to play his minister role straight and stay above suspicious. Ya know? —"

"Detective Wagner, " interrupts Kellum sternly. "Please be aware that you are speaking of Mrs. Moore's husband when you explain, and refrain from the sarcastic characterizations." Wagner looks at Olivia. He snaps out of it.

"Sorry, Mrs. Moore. I'm very tired. I've not had more than an hour or two of sleep in any night in weeks. I...just." She tells him that she understands and asks him to continue.

"Well...Burke...he wants insurance. He is under pressure 'cause he's into Joe Gags. One, he can't be late. There's no late with Gags. Two, and the main reason is, it's a windfall. He doesn't want to lose it. He's a...never mind." He refrains from another characterization, even of Burke.

K-9 look at Wagner. "I'll go, " explains K-9 to save time. "Joe Gagliano, aka, Joe Gags, is a loan shark. Joe Burke is a gambler, on sports. He doesn't win—"

"Super Bowl III." Wagner has the detail.

K-9 and Micky start falling over. Harrison is shocked, but in control. "What?" demands Olivia.

"Colts are like two touchdown favorites—" K-9 tells her, not helping much.

"Eighteen points to be exact."

"Detective, " K-9 nods, acknowledging the exact number. "Eighteen it is. Colts didn't even score eighteen. They had seven. Burke must have gone deep into Joe Gags pocket to get the money to bet, and he lost. " He looks back to Wagner.

"Twenty large." Wagner has everything. "Twenty thousand dollars." He clarifies at the question in her face.

K-9 whistles. Olivia is tracking, just barely. This is the big football game. Burke lost a bet. Borrowed money. Owes a gangster. "Okay. The letter?"

"He takes the letter that Reverend Moore has. He has a copy. He Xeroxes the letterhead and the signature onto his own letter using a few details that he had from Moore during their planning on the public relations campaign." Olivia is replaying his words. It makes sense. Burke is adding his own touches, unknown to Charles.

"There are very faint trace lines that can be seen, under a microscope, lines from the edge of the paper and what was likely multiple copies." Harrison Keller explains.

"Microscope?" Olivia asks, but they're all surprised.

"The Defender deals in a great many documents of historical importance in the development and printing of our news. Authenticity is critical. Yes. Microscope."

Silence follows Harrison's last words. She looks over at him. He's the only other person in the room who knew Charles Moore. Isn't he shocked, her eyes ask? Maybe, but more than that, his eyes say he's sorry for her sake.

"I've learned some things, too, that corroborate what Detective Wagner is saying. Charles, for instance, kept the phone number of Burke-O'Malley Realty in his planning notes, but not Avenue's. " Wagner nods, but doesn't offer that he's seen the phone records. "These notes imply a plan to use the march and other..." It's hard to say. "harassments. There are dates and an order. They imply that he had knowledge of the march before it happened. " *Please don't let me fall apart, until they're gone.* "He might have taken some money from the church." Like a hammer, it hits. Harrison leans toward her then stops himself. It's not his place to offer comfort. And she's not asking. "This might make sense regarding a need to pay Elijah and anyone else involved, especially if Mr. Burke was strapped. " She waits. She has to say one more thing. "Motive. As I said at our last meeting. It starts there. I believe that he wanted to use the whole thing, including the fire, to place himself into national prominence so that he could truly resurrect the Civil Rights movement and continue as its leader. He was frustrated with the stalemate at the SCLC. He was frustrated with the city and thought likely they will just assassinate the gang leaders, only to leave others take their place. It's won't solve the problem, he thought. The money...I think the money from the expected windfall...was secondary, and just something he wanted to provide for me. He didn't do it for himself." She protects him. *He did it because he loved me.*

The air is thick and silent. No one knows what to say to her. Micky can't let it go. "Everything I've seen, that I know about Charles Moore says standup guy. He gave his life for others, for black people. The one thing powerful enough to make him want money would...be...you." She looks to see if he's just being kind. She sees that he means every word of it. She's grateful.

"Olivia, I've said before that Charles and I knew each other a long time. Nothing inspired him more than you. You opened possibilities to him. When he spoke of you, his soul was on fire. You showed him grace and elegance driven by a pure heart." With a tremendous strength she holds herself silent. *I will be that for you, Charles, even now.*

Quickly, they turn to the next step, the important thing. Find this killer!

CHAPTER 37

T his killer needs to be either brought to justice or to have justice brought to him. Micky prefers the latter. He's way ahead on the Cerone study. Diamond has it in his files. No questions on it yet. He hasn't written a column in a long time. He won't write this week either.

They've agreed to meet at Micky's CST office. A thick file from the police department, courtesy of Detective Wagner, lays bound with large rubber bands on Micky's desk at CST. Two more Xerox copies lay on top. Three chairs surround have been positioned to accommodate the team. He's only expecting two, but Wagner, who lives this chase to the point of obsession, might show after all. He lowered the black blinds that cover the two storefront windows. Pencils, paper and a cork board for posting are all stationed or within reach. A pot of water stands ready to percolate its way into Folger's coffee. He's set. In pops Mary Lee.

Greek lighting, " she says. Her photos drop in front of him with a light slapping sound. He's been expecting these, but not looking forward to it. The

Greek-owned Austin Delight restaurant was burned badly and beyond repair yesterday. No one was hurt because they were closed. They never close, but they did yesterday. Open 24 hours a day every day of the year, except yesterday. And that's when they had a fire. A Greek-owned restaurant is a cliché, but the real cliché is, Greek or not, this happens to restaurants that are in neighborhoods which are 'changing', like Austin. There's insurance. It's all turns out great, a fortunate misfortune. They never reopen at the same location or anywhere nearby. Austin Delight is the third area restaurant in the last year to have a fire when it was closed. No one was hurt in any of them.

He looks the photos over and picks two to run in the next edition of the Central Standard Times. One shows the fire trucks blocking the streets in front of the restaurant, hoses spaghetti strung across all sides of the building and the whole intersection soaking wet. The other prominently shows the owner, William Pistorius, face scrunched behind thick glasses and below curly salt and pepper hair, despairingly surveying the damage. Everyone will want to look closely at his face for telltale signs of acting because everyone knows this was arson, signed sealed and delivered per contract. The policies are built to be an exit strategy.

"John and I are going to move," Mary announces uncomfortably. It feels a bit like desertion, but it has to be. They've been close to making this decision, anyway. Maybe this fire was a nudge? She and her husband expect to start a family soon. Austin isn't the safe bet. "I can still work here. We're looking at the North side, Northwest, around Cumberland and Diversey or maybe Central and Bryn Mawr." A handful of miles gets you to the new world. He wants to show her it's okay.

"I understand, Mary. So glad you can still be here. Who knows? Maybe you'll be close to the new Northwest Delight? " She smiles at him, understanding the implication. Austin Delight will never reopen here. It's ending. This neighborhood is on its last legs. "I'll see you tomorrow."

"Need anything? Want me to stay?"

"Tomorrow, I'll want you to photograph some of the work we do tonight. We'll be changing things. I need a record." He leaves out 'but that's all', protective of her feelings. She answers him and heads out.

Micky walks outside to stand in front of his office. Trees herald the favorite time of the year, autumn. It's particularly appealing in the waning afternoon light. He spots K-9, hands in pockets, long sleeves, but without a jacket walking his way. They move inside. K-9 offers a simple greeting, leaves the jokes aside, and selects the chair he wants. He tilts his chair back, puts his feet onto the edge of the desk, and places a copy of the file on his lap, leaving it unopened. The sound of a car parking brings

Micky back to the door. Olivia cranks up her windows and reaches out to all doors to push down the locks on her 1965 Ford Fairlane. Curious mostly, he spies both ways to see who takes notice of her. Who follows her with their eyes? No one takes a second glance.

"I briefly looked at this file." Micky passes a copy to Olivia before her coat is off and opens his original. "Here's what I like. One, the Jobs Two, the Schools. Three, any friends, including those from prison. These are connections for him. We sort everything we have into those piles.

"That's good. I'd like to add a fourth, theories. You know, like left town, didn't leave town. For didn't leave town, we have all those possibilities you mentioned. For left town, it's a matter of where he could slip in and how we get notice to them.

"Sounds good." It really doesn't. There's only here, in the city. " Remember, it doesn't have to be pretty. We'll just use as many ideas as we like and, either move, eliminate or combine them until we're settled." Micky, anxious not to stumble or get bogged down in too much organizing, is glad that this doesn't bother either of them.

"We need photos, too, to add to what we picture." K-9 chips in.

"Wait. There's a file in here on the mother, Mikala Leonard." K-9 looks to Micky for an explanation.

"Yeah. I saw that. Wagner put this together. A police department profile, especially when they are looking for someone, is more than a rap sheet. The mother's life may include contacts or places —something, that Elijah would visit. The mother's been examined under accusations of abuse. A lot of the report are her stories of her own life and some notes from the psych evaluations. Some of it, though, goes all the way back to her childhood."

Five minutes into the reading, Olivia bursts. "It corroborates what we thought. It's the grand-father, Elmer Washington. He so hated the Lewis' mother that her life became toxic." She uses his birth name. "Abuse. Humiliation. He tried to get her to take her own life." She stares at each of them in outrage, as if to say, 'can you imagine!'. He called her the filth. She had nightmares about being filthy. She stuttered for some period. Bed-wetting. Her clothes were ragged. There is another comment in here that a teacher told her she looked 'repulsive'." Micky expected that this might be her response. He's trying not to allow himself to be sympathetic, even if he'd like to jack this guy up. *Repulsive? Who says that to a kid?*

"We're looking for a killer, a brutal and sadistic killer. We can't solve the history. We need to stay on that aspect."

"What about the mother, the grandmother,

Irene? Couldn't she help?" K-9 asks, looking to provide Elijah an out, and not leaving the history.

"Help keep Mikala flying straight? Not enough to tell, at least yet. I suspect he threatened her with being tossed out. A woman in the 1920s as victim of a rape by a white man would not stand much chance. I think she was a homemaker all the way. She would have no job and nothing. Maybe she stayed and tried to make it right. She couldn't." Olivia defends the Irene Washington.

"Let's look for the clues to get to Elijah." Micky moves them back to the point. They accept his soft direction.

Over the next two hours, with each of them reading their own copies and noting details to capture, a gruesome picture of a child's life emerged. The corkboard is pasted with dozens of scribbled notes. It makes sense to them, only them.

"What do we have that we can act on?" Micky asks trying to summarize.

"Not much." K-9 looks to Olivia to see if she has something.

"I start with the reward money? Mrs. Murray wouldn't take any, even though she earned it. She asked that it be given to Electra Alexander who kicked it right back into the fund —he's not found —which is now a cool eight-grand. That will get the attention of some eager Sherlocks, I should imagine

—"

"Right. A new car, like, say, a Cutlass," K-9 shoots a glance to Micky, " is like $3,500. You can well get into your own home for eight-grand." K-9 is current on the value of money.

"Okay. I will emphasize what we know. A killer, gang member, alleged arsonist and career criminal. I drop the names of the goons that jumped me. I hit the reward and the place to send the information. WJLO is setting up and staffing a hotline." They're all glad it's not the paper.

"That's reasonable for the broadcast," K-9 answers. Olivia shakes her head in agreement.

"Next, I trace the jobs, going backwards, starting with the Sears warehouse. I'm sure those guys will say he was a loner and kind of nuts, and we left him alone. But what if we trace the job app back to other places he worked, maybe we find someone who would hide him."

"Micky, I'd like to go back to Richie. His people don't necessarily watch the news or talk to cops. The 8 thou is quite a deal for them, too." Before he can say that he agrees, the doorbell rings, and they all jump halfway out of their skin. No one ever rings that bell. Micky thinks to reach for his gun but settles himself. Surprise attacks don't ring the doorbell.

It's Wagner.

"Gentlemen. Ma'am. Anything?" Micky is close to him. He didn't shave. Mouthwash tries to cover a whiskey breath.

Micky answers. "We're going to leave the out-of-town option to you, the police. Also, talking to the other goons, probably, is better with you." He looks at the others. They didn't actually discuss this. We can talk with the C-Notes." An idea enters Micky's head, but he waits. "And we'd like to look at the job application for Sears to see what previous jobs he put down. It might be more likely that who-ever is hiding him—we think that's the top option — is someone he met early on 'cause he's been too dangerous to be friends with for a long time, and the gangs cut him loose." Wagner starts to respond, but is cut off

"Plus, he's too hot to handle. Hiding him is ac-cessory to murder. Not to mention the Olds and the down payment." K-9 adds another reason and feels good about his obscure reference.

"Right, " starts Wagner, obviously ready to say more and wise enough now to leave K-9 to his own ways. He looks at the board and sees the three theories on where Lewis Leonard is. His eyes look to the floor. "Samuel Gallagher. He was an associate of Lewis Leonard's. A smattering of blood found on the chair in the basement, Lewis Leonard's basement. His blood type matched the blood on the chair. His fingerprints are in many places in that room. With

Leonard's identify known, the 'goons' as you call them." He nods to Micky. "They sung for crumbs. They gave us leads for an agreement not to be accessories and we found the body, brutally assaulted before death occurred." He thinks of Burke's face when he told him the condition of that body but doesn't add it here.

"Detective?" Olivia has a question. "The family. We've seen the information you included in the report. Horrifying. Don't you think that there might be some connections that they could suggest, with a second round of talks? And what about Detective Holder? Anything from his end?

"The last one, first. Holder is using a method you might call 'squeeze the tube from bottom up'. He's rousting up gang members, putting them in jail for small stuff, and trying to get leads to the next guy. His focus is the gangs. They've seen this method and he's running all over town with no results. Regarding Mrs. Leonard and Mrs. Washington..." He stops carefully thinking about his next words. He doesn't want to tell them that he has revisited them. They talk of Lewis. There are names. Mostly, though, he's trying to find a way back for the two of them now that Elmer is dead and gone.

He smiles, offering these last words before heading off. "Irene makes good soup."

CHAPTER 38

Micky drives to WJLO studio for his television appearance. The mid-day traffic is light making the increased presence of the blue and whites circling seem near parade level in and around the area of Austin. The sight makes everyone more nervous. They're all taking extra precautions. Some stay away, just the other side of town even. Doors and windows are checked. Those that haven't been locked in a long time are nailed shut. As twilight approaches, the streets become empty and quiet. Stores close early.

Station WJLO has told him that they'll put him on live at 4:30. They'll re-run piece at 6:30. The 10:-00 won't cover it. He wears a dark blue suit. It's the only one he has, but unless you've been to a funeral or wedding with him, you haven't seen him wear it. He was instructed to wear a light blue shirt. It'll look white on television they told him. Pure white often strobes on camera. He's been in the green room for television many times, but he's never been in front of the cameras.

They fuss over his hair and dab makeup on his

face, apologizing for doing so, telling him it's just to reduce shine. The microphone is last. There's a quick check, after it's routed from his tie, which he bought just for this. The two ties he owned made him look like he came to take a picture for the school chess club. None of it means much to him. What he keeps thinking is that Elijah will be watching.

Joel Albertson looks straight ahead and reads the copy. Micky can see the words himself, making it all seem very fake.

"And with our first edition regarding the fugitive calling himself Elijah, who is wanted for questioning in the murder of Effie Alexander, we go to John Wolford. "

"Thank you, Joel. Good afternoon, everyone. " He drops his voice for effect. "The murderer of Effie Alexander remains free." Micky thinks that they try to say murder as often as possible. It makes him a bit nauseous. "The police continue to chase leads, but, so far, to no avail. WJLO has established its own hotline to track tips and we're here with reporter and publisher, Micky Mulvihill, who has been leading the non-police effort to capture this killer since the beginning. "Micky, thank you for being here. I know how this story is personal for you. Can you remind the folks, as this is our first time with this feature, just how you became involve and how you knew Effie Alexander?"

The camera swivels at him and the red light comes on. He stares directly at it, momentarily, forgetting that people are watching him through this large black and chrome camera. "Yes. Thank you, John. The Alexander family are friends. They first contacted me after an intimidation march by black youths on the sidewalk in front of their home. It was from that march that Effie Alexander was able to identify Elijah. I also received information from Reverend Moore through my job at the Daily News about the march alleging a dangerous collusion." Micky can tell that Woolford doesn't seem to like the name-dropping of another news agency. *Too bad.*

"What's the latest and what do you want to ask people to do?"

"The latest is that police are working through the streets, trying to get informant information, and Central Standard Times is checking Lewis Leonard's work history, backtracking through all of his applications to find a contact that might be hiding him. There are also several neighborhood organizations that are keeping a vigilance." He doesn't say that the C-Notes gang and the Chicago Outfit are who he means.

"What, exactly, can people do to be vigilant"

"Someone is hiding him, or he's taken their home. What's not right? Who's missing? Individuals and stores, particularly grocery stores or restaurants. He's got to eat. Is somebody buying food that's very different? Now, please don't overreact. You have to use common sense to what is really different. "

"And there's a reward? Where is that at now?"

"Yes, there is an eight-thousand-dollar reward for information leading to the capture of Lewis Leonard."

John Wolford announces the hotline number that WJLO has established. He's offered anonymity and mentions that some people may be more comfortable talking with the media than the police. He turns it back to Joel Albertson. They're free.

"You did great. Let me show you our hotline setup."

The premises are only a handful of years old. It's much different than the ancient Daily News offices. They work their way through narrow hallways to a small room with a bank of phones. Only two are staffed.

"The phone numbers were established for this effort, specifically. All 4 lines hit both of these phones. We'll add people if the call volume gets high. Look. Something's coming in already." He watches as the two staff both get calls. They answer each line as soon as it blinks.

"Mr. Mulvihill?" It's one of the two staff holding a phone out toward him. "It's for you. I guess he wants to speak directly with the star." He smiles. Micky, tepidly, walks over and takes the receiver in his hand placing it to his ear, clearing his throat a little.

"This is Micky Mulvihill. To whom am I speaking?"

"Did you go to Cicero and Lake to look for Elijah like I told you? Did you follow up on '58 green Ford Fairlane? —Don't let anyone know or there'll be another death on your hands."

It's HIM! "Uh, yes, that's right an eight-thousand-dollar reward if the information leads to his capture." He covers the phone and pretends it's someone else, "I think they just want to talk. Not sure they have an actual tip." Wolford smiles. It's just a general caller, not important. He leaves him be and signals that he has to go. Micky nods okay.

"What do you want to tell me?" The phone staff are barely paying attention.

"You are part of the rapin' white boy that made the woman that gave life to me. God gave her a son and directed my life to come to this moment to atone for that sin. It wasn't coincidence that you were in the church, and that your name was brought forth. God killed Reverend Moore because he was false. The fire was set to start in the evening. God pulled you there and took control. It was my destiny. Now it's going to be yours. " Micky's heart accelerates. He steadies his emotions moving from angry to deadly.

"Yes. Terrible. And the little Alexander. Whatever the message from this creep was, that must have been an oversight, a tragic and disgusting oversight."

"Effie? Oh, no. I thought about that and it was perfect. You used her to attack me, God's messenger, but you couldn't protect her, not from Him. I am guided." His laugh sends a

"I understand. That's very sensitive, over the phone and all. Would you like to meet me somewhere in person?"

"Tomorrow night at 7:00 sharp. Come alone. Northwest Incinerator. I have a sacrifice. If you tell anyone, the sacrifice is dead. Just you and me, and our Gods. Park on Chicago Avenue and walk to the front. The gate will be open. If you're not there on time, she'll be sacrificed." *We have your phones tapped, at home and at work. Not here, though.*

"Sure. That's fine. I'd be happy to do that, actually. I'd like to meet you as well and hear all about it. " He turns to the staffers, covers the phone and says, "Wants to tell me about his personal experiences as part of a neighborhood patrol." He rolls his eyes. They quietly laugh.

Micky hangs the phone up. "Let me write the

call down for you, though, just like all the rest." He proceeds to document a fictitious caller using Kathleen Noonan's name and address.

He goes through the options, which seem to number only one. The police would cost someone their life, even Wagner would. He can't risk going against the instructions. What is the sacrifice, he wonders, or rather who?

CHAPTER 39

"What the hell is this?" Tony Pagnini explodes easily. That's the way he's kept Lexington Grocers in business for thirty years. Or so he thinks. No one that he works with actually gets too excited about his routine outbursts, but they do respond. He's the boss. So is his brother Angelo, who is calmer, but no less firm, when it comes to business.

"What's the matter?" Angelo asks, poking his head around a corner in the back room where two twelve-inch board are fastened together and bracketed to the wall to make the desk for their office. A two-drawer cabinet sits underneath, and a telephone sits on top. Together that's the office. He's completing the ledger with the monthly revenues

"The kid? Bruno. Is he working? Tony answers not explaining.

Angelo thinks about playing twenty questions with his brother to see what's wrong and decides against it. "I'll cover the register and send Eileen back." Eileen Sullivan is the head cashier. She also manages the delivery boys, of which Bruno is one. Tony's grunt means 'good enough'. He stays un-happy until things are perfect, as a general rule.

Less than two minutes later, Eileen comes in, shoulder-length dark red hair coiffed in a flip and bouncing, she wears her most optimistic and help-ful expression to greet him. In her heart, she thinks that whatever is the problem, it likely could be handled without making it a yelling emergency.

Tony shoves a signed receipt for delivery of groceries in her face. "What's that? Do you know? Do you look at these receipts before you give them to me? I can't have Bozo the Clown signing them, you know."

Eileen braces herself and then looks at the sig-nature. Tony's asking her if she thinks that's funny. She's reading it over and trying to understand. The name at the top is scribbled. She grabs the box of index cards and looks to confirm using the account number. Tony's still blistering her on due diligence and the importance of accurate bookkeeping. The look on her face turns serious, slowing him up. "What is it?"

"I think this is a message asking for help."

◆ ◆ ◆

The flash of blue lights alerts him, crouching low in her back seat. He dares a peak and sees a police patrol car heading toward Gladys Johnson's home. A second one speeds by. Staying close behind her, Lewis Leonard whispers into her neck. "Slow down." Sirens blare increasingly and from all directions. "What did you do?"

"Nothing. They must have figured it out. I didn't do anything. " They're not at home. They went out to cash her pension checks, make a deposit in her checking account and mail out payment checks as she always does. She doesn't know how he'll react to this.

He directs her where to drive. She fears that she is driving to her grave. The parking lot for Brach's Candy is only one third full, and not guarded. He instructs her to park on the nearby side-street, close to the tracks. He rips part of her dress as she shivers in fears. Her breathing remains heavy as he ties her hands behind her back and covers her mouth. One more shredding of her slip and he has enough to tie her feet. With a Phillips screwdriver and a hammer, he punches a few holes in the trunk. "Don't make a sound for an hour, and you'll live. If I hear you before that, you won't. " He doesn't look at her. He knows that she'll obey. She's demoralized and will accept any opportunity to escape him. The trunk closes like the lid on a coffin. Trembling, she tries to count off the time.

I have been spared yet again. Divine providence guided me out of the house today. Their attempt to capture me is defeated. It's time.

CHAPTER 40

Addie Mae sits quietly looking out the picture window in the living room of her parents' Washington Boulevard brownstone home. Her half-day of school ended some hours ago. Garfield Goose and Friends is on the television. She notices the crown that Garfield wears as King of the United States. It is off to one side and very near his right eye. She hopes that it doesn't slip further. It might hurt him.

Addie Mae has had her right eye surgically removed. She wears a patch. Soon she will be fitted for a prosthesis, a glass eye. She needs to be completely healed though. Almost there. It won't be long, just a couple more months. She doesn't really understand that she won't be able to see out of the glass eye, even though it's been explained. She has a bigger problem, anyway.

The black patch that she must wear to cover the hole where her eye once was makes her look like a pirate. They're thieves and not very nice at all. She doesn't want to look like one of them. Are there any angels who wear eye patches she asked her mother once looking for a better model? Probably, her mother, Carolyn, had answered. It would have to be, she added. In fact, I bet it's quite common. That was the right thing to say, but Addie Mae doesn't see any, in pictures or on television. Carolyn and her daddy, Womack, who goes by "Mack", never leave her alone. Mack will soon be home and today, they have a surprise for her.

◆ ◆ ◆

"Addie Mae, come into the kitchen please, " shouts her father after he assures Carolyn that he has it, the surprise. They are very hopeful that this will work and that it will make Addie Mae feel much better. She never sees their pain. They have put it aside to be happy in front of her to help her with this trauma. She couldn't know what that takes. Treat her normally. Have her do all the things that she was doing, including all her chores. Don't ignore it, though. Talk about it from time to time, but not too much. It was like walking on egg shells, but they would walk on 6-inch spikes, on large spears, if it helped.

Addie Mae is their only child. Mrs. Wesley does not easily bear children. There have been many miscarriages. But they made it. They have her. God blessed them with her.

"Hi, sugar. We've got something for you. I think you might like it, " says Mack, his voice generates a little enthusiasm for her. He brings out a brown paper bag that he was holding behind his back. Then he reaches in and pulls something out but doesn't show it to her.

"What is it, " she asks, curious, and showing, at least, a glimmer of hope?

"Look! " Dad opens his palms and cupped inside is a pink eye patch, made of soft felt, with a white bunny rabbit stitched on it. The rabbit has one beaded eye, like Garfield Goose. "We talked to the ladies at church, the sewing ladies. They were very happy to make, not only this, but many others for you. He empties the paper bag and out pours an array of patches with animals and cartoon characters, and hearts and flowers, too.

Addie's eyes grow big and she touches them. "All of them are for me, " she asks innocently? She can't see that the question breaks her parents' heart — who else? — and they don't show it.

"Yes, and any other special ones, if you want them." After asking if she could try them on, Addie Mae carefully removed her black patch. Mom and dad kept beaming encouragement even as they looked at their precious daughter's empty eye socket. Addie Mae slips on the pink one with the bunny. It wasn't necessarily her favorite, but it seemed to her she was supposed to wear that first. She looked up at her parents for their reaction, hopeful, but a little unsure.

"Oh, that is so darling. It's amazing, That's clearly not like a pirate." gushed Carolyn. She would sooner die than reflect anything except that this sweet sensitive child is beautiful.

"Very charming, my dear, " dad adds. "You know, soon you'll have a replacement and not need to wear a patch at all. It will match perfectly and even you won't be able to tell. In the meantime, you're quite the little star." Addie Mae smiles. She does like it.

Her life becomes less frightening each day. She doesn't remember much about the day of the fire or her first stay in the hospital. Carolyn and Womack have been careful to filter the response from the public and to shield her from potentially hurtful interactions. At the same time, the cards that have come in signed by other children, not only in Chicago, but around the country, are welcome. They make her feel like she has lots of friends.

She can still work on her reading. She could still watch television. She can see the people and things that she loves. She can even still play with her friends, in some of the games, anyway. Although, she has been told that there shouldn't be anything too physical while she was still healing. Can't risk another injury right now. Healing is a good word. It means getting better. It doesn't mean putting up with having vision in only one eye, losing friends and missing some boyfriends because they don't want to be with a one-eyed girl.

When it's time for bed, she takes her new patches and places them in a special box that she keeps on the dresser. God has a plan for me, she thinks, for everyone. I'm still part of everyone. He'll take care of me. She trusts that everything will be all right. The other kids, maybe they would like the patch. *Maybe they would? I know Cecilia will say something nice.* She drifts off to sleep with all these wonderful thoughts in her head. When the police arrive, responding to the emergency call, the box was still there, Addie Mae was gone. Detective Wagner and the Addie Mae's parents were punctured and gouged, and half-dead from loss of blood. Wagner, with the blood-drenched phone still sitting in his hand, looked at the first officer to enter, and spoke, even though he had a pierced lung. He wheezed, "Elijah."

CHAPTER 41

Micky had never heard of the Northwest Incinerator, and for good reason; there isn't such a place. At least not yet, anyway. When the phone book fails, a little search at the Daily News tells him that it's under construction, only not today. Environmentalists are pitching quite a war over development of the proposed site. They're already looking to shut down similar sites for nearby Medill as well as Calumet and on the South Side, at 34th and Lawndale. The standards aren't that clear and Northwest is going to burn everything and sort it out later. Historically, the mayor would step in and make everyone see the value of compromise. Today, he might not wield that kind of power. Nothing moves while they argue. One way or another, they'll get it done. Money talks. There's construction money, job money and, besides, landfills are not going to be enough. Micky thinks this 'burn it all and let God sort it out is a perfect place for Elijah to pick, and to die.

Northwest Construction will cover a half-mile between Chicago Avenue and Lake Street on Kildare. There aren't that many families. It's a kind of industrial corridor. That's why it was chosen. He knows that area.

He's made many phone calls and left contradictory notes with K-9, his parents and Maggie, not wanting them to know where he is. He's really at a little dive hotel near the Daily News at Madison and Wabash. No one will call him. Through the night he rests, putting the guilt over Effie aside to focus on his objective, getting his hands-on Elijah.

Today, Jim Diamond will be a guest on the WBZZ, the local Public Broadcasting's show, What Chicago Wants to know. This week, what everyone wants to know about is The Chicago Outfit from Big Jim Colosimo to today. This is why he had Micky legging out the details on Jackie the Lackey, to prep for this.

He'll just hang in the green room, answer any questions for Diamond before he goes on and, generally, be like his second at a dawn duel. The one with the sharpest facts today will be the star. Diamond wants that. It's who he is now, personality and entertainer.

Micky arrives, flashes his credentials and meets Diamond. They talk casually. He knows the fight plan. He both wishes him luck and tells him, encouragingly that he's going to be great as he heads out to the show.

Diamond looks sharp. His suit is new and the

color blue that everyone likes. His haircut is downtown. He looks ten years younger than he did last week. When he wants to, like for today's show, he can stop drinking for extended periods.

He'll catch up, though. It'll be somewhere quiet. He's not interested in the fanfare he might get from other customers. He will only want to drink, and he won't want to be bothered. Diamond has been with the Daily News for over thirty years. If it's just you and him, when he's drinking, he'll tell you about how he knew Carl Sandburg, who also worked at the Daily News. Micky has now read Sandburg's columns on the 1919 riots, but Diamond has the personal stories. Maybe that's who he wanted to be, instead of this.

A major difference in writing ability probably limited that. Micky's journalism teacher at Wright Junior College always talked about how great writing came from finding a place of truth. Diamond likely never did. And now he's an in-person encyclopedia who will perform at your party.

He's charming, articulate and exactly what they wanted. Even the other guests are deferring to him. He exits slowly, to make sure everyone has opportunity to glad-hand him for the job well done.

Bursting back into the green room, he looks at Micky with the smile of a man whose horse just won the Kentucky Derby. "Your stuff was good. Big help, Mick. Better than good, in fact. They even used some of your photos." The compliment is good. Adding his smile to it is nice. The use of his name cements it. We're in a good mood. Micky feels obligated to respond in kind.

"Well, you're the one that has to remember everything and add it to all the other knowledge. And then, deliver it on queue. Television doesn't like people stumbling around to remember the facts. " Diamond is still smiling when a staffer breaks in, looks at them and says, "Telephone call. They say it's urgent. " Diamond beams and straightens himself. Then his bubble pops when, as he moves forward, the staffer, adds, "It's for him, Mulvihill."

Micky thinks that this is one more taunt and, possibly, a change of plans —something he definitely doesn't want. "Mr. Mulvihill, a Detective Peter Wagner Chicago PD, was admitted to the hospital this morning. This is Rush-Presbyterian. He's in intensive care. I'm not sure that you'll be able to see him, but he's asked for you several times, really, each time he's been conscious. "

◆ ◆ ◆

A uniformed cop is there outside intensive care. Micky knows him from the times that he comes into the station to get information for the Blotter. He's the one that called when Wagner got access to Elijah's apartment. It's O'Leary, the desk sergeant from the 15th. O'Leary recognizes Micky, too.

"We've not met. I know ya. Michael O'Leary." He extends a hand, recognizing not more than a second-generation brogue.

"Hi, Micky Mulvihill, " he adds, unnecessarily, and slaps in for a strong handshake, as a matter of habit.

"This is what I know. He's been spending a lot of time with the black ladies. " Micky shoots him a quizzical look. "Mrs. Irene Washington and Mrs. Mikala Leonard, the family of the black heart himself. And Dr. Olivia Moore, the psychiatrist."

"Mrs. Moore? She not a doctor or a psychiatrist. " He doesn't seem to believe Micky, but it's not a time to argue credentials.

"Anyway, Mick, they all talk, about this Elijah and what he'd do. A sacrifice it is. —Can you imagine? Da barbarian. —Anyway, Mick, it's got to be something good. I mean someone that is good. You don't sacrifice, well, like a bad priest, or some damn thing. What's good in all this mess? The girl. That's what he t'ought. So, Peter's been hanging at her house for weeks. Last night, the son of a bitch came. Quite a damn battle it was. He caught a screwdriver in the lung, Peter. The family, the parents of the sweet thing, hammered in the face, and I mean hit in the face with a hammer with the claw end."

Micky thinks of Effie. "Their necks were gouged with that thing, but Peter he heard it happenin'. He bust in, but he couldn't get a clean shot. Then he did. Just missed blowin' his dear stupid head straight off so his evil soul can go to Hell, where it belongs. Not what it could have been, though. What could have been is they're dead. He got to them, Peter. He thinks he shot his ear off." He smirks. "It's a start."

"But Elijah got away with the girl?" Before he can confirm, a nurse walks in on them.

"Mr. Mulvihill? Mr. Mulvihill, Mr. Wagner would like to see you." She adds, "Only for a minute, sir. He's stable, but still critical."

As he's leaving, O'Leary adds, "He saved the parents. They'd be dead for sure." Micky nods. He adds still more, almost at a yell. "This has near killed him. It'ought he'd drink himself in a hole. I've known him ten years. Nothing like this. A good cop is all. They'd be dead, mind ya." Micky nods again. "Tell him I said he sounds like bagpipes when he talks, and him bein' German and all. What a thing is that?" Micky gives a thumbs up sign.

The room is too warm. Its dark, too, except for a light behind Wagner's head affixed to the wall. It shines in and down, not out, leaving the room in a silent twilight. He walks very lightly, calling just above a whisper. "Pete?" His head turns. When he sees who it is, he smiles.

Wagner calls him close. He whispers in short bursts. "He...has...the girl"

"I know."

"Sacrifice." He nods, understanding. "Wants...you...will...contact."

Micky knows that he shouldn't, but he does. He leans in and whispers. "He has. It's tonight. " Wagner's face darkens. "He gave me 24-hours to plan. Can't tell anyone or she's dead. Remember, it's like you said. He's evil. He's got some skills. But he's not smart. Once I get the girl," he stops for a moment. "Once I get the girl, he will beg his God for me to stop."

Wagner looks Micky dead in the eye, still the cop. "Get the girl." Micky nods.

Micky says goodbye to O'Leary. He's heard that the Wesleys are going to be all right, too. This is kidnapping. The FBI has been contacted. They likely have been to the home and talked with neighbors. When they called the hospital, they were told that they have to wait until he's better. The staff will let them know. Wagner made sure he spoke with Micky first. Darkness approaches.

He's never been readier.

CHAPTER 42

E lijah removes her eye patch and puts his finger in the socket. "When you are with God, you will have both eyes again." Addie Mae is barely conscious. He has been keeping her that way with chloroform. Lying flat, she looks confused, staring at this man with the top part of his ear missing. Only the sky is visible. He laughs.

She looks down and is terrified but cannot scream. Her mouth is stuffed with cotton and tied with cloth. Elijah and Addie Mae sit ninety-four feet about the ground on a metal grating, a walkway, that surrounds an incinerator tower. When it's operational it will spread the smoke of burnt refuse high into the air on the West Side. It is the smoke from fires that clean

Construction calls for two equal height round towers made of brick. On each of them there are two metal walkways that circle the tower. One is halfway up, at forty-five feet. The other, where Elijah and Addie Mae are, is at the very top. He carried her climbing up the metal rungs that that are forged directly into the brick on the outside of the tower as a ladder. He's been there all day, watching for signs of police, and completing his plans.

"It's time to go to the bottom. He places a chloroform-soaked cloth over her nose to knock her out. Then he throws her over his shoulder and proceeds to climb down. Near the bottom of the tower, but five feet above ground is a metal door. He opens it and carries her through. He ties her to the inside metal frame. It's the altar of sacrifice.

Dead tree branches have been gathered and drenched in gasoline. They lay on the floor of the incinerator eight feet below. A thick rope has been drenched to serve as a wick.

With the money that he stole from Gladys along with his own, he hired two degenerate street criminals. For a few hours of work, they'll each earn a thousand dollars. He gave them half up front. They know the danger. They know the ugliness of it. They only care about getting the other half of the money, and not getting caught.

He waits on the tower. A Chevelle pulls onto Chicago Avenue and parks. *Mulvihill!* Elijah and the other two position themselves out of sight as planned. A cyclone fence surrounds the site. Two gates rest on rollers and are secured together by a thick chain with a heavy padlock. The fencing was erected by the construction crew. A green plastic canvass covers the majority of it to prevent anyone looking in. The fence will be removed and replaced with a stone wall when the work is finished.

They hear Mick approaching. Sand from the construction work forms a thin layer over the nearby sidewalk. The grains twist slightly under his feet. Closer. He stops in front of the gate. He listens. He bends to look under the plastic canvas for feet. He preens above to see what's behind the gate. He slides the chain off, remaining outside. He stops again to listen. Elijah hopes he doesn't hear any of them breathing. *Just enter.*

With a shove he blasts the gate open and rushes to the inside. A mesh netting drops to snare him. In the few moments it takes them to realize that they've snared a boxing heavy bag, he crushes one pounding all his weight in the side of the knee, breaking it. The other man drops the net, pulls a gun and fires. His aim is off as the saw-toothed pilot's knife slides in under his ribs. Elijah's position is farther back, near the tower. He yells out.

"Do you have him?"

Prodded by whispered instructions enforced by a knife to his throat, the man with the broken knee yells back, in obvious pain, "Yes, but he broke my leg and killed William. William shot him in the arm. I clubbed him. He's barely conscious."

"Can you bring him to me?"

"I'll try, but I can't really walk...No. I can't" Elijah walks forward carefully. He lights the wick.

He can make out the bulky shape lying on the ground. It's covered with the netting. He can see the man who talks and then the other lying on the ground. He carries a hammer in his right hand.

He sees the movement but has no time to respond. It's like a wild boar low and rushing toward him. "Uhhf." He's hit mid-section knocking the wind out of him. He can't breathe. *MULVIHILL!* Micky has grabbed hold of his wrist where his hand bears the hammer, forcing it back until it must release. He punches and kicks at Micky furiously. It has little effect. A chop to his throat. Elijah gags unable to breathe.

"Where is she? Tell me or I'll rip you open and pull the bones out of you one by one."

He tries to speak but is limited. Micky stands him up, slapping him open-handed. "Where is she?" he yells with a fury.

Elijah smiles and croaks out, "Call your God to stop the fire." Micky puts him in an arm lock and breaks his elbow. Elijah, tears in his eyes, whimpers in pain. Micky continues to press. He the points to the tower.

Micky can see a rope wick burning just outside the door. "Call Him. He won't answer. He protects me. " Micky throws a ferocious right-hook to Elijah's jaw, which slides a half-inch left, unhinging. He slumps unconscious from the blow. Micky runs for the tower, watching the wick. He's not going to make it.

A cement pillar catches him across the chest and stops him dead. "Nooo, " he screams in anguish. The tower explodes in fire tearing his heart to pieces. He sees the shape. It's not a pillar. It's a man.

"Easy, Mick." The man is the Volkswagen. "We got the kid." Micky can make out that he's smiling at him. A small army of men start to walk out from every corner. One of them holds a pistol on the man whose knee Micky broke.

The Nassau Blue Cutlass walks close and gives a sign. Two men grab Elijah who awakens writhing and crying in pain. He can't speak. Turning back, the Cutlass cracks, "You don't tail people well. But we do. That hotel deal was a pretty big tell that it was going to happen. We came in from several angles while you were introducing yourself at the gate. You weren't going to lose that fight, but it was nice to watch you win it." Micky stares trying to understand. The men all laugh at his confusion.

"Look. We know things. One thing we know? This guy wants you. Right? You told us. We watch you. You go into the dive hotel. We know it's not your get-away vacation. Capisce?

"Yeah. I understand."

"How's the kid?" He turns to a man carrying her in his arms.

"Well, she's breathin'. But this kid's got one eye. So, I'm not gonna say she's GOOD."

"Don't you know nothin'" The Cutlass turns back to Mick. "He don't know nothin'. Look, Mulvihill, take the kid over to Rush. Get her some medical attention. Here's the story. You came. Had to be alone. Got the jump on the two of them 'cause that other guy who can't walk well and has hobbled down the street— he was never here. The guy you stabbed— "

"I'll take him to the hospital, too. "

"Suit yourself, if he's still alive. He don't know what happened. Anyway, you busted up Elijah, but he got away. And you got the kid back. The parents are still there, at the hospital. That Dick, he still there, too." He means Detective Wagner.

"What about—" Micky throws his thumb towards Elijah who has regained consciousness. He tries to talk but the paralyzing pain shoots through his jaw. The men laugh again.

"Bright eyes? You'll see him again in a couple of days. In the papers."

"Yeah. In the funny papers, " one of the men adds. It's stupid. No one laughs.

A small protest rises in Micky. "Look, Mulvihill. We can't have this. There's none of this. He's got to go out proper, sending a little message. You're a good kid. You got a brain. Use it. You did this, saved the kid and chased Elijah away. When the saint that ain't shows up, when his body is found, it closes, and everyone relaxes."

Micky nods. He pulls his car to the front gate and picks up Addie Mae, the stabbed henchman, and his heavy bag. He walks back to Elijah. An inch from his face, he says, "Here's one from the Bible, an eye for an eye." It crushes easily under the force of his powerful hand.

◆ ◆ ◆

As he walks towards the doors to Emergency at Rush-Presbyterian, the staff spot him, haggard and carrying a limp child. "Her. Not me," he says to indicate where their efforts should go. They wheel her off but continue to try to get him to take help. A cop, stationed for trouble, comes over.

"The girl is Addie Mae Wesley. She was kidnapped yesterday. I'm Micky Mulvihill. I'll give you the rest later. I'm going to see her parents and the cop who saved their lives. Upstairs." The cop seems unsure about letting him just go. "Barring shooting me, that's what's going to happen. Micky Mulvihill." He pops out his wallet. The cop writes the name and address. He knows now who this is. Micky sees him looking at the blood dripping from his right thumb and hand. The cop lets it go.

Mack and Carolyn Wesley share a semi-private room. They're due to be discharged in the morning. The television is on. The radio is on. They're looking for news. They recognize his face. His beaten and bloody look frightens them.

"What? What is it? Please. Oh, please" Carolyn Wesley jumps out of bed and implores Micky.

"Addie Mae is okay. She's kind of out of it, but she's getting help here, right here at Rush."

"Addie Mae is okay? She's here? What do you mean out of it?" He confirms that yes, she's here in the hospital.

"Unconscious is all, drugged or something." Mack is six inches from his face, wanting to believe, but it's too good. He's careful.

"I just dropped her off in ER. Find out where they took her." A million questions on their faces. "Go. Details can follow. You're all right. She's all right. And Elijah will bother no one ever again. Go." They thank him, trying to impart their gratitude, mumbling thank-you and thank God and just thanks. It's not a look he's ever going to forget.

◆ ◆ ◆

Peter Wagner has a tube sticking out of the right side of his chest to take pressure off his lung and allow it to heal. The intensive care beds are enclosed by glass walls to let the nurses see one patient while attending another. They spot Micky and rush over.

"You can't stay here. Mr. Wagner is resting"

"I'll just be a minute. Need to tell him something."

"I'm sorry. You can't. I'll call security."

"You can call King Damn Kong and Magilla Gorilla, too, for all I care. Mr. Wagner wants to hear this. He needs to hear this. And he will rest much better once he does hear this." They lock eyes for a moment. Then she turns and heads to the nurse's station.

"Pete. Hey. Pete." Wagner doesn't move.

He moves closer and pinches his ear. Softly, he whispers, "Pet-AY. PETE. Yo. Petey-Pete. Hot dogs. Hamburgers. Spaghetti and meatballs." Wagner's eyes open.

"It's me. Mulvihill." He gives him a few moments to adjust. When he does, his eyes sharpen. Micky sees the fear.

"It's okay. I got the girl. She's here, getting help. " His eyes ask if it's really true. "That's right. I got the girl." His eyes ask one more question. Micky understands. "Elijah is no more." Slowly, Wagner lifts his left hand toward Micky, who takes it. He nods his head yes. Wagner follows. His eyes fill. "Listen. They're going to pin a medal on your chest. Try not to puncture it again. The Wesleys are with her right now. That little girl could use some mom and dad. The only other thing that has to happen now is that you get some rest so that they can thank you for saving their life. You're a good cop." He means you're a good person, who is a cop.

Wagner looks like an anchor has been lifted from his neck.

CHAPTER 43

December 1969

O ne week ago, Fred Hampton was killed by Chicago police in what black leaders are calling an assassination that came under the direction of Mayor Daley and his State's Attorney, Edward J. Hanrahan. Police executed an early morning raid on the Black Panther West Side office space and Hampton's living quarters. Police claim they defended themselves. The forensic evidence isn't supporting that. An inquiry is underway.

Micky's desk is strewn with the coverage from various newspapers each day since it happened. *It was only five months ago that Reverend Charles Moore predicted such events. He told Olivia that Mayor Daley and Edward Hanrahan would assassinate the leaders to stem black violence. He had heard Daley say, "If we can't control and curb these gang structures, society will demand that we take the necessary actions." Moore had challenged Daley on making such a statement and used the Chicago Outfit whom the city lets have their violence as a comparison.*

This is why Charles felt he needed to do something on his own, to create a neighborhood that would work for blacks that were coming of age. He knows now that Moore didn't want integration, not in Austin. His idea was to have a black neighborhood that could set an example. After that, we can talk about integration. *He made two mistakes. One, he got greedy, or maybe he got human, and that put him in with some bad people. Two, and the biggest mistake, was that he tried to take someone else's neighborhood to do this. My neighborhood.*

The green light illuminates the words On Air.

"Good Afternoon, Chicago, and welcome. This is WJLO Radio News. Today is December 11, 1969. I am reporter Micky Mulvihill. Today, in our first topic, we'll continue coverage of the developing story of the deadly shootout that took the lives of Fred Hampton, 21, who was leader of the Black Panthers of Illinois and Mark Clark, 22, a member of the Panthers. Stay tuned for all the latest." The show's music leads into two commercials. Then he'll be back on. Micky hates the hyped lead-in, but the show gives him a lot of latitude to call it like he sees it.

Barely visible through the studio windows he sees the top half of the head of Forty-Eight. The door to the broadcast booth unlocks when the On-Air sign goes off and the commercials start. She enters.

"Hey, Mick," He doesn't even have to ask if she's ready. She always is.

"Hey, Kath. Right on time as usual." She only smiles a thank you back at him.

Micky moves close to the microphone. His headset is in place with the copy of what he's written directly in front of him. He doesn't even look as he begins.

"The Black Panther Party for Self-Defense is the full and correct name of the organization for which Fred Hampton led the Illinois chapter. The very wording implies that they're in a war with someone. That someone is the police. Their first and primary job in developing this organization was to patrols neighborhoods in Oakland to help defend against police brutality. This year, the Black Panthers expanded to community programs like free breakfasts for kids and health clinics. But it's still a war.

"Fred Hampton was the leader of the Illinois Chapter of the Black Panthers. Hampton's rhetoric was to tell blacks to arm themselves. The Black Panthers were a lot like a militia. The battle grounds are the cities: Chicago, New York, Los Angeles—all the places that large populations have blacks migrated to avoid the Jim Crow South.

"Police say that they were on the premises to serve a warrant for illegal firearms. And there was an arsenal on hand. Police also say that three separate times they announced themselves and their purpose, which was to serve a warrant. Police say— in fact, State's Attorney Edward Hanrahan himself says— the police did not fire until fired upon. Others aren't buying that story. They believe Fred Hampton was assassinated. The American Civil Liberties Union has alleged that this was an assassination and part of a plan to rid the city and the country of militant black organizations. Famed Defense Attorney William Kunstler, in Chicago currently leading the Defense team for what is known as the Chicago Seven trial, has also called this murder. More on this story from WJLO street reporter, Kathleen Noonan. Kathleen, what do we know today?"

"Thank you, Micky. The raid was, indeed, organized by the office of State's Attorney Edward Hanrahan, famous in Chicago for the statements regarding war on gangs.—"

Micky interrupts. "And adding to that statement, Kathleen, Mayor Daley, himself, has also said that if the violence doesn't subside—and it certainly hasn't —that society will demand extreme measures be taken. Isn't that correct?"

"That is correct, Micky. And many are worrying that these actions with the Black Panthers may be the intentional escalation toward those extreme measures." Noonan doesn't miss a beat returning to her report. "To that end Renault Robinson of the African-American Patrolman's Association has raised the question of tactics. We have his statement.

The broadcast cuts to a tape of Robinson's earlier press conference where he said that the police did not need to fire at all, that the use of tear gas would have forced the Black Panthers inside the building to come out. They cut to a tape of Robinson's press conference elaborating on just that point. When the tape ends, Kathleen picks it back up. "The physical evidence is being examined closely. At this point, it's not supporting the police version as all bullets, except one, appear to be fired from police weapons. That one has been, again, at this point, fired as an involuntary reflexive squeezing of the trigger after Fred Hampton was shot. I'll be following the forensic reports on this. Back to you, Micky."

"Thank you, Kathy. I think this is a story we'll be reporting on for a long time. A lot of political power is behind that police raid. A lot of people don't want to let this go."

Off the air again, he asks Kathy what she knows that she can't say publicly. "Well, Mick. There's a lot of FBI hanging around. It seems that they're not disappointed by the death of Hampton."

"You think that they maybe had a hand in it? Was it murder?"

"It's not known. This is going to take a long

time to sort out and the city doesn't want a bad rap." Micky's thoughts go to Frank Kulak, for whom the city took extra precautions to capture alive despite the fact that he had killed two cops. Then he thinks of Ernest Johnson who has been living with city coverups for fifty years.

His last segment before signing off on his 30-minute show is sports. He brings in K-9. He's pretty jacked up about a proposed match between Joe Frazier and Muhammed Ali just three months away. He usually adds a trainer's tip at the end.

Micky signs off. "You going home?" K-9 asks.

"Yeah. I'm going to catch forty winks, or however many winks give you a short nap. Then I'll hit CST, after which I am going out to dinner with Maggie. We have a reservation at the new Austin Delights opening week. It's North by Northwest Delights. —I'm kidding. It's Hera's Grille., with an 'e' at the end, so you know to dress nice. Somewhere way out west on North Avenue. I'll probably get lost. Anything past Manheim is like Iowa to me?"

"Aren't you lovely, with the dinner reservation and all. You going to join the East Bank Club?" He's not serious with the question.

"No." A sixteenth note, short and flat.

"Your own show now, downtown. East Bank's a downtown place. Get to sweat with a lot of swells."

"I like my parent's garage. —What's with the 'swells'? You watching old Cagney movies again?"

"And mom's cooking, I'll bet, which I would guess, is a lot cheaper than the East Bank Club.—And it's Jean Harlow. I seriously love her. Ser-i-ous-ly. She died like 30 years ago making it an impossible dream. And, somehow, making me love her even more."

"Undoubtedly. Myself, I couldn't pick her out of a lineup, but I know the song reference. It's from Man of La Mancha." Smirks all around.

He doesn't mention that the reservation is for four. Olivia and Harrison Kellum will be joining them.

◆ ◆ ◆

"Are Olivia and Harrison Kellum a couple now?" Maggie asks, trying to clarify things with Micky. They've never been out with these two before, although she's met Olivia.

No. They're friends," he answers.

"Okay, but It's going to happen. It's just that the pace is going to be slow." He looks at her and she returns a nod. She knows.

"Like the Courtship of Eddie's father. What'd that run for 3 years? And I don't know if he ever did get with anyone."

"You watched that, the family show with the eight-year-old?" She slides a challenging look his way.

"Guy had a great pad, cool kid, a housekeeper who did everything and he dated a lot of great looking women. I can kill some time with that." Challenge met.

They park, and he spots Kellum's black Grand Prix. "Naturally," he comments, a nod to Harrison's impeccable timeliness.

As he explains to the host that they're meeting other people, he spots Olivia. "That's them." They run the switchback of tables. Menus are already on the tablecloth.

After a couple drinks, most of the awkward moments have passed. Maggie, in response to Olivia's general questioning, has explained her life goals. She wants her own business, but not a bar or a restaurant. Maybe office supplies? They all push a little further. Maybe a realtor? That injects some energy into the group. He thinks she has something else in mind, but wisely, she doesn't want to say it. Keep those things within a tight circle, Micky thinks.

"And how about for you, Mick? WJLO Radio News. Guess you're doing all right?" He sees Olivia looking closely at him, to see if there's any cracks when he answers.

"Yeah. It's great." He can't hide well from her, but she leaves it be.

"Well, for me, I have accepted an offer from the Art Institute, to teach, and be part of a team to develop exhibits by black artists." Micky sees her start to say something more but stops. She looks at Harrison, who encourages her to continue. "And I came to an agreement on...on the church funds, which I was able to pay because of this new job." She looks at Micky to see how much he might have said to Maggie about it. Nothing, she gathers. No one else knows either as it was agreeably concluded before it needed to become public.

"Some silver linings, at least, to be thankful for, " Harrison adds with a stoic demeanor. She gives the best smile she can under the conditions.

"I'm going to visit Mrs. Washington tomorrow. Her daughter, Mikala, will be there, too." Olivia's announcement isn't a surprise. Micky's aware that a trust has developed between them and they're helping each other.

"You know, there's one question that I want to ask both of them." Micky would like to join them but doesn't know if he'd be welcome.

"Well, come on over after your show. We'll be there all afternoon." Olivia is dead serious.

"Really? They'd let me come, and ask questions, too. "

"Yes. We get all of our questions out. Sometimes there's no answer, but it's good. Besides, it's like Irene said. 'Ain't a lot of white men that would put their life on the line for a little black girl." With his skin, his blush is very noticeable. Maggie starts the giggle. Then it's all of them. He knows.

"Fine. Fine. Just...just....fine."

CHAPTER 44

Micky rings the bell and Peter Wagner answers. Surprised, he jokes. "Holy crap! You're still alive?"

"Much to the dismay of many, " he answers. They laugh and shake hands, like friends. Micky follows him back to the kitchen. While he's saying hello, he adds, "The kitchen is where everyone is most of the time at my house, too. " He means his parents' house. Where he lives is separate from 'my house'. That's wherever his parents live.

Wagner is dressed casually, but his clothes are clean, and he smells like soap, not whiskey. "I'm not on the force, anymore." Micky blanches, in total shock.

"You mean they—"

"No. I quit. I became a cop to get bad guys. I wanted to get bad guys because they hurt good people. It's really people I want to help. The Department is too political. I just want to do the job. I'm looking. Nothing has popped up yet." Micky has an idea, but he'll wait until they're alone.

Irene made coffee. Micky, given the chance up front, says that he doesn't like tea. Olivia puts her hands on her hips in mock anger. "Just sayin'..." he explains. There are no hard feelings. When the moment is right, he asks the question.

"Mrs. Washington, how did your grandson come know Reverend Moore? There's some vague thought about gang connections going back to the letter that Charles wrote to the Daily News, but it doesn't seem right. The years are off."

She looks to Mikala. She lowers her head. "Okay." Irene takes her hand and looks in her eyes with the love of a mother. She seems to be saying 'go ahead'. "Okay. Um. Okay. Reverend Moore was my minister a long time ago. I had a son who needed Sunday school teaching and all. I started to go. Reverend Moore, he could see we needed some extra tendin' to. We became close."

"Wait. When was this?" Olivia asks.

"I expect it was before you knew him or before you were married, anyways." Olivia nods. "You know my daddy hated Lewis, worse than me, 'cause he was a boy. Too much remindin' for him, looking at that boy. "

"That's all in the past now, Mikala." Wagner's comment gets a look from Micky. He's surprised he would offer that kind of boost and surprised more that she would accept it.

"Yeah. I know. But this time..." She starts to softly cry. "this time was too much. I can't never forget it." She looks to Micky who is quiet and sympathetic even without knowing why he needs to be.

"Lewis was slow. He would be held back in school. Daddy snatched him up one day and drove him to Maryland, and a place he knew of. It was a place that they'd scare all the children with in Indiana, all the black children. 'if you don't act right, child, I will take you to...'" She has to stop. "to the Crownsville Hospital for the Negro Insane. He'd threaten Lewis, too. And then one day, he did it. He had him committed there without me. No one asked. Mama's dead, he told them. This is my boy and he's insane. They didn't have no children there. Oh, some teenagers, but not any children. Lewis was eleven. He lied and said he was sixteen. They must have knowed, but he gave them some money. " Micky's heart is pumping furiously.

"Your husband?"

"Happy to be rid of him. Mostly, he wasn't around even when he was around."

"I see. And you asked Reverend Moore to help." Micky guesses the rest. Mikala nods yes, crying.

"He got my boy back. He told them I was

alive. He had a letter from me. He had that boy's birth certificate. He was a man of God that day. He brought my child home. Lewis, maybe he was slow, but he was made insane by Elmer Washington. God forgive me, but Goddamn that man. That place was too much. I've read about it. Overcrowded. Terrible conditions. Treating people like animals. He wanted to punish him to get back at someone else. Reverend Moore, he kept with him over the years, trying to keep him out of trouble."

"Hate ate a hole in his heart. My husband was just eaten alive by hate of a white man who did a terrible thing to me. Grace of God could have saved him. He wouldn't let none in. Too busy hatin'." Micky can't tell what Irene Washington's emotion is. There are too many years and too many things for him to understand that.

"And later on, he killed a Disciple, started a gang war. Reverend Charles stepped in again. He got a truce, and he and Lewis remained close, as close as anyone could get to Lewis." Mikala's voice drifts off, remorseful of a failure to reach that level with her own son.

Micky is stunned, but Olivia is affected more. That's a story she needed to hear, too. She shakes with emotion until she and Mikala stand and hug. They continue to hold. Everyone is very emotional.

"This probably happens here a lot, right?" Micky adds with perfect timing and taste, breaking them into laughter.

After they've had all the coffee, talk and cup-cakes that they can handle, and then some, it fin-ishes. They do a slow walk toward the front. Right at the end, Irene touches Micky's shoulder. "Would you stay just a minute longer?" *What now? Please let this be something easy.*

They sit together on the living room couch. "Mr. Mulvihill, I need to tell you. I know that you have spoken to Peter about what happened to me. I told Peter that the man's name was Mulvihill that did this to me." The thought that no one wanted to say out loud, but Micky knew. He nods to show her that he knows. "I told Peter that he was stopped, that a man like that makes lots of enemies and one of them stopped him. That much is true, but it's not the whole truth. "

She goes slow purposely. "Go ahead, Mrs. Washington. It's all right."

"It was me that stopped him. "

"What? What do you mean?"

"I pushed him in front of the same trolley I was riding at the same stop. He was there quite a bit. He was everywhere quite a bit. His whole day was going around trying to start trouble." She stops suddenly, embarrassed to be talking like that about someone in his family.

"I…uh…it's okay. I never knew the man. He was long dead before my time." And he's glad of that.

"No. He's not dead." He's disbelieving. "James Joseph "JJ" Mulvihill lost both his legs that day. He's just across the border in Calumet. It's a house where the woman takes people in. She has some help, and I think the police know, but the only people she has a are people who can't go anywhere else. There's a money fund that pays for him."

"This can't be. My family would have said something."

"They buried an empty casket. I knew the woman who cleaned for the funeral home. She knew. Your grandfather put his brother in a home out of state. After a while, whether it was expenses or questions or what, he moved him where he is now.

"But, I'm sorry—"

"I've been there. I've seen him. And he's seen me. He's senile and he'll not be there much longer, anywhere, that is. He has suffered for the many things he's done. And now may God take his soul quickly. I thought it's best that you know and that there's no secrets because something put a connection between us. That man, JJ Mulvihill. It was him. I gave birth to your second cousin, Mikala. And her son was Lewis Leonard. You and Lewis…" She looks at Micky, who nods an understanding.

◆ ◆ ◆

Micky sits in front of an ancient two-story red brick home. There's a front porch on both levels, each painted a dark grey. The first level has sofa chairs. The second, which has no roof has metal lawn chairs that are at least thirty years old. There are no screens on the outside and no blinds on the inside of any windows. The curtains look like white sheets that have been sewn to cover a rod.

A black child wearing a neat plaid shirt and navy pants answers the door. He looks like he probably is still dressed from attending school earlier in the day. "My name is Michael Mulvihill. I'm here to visit my great-uncle. " The boy closes the door leaving him stand outside. As he waits, he looks out on a very old neighborhood. Railroad tracks block through traffic at the end of the block.

"Hello. Can I help you? " He repeats who he is. "Do you mind if I look at your driver's license. That man ain't had but one visitor in Lord knows how many years.

"Yeah. Sure. I mean, no. I don't mind. " As he reaches, he thinks about saying that he just found out that his relative was alive, but he decides to leave well enough alone and avoid any potential further explanations.

She asks Micky to come in, but to sit in the living room for a minute. Apparently, she needs to get him and/or a room presentable. When the time comes, and he walks up the stairs, he wonders how many years it's been since JJ was off the second floor even. She turns right, and he follows. The floor is hardwood, last varnished when Hoover was President. Kids scream lightly and laugh, playing in a back room. The hallway has some toys laying loose.

"JJ, you have a visitor." She leans close to him and repeats it twice more. This is an upstairs room like he's never seen. Maybe it was some type of sitting room, or a drawing room. *Whatever that is?* It has a television which is on and blaring. Two other older men, both black, sit watching from a couch.

"I'm Micky Mulvihill, Martin's son, Leo's son, Martin had some children. I'm one of them. Micky.

"That's right. That's good. Nice to meet you." Micky could have said he was Rumpelstiltskin and received the same response. Both legs are missing from just below the knee. He watches him, but they don't speak again until his says goodbye. Staring at this man whose heinous act created so much destruction, he wonders and who else had their life ruined by you. *I'm not related to you. You're not even in my species.* He had asked to see his room. She said okay, but she isn't watching him.

Old photos sit on a dresser. He recognizes his

grandfather in a picture together with JJ. There's a small card, like a business card, with a birth date and location and signed. The date is March 5, 1890. The hospital is Mercy Hospital 2537 S. Prairie in Chicago. *Makes sense. Close enough. Catholic.* The signature isn't that easy to read, but MD after the name is clear enough. It occurs to him that JJ's birth is barely thirty years after slavery. It was barely any time past Reconstruction of the South and carpetbaggers. All in one man's lifetime.

"His time is almost over, " he says to the woman who runs the house. "What happens then?"

"What do you want to happen?"

"Burn him. That is, I mean, cremate. Throw his ashes out." She looks at him without emotion. Sad cases have come her way before. "Here's a card. Whatever money might be left, I'll work something out with the bank, if there's any need. Maybe some of it can go here for things you might need?" He's grateful that she helps people. He just doesn't care about this man, blood kin or not.

Micky walks out and takes a lung full of air, exhaling the death that is inside that home. He hasn't yet said anything to his parents and he probably won't.

◆ ◆ ◆

"Hello. This is Pete." It's funny. Most people

don't give their name answering at home. He answers the phone like he's still a cop at work. Until this recent case, he hadn't had much practice. The job worked him. He'd become so focused on the Department way of doing things, he forgot what it was all about. He has friends, from work, that he only sees at work, or directly after.

Micky thinks that there have been a few silver linings in this mess, too. Wagner is one of them. He's cut free. Of course, he's twenty years older and with less hair and besides work, which he just quit, his life is empty. A middle-age crisis customized just for him. *What's the Chinese symbol for crisis? If I remember, it's a mix of danger and opportunity. Let's get the opportunity side going because danger has a pretty good leg up.*

"Hi. It's me, Mick. Something you said yesterday...well, same kind of thing has been on my mind, too."

"What's that? How great cupcakes are?" *A joke? That's a good sign.*

"Well, yeah, but that's the second thing. The first is that part about quitting the job, and it being too political. How serious are you about that? I mean, are you going through a phase?" He emphasizes the last word as a joke. "Going to run back and say please give me my job back in another two months or what?"

"Oh, that thing. No. I've realized how wrapped up in it I was. You know, I've known O'Leary for like ten years. Never seen him out of a cop uniform."

"Hmm. Are you wanting to see him without his clothes on?"

"That's between him and me." He laughs quietly. Anyway, enough of me explaining myself into trouble. What is it you want to say?"

"Well, the same thing is true for me. The radio gig is cool. Somebody called me a rising star the other day. But it's political. It's about ratings. They're slowly moving toward grooming me into their kind of guy. I have to chop up what I say too much. I'm not going to do it forever. I have something else in mind.

"Yeah, you said. I might need to shave again before you get to it."

"Okay. Okay. I now have the bug for investigating. For the first time, I was working on doing something about something, not just writing the facts of it, or even my opinion.

"Oh, Christ! You want to become a private dick?"

"No. Definitely not. I want to keep writing. Have to. I want YOU to become a private dick and work with me. I want to start a magazine that re-